SAMANTHA H

THE
LIAR'S
WIFE

bookouture

Published by Bookouture in 2018

An imprint of StoryFire Ltd.

Carmelite House
50 Victoria Embankment
London EC4Y 0DZ

www.bookouture.com

ISBN: 978-1-78681-669-6
eBook ISBN: 978-1-78681-668-9

For my dear friend, Deb, with love.
You know why…

Of all the liars in the world, sometimes the worst are our own fears.
Rudyard Kipling

PROLOGUE

I glance at the office clock then check the time on my monitor for what feels like the hundredth time. I swear the hands are moving backwards. The conversation brewing around me is making me anxious, worrying how I'll deflect yet another invitation without seeming rude, stand-offish, ungrateful.

I just want to go home.

'We could make a night of it,' Wendy says to someone as she walks past my workspace.

I cower down, pretending to be immersed in the project I have open.

'Depends if you want to be a functioning human being tomorrow, or not,' a male voice chimes back from between the office partitions.

There's laughter, a few other comments, a plan forming – leave work at 5.30 p.m. on the dot, head to the bar around the corner, have a few drinks, maybe get some food, more pubs, crawl home, sleep it off. I can't help the shudder as I stare at my screen, playing the same ten-second clip over and over again. I don't know if it's the film sending shivers through me, or the talk of a night out.

Work, home, sleep…

'What say you, Miss Sinclair?' comes a voice from behind me.

I don't need to turn around. I know it's Adam. He rarely uses my first name, though he does for everyone else.

'About what?' I reply, leaning into my screen, pretending to concentrate, tweaking the film clip for the sake of it. Anything to make him think I'm busy.

'A piss-up after work to celebrate Helen's engagement?'

He comes into my little cubicle, plonking himself down on the corner of my desk. I slide my coffee cup away from the edge.

'But Helen isn't in today. She's gone on a course.'

'So?' Adam says, shrugging. 'Doesn't mean to say we can't celebrate without her.'

I look up at him, my heart flipping an unsteady beat. I'm pretty sure they only ask me out of duty, but I'm running out of excuses.

'Any excuse for the pub,' I say, adding a smile. 'But I'm sorry, I can't. I really have to finish grading this clip. I'm running behind as it is.'

Adam thinks about this, pulling a 'fair enough' face. In the past I've used sick relatives, hospital appointments, tiredness, sore throats, vague, nondescript plans and lack of money as reasons not to join in with work gatherings. They don't push it. It's generally accepted that 'Ella never comes'. But still they keep asking.

I know it's not them. It's me.

Adam folds his arms. Shows no sign of leaving. 'That's the school fire-safety film, right?' he says, squinting at my screen.

'Yes,' I say, replaying the clip yet again, skipping past *that* bit. It never gets any easier. 'I'm just struggling with the animated section in the middle. I know it's for kids but—'

'You do know the deadline has been put back, don't you?'

I stare up at him, swallowing. The clip plays on – the sound of crackling, popping and then roaring somehow even more disturbing without the images. I close my eyes for a second but, behind them, the flames are still there.

It only takes seconds for a fire to spread… the voiceover says. *How long does it take you to get out?*

'Oh… I…' I say, choking, coughing. 'I didn't realise.'

'So in that case, Miss Sinclair, why don't you down tools, shake out your hair and come and get lashed with the rest of us?' Adam says, leaning forward. He reaches over, his armpit in my face as he takes hold of my mouse, about to log out of the system for me.

'No!' I swipe away his arm, knocking over my half-finished coffee. It spills all over my keyboard. 'Christ,' I say, leaping up and grabbing a bunch of tissues from the box on my desk.

Adam quickly raises his hands, backing off. 'OK, OK, I get the hint,' he says, adding a laugh. 'Just thought the real Miss Sinclair might want to, you know, come out to play.'

I drop my head, my hand pressing half a dozen tissues onto my desk and keyboard, waiting for the mess to soak up. Then I turn, catching sight of Adam as he leaves, shaking his head.

'No,' I say, too quietly for him to hear. 'No, she doesn't.'

It's amazing how much mess half a cup of coffee makes. After I've unplugged my keyboard, dried it out, wiped all around, dabbed the papers that got wet as well as putting back everything just as it was, I sit back down, head in hands. 5.23 p.m. Seven minutes until the others leave. Seven minutes until I'm off the hook. And Adam was right. Looking at the time schedule for this job, I see the deadline isn't until the end of next week now. So many projects come and go that it's easy to lose track of the ones that change. But this one… well, it's not been easy and I had hoped it would have been assigned to another editor. The fire service, in conjunction with the local education authority, commissioned a series of safety films to show in schools. *Know Your Exit* is the film's title and, if the campaign saves even one life, then it has been worth it.

I rest my head in my hands. Sometimes, there is no way out.

'Don't flog yourself all night, will you, Ella?' a voice says from behind.

Not Adam this time. I swing around, give him a little smile. Liam's OK.

'I won't,' I reply.

He has his jacket on, a work bag on his shoulder, an expectant look on his face.

'You sure you won't come to the pub?' he adds, hesitating.

I admit, it's almost tempting. Anything to get away from this project.

'I'm sorry, I'm really tired,' I say. 'Anyway, I left my purse at home this morning.' The truth, at least. 'And I don't want to be cycling home too late. The rain's getting heavier,' I add, glancing out of the window.

'Well I'm happy to buy you a few drinks. Or lend you some cash if you prefer?' There's hope in his eyes.

'Really, it's fine,' I say, shaking my head.

'How about a lift home then?' Liam says, persevering. 'I'm borrowing my mum's car today. I'm sure we can get your bike in the boot somehow. And, to be honest,' he says, glancing at the others gathering by the door, lowering his voice, 'I'm not fussed about going out either. I can't drink because I'm driving. You'd be my get-out-of-jail card.'

'Thanks, but I'll just finish up here then get home. You have a good night.' I turn back to my monitor, hoping that's the end of the conversation.

'Maybe another time then,' he says before leaving, though I sense he waits a moment in case I change my mind.

When he's gone, when the others have all grabbed their stuff and headed out towards the lifts, when the office is finally silent, I lay my head down on my desk trying hard not to cry.

The cleaner is vacuuming and emptying bins, her headphones in. Finally, I log out and shut down my system before fetching my backpack and waterproof jacket from a locker near the entrance. Space is at a premium here, with most of the work areas pretty cramped, so the office manager agreed to staff storage last year. I think I'm the only one who uses it, and the only one to leave sandwiches in the ancient fridge in the staff kitchen upstairs. I glance at the clock again – 6.43 p.m. already – later than I'd intended to leave, but I'd decided to try to figure out why the film wasn't working, so I didn't have to think about it next week.

'It's just not *real* enough,' I'd whispered to myself under the noise of the vacuum, watching the clip for the hundredth time. Though it had occurred to me that maybe it didn't seem real because I was watching it through a personal filter. Detached and numb. In the end, I'd given up, hoping inspiration would strike next week.

Outside, the rain is coming down harder – the earlier drizzle now a downpour – and it's getting dark too. I wonder whether to wait it out, perhaps even head around the corner to the pub after all, see if the others are still there. But the lurch in my stomach tells me not to, that I just need to get home. Going to the pub would mean chatting, listening, being asked questions that weren't to do with work, and having to share stories, revealing little details about my life. Stuff about *me*. And there simply isn't anything to tell. Not that I'm willing to admit, anyway.

I unlock my bike – the last one left at the rack – and wriggle into my backpack, zipping up my cycling top to the chin. I've had it for ages and it's not very waterproof, but I'm not good at shopping, at choosing new things for myself. Twice a year I'll order a few new things online in the sales, venture to the shops only if absolutely necessary. I'm clean and unnoticeably smart, but I don't need to look attractive. Not any more.

I brush the water off my saddle, wondering where the huge sigh comes from as I stare down the busy street – people hurrying home, couples huddled under umbrellas, taxis being pounced on, the sound of tyres on the wet road. It's probably the rain making me blink so much, but I can't help wiping my eyes anyway as I head off, pedalling hard, weaving into the traffic, my wheels splashing through the puddles. I imagine the warm bath I'll slip into, the macaroni cheese pinging in the microwave, and perhaps I'll watch a documentary later or pick up that book I started the other night.

The perfect evening. Quiet and alone.

The same as *every* evening.

I head through the city centre, knowing the route so well that I barely need to think about it. I glance back over my right shoulder, waiting for the car to pass before I change lanes, silently cursing myself for forgetting my helmet this morning. It's not at all like me to be disorganised, to leave things out of my backpack, but my routine was broken, my sleep disturbed. I tossed and turned all night, that blasted film playing on my mind. The flames in it engulfing everything.

Suddenly, a horn blares.

The driver glares at me, giving me the finger as I swerve to the left, my mouth open in shock. I pedal on but slower and steadier now, taking more care as I wipe the rain from my face, trying to ignore the damp seeping through my clothes, the mud splattering up my legs and back. I just want to get home and shut out the world.

Twenty minutes later and I reach the final roundabout before the downhill run home – less traffic now that I'm well out of the city, and much safer, even though the streetlights are further apart, the roads not as well lit. But the roundabout is clear, so I kick up my pace again, taking out the day's frustration on my legs, pushing myself to the limit as I lean into the curve, cycling around until my exit comes up, squinting against the rain as it stings my face. I hear my breathing as I push on – deep, laboured pants as I pedal. Then, out of the blue, that film is on my mind again, along with everything else that goes with it.

Suddenly, it's as though I'm not cycling at all – I'm running, screaming and panicking as the flames take hold, the horror of what I've done gripping me by the throat.

I cough and screw up my eyes, forcing back the tears.

Please, just let me get home…

I don't see the van pulling out until it's too late – wipers flapping, exhaust belching, the driver looking down, not concentrating as he speeds towards me. I brake hard but there's nothing I can do to stop him hitting me, crying out as I go down, my hands flying out in slow motion, my leg crushing beneath metal. The pain is so intense it doesn't seem real.

There's nothing I can do at all as the world goes completely black.

Everything extinguished.

CHAPTER ONE

Ella

Ella is not dead. She knows this much. She senses something, aside from the ripping pain in her body, that tells her she's still alive.

It's her thoughts. Her mind. Her unconsciousness bleeding back into a conscious state, punctuated by occasional noises – so *loud* – and flashes of light behind her eyelids, something brushing against her skin.

I'm not dead.

She goes with it. Relief that thoughts are now forming into silent words, sentences even, rather than primal feelings swirling inside her head.

Then she hears more words, someone *else's* words. Comforting words.

'Ella, love…'

A hand on her forehead.

'Ella, it's OK. You're in hospital. Can you hear me?'

A hand on her shoulder.

'Open your eyes if you can, Ella. You're going to be OK…'

Someone adjusting the sheets. Sandpaper on her skin.

She tries to move her lips, open her eyes, but nothing happens. Or maybe her eyes *are* open, her mouth forming words, but her brain hasn't reconnected to them yet. She twitches a finger.

'That's it, Ella… move your hand, love. Can you open your eyes?'

Ella tries but her eyelids are stuck together. Sewn up.

What happened to me? she wants to ask, but nothing comes out, so she searches the depths of her mind instead. It must all be in there.

Sheeting rain… the roundabout… pedalling hard… darkness…

A shudder runs the length of her body, as though someone's fed an electric current through her, igniting every cell.

'I didn't want to go to the pub,' she hears someone whisper, breathy and barely there.

It's her own voice. She spoke.

'There was a fire…' she says. Nothing makes sense. 'It hurts.'

'There was no fire, love. Where's the worst pain?' The other voice is kind, soothing, making Ella feel that, while she knows something terrible has happened, it somehow seems bearable as long as that voice is there.

But still her eyes won't open.

A hand on her forehead again, stroking.

'My leg. Everywhere,' Ella says, wincing as the shrillness of her voice cuts through her head, even though she's only whispering.

'I'll top up your pain relief,' the kind voice says. 'You're due some more. I'm Sue, by the way. Your nurse.'

Ella hears noises around her, then another, different voice. Everything is so loud.

'Is she coming round?'

'Does Mr Hicks know?'

'You going out to Malc's birthday drinks after shift?'

None of it makes sense.

'I've just topped up your meds through your drip,' the nurse says.

Ella feels her breath on her cheek. Warm and sweet, as though she's recently drunk sugary coffee.

Then she hears a chair being dragged close, feels the nurse taking her hand. She wants to scream out that it hurts – her leg, her arm, her head – but she doesn't have the energy. It takes all her resources just to breathe.

'Can you hear me, Ella, love? Squeeze my hand if you can.'

Ella does as she's told, forcing her fingers to clench. The nurse's hand feels warm and soft, full of life, as her brittle fingers clamp around it. Gripping on.

'Well done, Ella. You've been in a medically induced coma for several days, my love. You're going to be fine, but you had an accident. Your leg is broken and your wrist has several fractures. The doctors decided a coma was the best place for you to recover from the brain swelling.' She pauses. 'You weren't wearing a helmet.'

Ella doesn't know what she's talking about. She searches her mind but only finds fragments of a puzzle, little disconnected pieces that won't yet fit together.

'Accident?'

'You were knocked off your bike, love,' the nurse goes on.

That's when Ella sees herself, as if from above, cycling onto the roundabout, pedalling hard, nearly home.

And then the van.

For a second, she remembers it. Two bright saucers of light, the sheeting rain making her squint, the wipers flapping fast across the windscreen.

Ella just wanted to get home. Pedalled harder. Leant into the curve of the roundabout to get past. But…

'*Oh*…' She hears herself sobbing as the memory comes. Screws up her eyes, even though they've not opened yet. Her chest is tight, her breathing hard.

'Just try to relax, love. The morphine will start to work in a moment.'

The sound of the monitor returns to a steadier beep as Ella consciously slows her breathing, tries not to dwell on the reforming memories in her fuzzy mind.

'I can't move my leg,' she says, willing her body to move. But the right one feels like a dead weight, clamped and heavy. Filled with pain. The left one moves a little when she forces her muscles, the sheets rustling as her foot twitches.

'You had an operation,' the nurse says. 'They had to put a metal pin in your knee, so you'll be making good friends with airport security officers now.'

Sue laughs but Ella can't understand why. Is she going somewhere? Ella doesn't think she's been on a plane for a long while. Has no desire to.

Work, home, sleep. Work, home, sleep.

All she wants is to be alone and for the pain to go away. No, she won't be going on any planes.

'Why don't you try to open your eyes, Ella?' Sue says. 'You're in Critical Care right now, so don't be alarmed by all the equipment. Just try to get your bearings a little.'

Bearings? Ella thinks. She doesn't want to get her bearings, not here anyway.

'I want to go home,' she manages to say.

'That's a good sign,' the nurse says with a little laugh. 'But one step at a time, eh? Maybe you could manage a few sips of water? Your throat must be very dry.'

'I don't understand,' Ella says, her mind swimming with thoughts that don't even seem like hers. 'There was a fire,' she hears herself saying.

'No, love. There was no fire,' Sue says again, dabbing something cool and wet against her lips. 'You can suck on this if you like. It's just a little sponge dipped in water.'

Ella opens her mouth, allowing the wetness to dribble onto her lips and tongue. It feels good.

'If you can manage to open your eyes, you'd make a certain person very happy later,' Sue goes on.

Ella doesn't think she's made anyone happy in a long time.

'Your lovely man has visited you every day since the accident.'

Ella thinks about this. Allows her brain to search and scan, seeking out the image of a 'lovely man' – or, indeed, *any* man who would visit her in hospital, let alone every day. She can't think of a single one.

'Lovely man,' Ella repeats, hoping it will jog her memory. Her mind remains blank. 'I-I don't know?…'

'Your husband,' Sue says kindly. 'Unless you have lots of lovely men in your life?' She squeezes Ella's hand, giving a little laugh.

'*Husband?*' Ella repeats, trying to process what the nurse is telling her. There's a gap, a blank zone in her memory. The puzzle pieces won't be forced together.

'He's hardly left your side since you were brought in.'

'Oh,' Ella says, still confused.

'He's a keeper, for sure.'

Ella feels her hair being tucked behind her ear then, her cheek stroked.

'And quite a looker, too,' Sue says in a whisper, giving her hand another squeeze.

But Ella can't recall if he's a keeper, a looker, or anything else for that matter. Because right now, lying in the hospital bed, scarcely able to move a muscle, Ella doesn't even remember getting married.

'What an awful thing to happen to newly-weds. You were all over the local news by morning,' Sue goes on, oblivious to Ella's lagging thoughts.

She needs to catch up, needs to figure out *who* her 'lovely man' is – perhaps a quick snapshot in her mind of their wedding day. Tap into an image of them together.

But there's nothing.

Ella wants to say something, wants to ask the nurse who he is, what he looks like, tell her that she can't remember anything about him, let alone marrying him – and she certainly doesn't want to have been on the news. But the sick coming up her throat overtakes the words as she retches and gags. Suddenly, her upper half is twisted sideways as Sue angles her head down, the nurse's strong hands supporting her.

'Let it out, my love,' she hears her say. 'It's OK. I've got a dish here.'

Ella's stomach clenches and knots, sending up watery, foul-tasting bile. There's nothing in her.

Gently, Sue settles her back down. Ella feels too exhausted to speak, let alone ask about her husband.

'Don't worry,' the nurse says, wiping Ella's mouth with a tissue. 'Sickness is common. I'll get something written up for it.'

She makes it sound so normal, Ella thinks. Drugs. Vomiting. Broken bones. Husbands. Operations and comas. And to her, it probably is. But this isn't normal for Ella; she knows that much, at least, as she searches her mind for answers. She cycles to work… an office, yes, with lots of equipment. Sandwiches, headphones, colleagues, the bank of monitors on her desk. Every day the same.

Work, home, sleep…

'He was reading to you, you know. Poetry.'

Ella hears the nurse flipping through a book.

'Sylvia Plath,' she says.

'Sylvia,' Ella whispers. There's a woman at work called Sylvia, she remembers – shards of life filtering back.

'He told me it was your favourite. Though it looks a bit…' The nurse trails off, making a puzzled noise in her throat.

Ella hears the book dropping onto a surface beside her. She knows for sure she's not read any Plath since… well, since way back. She feels sick again.

Open your eyes, she begs herself. *Please…*

'Anyway, he'll be here soon. He brings you something lovely every visit. Though we couldn't let him leave the flowers. They're not allowed on the ward. Yesterday, he gave you a foot and hand massage with aromatherapy oils,' Sue goes on, oblivious to Ella's confusion. 'Well, the ones that aren't in plaster,' she adds, with a chuckle.

Ella wonders if it's the shock of hearing all this that allows her to catch a flash of light in her left eye. Then, suddenly, both eyes are open. Everything's so bright, so blurry as her vision swims in and out of focus. The ward seems huge around her – like a football pitch. Or maybe it's her that's small now. Tiny. Insignificant. Almost gone.

So bright!

'A massage?' Ella says, trying to turn her head. 'I don't understand.' Her eyes feel swollen and painful in their sockets as she looks around at Sue. She's older than Ella pictured. The world is still a blurry, unfamiliar place.

'He brought you these,' Sue says, holding up several glossy magazines plus an expensive-looking box of chocolates. 'It's amazing none of the night staff have helped themselves.'

Ella tracks Sue's hand as she puts the gifts back on the bedside locker. Then she sees the card.

'Want to have a look?' Sue says, picking it up.

Ella takes it, her hand shaking. On the front, there are flowers. A photograph of a huge embossed bouquet with gold writing above

Get Well Soon, Darling

She opens it, revealing the message, trying to focus.

'"To my darling Ella",' Sue reads out loud for her. '"Nothing will keep us apart – the fire in our hearts will burn for ever. All my love, Jacob." And he's put loads of kisses at the end, see?'

'Jacob...' Ella says, trying to remember. And, just as she spots the gold ring on her left hand, part of her thinks she does.

Ella doesn't know how many hours or maybe even days later it is, but Sue is still here, attending to her regularly as other members of staff come and go, doing their jobs around the ward. Banks of machines and monitors surround her, lines running to a drip stand from the back of her hand.

'Was I asleep?' she asks, trying to sit up but overcome by dizziness.

'It's normal,' Sue replies, nodding, smiling down at her as she changes a bag of saline. 'Your body's doing a lot of healing.'

Ella looks down the length of the bed, one leg fatter than the other. The cast. Her right arm is similarly plastered from mid-forearm to her fingers. 'Why do I feel so?...' she says, trailing off, not knowing exactly how she feels. Just that it's not like her.

'Tired?' Sue says, sitting down.

'Yes, but that's not all. I-I mean, I know who I am and everything. But some bits just don't make sense. And... it's scaring me.'

'Imagine what your brain's just been through, my lovely,' Sue says, rubbing her hand. 'Memory is a funny thing but it'll come back. Mr Hicks will check on you tomorrow. You can ask him about it.'

'But there's nothing wrong with my memory,' Ella says, frowning. 'I know exactly—'

'Ah...' Sue says, suddenly standing up. 'What good timing.' She leans down then, sweeping some hair off Ella's face. 'Jacob is here, Ella,' she whispers. 'You'll feel better now.'

Ella looks over, her vision still blurry at distance. Several visitors are coming and going, nurses attending the other patients. Then she sees the shape of a man in the doorway at the other end of the ward – a tall and commanding figure. He comes closer, briefly blocking the bright light from the window as he approaches, finally standing at the end of the bed.

'Good news,' Sue says, going up to him, touching his arm as if she knows him well. 'Ella's awake, look. The doctors were so happy with her progress, so they decided to bring her round early.'

Ella hears a voice. Deep and low. She can't tell what he says. Can't make out who he is.

Or perhaps she doesn't *want* to.

'She's in and out of sleep still and quite confused,' Sue says to the man. 'Ella, your husband's here, my love,' she adds, turning back to the bed. 'Say hello to Jacob.' She fiddles with Ella's hair again, as if it's her duty to make Ella look presentable, even though she can still smell vomit on her chest.

Jacob…

The figure slowly comes closer, his features gradually resolving, taking Ella's breath away as she stares up, unable to take her eyes off him. Maybe she's still in a coma, she thinks – *prays to God she's still in a coma* – and if she's not, then she feels like she'll pass out again anyway.

'Jacob…' she whispers, her expression crumpling into a frown. '*Husband…*' she says, meaning it to sound like a question, even though it doesn't come out that way.

'I'm here, my darling,' he says, not taking his eyes off her.

He bends down and cups her face in his hands, giving her an adoring look before kissing her tenderly on the mouth. When he slowly pulls away, his eyes are still closed as if he's just feasted after a famine. He takes Ella's hands, burying them in the warmth of his.

She feels his perspiration.

'I'm here now, my darling, and everything's going to be fine. Just like it was before.' He sits down on the chair beside the bed, not taking his eyes off her.

He's not my husband! I've never been married! Ella wants to scream, but she can't say a word. Can't move a muscle. Nothing works. She's completely frozen.

'I'll leave you two lovebirds alone for a while,' Sue says, smiling, closing the curtains around them.

A moment later, Ella throws up again.

CHAPTER TWO

Ella

Ella stares up at him, watery vomit dribbling down her chin. He plucks a couple of tissues from the box beside the bed and dabs at her skin gently, cleaning her up.

'I've been so worried about you, darling,' he says, his voice quiet and deep, as if he doesn't want to be overheard. 'I thought I'd lost you for ever.' He throws the tissues away and sits down again, stroking her arm. 'And I couldn't bear that. Not again.'

'What... what are you?...' Ella wants to say *doing here?* but her brain, her thoughts and her mouth aren't properly connected. Fear tears through her, consuming her, as she stares back at him, not believing what she's seeing. *Who* she's seeing.

Husband...

She touches her forehead, praying that her brain will start functioning properly, that this feeling will go. That any moment now she'll wake up.

'I've come to take care of my beautiful girl, of course,' he says, leaning forward and kissing her again just as the nurse comes back.

'Oh, you two,' Sue says, eyeing them with a smile. She places a new cardboard dish on the table at the end of the bed. 'Just in case.'

'I'll take good care of her,' he says, smiling. He grips Ella's hands in his again, his sweat seeping into her skin.

Poison.

'You're a lucky girl,' Sue says, hands on hips. 'My man doesn't even make me a Lemsip when I get ill.' She rolls her eyes, grins, goes off again, pulling the curtain closed.

'Why are you?…' Ella mumbles, staring at him. Her lips are chapped. She can feel the dry flakes sitting between her words. Isn't even sure if she said them.

'Alive?' He gets up and slips off his jacket, draping it over the back of the chair. Then shifts even closer. 'Because I'm a survivor, Ella-bella. And I told you. I've come to take care of you, of course. And when you're well enough to leave hospital, we'll be together again. Just as we should be.'

'But—'

A finger presses against her lips. She wants to bite it off but it pushes down harder, hurting her now. A second later, his whole hand is covering her mouth and nose. He leans down on her, the pressure making it impossible to breathe. Ella tries to cry out but can't.

'No buts, Mrs Ella Sinclair. I want you to listen to me very, *very* carefully, OK?'

Ella nods frantically, grabbing at his wrist with her good arm, trying to get his hand off her mouth, but he slams it down with his free hand, trapping it on the bed. She sees the anger in his eyes as she shakes beneath him.

'I am Jacob Sinclair. I am your husband. Never *ever* call me anything else. Understand?'

She nods again, terrified and barely able to move as he forces her head into the pillow. She twists to the side, trying to break free, but it's useless. Her left leg thrashes.

'Good girl,' he says, keeping the pressure on her mouth. 'You are my wife. You still love me, don't you?'

Ella stares up at him, her eyes blurry from the tears. *He's not real, he's not real…* she tells herself over and over, but she doesn't believe the terrified voice in her head. She just wants to be able to breathe.

'*Don't* you?' he whispers, spit landing on her face. He glances across at the curtains around the bed, shoving her face again.

He swims in and out of focus, the present mixed up with the past.

She wants to shake her head, scream out: *No, I don't love you. I hate you!* but she can't.

Tell me… he mouths at her, finally releasing his hand.

Ella sucks in hard, gulping air. She can hardly move, let alone speak. 'Yes,' she pants breathlessly. 'I love you,' she says just as Sue comes back inside the curtains.

She grins at the pair of them.

'Just checking the monitors, love,' she says, squeezing past Jacob. 'Oh… does your breathing feel OK?' she asks Ella, glancing between her and the screens.

Ella manages a small nod as the blood pressure cuff squeezes tight around her arm. It keeps on gripping, just like the pressure she feels in her head.

'All fine,' Sue says, clipping something on to the end of Ella's finger. She frowns, makes notes and leaves again.

'I know it's a shock,' Jacob says when she's gone. 'Seeing me.'

Ella stares at him – can't bring herself to call him Jacob. Can't bring herself to call him *anything*, because that would mean acknowledging that he's real. And he's not. He *can't* be.

'I read to you while you were asleep, you know,' he says, tapping the book on the cupboard beside her bed. 'I know how much you love *Ariel*.'

'I don't,' Ella forces herself to say, turning her head She loves nothing about that time in her life.

'And I played you Debussy. And Kate Bush.' The smile again. 'You can't tell me you don't love *them*.'

Ella doesn't love anything any more; hasn't for ten years, making sure her life is devoid of things to have an opinion about. She feels a hot tear dribble out of one eye.

'Oh don't cry, my darling,' he says. His hand is on her cheek, tilting her head back round towards him. When she puts up resistance, he forces her to look at him. 'When we're home, I'll get you all your favourite treats. Iced coffee? Dark chocolate with cherries? Toast and honey at midnight?' He laughs then – a little secret shared. Lines that never used to be there crease the corners of his eyes, marking the passage of time, even though he's been dead for a decade.

Ella turns away, staring down at her feet. She sees the plaster cast poking out from the end of the sheets, her numb toes showing.

'Well, whatever it is you want, I'll make sure you have it.'

'I don't want anything,' she says. 'Please go.'

'Don't be like that,' he says. 'You know you don't mean it.'

Ella stares up at him, feeling nauseous again. She thought she'd escaped. She thought she was free. 'I am not married to you,' she whispers. 'I never will be. And I'm not going home with you.'

'Ella, Ella, *Ella-bella…*' he says, giving her a look just as the nurse comes back again. He lifts her left hand, touching the ring on her finger, turning it round and round. 'I'm sure Sue here will tell you the medication can make you feel glum, a bit down. Isn't that right?' he says, turning to her.

Sue pulls the blood pressure monitor out of its small space, wheeling it towards the gap in the curtain.

'Definitely,' she says, her eyes flicking between Ella and Jacob. 'But we don't take our eyes off you here in Critical Care, love.' She gives Ella a wink.

It's been a long time since anyone did that, Ella thinks. Then she's reminded of someone from the office – a kind face, someone with a smile. She touches her head… *Liam*, she thinks, recalling him, how he'd make her coffee, often stop at her desk for a chat. But as quickly as the thought comes, she pushes it away. Real life has no place here, not with *him* sitting beside her. She watches as Sue leaves again.

'What do you want from me?' she whispers when they're alone, whipping her hand out of his. She tries to pull off the ring, but it's a tight fit and stuck fast.

'You.'

Ella stares ahead, trying to destroy the new reality in her mind, bring it back to the safe landscape she knows. But it's not working. She may as well be back there, that night, that summer. She swears she can smell burning.

'I love you,' he says. 'And I know you love me too. That's why I gave you this.' He touches the ring.

'*No*,' Ella says, her breathing quickening, tears welling up. 'I don't love you. I *hate* you and… I thought you were dead.' She turns away, not wanting to see him. She hears the chair scrape back, him doing something as if he's fumbling in his jacket.

Then he grabs her face, whipping her head around, his fingers clamped tightly around her jawbone as he forces her to look at him. He rams something up close – something square and plastic shoved under her nose. He rattles it, his face consumed by anger. When he holds it above her, she sees it's a small videotape – an old-fashioned one from a camcorder.

'Does *this* help you change your mind?' Jacob says, his teeth clenched, his jaw twitching.

Ella can't help the gasp when she sees it, her eyes growing wide as she reads the faded label.

Lake House 08.

And she can't hide the terror on her face as it dawns on her what it is, where it's come from. Jacob shoves her head as he lets go, smirking as he watches her reaction. They both know what it is. What it means.

'So,' he says, looking smug, 'we could have a movie night when you get out of here. What do you think?'

'I think you're crazy,' Ella says, shaking. 'Why do you?… *How* do you?…' She covers her mouth, imagining the horror recorded on the tape, fast-forwarding through that terrible night. She screws up her eyes but can still hear the screams, still feel the blistering heat on her skin.

'Bottle of wine and a pizza, perhaps? The pair of us cuddled up on the sofa as we watch. We could even light the *fire*, couldn't we, Ella-bella?'

But Ella can't speak. Her heart is racing and her mind frozen as she stares at the plastic box in his hand. If what's on that tape gets out… 'Oh *God*,' she whimpers, tears collecting in her eyes. She covers her face, fighting back the sickness again.

'So, it's agreed. When you're discharged, you will come home with me. You will be my beautiful wife and we'll finally, *finally*, be a proper family? It's what we always wanted.' He sits down again, making a throaty sound, shoving the tape in her face again. 'You really have no choice but to do everything I say, Ella-bella.'

No, you're dead, you're dead! She wants to scream, but instead she nods frantically, recoiling from him.

'Yes,' she whispers, terrified, staring up at him.

And I should know, she thinks. *Because I killed you.*

CHAPTER THREE

Ella

'So, tell me, how did you two meet?' Sue sits beside Ella's bed. Her face is keen, eager, hopeful of hearing about a chance meeting in an elevator, their eyes catching across a bar, or perhaps their dogs drew them together in the park. True love ever after.

Ella doesn't know what to say. Doesn't know what's already been said. She decides on, 'Long story.'

'The best ones always are.'

Ella thinks about this. How, in truth, it's been a life cut short. A book with the middle pages ripped out. And she never saw the ending coming. She screws up her eyes.

'What is it you do?' Sue says, pressing on, unperturbed by Ella's reluctance to talk. She probably puts it down to grogginess, the medication. Ella's been in and out of sleep since he left. Snatches of freedom, oblivion, until she wakes again and remembers, covered in sweat, shaking.

'Film,' Ella replies. 'Editing and post-production.'

'Ooh, interesting. Ever met anyone famous?' Sue says, checking her watch.

Ella manages a small smile. She's on solid ground talking about work. 'No, it's not that kind of film. I do shorter indie commissions, plus promotional and corporate stuff. Sometimes charities or other agencies wanting to get a powerful message across.'

The pain in her head presses against her skull, as if her brain is trying to get out. If she moves her eyes too fast, she sees shooting lights.

'Sounds technical,' Sue says. 'You were wearing a work lanyard when you were brought in, so someone left a voice message for your HR department that same evening. So they know what's happened.'

Ella gives a little nod, wondering who will have taken on her projects. Liam, she supposes. His face pops into her mind again – his stubbly beard, his kind eyes. She'd been fast running out of reasons not to smile back or engage when he poked his head around the partition. She hasn't wanted to seem rude, but it's what she likes most about where she works – that she usually has her headphones on, that they all have their own little private spaces, mostly sealed off from everyone else.

'But no one's been in touch,' Sue adds.

'It's a busy office,' Ella replies, feeling the need to make excuses, wondering if anyone's even noticed she's not at her desk. She reaches for her water glass, taking a sip. The nurses make sure everything's within her reach. Twice she's pushed the book of Sylvia Plath poems on the floor, and twice they've picked it up.

'Anyway,' Sue says, standing up, peering at the stats screen, frowning. She checks a couple of leads stuck to Ella's chest. 'Mr Hicks thinks you're progressing very well and that's what counts. You'll be out of here in no time, you'll see.'

'When?' Ella doesn't want particularly to be out of here, unless it's back to her flat, alone. In fact, being wheeled off to the morgue would be preferable to the other option – leaving with him, Jacob. She can see why he's changed his name – same surname for the newly-weds. Clever.

'Mr Hicks will assess your recovery day by day.' Sue makes a kind face. 'There'll be more scans of course. The neuros are a fussy bunch: Mr Hicks particularly. He put you in that coma for a reason – perhaps overcautiously, but necessary nonetheless. You'll go to the general ward soon and we'll take it from there.'

Ella doesn't understand.

'When you were brought in, the initial scans indicated that medical sedation was best, allowing your brain to heal. But further tests while you were asleep showed that things weren't as bad as they had first seemed. That's why they brought you round.'

'That's good then?'

'Indeed,' Sue says, turning to go. 'But you'll not be a hundred per cent for a little while yet. You can't just up and go after something like this. And besides, the physios have their magic to work on you.' She taps Ella's cast.

'But what if I want to go home now?' Ella says, knowing she'll find a way to manage on her own. She just needs to get out of here before *he* comes back. But she's so sleepy all the time, and disorientated – making her wonder if she was hallucinating earlier, if he was even here at all. Mr Hicks said that was normal – feeling muddled, experiencing missing time and even imagining things that aren't real. She crosses the fingers of her left hand, noticing the ring again. There's still dirt under her nails from the accident.

'I bet you can't wait to get back to your man,' Sue says, her face lighting up. '*And* your new home. It looks beautiful from the pictures. Jacob was telling me all about it.'

'He was?'

Sue comes back to her bedside. 'Plenty of space for a family.'

'But—'

'No hurry though, eh? You just focus on getting well. Jacob will take good care of you. Such a terrible thing to happen right before your move.'

Ella frowns, touching her cheek. It helps to feel her own skin, to know she's actually here, real, because nothing else feels that way. 'Move?'

'Yes, love. You don't remember?'

Ella shakes her head.

'Jacob was in the middle of packing boxes when he heard the news. What a shock for him, finding out about you like that.'

'I really don't understand,' Ella says, biting her lip.

'He came to the ward in a terrible state, desperate to find you.'

Ella wants to sit up, but can't. She tried earlier and it made her feel woozy. 'He did?'

'After that, he rarely left your side,' Sue explains. 'He managed your house move all by himself, in between visits.'

'What do you mean, "finding out about me like that"?' Nothing makes sense, let alone a house move.

'I already told you, love. You'd made the local news by the next morning. Just a small clip, and on the radio too. That's how poor Jacob found out.'

Ella sits up by pressing the button on the side of her bed. 'Sorry, I forgot.' She touches her head, knowing she keeps getting confused – even thinking it was still yesterday when she's actually been out of her coma forty-eight hours and today is a new day. She remembers her mother saying that: *Today's a new day.* It seemed to cover up the past, mistakes, things that weren't to be mentioned.

'Why was my accident on the news?' she asks, imagining Jacob's reaction.

'The driver of the van didn't stop.' Sue pulls a sympathetic face. 'It was a hit-and-run.'

Ella can't help the gasp as she sees snatches of the accident in her mind again – flashes of memory that, when she's not thinking about them, don't seem real. She can't control when they appear in her mind. *Rain... pedalling... the blow from behind... her back wheel skidding sideways... her going down. Her arm reaching out... her leg crushed...*

'The police were appealing for witnesses. They released your name and a picture of the accident scene, hoping someone, or the driver, would come forward. Such a terrible way for your husband to find out. He dropped everything and came straight here.'

Ella searches her mind. Comes up with nothing.

'He thought you were stopping at a friend's house the night of the accident, after a meal out, don't you remember? He said that's why he didn't worry about you when he couldn't reach you after work.'

Ella stares at Sue. *Friend? Meal out?* She has no idea what she's talking about.

'It was so terrible for him, seeing you intubated and unconscious. He said he texted you the next morning, but of course you were here. And your phone battery was dead by then. By the way, all the stuff you had in your backpack is safe.' She taps the bedside locker.

'I see…' Ella says, thinking hard, trying to make sense of everything. What if she *is* married to Jacob? What if everything she knows to be real *isn't* real – her job, her flat, all those years of keeping herself to herself, only enjoying life in tiny allowed snatches – sunshine in the park, a favourite TV series, her embroidery? But Ella is certain there's nothing wrong with her long-term memory. All of those things are real.

He is not.

She forces a little smile, resting her head back, closing her eyes again.

'Right,' the young man says. 'Shall we do this?' He's wearing a white polo shirt and trousers. He has a wheelchair in front of him.

'Do what?' Ella says, opening her eyes, though she wasn't asleep.

'Get you into this.'

Ella stairs at the chair hopefully. 'Am I going home?' It seems like she's been here for ever.

He laughs. 'Will a whizz around the ward suffice for now?'

Ella nods. *It's a start*, she thinks. *A step closer.*

'I'm John, by the way,' he says. 'One of the physios.'

He's young, Ella thinks. *Mid-twenties. Filled with get-up-and-go*, which is what she'd like to do.

'And it's my job to mobilise you. You can't lie in bed for ever.' He grins.

'Just tell me what to do and I'll do it,' Ella says and spends the next ten minutes listening intently, learning about her knee injury, how to sit up and get positioned for the transition into the wheelchair. To Ella, the gap between bed and seat seems as daunting as swimming the Channel.

But, with John's help, she manages it. The drip stand has to come with them, wheeled alongside. Everything hurts. She feels nauseous and light-headed.

'Ready?' he says.

'As I'll ever be,' Ella replies, feeling one-fraction more liberated.

But, just as they're about to leave the new ward she's been moved to, Sue comes in – she's already told Ella she splits her shifts between the two departments – with Jacob beside her.

'Just in time,' she sings out. 'Jacob, do you fancy learning how to steer your wife in that chair? You'd better get used to it.'

And to Ella's horror, John moves aside allowing Jacob to take the wheelchair handles. He leans down from behind, giving her a kiss on the head.

She can smell him – fresh and dangerous.

'I'd love to,' he says, unaware that Ella is fighting back the tears, her entire body shaking.

CHAPTER FOUR

Ten Years Ago

'Oh, I *just* want to sit out in the sun,' Ella said, chewing her pencil and gazing out of the window. A nerdy boy with glasses glared at them from the next table to where she and Meggie were sitting, a pile of books surrounding them, their laptops open. The two girls glared back, Meggie making a face as she stretched out her bare legs in the puddle of sunlight. It was their favourite spot in the library. They'd learnt long ago, at the start of their degree, that studying outside meant only one thing – distraction.

'He's always such a twat,' Meggie mouthed at Ella, rolling her eyes and making her friend giggle as she caught the boy's eye. 'How many words now?' she asked, cupping her chin in her hands.

'Five hundred left to do. Then I need to go through my referencing. It's all over the place.' Ella locked eyes with the boy sitting across from them, trying to outstare him. But she ended up looking away first, his eyes sunken and intense, his lips thin and pursed. There was something creepy about him. She didn't think they were making *that* much noise.

Meggie pulled a pained face. 'Goody two-shoes,' she said playfully. 'Two thousand left to write here.'

'What have you been *doing* all this time?' Ella asked, grinning, glancing across at the boy again. He was still staring. If there was a way to procrastinate, Meggie would find it. But she still managed top grades – a poster girl for being amazing without having to try. And she was stunning, too. Boys fell at her feet.

Meggie forced a guilty look which ended in another giggle.

'*Sshhh*…' Nerdy Boy hissed, not taking his eyes off Ella, even though Meggie was making more noise.

'Sorry,' Ella mouthed back, while Meggie gave him the middle finger. She leant forward across the table, whispering. 'We've seen him around for several years and I still don't know his name.' She gave the boy another glance. He was tapping his finger slowly on the edge of the desk.

'Yeah, his name's Twat Face,' Meggie said at normal volume, spraying out laughter. 'Anyway, I'm busy writing an email,' she confessed to Ella, whispering again.

Ella rolled her eyes. 'Get. On. With. Your. Essay. The deadline's midnight tonight.'

Meggie pulled a stony expression then folded her arms, which Ella took to mean she wanted to be grilled about the email.

'Harry?' Ella whispered, still hopeful he and Meggie would get together.

Surprisingly, Meggie shook her head. Ella knew she fancied him like mad.

'Can I read it?'

'Nope. Anyway, it's not about me. It's about *you*. And it's not finished yet.'

'Neither is your essay,' Ella said, covering her mouth when she realised she wasn't whispering. She heard the nerdy boy say something under his breath, though couldn't make out what.

'Fine,' Meggie said, switching back to her Word document. 'I'll just copy and paste stuff from the Internet and change bits here and there.' If anyone could get away with it, Meggie could.

Ella began typing again, trying to concentrate, but she couldn't.

'You can't just leave me hanging. An email about me *what*? And who to?' she said five minutes later, giving Meggie a playful poke with her foot under the table.

Meggie tapped the side of her nose.

'Tell me!' Ella whispered.

During their time at Durham, Meggie had made it her business to help orchestrate Ella's social life, believing she'd been holding herself back and not allowing herself the 'full university experience', as she put it. It always made Ella smile; she appreciated her friend's determination to get her to date, party more and live on the edge a little, but Meggie didn't know the half of it. She didn't know that, since starting her degree, she'd had more fun than she'd ever had in her entire life so far.

During the first few weeks at St Mary's College, they'd become close friends, despite their very different backgrounds. While Meggie's life consisted of public school, wealthy parents with a London home as well as a country house, a large allowance and lavish holidays, Ella had grown up on a council estate in Birmingham and attended the local comprehensive. Holidays were either spent camping in Wales, crammed into a tiny caravan with her twin brother, Harry, their mum and stepdad, or a long weekend at a bed and breakfast in Suffolk where they were allowed to take the dog.

English literature had initially drawn Meggie and Ella together. Each sharing a love of poetry, they'd hit it off right away when Meggie spotted Ella sitting alone during the first week with her nose stuck between the pages of a Ted Hughes collection. Wary at first, Ella had soon warmed to Meggie's outspoken, flirtatious and confident nature – the way she instantly put her at ease, including her in the circle of friends she'd already made, some of whom she already knew from school. Ella's quiet nature, her more reserved and cautious outlook on her new life – so very different to what she was used to – had been a good contrast to Meggie's exuberance. Meggie was the girl Ella had always dreamed of being – popular, funny and beautiful – and, she'd thought, if she couldn't be like that herself, then maybe she could experience it by being in Meggie's presence.

Meggie suddenly made a slashing sign in the air with her forefinger. 'Zed is for…' She winked, teasing, making a show of typing again. Ella's mouth dropped open. Dear God, *no*… It wasn't as though she didn't like to have fun in the same way the other girls did, having various crushes on boys or one too many drinks and being silly and flirty. It's just that she didn't take things as far as the others. It was the way she was, how she'd been brought up. Cautious. Observant. Safe.

'Don't you *dare*,' Ella said, actually meaning the opposite, though she'd never say. Meggie knew she had a crush on Zach, like every other girl in their year, but Ella had no intention of *ever* acting on it. For a start, there was no way he'd be interested in a girl like her – he'd dated some of the most beautiful girls on campus. But so far, none had broken through Zachary White's enigmatic veneer. He was either determined to stay single or had very high standards.

'Might be too late to stop me,' Meggie said, closing her laptop lid. 'Fuck this place, I'm going for a coffee. Coming?'

'Dear God, tell me you didn't send it?' Ella said, half standing and leaning forward on the desk, secretly hoping she had.

A couple of books dropped onto the floor. Nerdy Boy sighed, giving Ella his angriest look yet while covering his ears with his hands.

Meggie turned and made a face back at him, packing up her stuff. 'It was only a short one. I just told him to be done with it and ask you out already. I said that you really liked him.'

'But I barely *know* him, so how can I even like him?' Ella sat down again, slowly reaching for the dropped books. Her heart skipped a beat. In all this time, she'd only had a couple of brief conversations with Zach. She had wondered once or twice if she'd caught him looking at her, and then there were the handful of times he'd seemed to make sure he got a seat near to her during the formals they'd had. He was the only boy able to interpret a black-tie dress code as black jeans, a dinner jacket and a paisley cravat and get away with it. He had a roguish air about him; sort of devil-may-care, Ella thought. But, in the end, she decided she'd been imagining the looks, as well as the feeling he gave her inside. It was easier that way.

'Why didn't you just get Charles to say something to him instead? *Way* less embarrassing.'

'Boys are rubbish at communicating. Trust me, a flirty note from your bestie is going to get his attention far more than Charles sniggering in his ear about him giving you one.'

'No one's giving me *anything*,' Ella said loudly, quickly covering her mouth.

Nerdy Boy slammed his laptop lid closed and gathered his books, standing up to move to another table. She felt a tingle down her back as he walked past, coming unnecessarily close, bumping her shoulder as he passed.

'Oh do fuck off,' Meggie said in a loud whisper as he left.

'Shh, don't,' Ella said, suddenly feeling scared, rubbing her shoulder. 'He's weird as fuck.' Another shudder ran through her.

'Well, we'll just have to see what Zach replies, won't we,' she continued, ignoring the other boy and slipping her feet into her sandals. 'Come on. Let's see who's outside.'

Ella hesitated. 'I think I'll stay here for a bit. Get these last paragraphs done.' She smiled up at Meggie.

'Fine. But when you're all burnt out, don't come crying to me.' She slung her bag over her arm, clutching her laptop to her chest, pushing up her cleavage from within the short dress she was wearing.

'And when it's five to midnight and you've got a thousand words left to write, don't come begging me to do them.'

Ella returned to her laptop, trying not to smile when she caught sight of Meggie's tongue poking out.

'Laters,' she said and walked off.

Zachary White, Ella thought to herself, leaning back in her chair and staring out of the window. What was it about him she liked, she wondered? Was it that he was a bit different to all the other boys – the way he dressed, the way he carried himself, the way he spoke? She remembered instantly liking his voice, the way he pronounced his words perfectly, slowly, thoughtfully. He clearly came from a similar background to Meggie and her friends – that wasn't uncommon at a place like Durham University – but Zachary White seemed to take 'posh' to an entirely new level, making it seem cool rather than entitled. She knew he was from the south, possibly London, and she'd imagined him living somewhere like Kensington or Knightsbridge, though he'd probably gone to a boarding school in the country like some of the others in their friendship group. She tried to imagine what it must have been like growing up rich, what his childhood was like, but the only thing she knew for sure was that it would have been very different to hers and Harry's.

Despite being in the same college – St Mary's – and hanging out with a few of the same friends, they'd had little chance to chat or get to know each other properly. Given that they'd all be going their separate ways in a few months, Meggie's email might be her last and only chance.

'Zach, Zach, *Zach…*' she whispered under her breath. The more she thought about him, the more she realised she liked his crazy dark hair – the long curls brushing his shoulders – and those vivid eyes, the unusual way he dressed – not a carbon copy of all the other Jack Wills lookalikes. His trademark scruffy jacket looked as though it was from a charity shop (vintage and cool as fuck, as Meggie had said) with badges from bands he'd seen pinned on the frayed lapel, but his shoes were always smart and polished – a complete contrast to the rest of him. She admitted to herself that he'd always intrigued her because he wasn't afraid to be unique, and that chimed with her; she felt the same, though for totally different reasons.

Ella shook her head, gave a small smile and turned back to her laptop. These thoughts weren't getting her essay written. Harry would just tell her to get real, that they were from opposite worlds, that people like them didn't mesh with people like that. So Ella took a breath and got on with her essay. It wasn't going to write itself.

CHAPTER FIVE

Ella

Ella feels Jacob's breath on her neck as he leans down from behind, whispering in her ear. A shot of pain races through her body as he bumps the wheelchair against the door, pretending to struggle to navigate through it, though she suspects it was on purpose. She whimpers, screwing up her eyes from the jolt to her leg.

'I'm so sorry, darling. I need an L plate,' Jacob says loudly, laughing as John the physio pulls the next double doors wide open so there's no chance of it happening again.

'An OT will come out and suggest some temporary changes at your home,' John tells them. 'They'll sort out some ramps and grab rails,' he adds, making Ella's stomach lurch.

Home.

She can't stand the thought of leaving the hospital with… with *him* – Jacob. God, how she hates calling him that. But she has little choice but to go along with everything he says. Until she figures out what to do.

'May I take her outside?' Jacob asks in that precise way of his. 'It's so mild today.'

Ella prays the physio will say no. She doesn't want to get a taste of what's out there, what she can never have. She just needs time to think. To work out her new reality, how to get out of it.

But with her head this muzzy, falling in and out of a fog, she can barely trust her own thoughts.

'Up to you, Ella,' John says. 'Though I don't want you to overdo it.'

'I am quite tired,' she says, pretending. 'And I feel a bit sick.' The truth.

'Well,' Jacob says, sounding affronted. He always liked his own way. Usually got it. 'The garden at home is beautiful. South-facing so you can have all the time you need to sit outside then. Do you remember it, darling? Our garden?'

Ella turns to stare up at him. *No of course I don't*, she thinks, just as his hand rests on her shoulder, one finger digging into her skin, followed by his nail. She stifles a cry.

'Yes, it's… it's lovely,' she says, her voice choked. She thinks of her flat, how it doesn't have a proper garden, simply a courtyard out the back and a little patch of green at the front where some of the other tenants go to smoke. If the window's open, the smell drifts up into her kitchen, which she doesn't mind. Even if she did mind, she'd never tell them to smoke elsewhere. That would mean interaction, talking, confrontation.

'Our new place is nice and spacious,' Jacob tells John, swinging the chair round and heading back to the ward. 'Perfect for your new wheels, Ella,' he adds with a laugh as though it's all a game.

Ella begins to shake again, can't stop herself. John notices, looking concerned, and halts Jacob, pulling the pale green blanket up over her shoulders. He takes hold of the wheelchair handles then, which Ella prefers, and pushes her a little faster back to the ward. But she throws up down her front before they get there.

'I brought you these,' Jacob says after a nursing assistant has cleaned her up and changed her gown. She dashes off to deal with another patient – the staff are rushed off their feet in this ward. Ella is back in bed now, a hot thrum escalating inside her plaster cast. She doesn't know if it's good that she can feel something going on in there, or bad. They warned her about infection.

She watches as Jacob grabs a plastic bag from the top of the locker unit. He pulls out something orange.

'Eat them,' he says, holding up a packet. Ella stares at it, blank-faced. 'Jacob's Cream Crackers,' he says, handing her the packet with a wry smile. 'But now they're Ella's,' he adds, laughing at his own joke. But Ella doesn't laugh. 'I got you these to go with them.' He pulls out a flat round box – spreadable cheese triangles, plus a pack of disposable cutlery in a little cellophane packet. There's a napkin too.

'Do you remember?' he says, pulling off the wrapper.

'Yes,' Ella replies, forcing a smile.

He takes a cracker out, using the Plath book as a plate. Then he unwraps a cheese triangle, spreading it out. The cracker breaks in half. He pushes a piece up to her mouth.

'I'm not hungry,' Ella says, turning her head away, focussing on the steady beep of her heartbeat.

Jacob puts it in his mouth instead.

'No point letting it go to waste,' he says, spraying crumbs. 'Maybe you'll feel more like yourself when I visit tomorrow.' He glances at his watch.

'Don't come,' she says, holding her breath.

'Oh, Ella,' he says, leaning forward.

Ella prays a nurse will come, but she doesn't need such regular checks now and, besides, there are more patients for them to attend to here. She has to wait her turn.

'I know you're muddled still, but trust me, things will be fine. Everything is nearly perfect. It's all we ever wanted.'

'It's all *you* ever wanted,' she replies, flashing him a look.

'Don't deny your feelings.' Jacob sighs, balling up her unplastered hand, cupping it within his own. 'You did a bad, bad thing,' he whispers, leaning close.

Ella forces herself to look him in the eye.

'But no one ever need see the videotape,' he adds softly.

She feels his breath on her cheek, looks away.

'And you'll *love* our house,' he says. 'It's not grand like… well, you know. It's not Adlington. But it's grand in a perfect for *us* kind of way. I've had plenty of time to think. And to be honest, it's all I've done, Ella. Think about us. How to make it right again. Finding you was fate.'

Ella wishes she could throw up again. She's close, but she needs a bigger diversion than being sick.

'It won't be long before I'm taking you home, making everything all right again. You'll see.'

'Nothing can *ever* be right,' Ella says, snatching her hand from his.

CHAPTER SIX

Ella

Later, when he's gone, when the ward is quieter and Ella has scooped several mouthfuls of mashed potato and chicken casserole into her mouth in front of the nurse to show willing, to prove that she's keen to heal and recover, she allows her head to drop back onto her pillow. Allows her shoulders to relax. Since she was woken from the coma, they've been tensed up around her ears from anxiety, anticipation. Her heart on fire.

All the visitors have gone now and the patients are mostly settled – though the same one or two constantly call out for attention. She hears a couple of nurses chatting as they walk past, giggling about some doctor, a party after work. That's what normal lives sound like, she thinks, closing her eyes. Ella never goes out in the evening. Hasn't done for years. After the chatter and noise of the office, the constant demands, the deadlines, it's the cycle home she looks forward to – pedalling it all out of her system.

Damn that van driver!

She wonders where he is, if he knows what he's done. If he saw the story on the news or has come forward. Sue told her the police would come and talk to her soon, that Mr Hicks had fielded them until she was well enough to be interviewed. She doesn't want to speak to them, but will tell them what she knows. Which is nothing. About the accident, anyway.

And then *he* is on her mind again. His face clear and present even when she closes her eyes, screwing them up to make him go away. But he doesn't. He may as well be sitting here, spreading cheese on crackers. She feels the diazepam the nurse gave her earlier taking hold of her body, calming her thoughts, allowing her an hour or two of respite. Her shoulders drop another inch or two.

'Making everything all right again...' she hears herself mumble, repeating his words.

She wonders what Jacob's house is like. *Our house*, she thinks, as a drugged smile forms. She knows it's the diazepam relaxing her into the idea of going home with him, that really the thought terrifies her. But what choice does she have? He has the tape. If she wasn't like this, laid up in bed, two limbs in plaster, then maybe, just *maybe*, there'd be a chance of escaping. She could gather her stuff, leave the ward in the dead of night, not even bothering to discharge herself. She's an adult. She can do what she likes. She could move flats, go to a different country even. Maybe Canada or New Zealand. Become someone else.

But, in reality, she knows none of this is possible. She has a metal pin in her knee and her wrist is in pieces. And every time she moves her head, it feels as though it's going to split in two.

'Ella?' She opens her eyes. It's Sue. 'You were making noises. Are you in pain?'

If only you knew, Ella thinks. 'You're always on duty,' she says, smiling weakly.

'Long shifts,' she says, her tired face illustrating this. 'How was your lovely man today?'

Ella looks away. 'OK.'

'I know I keep saying it, but you're a lucky girl. Together, you'll get through this.' Sue connects the blood pressure machine to the cuff already wrapped around Ella's upper arm. It makes the familiar noise, inflating, squeezing, almost hurting. 'Good men are hard to find. You're still young, both got your lives ahead of you. There's lots to look forward to.' There's something wistful in Sue's voice.

Ella looks up at her again, teary.

'Look,' Sue says, sitting down, 'you're bound to feel low after what's happened. And especially as it's not been long since your wedding. But you're a strong woman, Ella. And you have a strong man beside you. Let him look after you.'

Let him look after me, Ella thinks, staring at the tiled ceiling, trying to make images appear in the random patterns.

Then she's back there, that summer as they lay on the grass by the lake at Adlington, watching the sky, the wispy cirrus streaking overhead. Not a care in the world.

She feels Sue's hand on hers, but imagines it's him, taking herself back to that day, the tingle of alcohol making her not care that there were ants on her legs, grass in her hair. In the here and now, it's the diazepam making her feel out of it, the morphine making her skin itch.

'There's a snake, look,' she'd said, pointing. 'A cobra.' It was true. The trailing cirrus flared to make it look like it had a reared-up head, staring down at Ella. There were even a couple of eyes, warning her, though she didn't see it then.

'That's cheating,' he'd replied. 'It's a vapour trail, not a cloud.' He'd turned on his side then, propping himself up on one elbow, facing her. Their mouths close. 'And it doesn't look much like a snake to me.'

Ella had looked into his eyes, holding the gaze for as long as she could. She knew what he wanted and it was seconds later that he'd kissed her. Tender, warm, the sun on their backs.

'So go on then,' Sue says. 'You said it was a long story. How did you two meet?'

Ella feels her lips twitch and she's not sure if it's because she's remembering the kiss that afternoon ten years ago, or if it's because she's wondering how to deflect Sue's question.

'Seems like we've known each other for ever,' she begins, thinking there's not much more she can say. It's the truth, at least.

'That's how the best love stories always start,' Sue says. 'Jacob told me that you went to university together.'

Ella gives a little nod.

'So romantic,' she goes on, wiping the tear dribbling from Ella's eye. 'Oh, don't worry, love. Before you know it, he'll be wheeling you out of here to take you home. Just you wait and see.'

Ella nods again, almost resigned to her fate.

CHAPTER SEVEN

Liam

Liam stirred his cappuccino. The others were all chatting away as usual – Sylvia nibbling through her falafel wrap, leaving half of it as always and asking if anyone else wanted it (why she didn't order something smaller, he had no idea) – with everyone conscious of time, of deadlines, of getting back to work before half past one. Marcus, their boss, was a stickler.

It was just a normal Tuesday. But not normal, either. Even though she never came out to lunch with them, Liam still felt Ella's absence, as though he'd dragged the emptiness of her cubicle to the café with him. Was he the only one who'd noticed she wasn't at work? Perhaps, he thought, he was feeling it more because he'd been given the task of completing her current project – a fire-safety film that was far from finished. In fact, he couldn't work out what Ella had been trying to do with it. He hadn't told anyone yet, but it was a bit of a mess and certainly not up to her usual standard of work, almost as if she'd given up on it.

Anyway, that aside, he'd stopped asking if she wanted to join them all for lunch, though had fully intended on asking again soon. Just in a different way. Maybe somehow make it seem more tempting than just scoffing a sandwich and necking a cappuccino in the short time they had left when they got there. He thought perhaps just the two of them. A walk maybe. He could pack a small picnic, eat it on a park bench.

Liam swirled his paper cup, gathering the last of the foam and chocolate in a final gulp. He'd heard Ella had had some kind of accident. No one apart from him seemed that bothered, though he'd overheard Marcus grumbling on the phone to the woman who handled the payroll that Ella had better provide a doctor's note soon. She might be quiet and keep herself to herself, Liam thought, but he couldn't recall her ever taking a day off work. Must be serious, he reckoned, hoping she was OK.

'Right, that's me,' Adam said, holding his stomach and pulling a face. 'Anyone walking back?'

'Me,' Liam said, rolling up his bagel wrapper and stuffing it into his empty coffee cup. He chucked it in the bin on the way out, leaving the other three still squashed around the small table.

'You heard anything about Ella these last few days?' he asked Adam as they headed back to the office. He didn't want to sound too keen, especially as no one ever really mentioned her. Just like they didn't comment on the potted palm in reception or how the carpet was a bit threadbare. These things just *were*.

'Ella?…' Adam repeated, squinting. 'No, I haven't.' Then he started talking about the project he was working on, how the client had wanted unreasonable changes at such a late stage.

'It must be serious,' Liam pressed on. 'For her to take time off. I heard there'd been an accident.'

'Poor Ella,' Adam said, before talking about the band he was going to see at the weekend.

Liam didn't go straight to his desk. Instead, he went up an extra floor to the HR department, which basically consisted of a couple of desks squeezed in beside the kitchenette no one ever used – apart from Ella. The fridge didn't chill things properly and the water had a habit of coming out of the tap brown. They took it in turns to do coffee runs to the café opposite when needed and occasionally sent out for trays of cakes for a morale boost. There was a great bakery just around the corner.

'I just need to check something on my last payslip,' he'd told Adam when he stayed in the lift.

Adam nodded, stepping out and heading for the editorial suites.

There were seven editors, three of them in post-production, including him and Ella, plus a couple of regular freelancers when things got busy. He'd been at Ghost Media for five years now, though he knew Ella had been there much longer. Since she'd done her year-long MA in Filmmaking right after university, apparently. She didn't seem one for change.

'Hi, Helen,' he said, drawing up to her desk. As well as handling staff matters, she did the bookkeeping and took care of the petty cash. He'd had to ask her a few times for money for leaving drinks and various other, well, petty things needed around the office. It seemed it was no one's job to change lightbulbs or restock the toilet paper. Liam didn't really mind.

Helen looked up and gave the kind of smile that people give when they want you to know they're busy.

'I was wondering if you knew anything about Ella Sinclair. When she'll be back to work?'

He leant forward on her desk, and her monitor started wobbling. She stared at his hands until he stood upright again.

'Who?'

'Ella Sinclair. Post-production. Do you know when she'll be back at work?'

'No, why?'

Liam took a moment to think about this. Should he tell her it was because he liked her, despite only having had a handful of conversations with her that weren't about work over the last five years? Or should he tell her it was because her empty workspace was doing something to him, gnawing at his conscience with the thought that someone should at least be bothered about her wellbeing and check how she was? He didn't think she'd ever mentioned family – a husband or kids. It struck him they should probably send a card, flowers even.

'I heard she'd had an accident.'

'Oh,' Helen said, clasping her hands in her lap. 'Yes, maybe.'

'Well can you find out?'

'Not really allowed to give out employee details,' she said, staring across at a grey filing cabinet.

Liam wondered if that's where she kept all the staff records. Helen didn't look the type to have everything computerised. He knew she'd been there as long as Marcus, right from when Ghost was set up. While the production side of things was slick and bang up to date with state-of-the-art equipment, Helen's workspace suggested otherwise. She even had a Rolodex.

'I'm not asking for her details,' Liam said, though he wouldn't have minded them. 'I just want to know when she'll be coming back to work. I'm dealing with her projects while she's off,' he added.

'Oh, I see,' she said, glancing behind him. 'Jan,' she called out.

Liam turned to see the other woman who worked up there edging in behind her desk. She had a baguette and huge milkshake in her hands. Some of the grated cheese dropped out of the bread.

'You took the message about Ella… what's her last name again?'

'Sinclair.'

'About Ella Sinclair, didn't you?'

'Mmm.' Jan's mouth was full, crumbs falling out. 'Hospital.'

'Hospital,' Helen repeated, turning back to Liam.

'Hospital what?' Liam folded his arms. It didn't sound good.

Jan swallowed, pulling a face. She drank some shake. 'There was a message left late last Friday night or Saturday morning.

Said that Ella had had an accident. They'd found out where she worked and called in.'

'And?' Liam was getting impatient.

'That's it really.'

'Didn't they say what had happened? Did you call back and follow up?'

'No and no,' Jan said, taking another bite. 'I'm sure she'll be in touch.'

On his way back to his desk, Liam passed Ella's empty workstation. He didn't want to be seen snooping, but he couldn't help slowing and stopping in the entrance. There was a navy cardigan draped over the back of her chair, one of her hairs stuck on the shoulder, but nothing much else personal apart from a small plant sitting beside her monitor. It looked as though it could do with some water, so Liam went to the cooler to fetch a cup.

When he poured it in, some dribbled onto the desk. He plucked a tissue from a box next to her computer and wiped it up. That's when he saw the coffee-stained bit of paper tucked inside the tissue box.

CHAPTER EIGHT

Ella

'Bravo,' Mr Hicks says. Ella stares at him. *Bravo what?* she wonders. Nothing much is bravo. 'Happy with your progress. Soon be on your way.'

Mr Hicks, the consultant neurologist, is a man of few words. He says things in short clipped sentences. Sometimes not even sentences. She puts this down to him being a busy surgeon. Saving lives. She wishes she could ask him how he could save hers. And she doesn't mean the knock to her head or her broken bones.

'On my way?'

'Home, love,' Sue says, taking notes from Mr Hicks regarding the medication she'll be discharged with.

'When?'

'No reason why not today.' He gives a rare grin.

Ella can think of plenty of reasons. It's been nearly three weeks since she was brought in – A&E then her operation and into Critical Care. After that, she was downgraded to the general ward, where two police officers visited her briefly, taking a statement about what had happened. She told them all that she could remember, which wasn't much, though they weren't hopeful of finding the driver. No one had come forward following the appeal.

'I...but...' Ella wants to tell Mr Hicks she doesn't want to leave, that where she's being forced to go isn't even her home, anyway. But John the physio has been visiting her daily, working with her, showing her exercises to stretch and tone her unused muscles, helping her keep as mobile as she can to prevent bed sores and DVTs. And she can even get into the wheelchair from her bed without help now. It was a mistake to learn that, she thinks. *They might have kept me in longer if I couldn't. If I was pathetic. Helpless.*

'Thank you,' Ella says quietly.

When the old lady in the bed opposite has finally quietened, when Ella can smell the lunches being prepared, and the doctors' rounds have been done and the drugs trolley trundled between beds, Ella remembers something Liam once said.

Sometimes OK is good enough…

He was referring to a project they'd been working on – a short piece about bullying – not just at school, but in the workplace too. What he said wasn't relevant to the film but it was appropriate to the situation they were in with the client. The work was supposedly complete yet something wasn't working.

'God, how do you know when to let go?' Ella had said, watching as Liam's face passed through various expressions. He was considering what she'd said carefully, as if her words were somehow precious. 'I'm really not happy with it, but I'm not sure I ever will be either,' she added.

The message in the film was coming across as clear as a bell, but their job was to perfect and polish. To take away all doubt. Ella wasn't sure they'd succeeded with this one.

'You know what, Ella?' Liam had said after a long silence. 'Sometimes OK is good enough.'

Most of the others had gone home for the evening. It was a Friday night about six months ago and she rarely stayed late. She didn't need to, she always hit her targets. But the few times she'd had to, she didn't mind. She compartmentalised these haywire evenings into boxes she could cope with, telling herself that tomorrow, the next day, the next week, would all be back to normal. Regular days.

Work, home, sleep.

'You think?' she'd said, not convinced Liam was right. They played the film again. Six times. Scrutinising second by second. Tweaking.

'Look, it's OK. We've done what they asked,' he'd said, pulling on his jacket.

Ella hadn't realised the time. 10.20 p.m. She'd never stayed that late before.

'We'll deliver on Monday.'

'But just *OK*,' she'd replied more flatly than she'd intended. Nothing had ever left her desk just *OK*.

'Miss Perfectionist,' Liam had said, going around the office flicking off the lights.

Ella had been struggling with the idea of leaving the project like that. To her, it felt unfinished. Though later, at home, when she'd thought about it, she hadn't been sure if it was the film Liam had been referring to or something else. She'd overlaid what he'd said on top of her life. She hadn't liked that the two matched up.

'Sometimes OK is good enough,' Ella says now, making Sue pause and turn back.

'Sorry, love?' she says, smiling.

Ella shrugs. 'Someone said it once. It stuck with me. I like it, but I don't like it.'

'Well, I think it's actually true,' Sue says. 'And contrary to what you might think, it's very apt around here. We're all stretched, all try to get by the best we can.'

Ella thinks about this. 'You're not like the other nurses,' she says, finally. 'You talk, but you also listen.' She glances over to the girl in the next bed – the *tss-tss* of music coming from her earphones louder than ever.

Sue smiles. 'Listening is important. Part of recovery.' She's about to go again but doesn't. 'I'm usually around,' she says, tapping her watch. 'Seven till seven.'

Ella nods, glancing at the clock above the nurses' station. Not long until Jacob arrives to fetch her at 3 o'clock. It's all been arranged.

'Thanks,' Ella says. 'Everything is OK.' And in her head, she convinces herself that that is good enough.

'Ella-*bella*…' he says, drawing close. She feels sick. 'Ellie-bellie, my love…' The hug is tight, consuming, painful. The right side of her body is still mottled with blue-green bruises and her joints are stiff, feeling as though they have broken glass in them when she moves.

She looks up at him, doesn't say anything.

'All packed?' He scans the area around her bed – the cabinet beside her, the stuff strewn on the table reaching across the bed. There's an unread newspaper, some balled-up tissues, a jug of water and a smeary glass. A lip salve Sue gave her plus some cream for her dry skin. Some wine gums from the trolley, too (there were a few coins in her pack), plus a carton of orange juice.

Ella can't speak.

'The car is close. Home is waiting.'

She feels sick. But there's something else welling inside her too – something that feels a lot like resignation. She doesn't like it. Wishes a part of her could rear up and scream out that she's not going anywhere with a monster like him. But she can't. She's trapped. As trapped as her right leg is in the cast. They gave her a new one two days ago. Slightly smaller than the first, reaching just above her knee. It would have been some kind of a relief had she not seen the volcanic landscape of her leg. Caught sight of the incision when they changed the dressing.

Still, she'd thought, as she was being replastered, it's not as if I ever wear short skirts or try to impress anyone. Grey flannel trousers in winter, linen in summer, plus half a dozen white blouses and a V-neck sweater for when it's chilly. She didn't want to be *that* girl. The old Ella. The one who had it coming. Then she was reminded of Sylvia from the office, the tiny dresses she wore winter or summer. She only stared because she'd wondered how she'd look with her legs exposed like that, her breasts virtually on show. Maybe it *had* all been her fault.

'I feel sick,' Ella whispers, fighting it back. Instead, she imagines saving it up for when they're in the car on the way home, Jacob furious that she's messed up the interior of whatever expensive vehicle he's driving these days, pulling over, yelling at her. And, when the car has come to a halt, she sees herself flinging the door open, barrel-rolling out onto the verge, leaping over a fence and running away, never to be seen again.

'What's funny?' he asks, stroking her cheek.

'Funny?'

'You've got a smile on your face.'

Ella stares up at him. 'Nothing,' she says.

'Right, you're all set,' Sue says with an encouraging smile. It's a proper send-off, with her and a couple of other nurses lined up by the ward entrance. A few of the other patients have already said their goodbyes, wishing her well. 'The instructions are all in there plus what to do and who to call should there be any complications,' she tells Jacob, handing him two large bags of medication. He hooks them on the wheelchair handles. 'But I'm sure there won't be.'

'Don't you worry,' he says, laying a hand on the top of Ella's head. She can't help the flinch. 'I'll take care of her. I won't let her out of my sight.'

Ella clutches her small backpack on her lap. It's splattered with mud marks from when she's cycled in the rain. One side of it is roughed-up and shredded from the accident. She squeezes it, knowing what's in there – a book she was reading during her lunch breaks, her plastic sandwich box, which still has the peel of a tangerine in it, as well as a couple of crusts. Mouldy by now, Ella supposes, but can't bear to look. And the waterproof jacket she was wearing when she was hit, the blood still on it. Oh, and her phone, she thinks, feeling the outline of it in the front pocket. The battery is dead now, of course, and her charger is back at her flat, beside her bed. She doesn't really use it much anyway, just has it for safety. Even if she could call someone, she wouldn't know who. No one can save her now.

Ella hugs the zip-up sweatshirt she's wearing around her – the one Jacob brought in for her, along with the tracksuit pants she has on. Sue had to snip a slit in the bottoms to allow the cast to fit through. The nurses smile and wave as she leaves, while Sue bends down, pecking her on the cheek. 'You know where I am, love,' she whispers in her ear.

'Bye,' Ella says quietly, glancing back. 'And thank you,' she adds, holding eye contact until Jacob wheels her away.

The corridor is long with a pair of lifts at the end. Jacob presses the button and the doors slide open, closing again, sealing them inside.

'Well,' he says, swinging her chair around ready to exit. 'Off we go.' And he leans down, giving her a kiss on the mouth, leaving his lips firmly in place until they reach the ground floor.

CHAPTER NINE

Ella

It's a BMW. A big silver one with leather seats. She should have guessed. He'd always hankered after one. Always loved nice things. She has no idea what he does for a living, if he works. Doesn't *want* to know because the more he reveals, the more real he becomes. Part of her is still hoping to wake up in her flat alone, a quiet Sunday to look forward to or a normal day at work. Anyway, it's not the car or what he does that makes her heart thump, it's the little pink teddy on the front seat that she sees when he opens the door for her. The ribbon around its neck with *Be Mine* printed on it.

Ella's mouth falls open as she stifles a gasp.

'I thought you might want it,' he says, grinning as he tosses it on the dashboard.

Ella can't breathe, can hardly speak. 'Where… where did you get this?' She looks at him, studying his face, but his expression turns blank again.

'From your flat, of course,' he replies, sliding the car seat fully back.

'*What?*' Ella squeals, suddenly frozen in her wheelchair, gripping the arms. As soon as she gets in the car, she knows her fate is sealed. No way back. 'You've been in my *flat?*'

But Jacob doesn't answer. He's moving stuff around in the car, making space for her. Ella scans the parking area. It's busy, cars cruising up and down, people coming and going, a couple of security men checking windscreens for tickets. She could scream out, of course, yell for help, get someone's attention – *anything* – instead of being driven off by Jacob.

But, knowing he's got the videotape, she can't.

'How *dare* you!' she spits as he pushes her right up to the car door.

The tasteless teddy stares back at her from the dashboard. She'd only kept it because no one had ever done anything like that for her before, or since, and, even though, deep down, she'd known it hadn't been intended for her, she'd imagined what it might have felt like if it had been. That someone *liked* her.

While she had to admit that it had left her feeling uneasy, sitting on her desk beside her keyboard that morning, it had also given her a flutter. Once or twice, she'd paused from her work, staring at it, wondering. It had arrived on Valentine's Day – she only knew this because she'd overheard the others in the office talking – which had added some kind of hidden meaning.

She'd pondered *Be Mine* for the rest of the day, concluding that one of her male co-workers must have left it on the wrong desk. It was probably for Sylvia, she'd thought, who worked two cubicles down from her. Maybe that guy from animation had left it – he wouldn't know Sylvia's exact desk, after all, but he was always hanging around. She hadn't really cared.

All she'd known was that the sickly pink teddy hadn't been meant for her, though she'd kept it nonetheless, feeling guilty as she was about to leave for home that afternoon, wondering who was missing out on their gift. The creature had stared at her all day, almost begging to be slipped into her backpack, to be given a home. It had sat on her bedside table ever since.

Until now. Until Jacob had been inside her flat and taken it. Ella shudders at the thought of him going through her stuff, knowing where she lived.

'Get in,' he orders.

She looks up at him, her eyes filled with tears.

'*Now*,' he snaps, his finger digging into her shoulder again.

Ella coughs back a sob as she heaves herself from the chair into the car, pain surging through her leg as she resigns herself to her fate. Even with the front seat pushed right back and her twisting sideways, there is barely enough room for her outstretched cast. It hurts from her toes to her spine as she clips the seatbelt in place. She closes her eyes as he slams the car door shut, listening as he folds the wheelchair and puts it in the boot.

'Off we go then,' Jacob says once he's in the driver's seat. He starts the engine, the car roaring to life before falling into a quiet purr as he reverses out of the disabled space. He has no badge in his window but something like that would never stop Jacob. Ella practises calling him that in her mind, knowing the consequences if she doesn't.

Jacob, Jacob, Jacob… Jacob Sinclair.

Shameless. Delusional. Entitled.

'It's not too far,' he says, inserting the ticket into the machine. The barrier lifts. 'And when we get home, I'm going to spoil you rotten. You'll see.' He glances across at her, grinning.

But Ella doesn't want to see.

Jacob swings the car onto the roundabout, turning right, and the pink teddy slides along the dashboard. She reaches out and grabs it before it falls into the foot-well, wincing from the pain in her leg. She digs her fingers into its soft fur.

'I've got some nice food in for you,' Jacob says, reaching out to take her hand. 'I'll cook for you.'

'I'm not hungry,' Ella says, whipping her hand away. 'You can drop me in the city and I'll make my own way home. Thanks for the lift.' She glances over at him, seeing one side of his mouth turned up, amused. His body jerks in time with his laugh.

'Ella-bella…' he says. 'No, no, *no*.'

'I want to go home. To *my* home,' she adds. It's worth a try, she reckons, praying that any moment now she'll snap out of the nightmare, be in a taxi pulling up outside her flat.

'We are going home, yes. But to your *new* home. *Our* home, Ella-bella. I should have done this a long time ago.'

Ella doesn't say anything for the rest of the journey. Can't. As they get further from the hospital, the roads and streets lose their familiarity as they head out to a suburb she's never been to before. Older terraced houses and corner-shop-strewn high streets give way to larger 1930s detached places interspersed with a few newer builds, large gardens, two cars on the driveways, until the properties turn into much more recent ones.

Then Jacob turns left down a private road, slowing down and waiting as the huge iron gates swing inwards when he swipes a pass over a sensor.

'Welcome to Green Leys, Ella, my dear. It's very secure.' And he points to a sign at the entrance – the name of the small estate emblazoned on a plaque.

Ella feels sick. She doesn't want to be secure.

The BMW slips into a low gear as Jacob cruises slowly down the slope, the curve of the street winding between large detached houses, each one a slightly different design.

'Do you like it?' he says, beaming, glancing across as Ella stares out of the window.

There are probably ten or so houses set back from the private road, she thinks, the frontages all landscaped with autumnal shrubs and trees giving each house privacy, while the wide driveways and grand porticos reek of money. Tasteless money. Ella thinks they're somewhere south of the city now. It's nothing like her area with its kebab shops, foreign supermarkets and laundrette at the end of the street.

She turns to face him, wincing from the sudden pain in her knee. 'No, I hate it. I want to go home.'

'Don't be like that, Ella-bella,' he says. 'You haven't even seen inside yet. All the things I've done for you. The trouble I've gone to.' Jacob slows as they reach the final curve of the close, creeping up onto the drive of what seems to be the least opulent house of the cul-de-sac. 'Home at last,' he says, switching off the engine.

'Why are you doing this?'

What she really wants to ask is: *How are you even alive?* She closes her eyes but all she can see is the fire.

Jacob turns sideways, facing her. 'There's not a day that's gone by that I've not thought about you, how I could make it up to you, wondering if you'd even want me. Do you know what that feels like?' He pauses, waiting, but Ella doesn't reply. She's thought about him every day, too, but only because she was trying to forget him. 'And when I heard about your accident on the news, I knew it was fate. The right time. I'd just bought this place. It's a chance at our happy ever after, Ella. We're meant to be together.' He clasps her hand.

She doesn't resist, even when his grip becomes tighter and tighter, cutting off the blood to her fingers.

'Yes,' she says quietly, trying to stay calm, measured, gathering herself. Escaping physically isn't going to work, but appeasing him, working him, somehow burrowing into his conscience will be her way out. It will take time. Probably hours. Maybe, at worst, several days.

He comes around to the passenger side, the wheelchair unfolded. 'In you get,' he says, helping her, ignoring the pain etched on her face. 'I should be carrying you over the threshold,' he jokes, wheeling her up the front path.

There's a low clipped box hedge either side of it and ornate white columns flanking the front door. He unlocks it. Ella doesn't think it reflects anything of the man she remembers. Nothing like what he was used to. The family home.

Jacob opens the door and Ella sees a spacious hallway beyond. He goes inside and returns a moment later with a large ramp, which he places in front of the doorstep. 'I made sure everything is wheelchair friendly,' he says, beaming.

'But…' Ella's heart sinks. 'John said I would have a visit from the occupational therapist, that someone would come tomorrow.' She was hoping, in her heart of hearts, that maybe she could somehow signal to the person about her situation, perhaps make her fear and predicament known but not in a way that would mean everything came tumbling out. In her mind, she saw them helping her, wheeling her away, taking her back to her flat alone. Everything normal again.

'No need,' he says, taking a run up the ramp. 'I cancelled the appointment.'

As they go inside, Ella feels the sickness welling again. Jacob goes back to the car to grab her backpack and the pink teddy. Once inside, he locks the door, checking it twice.

Ella looks around as he pushes her further in, spotting the packing cartons over to one side, the bare walls, the stair carpet still with its protective cover on from the removals company. There's a strange smell – something plastic, unlived in.

Escaping, she concludes, burying her face in her hands, is going to take more than she thought.

CHAPTER TEN

Ella

'Please may I have my backpack?' Ella says, her voice flat.

'Anything you want, my love, just ask,' he says, handing it over.

'I want to go home,' she says, flashing him a look.

'You are home,' he says, wheeling her through into the living room. 'There's everything here you need. Everything *we* need. I've delivered on my promise, Ella.' He bumps the chair against the door frame. 'Do you like it? I've unpacked a few things and the furniture was delivered a couple of days ago. What do you think?' He pats one of two black leather sofas. There's also a smoked glass coffee table in the middle of the room, a tall stand with some kind of plant on it by the window, plus a grey fluffy rug in front of the fireplace. Ella would think they were all horrid even if they hadn't been chosen by him.

But it's not the furniture that makes her want to retch. It's the other stuff around the room.

'I thought it only fair,' he says, when Ella doesn't reply, her mouth hanging open as he positions her wheelchair next to the ostentatious marble fireplace. Ella sees it's one of those fake gas fires, imagines the flames licking up out of the grate, getting bigger and bigger. All-consuming.

'What have you *done*?' Ella says, forcing herself upright in her chair, her hands gripping the sides. 'Why is *my* stuff here?' Ella stares at her belongings strewn around, haphazardly arranged to make it seem as though they're meant to be here when they're most definitely not. 'That's my throw,' she says, reaching out and whipping the patchwork blanket from the end of the sofa. It took her several months to make, knitting two or three squares a night, picking up odd balls of wool from charity shops. She didn't much like stitching them all together but the end result was pleasing, filled some time.

'And my china…' She wants to say that the cups and saucers look ridiculous on the mantelpiece, that they should be on a shelf in the kitchen like she had them at her flat.

'I could hardly leave it all behind, could I?' Jacob says, swinging her wheelchair around to face the sofa. He sits down.

'*What?…*' Ella says, shaking. She doesn't have many belongings but most of them seem to be here. She runs through an inventory in her mind. In the corner of the room is a small bookcase – some of the titles are hers, but some aren't. She starts to wheel her chair over to it, but Jacob grabs the handle, stopping her. She turns to face him.

'What do you mean, you could hardly leave it behind?'

Jacob laughs. 'I was so relieved to find out that the furniture in your flat belonged to the landlord. No disrespect but… well, we can do better than that, Ella-bella.'

'What are you *talking* about?' She bats his hand off her chair but he's not having it. She sees the strength in his arm as he tenses his muscles, holding on.

'Your landlord was very helpful. He understood the situation completely.'

'What fucking situation?' Ella dislikes swearing but can't help it. She throws herself back in her chair, making it rock. Her heart thumps.

'He was so sorry to hear about your accident and very sympathetic about you moving out. I told him you were coming to live here. Thank goodness you were only on a month-to-month contract. I paid him off, of course, and agreed to leave the deposit with him. Saved me having to clean up once your stuff was out. It wasn't exactly…' Jacob pulls a face.

'Wasn't exactly *what*?' Ella is on the verge of tears, her voice squeaking.

'Clean, Ella-bella. You'd let things go a bit.'

Ella reaches out to take a swipe at him but he leans back quickly. He grabs a cushion and hands it to her.

'I understand, really I do, my love. But take it out on this. Give it a good punch.'

'You're *mental*,' Ella says, hurling the cushion at him. 'I want to go home.'

When he lets go of her chair, she swings around, wheeling herself towards the door. She's still not very good at manoeuvring it, but he's not trying to stop her at least. She can wheel herself back up to the main road, towards the shops they passed. Maybe get someone to call her a taxi. She'll manage. She'll tell her landlord there's been a mistake.

At the front door, with her backpack still on her knee, she reaches out for the handle. But of course, it's locked. 'Open it,' she says. He's right behind her. 'Now!'

'No, Ella-bella,' he says, pulling back on the wheelchair handles, turning her round.

'I can't believe you've given up my flat. You had no right to do that!' The tears come then, hot and fast as he pushes her through to the kitchen. 'I fucking *hate* you and I want you to let me go. I'll call the police!' She lashes out at him again but misses.

'Of course you will, Ella-bella,' he says in a way that makes her shudder. 'And tell them what you did?' He takes a glass from the cupboard, filling it with chilled water from the fridge. 'Drink,' he says. 'You're working yourself into a state.'

Ella takes the glass and hurls it across the room. It hits the front of a cabinet, water arcing and spraying everywhere, followed by the shards of glass as it shatters.

Then the blow to her head. Short and sharp.

His face up close to hers as he crouches beside her.

'Be a good girl, Ella-bella,' he says. His breath smells metallic and stale. 'Don't make me hurt you.'

She's choking on her breaths, her chest heaving madly. Angering him is not going to work. She needs to get out. She *will* get out. It might not be in the next few minutes or even in the next hour, but she will be gone by this evening. She doesn't know where but she will make sure he never finds her again. She chokes back more sobs.

'Just do as I say and let's be happy together, Ella-bella. We deserve it. Your accident wasn't for nothing. It brought us together again. Imagine if I hadn't heard your story on the news.' He stands up again, shaking his head. 'Unthinkable.'

'Sorry,' Ella says, staring at her fingers, trying to control her urgent breaths. She hates herself for saying it but knows she has no choice. One phone call from him and it would all be over.

CHAPTER ELEVEN

Ten Years Ago

'Nope,' Meggie said, swiping through the wardrobe. 'Hopeless. Nothing here. Wait.' She was businesslike and direct about Ella having nothing to wear.

'Where are you going?'

'*Wait*, I said.' Meggie skipped out of Ella's room and returned a short while later. Her arms were full of clothes. She dumped them on Ella's bed. 'Good job we're the same size,' she said with a wink. 'Except, you might need this.' Meggie held up a padded bra.

'Why?' Ella said, looking horrified, but Meggie just made a silly face in reply.

'Try this on.' Meggie picked out a navy polka dot dress with a ruffle around the bottom and capped sleeves. Ella wasn't sure but Meggie thrust it at her.

'Too short,' Ella said, twisting around in front of the mirror once she'd slipped into it. 'He'll see my bum.'

'And?' Meggie said, giggling. 'I got you the date, so it makes sense I get to choose what you wear. Which is basically nothing you own. Have you ever bought anything that *wasn't* from a budget high-street shop?'

'No,' Ella replied without having to think. She stared at herself. 'It's nice but… it's too girlie. Not me.'

'Boys like that, trust me,' Meggie replied, tossing another dress her way. 'Try this one.'

Ella did as she was told. It was basically the same dress but in a different material. While she was changing, Meggie dashed back to her room and returned with a clutch of heeled sandals. 'Put these on and see how long your legs look.'

'But they're long anyway,' Ella said, rolling her eyes. She'd never been one for heels, always found herself stooping if she was talking to anyone. 'I must be over six foot now,' she said, wobbling as she strode around the room in the peach-coloured sandals.

Both girls burst out laughing.

'Good job Zach's tall too then,' Meggie said, tossing a long, flimsy skirt with a deep slit her way, along with a cropped top. 'Put those on and see how gorgeous you look.'

'Not bad,' Ella had to admit once she'd got them on, though she kept tugging at the top, pulling it down more so there wasn't any skin on show at her middle. She'd never worn anything like this before.

'It's meant to be like that, silly, and you look stunning. That's the outfit.' Meggie supplied her with some black kitten heels and a matching bag. All the items were designer brands and the quality was like nothing Ella had ever known before.

'You're really sure?' Ella said, spinning around in front of the mirror. She was still wary about her midriff being on show. 'I'd have ended up wearing jeans and a T-shirt otherwise.' A part of her liked the way she looked – sophisticated, confident, sexy – even if she didn't feel it inside.

'Exactly,' Meggie said and set to work on her hair and make-up.

It was just before seven thirty when Ella left the college, walking as elegantly as she could manage to where she'd agreed to meet Zach. Well, where *Meggie* had arranged they'd meet. It had all been conducted by email and text and, frankly, as she walked towards the bar, she felt a bit silly that they hadn't arranged their own date, that Meggie hadn't passed on her phone number. But that was Meggie – always in control. Orchestrating, making things right.

Zach was already in Cloisters – a vaulted, semi-underground place with dim lighting, bare brick walls with graffiti and old gig posters plastered all over. Worn flagstones had seen the footfall of thousands of students over the years, while the bar boasted unusual gins, craft ales and an extravagant cocktail menu. She'd been into Cloisters a few times since she'd started at Durham, and had always felt a bit out of place. She knew Zach and his crowd hung out here often, had seen them coming and going many times. But tonight, wearing Meggie's clothes, she had to admit that she felt more comfortable going in – as though she were someone else – almost passing as someone from Zach and Meggie's privileged world.

She'd not dated anyone at university. Before they'd started, she and Harry had made a pact that, having worked so hard to get to Durham, they wouldn't get distracted from their studies. It was Harry's idea, but made sense to Ella and, besides, she knew he had her back, just as she had his. Anyway, getting close to someone or being intimate wasn't for her. Not yet.

She'd only ever had one date with a boy in her entire life and that was just after she'd finished her A levels back home in the Midlands. A boy from her school had asked her out, they'd gone to a grimy club, and then she'd never heard from him again. She supposed she'd been blocked because none of the hundreds of messages she'd sent him over the next week or two ever received a reply. Eventually, she'd given up. Felt hurt. Decided she wouldn't bother again.

Zach stood up from his bar stool when he saw her approaching, slowly looking her up and down. He was chatting to a couple of guys she knew, who also gave her the once-over, making her squirm as she approached.

'Hi,' she said, almost inaudibly.

Zach carried on staring, appraising.

The first thing she noticed about him as she drew close were his shoes. Brown leather brogues. Polished. Expensive. The second thing was the scarf he wore – one of those black and white Arabic print things, draped loosely around his neck over a faded T-shirt with a vintage-style print. A band or something, Ella thought. But the thing that stuck with her the most, were his eyes. They wouldn't let go. Dragged her in. Had her captivated right from the start.

'Well this is strange,' he said finally, reaching out and touching her arm.

Ella was so used to everyone diving in for kisses since she'd been at Durham – the mwah-mwah on each cheek – that she felt thrown when Zach didn't lean in. She did, though, and instantly felt stupid, trying to disguise her faux pas by flicking back her long hair. It whipped someone behind her and, when she swung around to apologise, she bumped their drink. She felt rum and Coke running down the back of her legs but said nothing. Hoped Meggie wouldn't notice a stain.

'Strange?' Ella said, not knowing if he was being sarcastic. Zach's friends laughed.

'A strange way to finally meet properly,' Zach said, smiling, making those eyes even more melt-worthy – Meggie's description, not hers, but she was right. 'You know Charles and Stan, yeah?' he asked, nudging the boy to his left.

'Yes, of course,' Ella said, having encountered them a few times before at parties and college dinners, in the clubs too. They were friends of Meggie mainly, so she wouldn't say she *knew* them as such. They weren't on her course and, like Zach, they came from a different world.

'Harry's sister, yeah?' Stan said, making an approving face as he stared at her low-cut top. Charles just glared at her, as though she was interrupting something.

Ella nodded, felt herself blush. She stared at the floor, her insides turning to liquid as Zach asked her what she'd like to drink. His voice was chocolate smooth. 'And of course, it's not like *we* haven't seen each other around before, is it?' he added.

Ella forced herself to look up, just in time to see him winking, which she reciprocated with an involuntary twitch of her left eye. 'Yeah, I've seen you on campus,' she squeaked, shrugging and mentally kicking herself for saying such a silly thing. They'd come across each other a few times over the last couple of years, had even chatted before, and there was that night in Zoo when he'd come up to her, lacing his arm around her waist – though she doubted he even remembered talking to someone like her. She decided not to bring it up.

'Indeed,' he said slowly, picking up two drinks from the bar. 'See you two reprobates later,' he said to Stan and Charles, who were now talking to a couple of other girls. 'Come,' he said, leading the way to a small wooden table nestled in a dark alcove under the brick vaults. There was a candle in a small red jar on their table, giving off a flickering glow.

Ella took a sip of her drink. 'What's this?'

'Guess.'

'Not what I ordered?' She laughed then, not wanting to offend him. But she didn't really like it. It tasted of tobacco and stale nuts, nothing like vodka and Coke, which is what she'd asked for.

'You approve?' Zach said, tilting his head while sipping his. He'd ordered the same for both of them – an inch of caramel liquid in a bowl of a tumbler.

Ella nodded, sipping the fierce drink, not sure he was even referring to it any more. She hardly ever drank anyway, was clueless about what to have – everyone seemed so much more sophisticated than her – and besides, money was tight.

Years ago, she and Harry had discovered some homemade wine stashed in the garden shed, so they'd poured some into paper cups one evening when they'd been left alone – Ella thought they were about eleven, maybe twelve – and, even after only one measure each, they'd felt tipsy. They ended up drinking a lot more than the one cup. Their mum had run around in a blind panic when she came home later, finding their beds empty. Eventually she discovered them on the floor of the shed asleep. Well, Ella had passed out, with Harry in a not much better state. They'd got a right telling off for that, and a few good clouts from Ron, their stepfather.

'So, what are you studying?' Ella asked.

'Maths,' Zach replied. 'But you already knew that. I told you when we chatted in Zoo.'

Ella felt her cheeks pink up, her ears redden. He *did* remember. A familiar flush of embarrassment spread down her neck. 'I'm English Lit,' Ella said, trying to sound casual.

'I know.'

'We chatted about that too?' Ella looked at him as she sipped, wishing Meggie could whisper advice in her ear. She already felt out of her depth.

Zach shook his head. 'No. I'd already asked everyone in Mary's who the gorgeous, tall brunette was.' He paused for a sip, fixing her with those eyes over the rim of his glass. Ella felt like a specimen in a laboratory. 'But then Harry told me that you had a no-dating policy, that boys were off your radar. So does Meggie always play Cupid for you? And is your brother your keeper?'

'Oh, God no,' she replied quickly, laughing and flicking back her hair so he didn't get the wrong impression. 'It's the first time she's done it. I actually begged her not to.' Ella made a point of rolling her eyes. 'And my brother… he's cool. I've not really, um, had…' She trailed off. Whichever way she went now, it didn't sound great. She tried to imagine what a boy like Zach – worldly, well-off, privileged – would want to hear. That she was easy or not, had had loads of boyfriends in the past, or none? She decided on the truth, but Zach got there first.

'You've not done this before, have you?' He wasn't smirking exactly.

Ella stared at him. Then at her lap. 'I...' She felt a finger lift up her chin.

'Well, we can change that,' he said, leaning forward, planting his lips on hers.

Ella froze, turned rigid as his face loomed close. Not only had she never had a boyfriend before but she'd never kissed a boy, either – well, she had but that didn't count. She shuddered, freezing, unsure if it was from what had happened in the past or from what Zach was doing to her. Sitting there in Cloisters, the candle flickering beside them, it felt as though she was being swallowed up, eaten whole. Zach's full lips and tongue probed her mouth, searching out places that even she didn't know existed, giving her feelings she'd never felt before. It was so wet. So invasive. So warm. At first, she thought she liked it, felt something stir inside her, but then she hated it too, felt repulsed. Didn't want it.

She put her hands flat against his chest and shoved him away, a horrified look on her face as she gasped. It wasn't how she'd been brought up to behave. And certainly not minutes after meeting someone. A switch had flicked.

'And now you know what a kiss is like,' Zach said, leaning back, grinning, watching her reaction.

Ella waited a moment longer – her eyes wide, her mouth hanging open – until her heart caught up with her mind. Then she grabbed Meggie's leather clutch bag and slid out from her seat behind the table, hurrying off as fast as she could in her designer kitten heels.

CHAPTER TWELVE

Ella

Ella watches as he cooks. He's positioned her wheelchair nearby, putting a wedge under all four wheels. When she leant down to remove them, he slapped her hands. She can't stop shaking. Everything is new here, she thinks, staring around – apart from the things he harvested from her flat. It makes her sick to think that he was in there while she was unconscious in hospital, rifling through her belongings, deciding what she was allowed to keep and what was to be discarded.

'You wouldn't believe how much of your stuff I took to the tip,' he tells her, turning from the hob.

She looks around at the sparse and clinical surroundings. Defending herself is futile, she realises. Would only fire up his anger even more and, besides, this isn't about material possessions any more. It's about possessing *her*. About getting her back. He could never stand losing anything. She must play a better game than him. She just isn't sure what yet, she thinks, watching him chop and stir. She eyes his back pocket, knowing the house keys are in there.

'You had no right to do that. It was *my* stuff,' she says, unable to let it go, even though there are more pressing fears.

'Exactly, Ella-bella.' He turns from the hob again, wooden spoon in hand, tasting the Bolognese sauce. '*Was*. And you're not going to need any of it now. I'll buy you anything you want, you know that. I want to make you happy. It's a fresh start for both of us.'

Ella decides not to argue, watching as he serves up the food. Then he wheels her through to the dining room and puts her dinner in front of her. It's a cold room and virtually empty, not in the least homely – a long, highly polished dining table with eight chairs sits in the middle, so reminiscent, she thinks, though of course on a far smaller scale. It's hard for Ella to eat properly because her wheelchair is too low but when she tries the upright dining chair, it's uncomfortable for her leg. Food drops down her front. She isn't hungry but doesn't want to anger him by leaving it. In any case, it tastes odd. Bitter. He was never used to cooking.

Ella bursts into tears.

'You really gave up my flat?' she asks, hiccupping through the sobs. She watches as he winds spaghetti around his fork, sliding it into his mouth without any mess.

'I did,' he says, glancing up, making a sad face when he sees her tears. 'There's no point paying for it if you're not living there. And without a job, you wouldn't be able to keep it on anyway.'

'But I *do* have a job,' Ella says, feeling nauseous again. She forces down another couple of mouthfuls when he tells her to eat up.

'No, Ella. You'll be more use around here, keeping house for us, making sure things don't slip... like before.'

Ella thinks she catches sight of something like remorse on his face, but knows it must be fake. It's layered over something else she recognises. Anger. 'OK,' she hears herself saying. 'You're probably right.' She gives a quick nod and eats up. It's safer to do as she's told.

After dinner, he gathers up the plates and takes them to the kitchen, coming back to fetch her. 'Talk to me while I wash up,' he says, kissing her head.

Ella is wheeled back into the kitchen, taking a good look around the hallway as they pass through. Even if she could get the keys, maybe when he's sleeping, there's a step up to get out of the front door and she remembers several steps down on the other side. She wishes the hospital had given her crutches, but they insisted on no weight-bearing activities for the time being. It could affect her future mobility, the surgeon said.

'What's the garden like?' she asks, trying to sound interested, craning to see out of the window. She needs to know what the rear exit is like, if she can get through it in her chair.

'That's more like the Ella I know,' Jacob says grinning. 'We can buy plants, put some bulbs in for spring, perhaps.' He dries his hands, reaching for a key on a hook above the door. Ella watches as he turns the lock. It's dark outside now, but he flicks a switch and the garden is suddenly floodlit. 'Ta-da!'

'It's big,' Ella says, seeing there are trees at the end. She wheels herself closer, gets a whiff of the outside. 'What's behind there?' She points down the garden.

'Lovely, isn't it?' he says. 'It backs onto a small copse. Part of the reason I bought the place.'

Ella nods, glancing at the threshold. Only one step down to outside. Doable, perhaps, but if she tips over, she'd be finished. 'Can we go out for some fresh air?' she says, hoping it might wake her up. She's feeling sleepy and needs to be alert for later.

Jacob pauses then smiles. 'Sure,' he says, taking the wheelchair handles and tilting her back. One wheel at a time, she's bumped over the step and down onto the paving. She looks back at the house as he pushes her down the path, making comments about where shrubs would look good, buying garden furniture. She desperately wants to lash out, to hit him, to tell him how crazy and sick he is, but she's more interested in the path down the side of the house, the gate at the end of it leading to the front drive. Her heart sinks when she sees there's a padlock the size of her fist attached to the bolt.

She breaks down in tears again, screwing up her eyes, covering her face so he won't see her frustration.

'Oh Ella-bella, my darling,' he says, crouching down. He wraps his arms around her, forcing her face into his armpit. She can smell him – a mix of deodorant and sweat. She forces down the gag. 'Don't cry. I know it's all new and strange but everything will be OK.'

Strangely, Ella finds herself wrapping her arms around him, pulling him closer. The shape of his body feels familiar – not comforting, but rather recognisable; a known landscape from years ago. Her hand brushes against the leather of his belt on his back as he draws her closer, reciprocating her unexpected warmth.

And, ever so slowly, as she's pressing her face against his neck, distracting him the only way she knows how, trying not to let his moan make the vomit come up her throat, her fingers creep down to his back pocket. The tip of the front door key is poking out.

'Thank you for being so kind,' she forces herself to say, hoping her words in his ear will drown out the sound as she slips the keys from his jeans, curling her fingers securely around them. 'Will you take me back inside now? I'm cold.'

CHAPTER THIRTEEN

Ella

Ella feels woozy as she's bumped back over the doorstep. Jacob struggles, grunting as he heaves her inside. He locks the door again, watching her face as he goes to hang the key back on its hook. But then he hesitates, hand outstretched, slipping it on top of the high cabinet instead.

Ella hangs her head. It's an impossible route anyway. She's already pushed the stolen front-door keys under her left leg, ready to use later. All she has to do is keep cool, pray he doesn't need to go out to the car, be pleasant and wait until he falls asleep. She knows a drink is the answer. He never stopped at one.

'Time for your medication,' Jacob says, reaching into a wall cupboard. 'Your nurse explained it all to me.' He pulls out the bag, rummaging through the boxes, running his finger down a list, opening a couple of packets, checking doses.

'What are they?' Ella says, staring at them as he holds out three pills along with a glass of water.

'They'll make you feel better,' he says, pushing his hand closer. 'Take away the pain.'

Ella knows the tablets can't do that but keeps quiet. She recognises the pills, swallows them, washing them down.

'Right, time to get you washed and ready for bed.'

Ella makes a noise, can't help it. It gurgles up her throat.

'Just like old times, Ella-bella. But so much better now,' he adds when he sees her shocked expression. He spreads his arms wide, as if to indicate their surroundings. 'We can put the past behind us, everything that's happened.' He crouches down beside her chair, clasping her hands. 'I *forgive* you, my darling,' he says, looking up at her, kissing her fingers.

But I don't want old times, she thinks. *I want my new times. Work, home, sleep.*

'How about,' Ella says in a voice that even convinces her things are normal. 'How about we relax first. Have a drink. That will make it much more like old times, surely?' She stifles a yawn, wishes she felt more alert. 'And thank you,' she adds along with a little smile.

Jacob glances at his watch. 'I suppose we could,' he says. 'And we could watch a movie, too, but it will have to be on my laptop because I'm still waiting for the television to be delivered. Along with the security stuff I ordered,' he adds with a look that turns Ella's stomach.

'A movie sounds good,' she says, trying to work out what he means by *security stuff*. 'Pour yourself a drink.' She eyes up the stash of bottles he has nestled on the counter. He makes a throaty growl, as if he's having an internal argument. She knows him too well.

'None for you though, Ella-bella. Not while you're on medication.' He grabs a bottle of Scotch and a tumbler and gives them to Ella to hold while he pushes her through to the living room. She sees a car cruise slowly down to the end of the cul-de-sac, its headlights fanning cones of light through the window as it stops and does a three-point turn before heading off again. Jacob whips the curtains closed before fetching his laptop and dimming the lights.

Ella wonders if the driver saw her. Nothing out of the ordinary to a passer-by, a casual onlooker. A woman in a wheelchair, her loving husband beside her.

'Let me help you onto the sofa,' he says, patting it. 'It'll be more comfortable.'

'Oh, I'm better off in my chair,' she says, knowing that she needs to be in it when he falls asleep. She can't risk waking him. Besides, the front door keys are still under her leg, and she needs to stay awake herself. Her eyes are already drooping, her body weak and lethargic.

'Suit yourself,' he says, sitting down and angling his computer screen so they can both see it. Ella pours him some Scotch, a large measure.

'Thank you,' he says, giving her a loving look. 'You're getting the hang of this already.'

She stares at him.

'It's the little things that matter, Ella-bella,' he says. 'Don't you agree?'

'Yes,' Ella says, watching him drink – familiar long glugs, not even wincing as the whisky goes down his throat. He puts a movie on Netflix, while Ella checks the bottle level before placing it on the side table. Three-quarters full.

She grabs a cushion off the sofa – one of *her* cushions – and hugs it against her. She breathes in its familiar smell, the slight mustiness of her flat (the landlord had done nothing to fix the damp), as well as a tinge of cooking smells. Not that she did much of that. She mostly ate microwave meals, but the cushion is some kind of comfort as Jacob starts the movie.

She runs her finger along the carefully embroidered flowers on one side of the cover – remembering how she'd spent ages stitching them last winter. It helped pass the long evenings, took away some of the crushing emptiness. The flowers go blurry, her fingers slowing, her head lolling…

Suddenly, she jolts awake. She wasn't quite asleep, but not alert either. *Dammit, keep your eyes open*, she thinks. But they're so heavy; she's so tired. She can't believe that this morning she was in hospital, Sue looking after her. It seems ages ago now. She glances over at Jacob. He's engrossed in the film, still seems wide awake.

'Here, let me top you up,' Ella says, pouring more whisky before he can refuse. She smiles at him.

'I treated myself,' he says, tapping the label on the bottle. 'I figured what's the point of having money if I don't spend it.' He strokes her hand. 'And now I have you to spend it on too,' he says, making a contented noise as he turns back to the screen. Ella glances at her watch, noticing him yawn from the corner of her eye. He pushes his hands through his hair, stretching out, making himself more comfortable.

Ella forces a yawn. 'Tired?' she asks, unable to help the next one.

He looks at her. 'It's been a tough week,' he confesses, not taking his eyes off the screen. 'But I've taken a few days off to look after you.'

Ella's heart sinks. In her mind, her being here stretches no further than the next couple of hours, let alone the next few days.

'That's kind,' she says, surprising herself as she reaches out and takes his hand. She strokes the back of it, wrapping her fingers around it, gently massaging his fingers. He gives a little moan, making her feel disgusted, but she continues anyway as she sees him relaxing.

But she's relaxing too, her shoulders dropping and her eyelids heavy again…

*

Her head suddenly jerks up. She doesn't know how long it's been but when she looks at him, he's asleep. Their hands are still joined, resting on the arm of the sofa between them. The laptop gives out a glow, changing with the scenes. The volume is low.

Slowly, Ella slides her hand from under his. Jacob stirs, so she freezes, watching as he gets into a more comfortable position. She can see he's drunk more whisky, but she's cross with herself for falling so deeply asleep.

When she's sure he's settled again, a soft snore escaping his lips, his head lolled back and his eyes closed, Ella reaches down for the wheels. Moving on thick carpet is hard but it dulls the sound. Slowly, she pushes herself backwards, reversing behind the sofa before swinging forward again, heading for the hall. A glance over her shoulder tells her he's still asleep.

Ella holds her breath as she crosses the polished wooden floor of the hallway. Thankfully it's wide enough to get up to the front door, but trickier navigating the deep brush of the fitted doormat. But still, she's there – nearly free. Her heart thumps and her hands shake as she slips the keys from under her leg, holding them in her fist so they don't jangle. It's dim but she can see well enough to get the mortice lock key in, to turn it. It gives easily. All she has to do now is reach up and open the Yale lock.

She prays that the ramp is still outside. If not, she doesn't know what she'll do. She gets her good leg ready to stand on, positioned to heave the front wheels of her chair up and over the threshold. Once she's on the ramp, she's as good as free. She'll quietly shut the door behind her, locking it to buy her some time, then she'll wheel up the street, praying it will be a while before he even notices she's gone.

Ella turns the final lock and pulls the door towards her, breathing in the first lungful of cool evening air as the door opens.

Then the alarm screams out around her – a shrill, piercing sound, making her cover her ears, screw up her face in fear. All she can do is wait, frozen to the spot.

CHAPTER FOURTEEN

Liam

After work, Liam didn't go straight home, still puzzled by what had happened to Ella and even more puzzled that Helen in HR didn't seem that bothered about when she'd be back. And, more worryingly, neither was Marcus, their manager. He supposed it showed how disposable they all were – that Ella's work projects had been farmed off easily enough to him and a couple of others and, no doubt, if he were in the same predicament he would be outsourced too. He wondered if the talk of redundancies several months ago might be inadvertently playing out. Management were dark horses.

The Dog & Whistle, smelt of beer and greasy food. It was comforting. A sanctuary from the day. He ordered a pint at the bar as well as a burger and chips and sat at his usual table over by the dartboard. Ken was there, mindlessly chucking arrows, some of them bouncing off the wires, others haphazardly sinking into the board.

'Improving, eh mate?' Liam said with a wink, pulling out from his pocket the stained slip of paper he'd found hidden at Ella's desk.

'Watch it,' Ken replied, coughing out a laugh, slicking back his grey hair. A moment later, he took a roll-up from his top pocket and went out of the side door to the alley where the regulars went for a smoke. A young couple stepped into his place at the oche and began a game.

It was a mobile number on the note, still just legible. Liam tapped it into Google on his phone but nothing came up – just loads of pages listing similar numbers. He tried Facebook too, but it didn't show anything. He took a swig of his pint, wondering why Ella had tucked it inside her box of tissues. He assumed it was important. He wasn't the nosey type at all, preferring to live a quiet life at his mum's place – gaming, going to the footie, hitting the climbing wall several times a week, plus having a laugh with his mates at the Dog and Whistle. And he'd only ever had a couple of girlfriends – nothing dramatic, heartbreaking or long-term. He'd probably have tolerated a bit of drama if it had meant having someone to confide in, to cuddle up with at the end of a day. Someone to buy a meal for or take to the cinema. He'd been thinking for a while that that person might be Ella but hadn't had the courage to ask her out, not on a proper date with just the two of them. He'd been building up to that. Figuring out her elusive ways, her quiet nature, trying to work out what she was into. He'd even been thinking about asking her to a football match, thought she might be the type to get excited about a game. But he'd have been equally happy to bring her down here, buy her a half, maybe play a couple of games of pool as they chatted. It was these feelings that made finding out how she was doing, what had happened to her after the accident, important. As though his tentative plans had been interrupted.

He hoped she'd got family and friends looking after her, supporting her.

He took a breath and dialled the number, adding in 141 first so it wouldn't show his details. But, of course, he also realised that the 'No caller ID' might put someone off answering. He took another swig of beer to calm his nerves.

After a moment, it rang out and went to a recorded message.

'Hi, this is Steve from Warner and Critchley Property Management. Sorry I can't take your call right now but leave a message or call my colleague Alison on...'

Liam grabbed the pen he kept in his top pocket and jotted down Alison's number on a beer-mat. A property management company, he thought, after he'd hung up. He wondered if Ella had been thinking of moving, or if it was something to do with where she lived now. He decided to call Alison, whoever she was, to see what he could find out.

'Hello, Alison Bailey,' she said brightly, answering after the second ring.

'Oh, hi,' Liam said, faltering, realising it was unlikely she would release details about tenants or clients to a stranger. 'I'm trying to reach a friend, actually,' he said, stumbling over his words. 'Her name's Ella Sinclair.'

There was a pause. *'I'm sorry, is it to do with a property?'*

'Possibly,' Liam said. 'She's been hurt in an accident. She's in hospital but…' Liam thought quickly. 'I want to take her some flowers. And make her a casserole or something, but I've mislaid her address. I found your number and was hoping you could help.'

'Oh… her,' the woman said, suddenly sounding annoyed.

'Her?' Liam repeated. 'You know Ella?'

'Not personally.' She sounded frosty.

'Can you tell me where I can contact her?' Liam said, wishing he'd thought this through more.

'Sorry, I can't disclose personal details,' the woman said. *'Data protection.'*

'I'm just a friend wanting to help out.'

'Then I suggest you contact a family member or someone she knows,' she replied. *'I can't help you.'*

Liam pushed it a couple more times but Alison was steadfast. After thanking her, realising he was on a hiding to nothing, he hung up. It didn't sound as though Ella had endeared herself to Alison, whoever she was, but he supposed he could try Steve again tomorrow.

But tomorrow seemed a long way off. He wanted answers now.

Ken came back inside and picked up his darts from the little shelf below the chalk scoreboard as Liam's food arrived. He did a double take at the young couple in his place at the dartboard, then glanced at Liam, who offered a sympathetic shrug back. Ken came over and sat down.

'They'll be jumping in me grave before I've gone cold,' he said, taking out a tin of tobacco, rolling his next smoke.

'They're just having a bit of fun,' Liam replied, laughing, not failing to notice how the girl had scored a double twenty and a neat treble nine to swiftly win the game. He pressed down on his burger bun and took a huge bite. 'Not stopping long, Ken,' he said, the itch growing ever stronger. 'Things to do.' It was hard to talk with his mouth full.

'As in what, lad?' Ken said, working the tobacco between his fingers.

'Work stuff,' Liam said, drinking more beer to speed up his eating. He stuffed some chips in his mouth. He glanced at his watch, hoping the building wouldn't be locked up for the night. He had access to certain areas, but not all.

Ten minutes later, Ken was back outside smoking again and Liam downed the last of his pint. He waved to the barman and headed off.

The walk back to work wasn't far – about the same distance from the pub and home. That's why he liked the Dog so much – that plus its local atmosphere, the unpretentious people, the same-old-same-olds who had likely been coming in since they were sixteen. He knew some of the lads in there from his college and school before that.

The night security guards at work were just swapping over when Liam swiped into the main entrance of the building. That part was no problem – he had a twenty-four-hour pass and could easily gain access to the editorial suite on the third floor. It wasn't uncommon for any one of the post-production team, or a group of them, to be holed up into the early hours, takeaways and drinks to hand, racing towards a deadline. It came with the territory, especially if they were working on a time-sensitive piece for television. To a point, they were paid overtime at Marcus's discretion, but mainly it was just expected.

Liam pressed the lift button for floor four, where HR was located. There was only a slim chance his pass would let him in, he knew, but he had to try. And even if he got in, he wasn't sure where to look or if he'd find anything of use.

The doors pinged open and he stepped out onto the landing, faced with the glass doors, beyond which were Helen's and Jan's desks, the small kitchen, and a spare office piled up with clutter. All the lights were off, the desks deserted with no one in sight. He rattled the door. It was, of course, locked.

He swiped his pass across the sensor by the door but the light flashed to red. He tried again. Same thing. 'Damn,' he whispered, annoyed for expecting any different.

'Y'all right, bab?' came the voice from behind.

Liam turned. It was the cleaner, struggling with the vacuum, a bucket of cleaning things, a mop and a bag of rubbish.

'Oh…' he said, thinking fast. 'Yeah, sorry. I can't seem to get in and I need to grab something before I leave. Stupid me got halfway home before I realised.' He rolled his eyes, flashing his Ghost Media lanyard but covering the editorial part with his thumb.

'Follow me,' she said, winking. 'But you can take Henry here for me.' She laughed, handing him the hose.

Liam gladly dragged the vacuum cleaner through the door as she opened it wide.

'I'll be here for at least half an hour if you need anything else, love,' she said, going into the kitchenette.

He stared around, faced with the two desks he'd been at earlier. Helen's workspace seemed the logical place to start, but there was no way he'd be able to log into her computer. Whatever it was he was hoping to find, it would have to be physical.

Liam glanced over his shoulder before getting stuck into the Rolodex. He'd never seen one before let alone used one, but he couldn't help smiling at the way all the contact cards flipped around in alphabetical order. He got to the S section and worked through them, hoping to find a card with Sinclair on it, perhaps Ella's address. But there was nothing, just a few contacts he recognised as clients rather than staff, and old clients at that. Useless.

He went behind Helen's desk, pulling open a few filing cabinet drawers. Most were accounting-type files, but then he saw it, underneath the desk. A much smaller, two-drawer cabinet with a sticky label saying 'Staff' stuck on the front.

His heart thumped as he pulled it open. He was pretty sure it would be a sackable offence if he got caught. The files, each labelled with the employee's name, were in alphabetical order. He skimmed past colleagues' names until he found Ella's file. It wasn't as thick as some of the others, even though she'd been at Ghost a long time. He pulled it out, along with his phone from his back pocket. Taking pictures would be the quickest and easiest way of copying information.

Bingo! he thought as, within the first few pages, he found out everything he needed. Address, date of birth, phone number, university transcripts, copies of her degrees, NI number… it was all there. But Liam was only interested in one thing, and that was where Ella lived.

After he'd photographed what he needed, he replaced the file, closed the cabinet, and called out to thank the cleaner as he left.

When he got outside, it was raining – a fine, annoying drizzle that seeped right through to his skin. Liam hitched up his collar, opening up Google Maps and searching the way to Ella's flat. A thirty-three-minute walk.

He set off, imagining Ella cycling the same route, day in, day out. Already he felt a little bit closer to her. A little bit more confident about telling her how he felt. Perhaps even asking her out.

CHAPTER FIFTEEN

Ella

Whiplash. Ella's head jerks back as the wheelchair handles are yanked from behind. She feels herself being hurled inside, away from the door. Freedom slipping away. The alarm siren screams out overhead, only matched in volume by Jacob's angry yells.

Once he slams the door shut again, he silences the alarm on a control panel inside the under-stairs cupboard, growling, angry and seething as he returns to her side. 'Fucking stupid *bitch*,' he yells in her face.

Spit hits her cheek.

'You want to alert the whole street?'

'Sorry,' she says, shaking. She presses down on her legs to stop them jiggling. Her knee throbs from deep inside the bone.

Then comes the blow to her head, the sharp cracking sound inside her ears as his fist knocks her sideways. She reels, crying out, grabbing hold of her face to stifle the pain. She takes a few deep breaths, trying to steady herself, make her eyes focus.

'I-I didn't know there was an alarm,' she says, trying not to cry. 'I'm so sorry… I just wanted some fresh air. I didn't want to wake you.'

'I put the door alarm on at night, to keep us safe. How the hell did you get *these*?' Jacob says, snatching the keys from the door after he's locked it again, thrusting them in her face.

'They were on the sofa,' Ella says, thinking quickly. 'They must have fallen out of your pocket. Please don't be cross…' She nearly uses his name then but checks herself, knowing it would rile him even more. 'I often sit outside at night, looking at the stars. Do you remember? This is my home now and I just want it to feel… to feel the same.' She stifles her sobs. Desperate. Saying whatever comes into her mind.

Jacob says nothing but wheels her back inside the hallway. When he stands in front of her, she senses he's thinking back. That night by the lake, perhaps. The stars, naming constellations together. Shared giggles as she'd concocted silly made-up names for the heavens. They were all there. The whole group of friends relaxing after exams.

Ella reaches out a shaking hand, tips her head to the side. She forces a smile even though her heart feels as though it's about to burst from her chest. He bats her arm away.

'Time for bed,' is all he says, bending down and scooping her up in his arms.

It takes all Ella's self-control not to cry out in pain as her bad leg is twisted and bumped against the wall when he carries her upstairs, all her reserve not to claw his eyes out, spit in his face and thump him. No, she needs to be much cleverer than that, she thinks, as she's forced to cling on with her arms around his neck, his face only inches away.

He takes her into a bedroom, setting her down on a huge bed. When he flicks on the light, she sees the room is decorated in white and grey. Stark and masculine.

'Get undressed,' Jacob says, standing over her. 'You need to wash.'

'But—'

'*Now*, Ella,' he says, looming over her.

She closes her eyes and crosses her arms, slowly pulling off her sweatshirt. She sits there in a T-shirt, praying he doesn't mean everything.

'Just bring me a wet flannel and I'll wash myself,' she says, not caring if she's dirty. She won't be here this time tomorrow anyway.

'We do things properly in this house, Ella-bella,' he says, his blue eyes flickering as he stares at her. 'And the rest.'

Her hands shake as she takes off her T-shirt, him helping her slip it over her head. She sits there in her white bra and jogging bottoms.

'And these too,' he says, tugging at the tracksuit pants. He goes to a chest and opens a drawer, pulling out something cream and silky. A nightdress. He lays it out on the bed next to her. It's short with a low-cut, lacy neckline and thin straps. Not something she'd ever dream of wearing.

'You can't put it on until you're clean,' he says, pulling at the ankles of the sweatpants. Ella hitches herself up so they come off. She's shaking, not from the chill in the air but from fear when he undoes her bra strap, making it fall from her shoulders. 'These too,' he says, pointing at her underpants.

Ella clamps her arms around her bare chest, screwing up her eyes, as he pulls off her knickers. Then she feels herself being carried into the bathroom, placed on a stool.

'My… my leg hurts,' she says, still not opening her eyes. 'And my arm.'

He says nothing, but Ella hears the basin tap running, soap being squirted from a bottle, his hands swishing the water about.

'There, there,' he says. 'Haven't the painkillers worked yet? Perhaps I should give you another dose.'

Ella keeps silent, although more painkillers – hundreds of them – would be preferable. An escape. She gasps as she feels the warm wet washcloth on her breastbone – him gently rubbing at her skin, working his way under her arms, rinsing the cloth in the water. She keeps her eyes tightly closed, doesn't want to see the look on his face, the same look when…

'*Oh…*' Ella cries, feeling like she'll throw up as her body remembers, convulses. Everything she's tried to block out is coming at her full pelt.

He wipes her face then, around her eyes, her ears, cleaning her cheeks and lips. More water and then he rubs down her body, his hand swiping over her breasts, her stomach, down between her legs.

Ella freezes. She thinks of embroidery and work. Thinks of the plants in her flat – wonders where they are, if they've been watered or if they got taken to the rubbish dump too. She thinks of her kitchen and the little window she'd often open to hear the chit-chat of the smokers below, their random conversation snippets making her smile. The tang of their cigarettes. She thinks of the project at work she was working on recently, the colour grading she'd begun but not finished. How the woman in the three-minute film had wanted to get away but didn't know how. How bad things had been happening to her. How there was no one to tell.

'All clean now,' Jacob says, patting her dry with a towel. 'Poor baby, you're shivering.' But he doesn't cover her up. Instead, he takes a toothbrush from the cabinet, squeezes paste onto it and hands it to her. Ella brushes, leans over the basin to half-heartedly spit. She doesn't bother to rinse.

She shivers uncontrollably as he carries her back into the bedroom, lays her on top of the downy quilt. She sinks into its thickness, wishing it was quicksand swallowing her up.

'Put this on, Ella-bella,' he says, holding up the nightdress.

Ella takes it from him and slips it over her head. It's better than being naked.

'Beautiful,' he says, looking her up and down. 'Climb in to bed then, darling. And don't take up all the space.'

Horrified, she does as she's told, not taking her eyes off him as he unbuttons his shirt, exposing a large scar across his shoulder and chest – the skin tight and stretched with red, sinewy roots spreading out. She can't help gasping – just the sight of it is enough to take her back to that night. Then, when he kicks off his shoes, steps out of his trousers and stands there only in his boxers, the penny drops. Her face freezes from fear. She can't speak or make a sound as Jacob turns off the main light and climbs in beside her.

She feels the mattress dip down. Doesn't do a thing as he leans over and kisses her neck. She can't even find it in her to screw up her eyes as he draws close, pressing his warm body against the length of hers – the scar rough against her skin. She almost feels the searing heat radiating from it.

'Good night, Ella-bella,' he says, his breath hot and moist on her cheek.

CHAPTER SIXTEEN

Ella

Jacob halts at the sound of the doorbell, his toast halfway to his mouth. '*What?…*' He slides off the kitchen stool and heads into the hall, his expression twisting into a frown. Ella watches him as he goes slowly towards the door, creeping like a cat. One foot placed carefully in front of the other. Hackles raised. It's the first time she's seen him nervous.

The bell rings again.

From her wheelchair, she can just make out the front door if she leans forward, can hear Jacob muttering expletives as he hesitates, not knowing what to do. On the third ring, which includes a knock as well, he takes the keys from his pocket and unlocks it, pulling it open a few inches.

'Hell*ooo*…' Ella hears a cheerful female voice ring out. 'Hope you don't mind me calling by unannounced,' the woman goes on, 'but I saw the car out front. Guessed you were home.'

Jacob says nothing. Just stares.

'I'm Liz from two doors down,' she says and, as she leans forward further, Ella can see she's holding out her hand to shake.

Jacob opens the door wider, finally reaching out and reciprocating.

Ella's heart thumps.

Someone is *here*.

Someone that's not her or him.

'Jacob Sinclair,' he says in that voice of his – confident, reassuring, charming. Disarming. He keeps hold of the neighbour's hand, switching into the person he needs to be. 'Very nice to meet you, Liz.'

'Rachel next door said that she'd popped round to see you just after you'd moved in. Said she'd taken a couple of deliveries for you,' Liz goes on.

Ella sees him finally release her hand. There's a pause, as if Liz expects Jacob to say something. But he doesn't.

'She said your wife has had an accident. I'm so sorry to hear that,' Liz says the last bit quietly, leaning forward. 'How awful for you both. How's she doing now? I couldn't help noticing you brought her home yesterday. I don't work, you see. And when I saw she was in a wheelchair and in plaster… well, what a terrible thing to happen. If there's anything I can do to help, anything at all – shopping, errands, cleaning, company, you must let me know.' She pauses again, waiting for Jacob's response.

There is none.

'Oh, and I made you these as a welcome-to-the-street gift.' She gives a nervous laugh. Waits. Definitely embarrassed now.

Ella wheels even closer to the hallway, peeking through the crack at the edge of the kitchen door to see Liz holding out a cake tin.

'Is your wife free?' Liz continues when Jacob doesn't reply. 'I'd love to meet her, welcome her to the street personally. And I'm happy to help out any way I can while you're at work.'

Jacob holds the silence for a while longer. Ella sees Liz shifting from one foot to the other, the tin still held in outstretched hands. Jacob makes no move to take it.

'That's kind, but no need, thank you. I've taken a few days off work to look after her. She's fine.' His voice is flat and cold.

'Oh, OK….' Liz laughs again. 'I'd love to just say a quick hello, introduce myself and give her these?'

Ella admires her tenacity, knows that Jacob will be itching to lash out, swipe her around the face. She holds her breath.

'She's busy right now.'

'Busy?' Liz goes on. Her voice has changed, too – questioning, confrontational. Ella admires that. She's just being a friendly neighbour. A rescuer without knowing it. She already likes Liz and it takes her by surprise. She's not allowed herself to consider if she likes anyone for a very long time.

'Yes,' Jacob replies, wavering, clearing his throat. 'She's busy feeding the baby, actually. He missed his mum while she was in hospital.'

Ella can hardly contain her gasp.

'A baby?' Liz says. 'Oh my goodness, that makes this all the harder. I'm so sorry this has happened to new parents. Just despicable. We saw it on the news and everything. How can that driver live with themselves?'

'Despicable indeed,' Jacob says. 'Ella is very tired, as you can imagine. And she wants to spend time with… with little Zach as much as she can now she's home. But I'll tell her you called by. And I'll tell her you brought the cakes.'

Little Zach? Ella thinks, nearly exploding inside.

She sees him pull the tin from Liz's hands, though Liz suddenly doesn't seem too keen to release it. She gives a small, awkward smile before glancing down the hallway and into the kitchen, briefly catching Ella's eye.

Ella sits back, quickly ducking behind the cover of the door.

'Well, wish your wife and son the best from me, then. From me *and* Rachel. We hope to meet her soon.' Another pause. 'We're all close around here, you know.' Liz clears her throat. 'Neighbourly.'

Ella hears Jacob muttering some kind of goodbye, a thank you, and then he closes the door, locking it again.

'Cakes,' he says, coming back into the kitchen and slamming the tin onto the worktop. 'From the neighbour.'

Ella looks up at him, trying to smile. 'That's nice,' she croaks. 'What a welcome. Feels like home already.'

Jacob stops, his hand on his coffee mug. 'You mean that?'

Ella makes eye contact. Full on. The kind of look that brings back a rainbow of horrors – things she didn't know were horrors at the time, but is certain of now. The kind she thought were over. Gone. Dealt with.

'Of course,' she says, smiling, unable to get rid of the image of Liz at the door. Another person. Wanting to meet her. To *help* her. Someone who doesn't even know her. Someone who doesn't know that she's trapped. Stuck inside her own nightmare.

Again.

'It's a lovely thing to do, but…' She's about to ask why he mentioned a baby, but decides against it. It would show she was eavesdropping. He wouldn't like that.

Jacob bites into the rest of his toast. Earlier, he'd made Ella a bowl of cereal, brought it upstairs when she was still in bed. Muesli. She hadn't slept a wink.

'You're right,' Jacob says. 'Liz was just being neighbourly.' He gives a satisfied smile, though he doesn't say if they're going to be neighbourly back.

'Plan for today,' he says. 'We're going for a walk. I will show you the area. The street. How lucky you are to be living here. How lucky *we* are,' he adds.

Ella agrees. Nods. She doesn't think it's lucky in the least. 'I'd like that,' she replies, glancing back down the hall at the front door. It will at least give her a chance to assess outside, the front, the street. The escape. To see where this Liz lives, plus the other neighbour, Rachel, immediately next door. The lay of the land, which she can't recall from when she arrived. She needs to plan more carefully.

'We *are* very lucky. And it's all thanks to you,' she says, looking away as she catches sight of the scar rising up his chest, visible at the top of his open-necked shirt.

Jacob nods in approval, eating the remainder of his breakfast. He takes two phone calls that seem, to Ella, like work colleagues. In hospital, she overheard him telling Sue he works in banking, but she has no idea what his actual role is. For a dead man, he's done well for himself.

Green Leys is all immaculate driveways, new cars and pretty front gardens. To Ella, it's a world apart. So very different to where she grew up – and, of course, Jacob too. Not that she isn't, and wasn't, aware of how other people live. God knows, she saw enough of that and the rest of it while at university. Adlington Manor was enough to make Green Leys look like an inner-city council estate by comparison.

She glances up at Jacob as he pushes her along the pavement, a blanket draped over her knees. He knows it all too, she thinks, sighing, her fingers knotting the wool throw. How she wishes she could leap out of the chair and run. Only a few weeks ago, she'd have been able to. But then a few weeks ago, he didn't know where she was.

'What do you think, Ella-bella,' he says, pushing her up the incline. 'Isn't it pleasant?' He sweeps his arm around, gesturing to the grand development of houses.

Tacky, Ella thinks. Tasteless and soulless. The stark tarmac, the manicured front lawns, the small shrubs and trees – none of it has grown out of decades of life, loves, people, or the continuing bustle or struggles of humanity. It's clinical, she thinks. Sealed off and separated from real life. And a complete contrast to what he – and she – are used to.

'Do you remember how we used to talk about getting a home together, our crazy plans?'

'I do,' Ella says without having to think. She can't deny it, all their chats, their hopes and dreams for the future when they were at university. 'And here we are,' she adds, hating herself for reaching behind and stroking his hand.

Jacob makes a contented growling sound, and Ella knows this is a good sign. The first step to breaking free, to escaping.

And deep down, as they head back to the house, as she catches sight of the neighbour next door but one peering out of the window, she knows that it's probably not going to happen today.

CHAPTER SEVENTEEN

Ella

Ella is lying on the sofa in the living room. Her eyes are closed, but she's not asleep. It's cool, even though the sun angles in through the bay window of the living room. Her leg is hurting – the same deep throb that has kept her awake at night since she was brought out of the coma. Though last night it wasn't simply the pain that kept her awake. It was him, lying next to her in bed, his steady breath on her shoulder as he slept soundly while she stared at the ceiling. She must have dozed off for maybe an hour or so as it gradually got light – long enough for him to take hold of her hand and her not to notice, to still be clasping it when she snapped awake, unsure of where she was. Until she remembered. The dread sweeping through her.

Easier to give up, she'd thought, lying there, terrified. *Just do whatever it is he wants.* She'd considered it. That perhaps a life of captivity here wouldn't be much different to how she'd been living the last ten years anyway. Alone. Trapped. Isolated. But at least that was self-imposed. This wasn't.

But, as Jacob had stirred, she'd batted the thought away. Slipped her hand from his sweaty palm. Lay there, hating him. She would escape. Somehow.

Ella suddenly hears a soft mewing sound – high-pitched and getting closer. She sits up, wondering if she imagined it.

Then Jacob comes in, a tiny tortoiseshell kitten following close to his heels.

'Time for your medication, Ella-bella,' he says, presenting her with a handful of pills and a glass of water. Two types of painkillers and an antibiotic.

'Whose kitten is that?' she says, watching as the little thing weaves between his feet, almost getting trodden on.

'Ah,' Jacob says, a warm look in his eyes. 'Isn't it sweet? It's yours if you want it.'

'But…' Ella doesn't understand.

'He chose us, Ella-bella. Came right in through the back door, meowing for food. I gave him some milk and shut the door behind him. Do you love him as much as you love me?'

She takes the pills, desperate for the pain relief, using the fingers of her right hand, pincer-like, to pop them in her mouth. She swills them down, staring at the kitten.

'So he belongs to someone else?' she asks.

Jacob doesn't reply, just picks up the kitten, placing it on Ella's lap. Immediately it nuzzles up to her face, licking her cheek, purring loudly.

'Someone's probably looking for it,' she adds, stroking the tiny creature. 'Why are you doing this?' she asks. '*Any* of it?'

The look on his face tells her she should have kept quiet, played along.

'Are you being ungrateful?' he says, banging the glass down hard on a side table. Then he grabs her right leg by the cast, yanking it high off the sofa.

'Ow-*www*,' Ella shrieks, reaching out to stop him. Then he lets go, dropping it back down. Ella cries out again and the kitten jumps down, hiding under the sofa. 'I'm not ungrateful… really I'm not,' she says, stifling the sobs. 'I just don't understand why…' But she checks herself, knowing she won't get answers. Doesn't actually *want* answers because the truth is too hard to hear. She knows what she's done. And so does he.

'What is it you don't understand, Ella-bella? Why I'm alive?' Jacob laughs then, sits down on the edge of the sofa. 'Oh, Ella-*bella*…' He leans forward, kissing her forehead. She smells the spicy notes of his deodorant. 'I already told you. I'm alive because I'm a survivor. We *both* are. Anyway, that's all in the past now. Let's put it behind us and pick up where we left off.' He makes a sound with his lips, calling to the kitten as it pokes its head out from under the chair, slowly coming over.

But Ella doesn't want to pick up where they left off because the last time she saw him was *that* night, *that* summer. She tries to block out the horror, like she's always done, but it's getting harder, seeping in. The vault of her mind cracked.

He strokes her forehead. 'Don't dwell on the bad, my darling. Just remember the good days.' He picks the kitten up again, pinning it to his chest.

Work, home, sleep.

'Do you remember the first time we all went to Zoo together? So bloody exclusive that your eyes nearly popped,' he says, laughing. 'All that champagne, all those famous faces. Rubbing shoulders,' he adds, handing her the kitten again before doing exactly that to Ella – rubbing her shoulder. She flinches at his touch.

And yes, of course she remembers going to Zoo. They'd taken a car – *a private car* – down to London, all courtesy of Meggie. At that point, she knew of Zach, of course – he'd caught her eye, as he had most of the girls in their year, though she hadn't yet got the measure of him or the way his mind worked. But she'd sensed he wasn't like the other boys, she'd been sure of that. She preferred to learn and watch from a distance, work out for herself how Zach saw the world one step askew of reality, almost as if he lived in his own perfect bubble.

'This is absolutely crazy, Megs,' she'd said, sliding into the car's plush leather interior. She hadn't even known what type of car it was, except that it was long and black, looked expensive and that it was at Meggie's beck and call. All she had to do was phone her parents' driver and she could go anywhere she wanted, take her friends too.

'Not as crazy as taking the jet,' Meggie said, giggling and huddling up close to her friend as the others climbed in. 'Love you, Els,' she whispered, her breath already zingy from alcohol.

'Love you back more,' Ella replied, giving her arm an excited squeeze. She'd often wondered why they'd become such close friends – their lives were worlds apart, after all. To begin with, at the start of their degree, it had been hard to accept that someone like Meggie would actually like her, want to hang out with her. But, over time, it had seemed Meggie had no ulterior motive, just that she was genuine, warm-hearted and that they got on. They chatted for hours – laughing together, crying together, and they both adored their subject. Ella admitted, she looked up to Meggie. Wanted to be like her. Though she doubted Meggie thought the same about her.

'God, I *love* this place already,' Ella squealed when they went inside Zoo, the bouncers letting them queue jump when they saw Meggie. She'd been determined to show Ella a taste of her life in London; her parents' Chelsea home, the restaurants, her fashionable friends, everything that was so familiar and easy to her – and so very far removed from Ella's and her brother's lifestyle. As ever, Harry had been there too, but would never admit that his eyes also popped when they walked in, that he'd been as nervous and in awe as she'd been. The pair of them had felt awkward, standing out in their budget clothes, not even knowing what the chaser was to their sparkling cocktails, let alone understanding how the cloakroom worked, and averting their eyes from all the famous faces that were dotted about the different levels of the club. No, unlike Ella, who couldn't help the starry-eyed gazes or contain her excitement, Harry had kept his cool.

'This place really *is* like a zoo,' she'd said into his ear as he stood rigid, holding his drink. 'Filled with rare species!' she added, shrieking and moving in time to the music.

But Harry had just smiled, looking out of place, though Ella had known he was pleased she was having a good time. Then, when she'd followed his line of sight, she'd seen he was staring at Zach across the other side of the dance floor, surrounded by his group of friends – including Charles and Stan. 'Just be careful, OK?' Harry had said, squeezing her hand.

A moment later, with his velvet jacket and slicked back hair, Zach had made his way over to them. Ella smiled up at Harry, nearly spilling her drink as Zach latched his arm firmly around her waist and guided her through the crowds to his table. His reputation preceded him as people got out of their way, wondering who the lucky girl was. Then the waitress had been swiftly beside them – tiny dress, tiny little nose, acting as cute as anything with Zach. She'd have done whatever he wanted. Anyone would have. Zach oozed charm. Right up until the moment he went off and talked to another girl, forgetting Ella even existed.

Bastard, Ella thinks now, looking up at Jacob. Wanting nothing more than to smash his face with the plaster cast on her arm.

'Zoo was fun indeed,' she says, having to admit that, at the time, it had been. Her first night at the club (there'd been more over the years), Meggie had got high in the toilets, begging Ella to try a line, getting pouty when she refused. They'd indulged in the free-flowing champagne poured straight from Meggie's parents' account; there was a world-famous DJ – the pulsing music thrumming through her entire body – and so much dancing, the hands all over her until she gave up trying to work out whose they were or bat them away. The chill-out lounge, the oysters and Bloody Marys. All a blur of the young and the beautiful, the rich and the privileged.

It had been the complete opposite to hers and Harry's lives. Not the light to their darkness and mundanity, exactly, but rather a different shade entirely. A colour she'd never imagined possible. Off the known spectrum. And it wasn't long before she'd begun to enjoy it.

But that was the problem, she thinks. That reckless summer. Too much fun to even see it coming. She was looking the other way when the high-speed train hit.

When the *van* hit.

Jacob stares at her, a warm glow in his eyes. He likes that she's remembering. It's triggering something in him. Something that's making him happy, content, calm.

I need to make him feel more like this, Ella thinks, *because happy people make mistakes.*

'Do you remember Charles getting wasted, the night before we went off to Adlington?' he says, stroking Ella's hair.

She tries to imagine it's not him, that it's someone else's fingers toying with the strands. Suddenly, Liam is on her mind. She'll pretend it's him. He's always been kind. Anything to take away her revulsion to Jacob's touch.

Of course Ella remembered that night. If she thought about it hard enough, she would easily be able to recall every single minute of those few weeks in full technicolour detail. Except, for the last ten years, she'd chosen not to. She'd blocked it all out instead.

Work, home, sleep.

'Oh yes, it was *so* funny,' she says, seeing Jacob relax further.

She hands him the kitten, watches as it settles down on his knee, curling up as he strokes it.

'That poor doorman. Vomit all over his shoes, down his leg.' Ella had secretly thought Charles was disgusting but had said nothing. She'd somehow become part of their elite group by being friends with Meggie, and so had Harry by default. And being in it had made her feel safe, wanted, accepted, as though she'd had people watching her back. Unlike school. Or home. Until then, it had just been her and Harry against the world.

Jacob sprays out laughter. 'Oh my God, yes. He refused the ambulance, didn't he? Said he'd only travel to hospital in the Rolls and called his father's chauffeur to take him. His dad was furious when he spray-painted the inside.'

Ella forces a laugh, disgusted with herself for playing along with him. Any further memories are curtailed by the doorbell ringing again.

Liz, Ella prays, holding her breath as Jacob cautiously goes to the front window, peering out.

'Ah,' he says, shoving the kitten back at Ella before striding to the front door, rubbing his hands together. She hears him talking briefly and then there's noise, as though stuff is being brought inside. Then the door shuts again, locks, and Jacob returns carrying a large box.

'TV arrived,' he says, looking back to the hallway. 'And this lot came too.'

He puts the box down on the floor in front of the fireplace, deftly slicing it open with one of the house keys. Ella watches, holding her breath, feeling Jacob's anticipation as he pulls out the packing materials. One by one, he removes several smaller boxes. The kitten jumps down to investigate.

'Just what we need,' he says, squinting around the room. 'One over there, I think. One in the hall and the kitchen, another in the bedroom. I can always get more if needed.' He opens one of the boxes. The kitten immediately jumps in. 'And this little beauty controls them all.'

'Controls what?' Ella says, trying to sit up, thinking that if he's got some kind of hobby, she should show an interest. *Get him onside*, she reminds herself.

'The cameras, of course,' Jacob says, standing up. 'How else am I going to keep an eye on you when I go back to work?' He pulls out his phone. 'There's an app,' he goes on, 'so I can watch you from wherever I am. Even if I'm on the other side of the world.'

And suddenly, Ella wishes he was.

CHAPTER EIGHTEEN

Ten Years Ago

Ella didn't go straight back to Mary's. Instead, she got far enough away from Cloisters before slowing down and dropping onto a bench in a small park. She didn't know where she was. Her feet hurt, so she slipped off Meggie's shoes, unable to help the tears. She dropped her face into her hands.

She hated herself. Hated herself for actually meeting Zach in the first place; hated that she'd acted stupid and unsophisticated; hated that she felt ridiculous in the skimpy top and heels; hated that she'd let him kiss her – in *public*. But most of all she hated that she'd run away. A frightened little rabbit.

Despite everything – her background, her family, her school and all the troubles she'd been through – Ella had never once done that. She was a fighter, a coper, had always faced her fears. Right now, all she wanted was to rewind time, be back in the bar with Zach, have him approach her for a kiss once again. She would stop him. Move away, halt him with her hands on his chest before he even had a chance to touch her. Tell him that if he tried it again, she'd be gone.

After everything she'd been through in the past, she'd vowed no one would ever cross that line again. Except somehow, Zach had.

*

Later, she ambled back to Mary's – barefoot and walking carefully, slowly. In the corridor of bedrooms, she walked past Meggie's room, listened, but couldn't hear any music or her friend talking on the phone. And neither was there the smell of smoke as Meggie hung out of the window, puffing slyly on a cigarette. She was relieved she was out, wouldn't have to explain. She could crawl into bed with a book, forget the stupid date with Zach that, secretly, she'd been hoping would turn into an evening of fun conversation, a few drinks, some appreciative looks and maybe, just maybe, if he walked her back to Mary's – a kiss on the cheek. Or at most, a quick one on the lips.

'Violated,' she said, draping Meggie's clothes over the back of her desk chair. Then she hung them up, taking a guess at what they'd cost. 'Twat,' she muttered a dozen times. But really, she was cross at herself.

Ella felt the tears brewing again as she leant over the basin in her room, brushing her teeth. She suddenly felt desperately homesick, yet home was the last place she wanted to be. She remembered the pact she and Harry had made aged eleven – to ignore the bullies, keep out of Ron's way and avoid his violent temper, work hard, get into the good grammar school and then work harder some more, finally making it to university. Even way back then, they'd dreamed of a life after *that* life. Ella never spoke to anyone about what she'd gone through. The only person who knew everything was Harry.

And here they were, doing just what they'd dreamed of. They'd succeeded and Ella wouldn't allow anything, or anyone, to get in their way. She knew Harry felt the same.

She'd just brushed her hair and climbed into bed when there was a knock at the door. She didn't know whether to answer it. What if it was Zach? Perhaps he'd come to tell her how silly she'd been, that they should go out again, that she should give him another chance. Or, maybe he'd come to get what he obviously thought he was entitled to: *Her.*

She shuddered, getting out of bed and slowly turning the lock. When she opened the door a crack, she sighed out in relief, almost wanting to break down in tears.

'Harry,' she said, opening the door wider. 'Thank God it's you.'

She could see straight away he was drunk.

'Date go well, did it?' he said walking straight in, dropping down on her bed.

'How did you know?' Ella replied with a strange feeling in the pit of her stomach. 'And not really,' she added, confessing.

He stared at her, giving her that look, the one they both shared as twins. It was a deep bond, almost as if they'd been born with it, always understanding each other perfectly, as though they had a sixth sense. It was hard to explain to regular siblings. But they'd grown up preferring it that way – no one knowing about their almost psychic connection. It was their secret. *One* of their secrets, and had helped them through tough times, making them closer and, above all, fiercely loyal to each other – despite everything.

'Tell me,' Harry said, stretching his hands behind his head, laughing. 'Is he not as gorgeous as me?'

Harry had always been the more confident of them, even at school when their lives were toughest. Ella sometimes wondered if her being the fall guy – at home and at school – had allowed him to flourish while holding her back. He'd done his best to protect her, of course, to watch out for her – Ella knew that. But she knew that the opposite was also true. Many times, unbeknown to Harry, she'd defended him, at a cost to herself, especially when it came to Ron, their stepfather. She'd taken the full force of his anger, his rages, confessing to things she hadn't done just to save Harry's skin. Ron always preferred to hurt a girl. She shuddered. She wanted a chance to bloom, too.

'He's kind of cute,' she said, trying to sound casual as she slid onto the bed next to him, allowing a coy smile. She didn't want him to get defensive or overprotective. Those thirty minutes between their births had somehow always given him that right.

'But?'

'But maybe he's not for me. You know.'

Harry's expression relaxed, no doubt a result of the alcohol.

'I'm tired, Harry,' Ella said, patting her pillow. If he stayed, there was more chance of him questioning her about the curtailed date, of things getting heated. And she mustn't forget that he and Zach hung out in the same group of friends. She didn't want it to be awkward for Harry. She just wanted to forget the evening and Meggie's stupid matchmaking and get some sleep. She should have known it wouldn't go well. She wasn't like the other girls.

'Fine. I get the hint. Anyway, I have training in the morning,' Harry said. 'Are you coming to the match?'

'Of course,' she replied, knowing how much it meant to him to have her watch.

'Zach said he'll be there,' he added, watching her reaction.

'*And?*'

Harry laughed, though he wasn't smiling. 'You know how unlike him that is. To slur his reputation by hanging out with a bunch of rowdy football players. He must *really* want to be there.'

'I don't know anything about his reputation, actually,' Ella said. 'In fact, I know very little about him.'

'He asked me if you'd be there.'

'When?'

'Just now. I bumped into him downstairs.'

Ella swallowed. She'd wondered what Zach had done after she'd run off. Been with his mates, no doubt, laughing at her. Or maybe he'd picked up another girl at the bar.

'He likes you,' Harry went on.

'What else did he say?' Ella's heart thumped. If the evening had gone on the way Zach had obviously wanted, then she'd be labelled easy. And as it stood, word would soon spread that she was frigid and cold.

'He said that he thinks you're intelligent, sweet, funny, pretty. He wants to see you again. The date must have gone better than you'd imagined. Are you sure you're telling me everything, Ella?'

She tried to read her brother's face, usually so easy, but he'd suddenly switched into blank mode, an annoying habit that he'd employ from time to time that not even she could read.

'You like him, don't you?' he pressed on when she didn't reply. It was barely a question. More an accusation.

'He's OK,' Ella said, shrugging. 'But I'm so busy with my studies, my music, friends and stuff. You know how it is. It's not going to go anywhere with Zach.'

'Well,' Harry said, getting up off the bed and planting a brief kiss on her forehead. 'You say that now…'

And then he left.

Meggie was standing at the side of the pitch, huddled under a huge umbrella. She beckoned to Ella, waving her over.

'Why didn't you reply to my texts last night?' she asked. 'Was the date *that* good?' Despite the rain, it was still mild. Early summer had been kind so far. 'Did you, you know… do it?'

'No, of *course* not,' Ella shot back, rolling her eyes, play-punching her friend. She didn't think she was a prude, but there was no way she'd ever do that on a first date, even if it was with Zach White. She didn't want it to be a drunken regret and, if she was honest with herself, getting to that point with a boy – *any* boy – seemed unthinkable. 'It was…' She wanted to say 'fine', to be noncommittal, but trailed off. She couldn't lie to her best friend. 'He tried to kiss me, Megs.'

Meggie sucked in sharply, making a show of it. 'Shock horror. Do go on.' She grinned, wrapping her arm around Ella's waist, huddling closer under the umbrella. 'Ooh, talk of the devil,' she said, squeezing Ella as her eyes flicked to the other side of the pitch.

Through the melee of boys training on the muddy grass, Ella saw an all-too-familiar shape on the other side of the field. Though she couldn't make out his face, the dark jacket, the trilby-like hat tilted down, the way he carried himself, all reeked of Zach. He even made standing still seem graceful. His hands were shoved deep in his pockets, his head bowed, yet Ella could sense he was scanning about to see who was there, the glint of his eyes flashing from beneath his hat.

'But I didn't *want* him to kiss me,' Ella continued, her voice serious. The feelings were stirred again. From somewhere deep inside.

'Of course you wanted him to. It's Zach bloody White. I could have gone for him myself now he's single again, but thought… well, I thought you needed a boost. Tell me you didn't waste the chance to snog the prettiest boy in St Mary's, perhaps the whole of Durham. The UK even?'

'No. Really, I didn't want him to—'

'Oh, wait. Look. Fuck. He's coming over.' Meggie fluffed up her hair, cursing the rain, changing her posture entirely as he drew up beside them.

'Hi Zach,' Meggie sang out.

Ella stared at the ground, wishing a sink hole would open up.

'Morning, girls,' he replied. She could sense he was looking at her, not Meggie. 'Ella…' he said.

She felt him touch her arm and then, to her horror, he leaned forward and kissed her on the cheek. The perfect gentleman. Had she imagined his forced kiss last night? Made up his advances to suit her own reality – her *fears*? Had he actually done anything wrong?

She glanced up, flashed him a look that was mainly a blush, heard Meggie talking to another of the girls who lived on their floor at Mary's.

'I'm sorry about last night,' Zach said quietly. 'I shouldn't have kissed you like that. I…' He reached out and touched her arm again.

So she wasn't imagining it. His face seemed earnest enough, she thought. She gave a little nod.

'Would you like to meet again?' he asked. 'Maybe for afternoon tea?'

'Oh,' Ella said, touching her cheek and turning away. 'I don't know…'

'Also, I'm having a sort of party in a few weeks,' Zach went on, his eyes flashing excitement as he stepped into her line of sight. 'I'd love it if you came.'

'Oh,' Ella said again, completely lost for words. 'I'm not really sure…' She curled her toes inside her shoes.

Something flared in Zach's eyes then – a dark sparkle that actually appeared blacker than his pupils, making Ella wonder how that was actually possible. She wasn't sure if his look was more dangerous than anything she'd seen before and she should run a mile – perhaps he wasn't used to being turned down – or if it made him the most enticing and alluring boy she'd ever encountered.

'When is it?' she added, not wanting to seem stand-offish.

Zach turned his face into the rain. 'It's after final exams,' he said. 'For a few days at my home in Oxfordshire. There's a whole group of us going.'

Ella suppressed her shock, looking at him square on, determined to face her fears. Now the end of her degree was approaching, maybe it *was* time to let go a little, perhaps even consider the prospect of having a boyfriend. She'd soon be moving into the next phase of her life after all, couldn't always rely on Harry to be there. The thought of having someone to share things with, to confide in and, maybe, one day, be close to physically – well, she couldn't deny her feelings.

She told herself she needed to stop acting like a silly girl, remember the person she'd been for most of her childhood – strong and determined. Zach White had just invited her out for a cup of tea as well as to his house party. It was normal, she tried to convince herself, and what most of her friends did without thinking twice about it. There would be others at the party too, and maybe she *could* go just for one night. She tried to imagine what his place would be like, what it would feel like to spend time inside his privileged world. She didn't know whether to scream for joy or run a mile. Either way, her mind was made up.

'Sure, I'd like that, thanks,' she replied, sweeping her hair off her face, unable to help her beaming smile. 'Both of those things.'

Later, she would blame his eyes entirely for drawing her in, for making her say the complete opposite of what she should have said.

CHAPTER NINETEEN

Ella

Ella watches on in horror as Jacob sets out all the equipment, laying it on the floor with great care and putting each set of instructions by its component part. She is still on the sofa, her leg raised up, stroking the kitten as it lies on her knee.

'I have to go into the garage to get some tools,' he says, staring at her. 'Don't move.'

Ella makes a face, pointing at her casts. 'I'm hardly going anywhere.' She wonders where the garage is, if it's accessible from inside. She hasn't quite got the lay of the house figured out yet.

Jacob stares at her then nods. Her wheelchair is in the hall near the front door and there is no way she can bear weight on her broken leg to get to it. Ella hears him go through to the kitchen, then something that sounds like a lock turning, a door opening. It slams hard, as though it's weighted to close automatically. *A fire door*. It must be an integral garage then, she thinks, constructing a mental map of the house.

A few minutes later, he returns with a plastic carry-case and a small toolbox. The kitten jumps down to investigate.

'You're well prepared,' Ella remarks, trying to sound light, even though she's horrified by what he's doing. 'Mr DIY.' She hates herself for dancing to his tune. In fact, she doesn't even know where it's coming from, the chit-chat, the little comments that send Jacob's face into a rainbow of approval. She knows it's not from recent experience, having little communication with anyone the last ten years, and she was never witness to a normal family growing up. But then neither was Harry, she remembers sadly. She misses him terribly. Wishes he was here. Her twin. The strong, capable, protective brother who would move the world to look after her. But he's not.

She's thought about him countless times over the years, of course, and has even written letters to him, screwing them up or hiding them in the box under the bed, along with the birthday cards she'd buy but never send. There was no point. It wouldn't have done any good, but her own birthday was always tinged with sadness. She wonders if a psychic message would somehow get through to him. Something to end this desperate situation. To get her out, put everything back to how it was. But, after everything that's happened, she knows it's too late. He's gone and she has to accept that. It was all her fault.

She shudders as Jacob takes out the drill from its case, wielding it with a loud rev of the motor. The kitten shoots from under the sofa, charging into the hallway and up the stairs.

'Looks easy enough,' Jacob says, leafing through the camera instructions. 'Once I get them installed, they connect by Wi-Fi to the control unit and then link to the app on my phone. I have to make sure you're safe, Ella-bella. I can't risk losing you again.'

She thinks about this, not realising that she'd ever been lost. But it's only now, sitting on the sofa, helpless and stranded, that Ella realises the only person she's been missing from all this time is herself.

*

Two hours later, Jacob is satisfied. Not only has he installed the monitoring system, but it worked first time. And he made Ella lunch, too. Chicken and tomato sandwiches. With mayonnaise.

And too much salt. Or something else that tastes weird. Afterwards, she feels extra sleepy, can't help drifting off as she lies on the sofa, her body almost melting into the leather. She doesn't like that she's relaxing, wondering if perhaps she's beginning to enjoy it here, being cared for, having someone to talk to. Surrendering. She read about that once, a girl who was kidnapped and ended up falling in love with her captor. She doesn't want to be that person, despite the way her body is reacting. She will fight it and escape, she thinks, unable to help the yawn.

'I need to put the system to the test,' Jacob announces, once he has doled out her next round of medication. He taps away on his phone. 'It's working while I'm here on Wi-Fi.' He shows her the screen. Horrified, Ella sees herself on the couch, her eyes taking a moment to focus. The image is clear, the camera capturing most of the living room. There are only a couple of areas where it doesn't reach. 'I'm going outside, check it works on 4G.'

'Good idea,' she says, her mouth going dry. Maybe she can escape while he's gone. She doesn't see how, though, as he'll be watching her every move. 'How does it look in the kitchen? The bedroom?' she says, trying to sound interested, peering at his phone. 'Thank you for caring about me.' She touches his arm. Hating herself.

Jacob taps the screen and shows her the other rooms. 'Pretty good, eh?' he says, proud of his handiwork. 'I can be home in a shot if need be.' He stares at her a moment too long, something sparking in his eyes.

Ella tries to remember the areas covered on the screen, even though her brain feels sluggish. There's a spot by the bathroom doorway that isn't covered by the camera, and another by the bedroom door. It's mainly the bed, the wardrobe area and over by the window. The kitchen camera is aimed at the back door as well as the door that she believes leads out to the garage. Most of the cooking area is off-screen as the kitchen is so big. The camera in the hallway spans the length of it, including the under-stairs cupboard where Jacob installed the control centre for the system and, of course, the front door is the main focus.

Her heart sinks. She won't be going anywhere.

'You've got it all sorted,' she says, laying her head back down, closing her eyes.

'No time for sleep,' he says, returning with her wheelchair. 'I want you to wheel yourself around the house while I go to the end of the street to test it. Make sure you give me a wave.' He smiles. 'And don't try any stunts.' He kisses her head.

'Of course not,' she says, shifting herself across into her wheel-chair, wincing from the pain.

'Go from one room to the next. Hallway, kitchen, back in here again. Keep doing it until I return.'

Ella nods, watching him leave. She hears the front door being locked. When she wheels herself past it, staring longingly at the exit, she can't help wondering what would happen if she slid the safety chain across and locked him out. But then she's imagining the smashed windows, the rage, the blows to her head. She knows the consequences, knows the time is not right. Not yet. Not even today or tomorrow as she'd hoped. Freeing herself is going to take something way more complicated than simply escaping.

CHAPTER TWENTY

Ella

The doorbell. Ella isn't expecting this. It's Jacob's first day back at work and he didn't say what to do if visitors called. He fed her as usual this morning – porridge today, bitter and thick, as if perhaps the milk was off. But she didn't complain and he watched while she ate it all, taking her back upstairs afterwards and washing her. She's a little more used to that now, him running a soapy flannel over her naked body, closing her eyes when his hand goes where it shouldn't. Her leg is a little less painful when he hoists her in and out of the chair, or helps her get onto the toilet, never turning his back as she does what she needs.

Every night for the last week, they've lain side by side in bed, his body always touching hers, feeling her presence. Ella knows it's only a matter of time.

The doorbell chimes again. Resounding through the house.

She doesn't know what to do. Slowly, she wheels herself into the hallway just as the knocks start up. Then a voice calls through the letterbox.

'Hell*ooo*,' it calls out. A woman. 'Anyone home?' Then silence, apart from the sound of Ella's breathing. 'I come bearing gifts.'

Liz, Ella thinks. She recognises her voice from the other day. True to her word, she's come back, is still trying to play the good neighbour. If only she knew.

And then fingers appear through the bristles of the letterbox flap, prising them apart.

An eye stares in.

'Oh, you poor love,' Liz says. 'Can you make it to the door and let me in? I'm Liz, a neighbour. Did your husband tell you I called by?'

She waits for a reply. Their eyes are at the same level, no hiding now.

'I saw he left early this morning all suited up. Back at work, is he?'

Ella doesn't say a word. As much as she wants to tell Liz to call the police, to beg for her help, she can't. Everything would come out.

'Yes,' Ella finally says, feeling stupid for talking to a letterbox.

'I made you some more brownies,' Liz says. 'Thought we could share a couple over a coffee. You must feel very isolated in there alone, just you and the baby. How are you coping, love?'

Ella senses that Liz is older than her, perhaps early forties, though she can't be sure. She feels tears pooling in her eyes. 'I'm OK,' Ella says. 'The baby is… is, um, sleeping right now.' She whispers the last part, to make it seem more real. *Me, an imaginary baby, and a kitten*, she thinks, clenching her fists.

'Perfect time for a cuppa then,' Liz says. 'Can you open the door?'

'Not really,' Ella says. 'He'll be waking up soon.' She has no idea about babies and what their sleeping hours are like. She's never even held one before.

'I could help you with him. I bet he's adorable,' Liz says. 'How old is little Zach?'

Ella feels a sweat break out.

'I don't need any help, thanks. Jacob left everything here for me, food and stuff. I can get to it all.'

'Are you breastfeeding?' Liz asks, making a sound then standing up a moment, as if she's stretching out her back. Then her mouth appears at the letterbox again. 'It'd be easier to talk without the door between us.'

Ella doesn't know if she is breastfeeding her imaginary baby or not. She can't picture it – a tiny thing being dependent on her body to stay alive. She can hardly depend on herself to stay alive right now, let alone be responsible for someone else.

'No,' she says, thinking it's safest. Babies can have bottles of milk too. 'I'm not.'

'How old is he?' Liz says. 'I'd love to meet you both. If it's not a good time now, perhaps we can arrange another day? Get a couple of the other mums from the street to come round, too? Green Leys is a really friendly place to live.'

'That would be nice,' Ella says. 'And he's about... about six weeks old,' she adds, thinking that if he was much more than that, then he probably wouldn't be a baby any more. She's not too sure.

'Oh, so tough for you to be going through this with a newborn. I'll leave you in peace now, love, but don't forget, I'm only a couple of doors down. I'll give you my number.' A moment later, a note is popped through the door. 'Bye for now then,' she says, and Ella hears her walk off.

She closes her eyes, her heart still thumping. She's about to go back to the living room, heave herself onto the sofa to think, perhaps have a little sleep – she's so tired all the time – but she doesn't want Jacob finding the note. She'd have to tell him that she spoke to Liz then, tell him how she had to cover his lie about having a baby. So she reaches down for the paper and wheels through to the kitchen bin. When she glances out of the window, she sees the little tortoiseshell kitten walking along the top of the fence before it jumps down into next door's garden. Jacob must have let it out earlier. As she opens the bin lid, she bursts into tears, wondering why the kitten is allowed to run free but not her.

*

Something wakes her. The clattering of keys, the door opening. As ever, it's a few moments before she realises where she is or remembers her situation. Her stomach knots. When she dragged herself onto the sofa after Liz left, it was morning. All she knows now is that it's dark and she's been asleep all day. Her back is stiff, her head hurting. And she forgot to take her antibiotic and pain medication.

Jacob stands before her, towering over her. His hair is soaking wet, slicked back and clinging to his head.

'Is it raining?' Ella says groggily, forcing a smile. She sits up, lifting her bad leg and propping it on the seat of her wheelchair.

He eyes her for a while, squinting, not giving anything away. Then he slowly reveals a bunch of flowers from behind his back. 'Who were you talking to this morning?' he says, ignoring her question. A couple of rose petals fall onto her lap.

'No one,' Ella says, her heart thumping. She hears her own cry before she realises that it's because he's hit her hard around the head. She reels as he hurls the flowers down on her lap.

'You're lying. I saw you in the hallway. You were talking to the front door. Someone was outside. They put something through the letterbox.' He holds out his hand.

Ella clutches her throbbing temple. 'I-I couldn't help it,' she says, trying not to cry. 'That woman, Liz, called round again. She-she was just being friendly.' Her brain thrums as she thinks frantically. 'It was just her number but I threw it away. Check the bin if you don't believe me.'

'What did she want?' His voice is demanding, inquisitive, angry.

'She wanted to know if I needed help.'

'What did you tell her?'

'I said I didn't,' Ella says. 'She didn't mean any harm,' she adds, praying he believes her.

Jacob paces about before going to the kitchen and returning with a large drink. He stares down at her.

'How was work?' she asks, shaking, trying to sound bright and cheerful. Trying to sound like a wife. She imagines him meeting with rich clients at the bank in the city centre, moving their funds around the world, advising on investments, then coming home to her. A snivelling mess.

'Busy,' he says, dropping down onto the sofa.

She wonders if she should massage his shoulders, keep up the act, but she can't bring herself to.

'I've been swimming,' he says, pointing to his wet hair. 'It helps me relax.' His voice is softer now, more like the man she used to know.

'Swimming?' Ella says, surprised. 'But I thought you hated swimming,' she adds, imagining him in his swim shorts, the burn scar stretching across his torso, alien-like.

'There's a lot you don't know about me, Ella-bella. I go every night after work. Except for Fridays.' He slings his arm across the back of the sofa, gradually dropping his fingers down onto her neck, walking them up through her hair.

A shiver runs down her spine.

'Tell me what else Liz said. And what you said to her.'

Ella looks up at him, staring straight into his eyes. *Those* eyes. Nothing in there. Empty. She looks away again. 'She'd made some cakes,' she says, smiling.

'She wanted to come in?'

'Yes.'

'And did you let her?'

Ella's mouth goes dry. 'No. No, I-I said that…'

She feels her head being pulled back, her neck straining as he wraps a fistful of her hair around his hand, slowly tugging back. Tighter and tighter. Tears well up in her eyes.

'I said that the baby was sleeping,' she whispers, gritting her teeth.

'The baby?' he replies.

'Yes. I'm sorry. I overheard you telling Liz about a baby the other day. I couldn't help it. I thought it would be the best way to get rid of her. I was so tired. I didn't want her to come in.'

Ella flinches, waiting for the clout around her head. None comes.

'The baby,' Jacob repeats, a smug sing-song tone to his voice. 'Our little baby…'

Ella watches him as he stands up, his eyes not leaving hers as he looms over her. She feels her body begin to shake.

'Maybe we *should* start a family,' he says, narrowing his eyes, appraising her, nodding in approval before going to fetch another drink.

CHAPTER TWENTY-ONE

Liam

Liam knew he was in the right place. To the side of the front door was a worn set of buzzers – five of them, one for each flat in the building – and the name Ella Sinclair was written on a faded piece of card inside the plastic cover beside number 4. The building wasn't anything to shout out about – a 1970-, perhaps '60s-type of place – but the state of it was OK. Reasonably well-maintained but nothing special either. Aluminium windows, grey cladding to one side, a patchy area of grass out the front where a woman sat smoking, holding a lead with a large dog on the end of it. None of it would have leapt out at him, made him stare, if he'd been walking down the street. It blended in with the other places around it, nestled within a mix of older Victorian terraces and assorted flats making up the mishmash of the area. He quite liked it. It was very Ella, he thought. Quite unnoticeable at first, yet he reckoned something interesting was inside. As he pressed the buzzer, he hoped the interesting stuff would be in the form of Ella answering.

He waited a moment, wondering if it had actually worked. He pressed the buzzer again, his nose catching the smell of the woman's smoke. Liam walked back a few paces, staring up at the front windows. A couple of them had net curtains across the front, but one on the first floor didn't. Just open curtains. He had no way of telling which was flat 4.

He tried again, this time jabbing it a few times in a row to make sure.

'Who you looking for?' the woman said, coming up to him. The German shepherd sniffed at his legs, wiping its nose up and down his work trousers. He didn't have many pairs and wanted to wear these tomorrow, so didn't want dog snot on them. He moved away, giving the dog a tentative pat on its head. It just stared up at him.

'Ella Sinclair,' he said. 'Do you know her?' He gave her a smile. Hoped she might be able to help.

'Which flat?' She pulled a puzzled face.

'Flat 4,' Liam said. 'She's been in an accident. I wanted to see how she was doing.'

'Ahhh… Miss 4 keeps herself to herself,' the woman said, laughing. She drew in on her cigarette again, the lines around her mouth deepening. 'Only ever seen her a few times and I've lived here a while. She sometimes says hello. Accident, you say?'

'Sadly, yes,' Liam said. 'I work with her.'

'Could be a dead body in flat 4, for all I know,' she said, letting out a throaty cackle followed by a cough. She chucked the cigarette butt on the ground by the wall. 'C'mon,' she said. 'I'll let you in.'

The woman hitched up the front of her sagging tank top, but her discoloured nylon bra still showed. She unlocked the entrance door and tugged on the dog's lead, the old creature following on, turning once to look up at Liam.

'There's no lift,' she said, glancing back. 'This way.'

Liam held back a bit as they trod the stairs – partly because the dog was slow, its claws clacking on the hard lino tread, but also because the woman was wearing shorts that Liam thought were probably, well, too short for a woman of her age. He also reckoned she must be freezing, dressed like that in autumn. But who was he to judge, he thought, as they turned the corner on the half-landing. Anyway, he liked people like her – open, willing to help a stranger, unaffected and sincere. Just how he imagined Ella to be once he got to know her. And her absence was making him all the more determined to make that happen.

'That's her then,' the woman said, pointing to a grey-painted door with a stick-on number 4 on it. 'I'm just across the hall here, and Nigel is in number 5 round there. There's two flats downstairs, three up. These ones are smaller, you see. Just the one bedroom up here.' Another laugh. 'You going to knock then or what?'

Liam was standing there, his arms dangling, his mouth half open. He was feeling strange and he didn't know why. It was almost as though he was trespassing, invading Ella's space – *stalking* her, even. He'd hate her to think that when all he wanted was to know that she was OK. Though, from what he'd heard and her not having been into work for nearly a month now, he guessed she wasn't. He wondered who was looking after her, pictured himself delivering hot meals, keeping her company. He shook his head.

'Yeah, thanks.' He was hoping she'd go but she just stood there, waiting with her dog.

Liam knocked. Looked at the woman and smiled.

'Sometimes them buzzers downstairs are broke,' she said, coughing again. 'Try knocking louder.'

Liam did as he was told but, even after another minute or two, there was no reply, no sounds from inside, no *Hang on, I'm coming…* if she was finding it hard to get to the door.

'Not in then, ain't she?' The woman shrugged, heading towards her own door. 'Try again tomorrow perhaps, eh?' she said, sticking in her key. A second later, she disappeared inside with her dog.

Seemed she wasn't that bothered about security after all, though there was nothing much Liam could do. He could hardly smash down the door. But he did reach out and turn the knob – one of those globe-like things where the key goes in the centre. It didn't give. He wiggled it to make sure. Locked fast.

Resigned, Liam turned to go back down the stairs but a man, about his age – early thirties by the looks of it – was heading up. He was carrying a bag of shopping in each hand.

'Sorry, mate,' the man said, coming up the last couple of steps faster.

'No probs,' Liam replied. He was about to head down but glanced back to see him heading towards flat number 5.

'You live here, do you?' he called out, suspecting it was Nigel. The man stopped, flicking his long hair back off his face with a tip of his head.

He looked like one of Liam's friends from the Dog – same friendly yet slightly gangly and awkward demeanour. Approachable, Liam thought.

'Yeah, that's right.' He grinned. 'You after someone?'

Liam pointed at flat 4. 'Ella, actually,' he said. 'Any idea where she is?'

The man was stony-faced for a moment. 'You with him, are you? Come to get the rest?'

'Sorry?' Liam turned back onto the landing. This man knew something. 'I'm not sure what you mean.'

'Are you with that guy from the other week? The one who took all her stuff.' He shook his head, as if he disapproved.

'No, I'm a friend, actually.' Well, I would be a friend by now, Liam thought, if only she'd opened up instead of speaking in clipped sentences. He didn't think it was anything he'd done wrong.

Damn, he hated that it bothered him so much.

'She's not been here for a few weeks now,' the man said.

'Oh,' Liam said, feeling deflated though also closer to some kind of truth, even if he didn't want to hear it. 'Moved out for good, you mean?'

The man nodded, rearranged his heavy bags. 'Reckon.'

'Any idea where she's gone?'

He shrugged. 'It was a bit weird, to be honest. Living next door to someone, you get to know their patterns, their movements. She was regular as clockwork. Left the same time every morning, most nights back at the same time too. Then it all stopped. She just wasn't here. Holiday, I thought at first, though in the three years I've been here, she's never done that before. Then this guy came. With the landlord. I was off sick that day so I heard it all.' The man suddenly looked sheepish, as if he shouldn't be saying anything. 'So you're definitely not with him, right? He was quite rude to the landlord.'

'No, no I'm not. I'm just a mate. Ella's colleague. So you have no idea where she's gone?'

He shook his head.

'Did you know she'd had an accident?'

'That figures,' he said. 'I overheard that man saying she wasn't able to sort out her belongings; that he had to do it instead.'

'Go on,' Liam said.

'That's it really. Guess you could ask the landlord where she's moved to. I can give you the number.'

Liam nodded, whipping out his phone. The other man put down his shopping and read it out from his contacts while Liam tapped it in. No new information. It was the same as the number on the piece of paper he'd found in Ella's tissue box.

'Cheers, mate,' Liam said, deflated, turning to go.

'Oh, wait,' the man called out. 'I heard them mention the Queen Elizabeth Hospital, if that's any help. Maybe that's where she was taken?' he said, giving a quick nod before heading round the corner to his flat.

Liam nodded in return and left, wondering what to do next.

CHAPTER TWENTY-TWO

Ella

Ella is in a hole. A deep, deep hole. Not literally, of course, though she thinks that that would be preferable. But a hole in her psyche – a sink hole in the fabric of her life. And it opened up the evening she was cycling home from work. The split second that changed her life. The van driver not seeing her, pulling out onto the roundabout, its wipers flapping, belching exhaust, Ella pedalling hard, hearing only the sound of her own breath, blinking against the rain, feeling the pump of her heart as she pedalled faster. She just wanted to get home.

Then agony. Blackness. Nothing, as if she were dead.

And now she's in this place. A new black hole, sucking her in. Far deeper than the hole she'd been in before the accident – her normal life. She's grateful, in part, that she'd lived a semi-underground existence before, because she's already conditioned to the feelings of despair and hopelessness.

How much deeper will she have to dig?

She shudders, thinking about last night, what he did to her before he passed out from alcohol – the reason the chasm inside her is deepening. It's been a decade since he, or anyone, touched her. She once read that all the cells in your body are completely renewed after seven years, that you're physically not the same person. She liked that, had thought about it a lot. When 2015 came, 17th June to be precise, exactly seven years on, she bought herself what the label claimed was a green detox drink from the corner shop on the way to work. Spinach, apple, ginger and lemon. It was very green indeed and, apparently, cleansing and renewing for a healthy body and a clear mind. It seemed apt. Seemed the right thing to do on the day that her body was, according to that article, suddenly completely new and once more untouched. While her mind was still trapped in the past, at least her body had, in effect, freed itself.

She'd gulped down the drink outside the shop, propping up her bike as she drank. It didn't taste very nice. She usually drank milky tea, water or diet Coke. But she took the drink's claims at face value and, combined with the science in the article (true or not), she felt pleased. Reborn. *Her* but not actually her any more.

And now she feels dirty all over again.

The clock reset.

Another seven years to go.

She shivers, lying on the sofa – the place where she's spent most of her time these last few days while he's at work. She needs the toilet, but it's near impossible to get the wheelchair close enough to the downstairs loo to slide onto it. She's taken to crawling along the floor, dragging her plastered leg behind her while trying not to put any weight on her broken wrist. Yesterday she wet herself.

As she makes her way across the hall, she peers up the stairs, wondering if she could make it up there alone, perhaps going backwards on her bottom. She wants to look around, see what's up there. The house is sparse and clinical, as though it was furnished in a rush, but there are a few boxes of unpacked things – things from the last ten years when he was meant to be dead. Besides, she wants to know what else he took from her flat, apart from what she's spotted downstairs. She wants to find her purse, her cards and the cash that was in it. She doesn't want to leave without them, she thinks, cursing herself for being in a rush the day of the accident, for being rattled by the fire-safety film, forgetting to put the usual things in her backpack and leaving her helmet behind.

She sheds a tear as she thinks of her little flat again. Being morose isn't going to help her get away and, whatever happens now, she can't go back there. She'll have to find somewhere new, maybe go to a cheap motel for a few nights until she decides what to do. She wishes she had a friend to call on – something she's never once wished in the last ten years (not that she'd admit, anyway). Thinking back to when she had them does her no good, only makes her sad. Then and now are different places.

A while later, back on the sofa, Ella hears a noise, making her half sit up. She's been dozing, doesn't know what the time is – there are no clocks in the house and the battery on her mobile phone is long since dead. She has no charger for it and, even if she did, he's not going to let her have it.

It's the front door unlocking. She knows that sound well enough now. It must be about seven, the time he said he'd be home after his swim. Ella hates that she's wasted another day but she's so tired. Her body healing, she supposes, sapping all her energy as her bones knit together again. Sue at the hospital warned her about that. But impatience is making her twitchy. She needs to work out a plan, a way to get out, though with the cameras on her, she can't move without him knowing. He'll be watching everything she does and, even if he's not glued to the app on his phone all the time, he'll be spot-checking.

Then a different noise.

A whimper.

A cry.

Ella twists round, staring over the back of the sofa. Jacob is standing in the doorway of the living room, his hair damp from swimming. She forces a smile. The good wife.

Welcome home, honey! Dinner won't be long…

'What's that?' she says, hardly daring to breath. He's holding something. She sits up properly, hoisting herself up, unable to take her eyes off whatever it is he's got in his arms.

She tracks him as he comes in, sits down beside her.

Whatever it is cries again. Wriggles.

'Is that?…' Ella can hardly speak.

'It's a baby, Ella-bella. A sweet little baby for us.'

She stares at it, frozen, her mouth gaping open and her eyes flicking between the bundle and Jacob's beaming face.

'What do you mean, *a baby for us*?' Ella's heart thunders in her chest. This can't be real, she thinks, her eyes wide. *Prays* it's not real.

Clumsily, as if he's about to drop it, Jacob lowers the baby – a small form wrapped up in a blanket – exposing its face.

It's definitely a baby, Ella thinks, horrified. Chubby cheeks, a fine covering of hair, hands with worm-like fingers poking out of the swaddling.

'Are you pleased?'

'I…' Ella thinks before she speaks. Focusses on her escape. Forces herself to keep on track. Keep him onside.

'Well, yes,' she says, placing her plastered leg on the floor. It throbs within the cast as she leans closer, taking a peek. 'I mean… whose baby *is* it?' She prays he's minding it for a friend for a couple of hours. Just babysitting for a colleague or someone from the swimming pool.

'It's *our* baby, Ella. Isn't he beautiful?' Jacob gently rubs his forefinger across the baby's cheek. It looks up at him, staring, barely making a sound apart from a few gurgles as he sucks on his bottom lip.

'Ours?' Ella shivers. 'What do you mean, *ours*? How long for?' She supposes that a night's babysitting wouldn't be the end of the world, that she could live with that if it went back tomorrow. But something in Jacob's eyes – a doting, adoring look – tells her that's not the case. She feels sick.

'For ever, of course, Ella-bella. He's our new little boy.' Jacob bounces his leg up and down, making the baby's head loll and bounce too. 'Zach, meet your new mummy.' He bends down and kisses the baby's head. 'Ella-bella, meet our beautiful little son, Zach Junior.' Jacob manhandles the baby, passing him across to Ella. She sits perfectly still, not knowing what to do. She doesn't want to hold him. She doesn't want anything to do with him, let alone be his mummy.

When she doesn't take him, Jacob lays the infant on her lap anyway – tricky with the cast. Reluctantly, she puts an arm on his body to stop him falling off. The baby begins to cry. A few short, sharp moans at first then his mouth opens wide and his eyes screw up as he works himself into a full-blown frenzy. Ella feels it vibrating out of his chest and into her legs. She doesn't know what to do.

'What are you talking about?' she says above the din. 'I'm *not* his mother. And I don't want a baby. Where on earth did you get him from?'

Jacob stands, pushes his fingers through the tufts of his damp hair. He strides over to the window, snapping the curtains shut, then paces back again. His face is a contortion of anger and hurt.

'You don't want a baby?' he yells, his fists balling by his side. His jaw tightens and his shoulders draw up to his ears. 'Of *course* you want a baby.' He laughs then, looks proud of himself, as though he's convincing himself rather than her. 'It's what happens when two people make love.'

Ella screws up her eyes, turns away. Climbs deeper into the hole. She can't think about that. Refuses to. For all she knows, nine months might have passed since last night.

'Whose baby is it?' she whispers, trying to sound calm even though she's not.

Jacob ignores her, going to the kitchen, returning with a large drink. 'Your medication is still in the saucer. Why didn't you take it? And you didn't eat the food I left.'

'I fell asleep,' Ella says, seeing his fist twitch, wanting to lash out at her. But he doesn't. Perhaps because she's holding the baby. 'I lost track of time. I'm sorry.'

Jacob paces about, thinking, looking agitated.

'Jacob, just tell me. Whose baby is this? We can't keep him.' She can hardly stand to think what he's done.

He sits down again, his legs spread, leaning forward on his arms, staring into his glass as he swirls the whisky around the tumbler. 'The stupid woman was asking for it,' he says, his mouth pursing. 'Leaving him alone like that.' He takes another mouthful. 'Who does that to a child?'

They stare at each other, each fighting their own thoughts.

'Like *what*?' Ella says.

'A poor, defenceless baby,' Jacob says with a defiant tone. 'I'd pulled up at the corner shop on the way home from the pool. The one at the edge of the council estate.'

Ella flinches. Hates the way he talks, the disgusted face he pulls when he says 'council estate'.

'I watched her go in. Her and her scumbag friend. Going in for their fags and cider, probably. They tried to get the pram inside but were too lazy to lift it up the step. Can you believe they left the baby outside?'

'You *stole* a baby?' she whispers, her mouth trembling as she bites on her lip. She can't believe what she's hearing.

'It's not stealing if someone discards something, Ella-bella. She didn't want her baby.' He takes a swig of his drink, wiping his mouth. 'Finders keepers, eh?' He stands up and heads to the kitchen to get a refill. The baby writhes and squirms on Ella's knee. He's about to fall off again, so she lifts him up, hitching him into a sort of sitting position. He tilts his head backwards, looking up at Ella. Something twitches in her heart.

'Look at you two,' Jacob says, beaming when he comes back. 'Ella, you're going to make a fine mother. I always knew you would.' He leans down, giving them both a tender kiss.

Ella stares at him and, in her mind, she sees the door to her escape closing even tighter.

CHAPTER TWENTY-THREE

Ella

Ella doesn't sleep. Of course she doesn't sleep. For one thing, she's been napping on and off all day, hardly able to keep her eyes open, but worse, there's now a baby to worry about. A stolen baby.

Jacob is sleeping beside her, softly snoring. Oblivious. The baby is in its pram – a dirty grey thing with luminous green and yellow zigzags down the side – next to her side of the bed. The bed she tries very much to lie at the edge of, furthest away from *him*. She thinks, if she ever did have a baby of her own, she wouldn't put it in a tasteless pram like this. Let alone one so dirty. But then she thinks of the poor mother, who she is and how she must be feeling right now. Beside herself with worry and guilt, and driving herself insane waiting for news from the police. How awful. How utterly, *utterly* unthinkable and awful. She sheds a tear for the mother. Prays she will get her baby back.

At first, Ella thinks it would be a good thing if, miracle of miracles, Jacob was caught on CCTV outside the shop taking the baby, his car registration logged. But she doesn't want the police coming here. She's been kidnapped, yes, held hostage, yes. But the ransom is her own freedom. She can't lose sight of that. She knows what she's done.

The baby snuffles and gurgles beside her. Ella has no idea what a baby needs, but she's certain they should have food regularly.

Special milk, she thinks, though she doesn't know how old he is or how much of it he would drink.

Earlier, Jacob had recounted the story of how he got the baby, as if he was some kind of hero – about how he snatched it from outside the shop, rescued it, he'd said, laying it on the front seat of his car before hauling the pram into the boot, as if he'd thought of everything.

Later, when he'd brought the pram inside, Ella had found a feeding bottle buried under some blankets. Before they'd gone up to bed, before Jacob had gone through his nightly routine of washing her – a ritual that seemed to soothe him more than it actually cleaned her – Ella had sent him to swill out the bottle in the sink. Then she'd told him to boil some milk from the fridge and let it cool down again. In an emergency, she hoped any milk would do.

Jacob had given the bottle to Ella, who'd been rearranging the fractious baby on her knee, not knowing how to hold him to stop him wailing.

She wished he had an off button. For his sake as much as hers.

But as soon as he'd felt the teat against his lips, his cries switched to contented grunts and throaty sounds as he guzzled the milk. He'd been starving. A chubby little chap. And heavy too, Ella had thought, as she'd held him on her shoulder afterwards. She hadn't known why, but it had seemed the right thing to do. Perhaps she'd seen it in films or noticed other mothers doing it. Or maybe it was just instinct. But seconds later, the baby had belched and spewed milk down her back and onto the leather sofa. When she'd seen Jacob tense up, his eyes beginning to boil, his fists twitching, she hugged the baby closer. Protection.

'I still can't believe you did this,' she'd said to him a thousand times during the evening. But he hadn't listened. Carrying on as if it was normal. He'd even brought two trays of pizza into the living room and a bottle of wine, which he'd drunk himself.

'You're a natural mother,' he'd said, ignoring her comments, chewing and watching her intently. 'Of course, having a baby is hard on the dad too,' he went on. 'Me busying around looking after you. It's not easy, having a new family.' He smiled, finishing the pizza. 'Am I doing a good job, Ella-bella?' He'd leaned forward then, tickling his finger under the baby's armpit and then its chin. The baby just stared at him, not crying, not making any kind of sound. As terrified as Ella.

'Yes, you are doing a good job,' Ella replied softly. She had to keep saying these things. 'But we can't keep him. The whole world will be looking for this baby. You have to take him back.'

'Give up our son?' Jacob had looked horrified. 'Only *wretched* parents do that, Ella-bella.'

Ella had given a little nod then, soothed the baby as he lolled on her shoulder. A while later, before he finally drifted off to sleep, she'd felt his body tense, heard a few soft grunts. And then the smell. She hadn't known what to do.

And now the bedroom is filled with the same stink again. Ella has never changed a nappy before and, even if she knew how, she doesn't have a spare one. She prays that, in the morning, Jacob will see sense and take him back, give him up, even if that means dropping him outside the shop or leaving him by a police station or at the hospital. She also prays, as she feels her eyelids growing heavy, that when she wakes, she'll be in her own bed, back in her little flat, and all she'll have to do is get ready for work and shake off the bad, bad dream.

Ella wakes. Someone is standing over her. Jacob is holding out a mug.

'Rise and shine, you sleepy heads,' he says, beaming down into the pram.

Not a nightmare, Ella thinks, filled with dread.

Her nose twitches. Coffee and shit.

'I've got some presents for you, my darlings,' he says, placing the mug on the bedside table. 'I've been out already.' Jacob goes out to the landing and returns with several carrier bags. 'All the things you'll need for a baby,' he says proudly. 'Thank goodness for twenty-four-hour supermarkets. There was a very helpful assistant there. Turns out she'd not long had a baby herself, so knew all the things we'd need.'

Ella sits up, peering into the pram. She vaguely remembers hearing the baby cry in the night, remembers pulling the pillow over her head to drown it out. Part of her wanted to push it down on the baby's face, to shut it up, but now she feels terrible for thinking such things. The helpless mite stares up at her, chewing on his fist. She thinks it means he's hungry again.

'His nappy needs changing,' Ella says, needing the bathroom herself.

When she's back in the bedroom, he puts the baby beside her, crooning over it, making silly noises despite the smell, despite the stains seeping through the towelling Babygro. His waist is ringed with brown. Disgusting, Ella thinks, but at the same time, she feels terribly sorry for him. Even sorrier than she feels for herself.

'Nappies, wipes, cream, clean clothes,' Jacob says, pulling things from the carrier bag. 'Everything you'll need. I also got baby milk, bottles, teats and a steriliser. Plus a few nice outfits for him for when we take him out and do family things together.' Jacob glances at his watch. 'Oh, and I got you this.' He pulls out a pink shiny box wrapped in cellophane. 'A little gift for you.' He stands there, holding it out and, when Ella just stares at it, he opens up the packaging and takes out a bell-shaped perfume bottle. 'For you, my love,' he says, spraying either side of Ella's neck. 'I thought you would like it.' He thrusts the bottle under her nose.

'Lovely,' she says quietly, squinting from the mist.

Jacob raises his eyebrows.

'Thank you,' she adds, forcing a smile.

Jacob nods, placing the bottle on the bedside table. 'Now, hurry up and change little Zach, Ella-bella, as I have to leave for work soon. Then I'll take you both downstairs for the day. There's food waiting for you.'

He's considered everything, Ella thinks, staring up at him, wondering where his mind is at. Part of her tries to truly imagine that he's her loving husband, the baby is their adored son, they have a beautiful home in a lovely street and he cares for her deeply. And that same part of her, just for a second, believes it, indulging in the security of it. At least the nightmare would be over if she accepted everything – that this is her life now, that she will be with him for ever. But then another part of her, the bigger part, can't even contemplate the situation. He's a sick and vile man – a man she thought she knew but didn't. Everything about this situation is wrong. Twisted. He's a stranger to her. Dangerous.

And then she remembers the videotape.

'Of course,' Ella says, taking a deep breath, watching as he heads off downstairs again.

When she's alone, she undoes the poppers on the baby's little suit, his bare arms and legs flailing everywhere. Judging by the sounds he's making, he's not happy. His face is puckered and his fists clenched as he squeals and thrashes. Beneath his suit, Ella finds his nappy. A very soiled nappy. Thick and heavy. How on earth is she going to look after him? She has no idea about babies.

She wriggles him out of the dirty suit and undoes the tabs at the side of the nappy, peeling away the thick padding. More of the same smell, but stronger, escapes, making her recoil, especially when she sees the extent of what's in there.

And especially when she sees that the little baby boy is, in fact, a little baby girl.

CHAPTER TWENTY-FOUR

Ella

Ella stares down at Zach. *Girl*-Zach. Before he went to work, she didn't dare tell Jacob what she'd discovered about his beloved son. That he's actually a daughter. She knows he'll be angry. Imperfection in the perfect family. He always had his heart set on a boy.

Her stomach cramps, making her want to throw up. The baby lying on her lap is stolen. *Stolen.* Taken. Kidnapped. But then, she thinks, the lap the baby is lying on is also stolen, taken, kidnapped. The difference between them is that girl-Zach hasn't done what *she* has. Girl-Zach isn't a murderer.

A sob forces up her throat, leading to a cry with no tears. She's beyond that. Has been for a decade. The baby stops gurgling and fist-chewing, staring up at Ella, frowning. Ella didn't know babies could frown. Her dry sob turns into a laugh – a pathetic laugh of disbelief. The baby then smiles, exposing a gummy grin with several teeth breaking through. Ella wonders if they need cleaning. She can't imagine they do.

'Oh, baby,' she says, stroking his – *her* – cheek. 'What in God's name are we going to do?' She doesn't like that her thoughts and plans are now in the plural. *We.* She is not responsible for this child, yet here she is, trying her best to take care of it. When she escapes, how can she leave it here, with him? *If* she escapes, she thinks. Until this baby came along, there were no ifs at all.

Ella covers her face, the baby propped on her legs as she lies on the sofa.

'Ma-ma-ma-mah,' the baby says – or rather, makes a noise that sounds like it.

Ella's hands slide down off her face. 'Did you just call me Mama?' she asks, almost expecting a reply. But the baby immediately breaks out in fits of hysterical giggles. 'Do you like that?' she says, unable to help laughing.

She covers her face again, quickly removing her hands.

The baby giggles, staring up at her, almost shaking with anticipation.

Ella repeats. Covers, reveals, and this time makes her eyes go wide, pulling a silly face.

The baby's squeals are louder. Verging on hysteria.

She does it again. This time with a 'Boo!' added in.

The biggest laugh yet, the baby's legs thrashing, her hands balled up in excited fists as she waits for Ella to do it again.

But Ella doesn't. She likes seeing the baby respond and look happy, but inside she's curling up. She can't sustain fake happiness for more than a few seconds, not when she knows she's got a kidnapped child on her legs. Not when she knows they're both in deep, deep trouble.

Ella knows what Jacob is capable of. The baby doesn't.

'There, there,' Ella says. 'Don't look so sad. We can play again later.'

The baby's face crumples into disappointment and she makes agitated sounds. Squirming. Ella is surprised at how much she can tell from her face, the noises, the little actions signed by her hands. She doesn't feel like a mother – has never *wanted* to be a mother – but there's something stirring inside her.

Just as the baby is working herself up into a mini-frenzy, Ella hears a voice. And then the chime of the doorbell. Her heart sinks.

'Coo-*eee*…' Liz calls again through the letterbox, even silencing the baby for a moment.

Ella doesn't know what to do. Then there's a tapping sound. Ella swings around. Liz and two other women are at the living-room window, waving, grinning, making gestures with their hands. Then they see the baby on Ella's lap and all make cute faces at exactly the same time. Ella feels nauseous again, especially when Liz signals with her hand, making an overstated turning action, her mouth saying something, making her look like a goldfish.

She's back at the letterbox. 'If it's hard to get to the door, we can let ourselves in,' Liz calls out. 'Just give a thumbs up to Rachel at the window and she can fetch the keys.'

Keys.

Ella's heart thumps. What does she mean, *keys*?

She stares at the window. A woman she's never seen before is standing there, grinning, holding a toddler on her hip, jiggling it up and down. Looking expectant. Without thinking, Ella gives her a thumbs up and a small, nervous smile. The woman at the window returns the thumbs up. Then disappears from view.

A couple of minutes later, Ella hears the front door being unlocked and then opened. She gasps, holding her breath, terrified the door alarm will sound. It doesn't. It must be true that he only turns it on at night.

Shit – the cameras! Ella panics. What if he's watching right now, sees them all, rushes home and… She can only imagine the scene.

Too late. Suddenly, the living room is filled with three women – Liz, the woman with the toddler and another woman – tall, with a baby in some kind of contraption slung around her front.

'Hell*oo*,' Liz says brightly. 'I hope you don't mind us calling round like this. Rachel used to feed the previous owners' cats when they were away and still has the keys. Turned out handy! Anyway, how good to finally meet you, you poor thing. Aww, just look at you.'

Liz tilts her head, makes a sympathetic face as she sees Ella lying there, helpless, on the sofa.

'And just look at your... look at your beautiful little boy.' She trails off, as though something is wrong. 'Anyway,' she goes on, shaking her head quickly. 'Meet Rachel – and Joey.'

'Say hello, Joey,' Rachel says to the lump of child attached to her side. He clings on harder, burying his face in his mum's shoulder, refusing to look up. Rachel laughs. 'He's shy,' she says. 'Lovely to meet you and sorry for the invasion.'

They're all still standing, looking down at Ella.

'I'm Steph. And this is Milly.' She strokes the bald head of her baby. It's much smaller than Zach. *Girl*-Zach.

'Hello,' Ella manages, terrified. Terrified not only because she's been kidnapped, the baby is kidnapped, but also because it's been a long time since she's taken on three people in a conversation. Maybe once at work in a meeting, she thinks, but that was uncomfortable. She never knows what to say. And besides, her mind is distracted by the keys.

Somehow, she has to get them.

'Is it OK if we sit down? We won't keep you long but we've been desperate to meet you and... and your little one. Hubby at work, is he?' Liz perches on the end of the sofa, next to Ella's feet, while the other two women and their children sit on the sofa opposite. The toddler resignedly climbs onto his mother's knee.

'Yes,' Ella says.

'How are you managing?' Steph says. She's slim, blonde, pretty. *Nothing like me*, Ella thinks as she watches her wriggle out of the contraption around her body, as though she's taking off a straitjacket.

'It's hard,' Ella says. The truth at least.

'And that's why we're here, love. You're never alone in Green Leys,' Liz says.

'What's your baby's name?' Rachel asks. 'Joey, why don't you go and say hello to the baby? You like babies, don't you?' She kisses the top of her child's head but he refuses to budge, shoving his thumb in his mouth and kicking his mother's legs as he swings his feet back and forth.

'Zach,' Ella says. *Quicksand*, she thinks. *Sinking up to my neck.*

'Is he good?' Liz asks. 'Sleep well?'

'Yes,' Ella says meekly. How can a baby be anything but good, she wonders? They've hardly had any time to turn bad.

'And how old did you say he was?' Liz goes on. 'My two are at school, by the way. Six and eight. One of each flavour.'

'Um…' Ella tries to remember what she said when Liz last called at the door. But her brain is muzzy, struggling to keep up with the situation, let alone knowing how old the baby is.

'Six weeks, didn't you say?' Liz prompts, looking puzzled.

'Yes,' Ella says, nodding thankfully. 'Yes he's six weeks old, aren't you, Zach?' she adds, tickling the baby's tummy, trying to act like a proper mother. But the baby's head is bent at an odd angle as it half slides off her legs, down between the gap and pressing against Ella's cast.

'Wow, he's certainly a bruiser,' Liz says, staring at him. 'You can't have stopped eating since the moment you were born, young man,' she goes on, touching his cheek. 'Here, let me take him from you. You look uncomfortable.'

'Thanks,' Ella says, glad of the weight to be lifted from her legs. She hoists herself up more, rearranging the cushions.

'Oh my, and what a weight you are.' Liz flashes a look at Steph and Rachel as she holds Zach up, her hands under his armpits. 'Such a big boy. And amazing head control. He just wants to stand up!' The baby pushes her feet down against Liz's lap, her plump legs pumping up and down.

'Six weeks? Wow,' Steph comments, finally untangling her own baby from the sling. 'About the same age as Milly then.'

Ella looks at Steph's baby. *Christ*, she thinks. It's tiny compared to Zach. Not as coordinated. And, as mothers, they'll know the difference.

'Are you sure you didn't mean six *months*, love? Maybe that's what you meant to say. He certainly seems more like it to me, don't you, you gorgeous little chap.' Liz nuzzles the top of his head.

'Oh… yes, of *course*. Did I say six weeks? Silly me. It's the drugs, they space me out. I'm not completely myself.' Ella can't believe she is having this conversation, but she has no choice.

The women seem satisfied then, not questioning Ella's mistake, but they're intent on asking her how she's coping now that her husband is back at work. No sign of them leaving yet. Ella glances at the camera in the corner of the room.

'What does your husband do?' Rachel asks.

'Oh. He's in banking,' Ella replies, not really too sure about his exact role. 'And all your husbands?' she asks, desperate to take the focus off her.

'Building company here,' Liz says. 'But he's more of a project manager now rather than down and dirty on site. Thank God. I've got enough washing as it is.'

'Andy's a surveyor,' Steph chips in. 'Me too, but I'm on maternity leave. We met at university.'

'And mine's a cop,' Rachel laughs. 'Though don't worry, he won't be checking your car tax. He's in CID. A detective.'

'A detective?' Ella says, tensing, her head swimming. The room goes blurry for a few seconds, though she's not sure if it's the part about Steph meeting her husband at university or that Rachel's husband is a detective that's making her feel light-headed. Both, she concludes.

'That's everyone's reaction,' Rachel goes on, laughing. 'How did you two meet?'

Ella is just about to answer, just about to convince herself to play the role of good wife when Liz laughs loudly, holding Zach out at arm's length. 'Oospie-daisy,' she sings out, making a face at the baby. 'Looks like we've got a real stinker here,' she laughs. 'Where do you keep the changing stuff, Ella? I'll sort him out.'

CHAPTER TWENTY-FIVE

Ten Years Ago

Afternoon tea – how quaint, how not like other boys, Ella thought with a smile when she remembered their teatime tryst after the football match that day. It was followed by a string of other dates (Ella supposed that's what they were) over the next couple of weeks since formal lectures had drawn to a close – everything from drinks in the pub, the cinema, meals out, walks along the Wear and ambles around the cobbled old lanes of the city. It seemed Zach went out of his way to do things she wanted, the things she enjoyed. In all her time at Durham, Ella had never explored the city in such depth and, even though Zach was from London, he seemed to have an in-built map of the place in his mind, sought out all the interesting spots to take her, never failing to enchant her with somewhere new, somewhere secret and off the beaten track. Everywhere they went, he paid. And not only that, but he had only ever given her a quick kiss on the cheek when they parted.

Perfect.

Ella was cautious but thought, perhaps, she might even be happy. A degree *and*, dare she say, a boyfriend.

'You're a dark horse,' he said as they sat drinking iced lattes in their favourite little place just off Framwellgate Bridge. The street was narrow, cobbled, though the sun still managed to angle in through the quaint window, casting a welcome glow over their table.

'I am?' Ella had bought herself a new lipstick a few days before, noticed the peach semicircle left on her glass mug. She wiped it with her thumb.

'You never tell me much about yourself, your family, your past. The only thing I know about you is that you have a brother, and that's just because he's a friend.' Zach sipped his drink, licking away the froth from his top lip. His eyes narrowed into appreciative slits.

Ella loved the way he looked at her, drinking her up with as much relish as he did the latte. She didn't give her trust easily but, with Zach, even in such a short time, she felt she could – despite the first-date false start. She'd quickly realised it was her own insecurities making her overcautious, that his intentions weren't sinister as she'd first believed. Ella had always listened to her gut but, since getting to know him, she felt it was time that her gut, for once, shut up. Besides, she was having fun.

'There's not much to tell,' Ella said, laughing.

'Harry seems older than you. I assumed he'd taken a gap year after school.'

'Thirty minutes older, to be precise,' Ella said with a fond look in her eyes. Then she took a deep breath. Reckoned she'd open up a bit. It felt right. 'Our dad died when we were very young. Harry and I don't remember him. It was really hard for Mum as a single parent with twins. We weren't well off when Dad was alive, but things nosedived after he passed away.'

'What did your dad do?' Zach reached out and took Ella's hand. The face he made wasn't pity. It was… it was *understanding*. It stirred something inside her.

'Train driver,' she said pensively. 'When he was growing up, that's all Harry wanted to be.'

'And what did *you* want to be?'

Ella thought about this. In fact, she'd been thinking about it a lot recently and only ever concluded that she had no idea. An English degree from Durham was all very well, but what was she going to do with it?

'I love movies,' she said, not wanting to sound dull. And she knew Zach loved them too, as well as photography. He was always taking pictures, aiming a camcorder at something. She liked that they had this in common. 'So a job in filmmaking would be amazing.' She thought she saw something flicker in his eyes – almost something wistful – but when Zach didn't respond, she felt silly. It was a pipe dream. He probably thought the same. Their degrees would take them in other directions – *sensible* directions such as marketing and finance. 'What about *your* dad? What does he do?'

Ella didn't know that much about Zach's family either, she realised. Or, more to the point, how they'd made their money. When he'd shown her pictures of his family home in readiness for the house party, she knew that they must be incredibly rich. Not just the type of rich where you can afford dessert in the restaurant as well as a nice bottle of wine. Not even rich where driving a smart car is possible as well as taking several flash holidays a year. No, from what she'd gleaned, Zach's family took rich to a whole new level. His home was nothing short of a mansion – even more mind-blowing than Meggie's. Anyway, Ella had no idea what excuses she would give if Zach ever delved deeper into her past. Only she and Harry knew the truth.

'Banking,' Zach said, rather grimly.

'Don't say it like that.' Ella smiled.

Zach rolled his eyes. 'And I don't mean bank teller, either. No one really knows what he does, to be honest. It's like, well… he goes to Switzerland a lot. The Bahamas.' He laughed then. Trying to brush it off. Trying to play it down and sound… well, normal, like her. 'He wants me to follow suit.'

'And what about your mum?' She liked that he was coy about his family, that he didn't splash his privileged upbringing around like some of the others. There were all sorts at Durham, but many had come from top public schools. She knew Zach had been to Eton.

'Sod our parents,' Zach said. His eyes beamed out from beneath his hair as it flopped down over them. 'It's *you* I want to find out about,' he said, being as evasive as she had been. 'Tell me three things about yourself I'd never guess.'

Ella stirred her drink, scooping up the froth on her spoon, licking it off. She was about to answer his question, but the weird boy from the library came into the café, deliberately kicking the back of her chair as he walked past. Ella jumped, spilling some of her coffee.

'Watch it, mate,' Zach said, half standing, leaning forward on his hands. He glared at him.

'It's fine,' Ella whispered, touching his arm.

The boy – skinny and pale despite the recent heatwave, with dark circles under his eyes as though he'd been studying all night – stopped and stared back at Ella, sending a shudder down her spine. His lip twitched as he glared at her. She quickly looked away, mopping up the spilt drink.

She hadn't told anyone, not even Meggie, but the last week or two, it seemed he was everywhere – everywhere *she* was. She put it down to pre-exam nerves, that she hadn't been getting much sleep, that she was probably imagining it. But the last time she'd encountered him, only a couple of days ago, was in the ladies' loo in a department store. Meggie had been browsing the make-up and Ella had been desperate, so had dashed in. When she'd come out of the cubicle, Nerdy Boy, as she and Meggie referred to him, had been leaning against the basins, staring right at her. No one else had been in there, so Ella just washed her hands, not bothering to dry them, hurrying past him as she left. He'd said nothing. Not a single word, even as the door banged behind her.

'You want something, or what?' Zach said to him when he made no move to leave. He was doing exactly the same now, Ella thought – just standing there, saying nothing, staring at her. Zach stood up again, getting up close to him, and finally he turned and left the café, still without saying a thing.

'Weird,' Ella said, laughing it off, flicking her hair over her shoulder. But her heart was thumping. 'Now, where were we?' She swallowed, stirring her latte.

'Three things about you,' Zach said, a frown still on his face as his eyes tracked the boy's path through the window.

Ella sighed, thinking about what to say. There was simply nothing she wanted to reveal. No huge houses, no exotic holidays. No inspiring stories about a gap year, or travelling, or crazy friends from school. She hoped a flirtatious look would suffice.

'Well…' she began, licking her lips. She supposed she could have told him that their stepdad, Ron, had started being violent to her and Harry pretty much from the moment their mother brought him into their lives – only six months after their dad died. But to be fair, he only clouted them when their mum wasn't around. In the end, she and Harry had got so used to it they thought it was normal.

'Let me think,' she went on, stalling, still feeling unsettled by Nerdy Boy.

She racked her brains, but instead her mind was flooded with things she wanted to forget. She didn't want to tell him that often they scarcely had money for food and certainly not luxuries. Occasionally, if there was a spare coin for the electricity meter, enough to fuel the immersion heater for half an hour, Ron always got first dibs on the bath. He was the one who went out to work, after all. Got sweaty on the building site. Her mum would sit in the grimy water after him, and then Harry and, finally, if she wanted it, Ella was allowed the cold soup to bathe in. She never did, preferring to stay in her bedroom, reading books from the school library, with Harry checking in to make sure she was OK. Other times, when she wasn't escaping in a book, she'd sit and stare out of her bedroom window, wondering what was out there in the world. She'd hoped one day she'd find out.

'Ells?' Zach said.

She jumped as he touched her hand.

'It's not a trick question.'

'Oh, sorry,' she said, laughing, grounding herself. No one had ever called her Ells before. 'OK, number one…' she took another sip of her latte. 'Number one is that I truly dislike ice cream. With a passion.'

'Shock horror,' Zach said. 'Dig deeper, Ells.' He laughed then, but she could see he meant it.

'I know, I *know*…' She gave a cute smile. 'Number two, I have a major girl crush on Sylvia Plath.'

'Better,' he said.

'And three…' Ella was floundering as she tried to hold back all the stuff that was dying to burst out. *Needing* to burst out. Everything she imagined telling a friend. Not a friend such as Meggie, who she did confide in to a point, of course – though usually just about boys, clothes, their studies and going out – but rather a friend who'd truly listen when you wanted to go *deep*, as Zach had put it. Someone who'd hear you when all the darkness came out.

'Three,' she said, biting into another brownie. 'Number three is that I never reveal everything about myself until I *truly* get to know someone.' She prayed that would do for now, because anything else would have made him run for the door.

As spring transformed into early summer, Ella immersed herself in revision. But that, in turn, she suspected, was a reaction to overinvesting in Zach. He'd taken up a lot of her time these last few weeks as well as much of her headspace. But the more she refocussed, the more she tried to stay balanced and sensible, the keener Zach got. She had zero experience of relationships, didn't know what a good one felt like. To an extent, she was cross with herself because she hadn't survived her entire degree without becoming involved with a boy. But she kept reminding herself that this wasn't just any boy. It was Zach White. And everyone knew, he was an exception. To *any* rule.

'Fucking hell,' Meggie said, taking off her light cotton jacket as they left St Mary's. 'It's too hot for studying.'

But despite the temperature, despite impending exams and any misgivings she had about Zach worming ever deeper into her heart, Ella couldn't deny the spring in her step, as though she had her own internal heater.

'It is indeed,' she said, grinning, glancing sideways as they headed to a revision clinic on American poetry.

'Fine for you. You're all loved-up and hot under the collar anyway,' Meggie said, walking sideways into her on purpose. 'Summer's no fun when you're single.'

'Oh, Megs,' Ella said, linking arms with her. 'You literally have boys falling at your feet.' Meggie remained silent. 'Anyway, you can tell?' she said, wondering what a loved-up version of herself looked like. Perhaps it was just as she was now – that perfect spot between self-doubt and perfection: a point between denial and surrender.

She couldn't deny that she really liked Zach – and maybe it was more than liking – but she hadn't yet surrendered to it. She liked being wanted, but not being taken.

'Fucksake, Ella, you've been going around with your head in the clouds these last few weeks. Dreaming your way through the last of our lectures, no doubt writing love poems instead of study notes. I've hardly seen you. You're always busy with him.' Meggie pulled her arm away.

Ella stopped in her tracks, reaching out to Meggie again, halting her too. 'It's his house party soon,' she said. Saying it out loud suddenly made it seem so real. For Ella, it was a big deal. She knew Zach would want to get close. *Closer.*

'And?' Meggie said, her expression suddenly thunderous. She walked on.

'Why the weird vibe?' Ella called out, catching up with her. 'Megs?' But Meggie kept walking. 'Aren't you excited too?'

'Excited about what?' Meggie said, looking straight ahead. 'That you'll be there?' she added, giving a tight smile.

'What are you talking about?' she replied, shocked, her mouth hanging open. 'Meggie?' she said, though too quietly for her to hear.

Ella's arms hung by her sides, her pack weighing heavily on her back as she watched her friend stride off. She didn't understand. While the thought of mixing in Zach's privileged world terrified her, spending time back home in Birmingham once they'd finished university terrified her more. After nearly three years at Durham, her childhood home seemed a million miles away. She was really looking forward to the party.

'What's your problem?' she called out, but Meggie ignored her. After a moment, Ella continued on to the tutorial alone, dragging her feet and feeling stupid. She didn't understand. She'd never seen Meggie like this before. 'Probably jealous,' she muttered under her breath, glaring at her up ahead, then disliking herself for thinking that about her best friend.

She picked up her pace and finally caught up with Meggie, drawing up beside her as they entered the building. She'd had enough of feeling different, of always being the girl who didn't join in, the one who went to bed early. The *good* girl. And she certainly didn't want to be singled out for her background. As far as she knew, she and Harry were the only ones in their group of friends from a council estate, the only ones not from public school. But, in a way, she had to admit, that kind of made them cool. Different. Enigmas.

Or specimens, she wondered.

CHAPTER TWENTY-SIX

Ella

Ella is frozen, not knowing what to do. Finally, she manages to speak. 'Really, Liz, it's fine. I can manage. If-if anyone but me changes his nappy, he cries for ages.' Ella doesn't know if that's likely – babies even knowing who's cleaning them up, but it's worth a shot. She just wants them all to go. Just wants Liz not to change that nappy. And God knows what will happen when Jacob gets back. He's probably watching all this on the cameras right now. Could be back at any moment.

'Nonsense,' Liz says, holding the baby out at arm's length again. 'You've done a big poo-poo, haven't you little one?' She rubs noses with him, making silly sounds. The baby does nothing, apart from a few little leg kicks. 'Who wants to sit in a stinky nappy, eh?' More inane noises. Liz stands. 'Is his kit upstairs?'

'You know what?' Ella replies. 'I'm really tired. I didn't sleep much last night and—'

'Are you breastfeeding?' Steph asks. 'It can make you feel totally knackered. And especially so if your body's recovering from an accident.' Steph lifts up her top as her baby squirms and fusses on her knee. 'Just a moment, sweetie, Mummy's coming.'

Ella just sits there, her mouth gaping as Steph lowers a flap at the front of her bra, revealing a huge, swollen breast. So full it actually looks hard. Watery milk leaks from it as Steph positions the baby's mouth against her nipple. Milly instantly stops crying, making gurgling sounds instead.

'Bottle,' Ella says quickly, looking away. She's not sure it's the done thing to stare.

'Shall I make us some coffee?' Rachel says. 'While Steph's feeding and Liz is sorting out young Zach here?' She stands up, not waiting for a reply. 'Come on, Joey. You can help me. Kitchen this way, is it, Ella?'

Ella nods. Resigned. Helpless.

'Ahhh, here we go, little Zachy!' Liz says, spotting the plastic bag of items that Jacob bought earlier. 'Wipes, nappies, cream.' She kneels down on the grey fluffy rug in front of the fireplace, laying it all out. 'Your mummy needs a nice nappy bag for you instead of this, doesn't she?' She looks around. 'Do you have a changing mat?'

Ella shakes her head.

'Well, this plastic bag will have to do for now.' She spreads it out on the rug, placing Zach down carefully on top of it so her bottom is over the plastic. 'Ooh, it's gonna be a bad one in there, I think...' Liz laughs.

Ella watches on, horrified.

'Who's a good boy then, eh?'

The baby starts to fret as she's laid down, her face reddening and her fists clenching. She lets out loud, individual shrieks that eventually join together into one long bawl.

'See what I mean?' Ella says, silently thanking the baby. 'He only likes me to do it. Why don't you leave it?'

'Hey, hey, hey,' Liz says, rubbing the baby's tummy gently. 'No problem, I'll sort him. It must be so hard for you with those casts on. Nigh on impossible, I'd have thought.' She pauses for a moment. 'Where are all your toys then, young man? Ella, do you have a rattle or something to amuse him while I do this?' She glances about. No toys in sight.

'Oh… I, well, not really. Not down here.' Ella's cheeks redden to match baby Zach's.

'Joey won't mind if you borrow this, I'm sure,' Liz says, reaching out for a chunky plastic figure that the toddler has left on the sofa. 'What's this then, eh?' she says to the baby, waving it above her face. She instantly stops crying, reaching out.

'God, that feels better,' Steph says, sinking back into the sofa as her baby suckles. 'I thought I was going to explode.' She gives a big smile. 'So tell me, Ella, do you work? Are you planning on going back or are you going to be a stay-at-home mum?'

Ella doesn't know what to do as a mug of coffee and a plate of biscuits are thrust at her by Rachel, who's returned with a tray. 'Good boy, Joey, you eat nicely now.'

The toddler grabs several biscuits and shoves them into his mouth, crumbs falling everywhere. Jacob will make her pay for this, Ella thinks, glancing at the camera again.

'I-I used to work, yes.' It's the truth, at least.

Liz undoes the baby's towelling suit. Pop, pop, pop.

Ella stares at them all – Liz kneeling down on the floor with the baby, Steph feeding Milly, Rachel doling out the coffees and trying to stop her son grabbing all the biscuits as she sits down. The toddler whines, climbing onto his mum's knee. Just a normal coffee morning in a normal family home, Ella thinks, feeling as though she's about to throw up.

'Oh what a mess you're in, little one,' Liz says, as brown runny stuff seeps out around the baby's legs. It's still the nappy she had on from earlier. Ella doesn't know how often they need changing.

'Has he got an upset tummy?' Liz asks. 'Looks like he's eaten something that doesn't agree with him. Is he on solids yet?'

Liz peels back the tabs on the nappy. Pulls the front flap forward.

'I-I'm not sure if—'

'Oh!'

Liz rocks back on her heels, reaching for the pack of wet wipes. She pulls out a few, wiping away the worst of the mess. Then she turns to Ella – her voice part curious, part accusatory. All eyes are on her.

'Ella, my love, you do realise that your baby is a girl, don't you?'

CHAPTER TWENTY-SEVEN

Ella

Two hours, Ella thinks, exhausted. They were here for *two long hours*.

And now they know Zach is a girl.

Since they left, Ella has managed to eat some of the food that Jacob put out for her – some soup to warm in the microwave. It wasn't because she was hungry, but rather because she knows she will need the strength to escape. She feels so tired all the time.

The baby gurgled as she ate then, moments later, she fell asleep on the sofa, the baby sleeping too, lying prone on his – *her* – front on Ella. She wrapped her arms around her little body so she didn't fall off. Though sleep wasn't much of an escape when all she dreamed about was the baby's poor frantic mother and the police hunting down the child. Getting ever closer. Hammering on the door before breaking it down, taking the baby while dragging her away to a cell.

Ella jumps, suddenly waking – hot, sweaty and in pain. The baby is squawking, gnawing on her fist, which Ella knows means she wants a bottle. She can hardly be bothered to get it – she's so tired still – but she can't stand to see the little mite distressed and hungry, so she drags herself to the kitchen, literally, as she doesn't have the energy to grapple with her wheelchair. She takes a pre-made bottle from the fridge, the last of the ones Jacob made up this morning.

The baby doesn't want it at first – too cold, Ella suspects – but, when it seems to be the only option, she reluctantly drinks. She wonders if it was the regular milk that upset her tummy, caused Liz to use almost half a pack of wipes cleaning her up. It's odd, Ella thinks, watching the baby's face looking up at her as she feeds, how she's tuning in to her needs. Sensing what she wants. Mostly, she's content, pretty placid and satisfied with taking in the world around her. She relates to that, she thinks, as the baby's ever-moving hands search out the bottle, gripping onto it.

She thinks back to earlier, when Liz saw that Zach was a girl. They were all staring at her.

'It's… it's complicated,' Ella had said, feeling her cheeks burning red. And then one of the short films she'd been working on with Liam recently popped into her mind, at just the right moment. 'The thing is,' she went on, stumbling over her words when the others remained silent, trying to allay the look of bewilderment on all their faces. 'And please don't tell him I said this – but Jacob's always wanted a little boy.' She whispered the last part. The film that had come to mind wasn't a direct correlation, but was inspiration enough for the quick cover-up. The three-minute short told the story of fifteen-year-old Michael, who'd actually been born Michelle.

Ella watched Liz's face turn from shock to almost understanding.

'That must be hard,' she said. 'For you both.'

'He's getting help with it,' Ella said, trying to sound genuine, though not sure she was pulling it off. 'What with the baby coming along, moving house, and then my accident… Jacob's had a lot to deal with. I figured letting him go along with having the son he always wanted was the least I could do.' She lowered her eyes, hung her head.

Liz gave a tentative nod, along with the others. And contrary to what Ella thought they would do – pack up and leave immediately, perhaps even report her to social services – they stayed another hour or more, chatting, telling stories and being completely understanding.

Ella quite liked it.

Liked that they didn't judge, that they didn't question her. That they made sure she had everything she needed close by before they left, even washing up the cups and plates as if they'd never been.

But Ella didn't get the keys.

After everything, she didn't like to ask.

Now, the front door is opening – the familiar click of the handle, although without the rattle of keys. Liz must have forgotten to lock it. She forces herself to snap out of her drowsy state. She hadn't realised it was so late.

'So,' Jacob says, looming over her, briefcase in hand.

He knows. She can see it written on his face, and, if Ella didn't know any better, she could almost believe he was the perfect husband as she looks up at him. Perhaps his swim (his hair is wet again) washed all the bad out of him, though his stern voice indicates otherwise. His eyes, although still piercing, and his mouth, although shaped into an accusing pout, are – she can't deny – beautiful. Somehow cleansed. Yet also evil.

She never noticed before, when they were at university.

Love is truly blind, she thinks.

She prepares for the blow to her head.

'So?' she says nervously, offering up a smile.

Sure enough, the swipe comes. Hard. She deals with it, breathing through the pain, gripping onto the baby, shielding its downy head with her arms. It's only a few seconds of deafness, her vision temporarily blurry, but she doesn't want the baby hurt.

'You *know* what I mean, Ella-bella.' He sits down, making her bad leg roll into an awkward position. He glares at her, which is almost more uncomfortable than another blow. He smells of chlorine. 'How's our beautiful little boy been today? Is he happy?'

Jacob pulls the baby from Ella's grip, holding it vice like. The baby cries, reaching out for Ella. Her heart twinges.

'He... he's been very good.' It feels a betrayal, calling her a *he*. 'I-I'm sorry the neighbours came in. I couldn't stop them.' Ella hangs her head. Her heart thumping, thinking a confession is for the best.

Jacob lunges forward, grabbing a fistful of her hair. 'What are you talking about – *came in*?' His spit gets on her face.

Shit, she thinks. *He didn't know.* Perhaps he isn't glued to the app on his phone as much as she thought. He has a busy job, after all.

He's hurting her, but she stays one step ahead. 'It was unexpected. I could hardly stop them knocking at the door, could I? You know what Liz is like – one of *those* neighbours.'

She winces, her scalp feeling as though it's about to come off her skull. She leans closer to him to try to release the pressure, but he just pulls harder.

'And-and then one of them tried the door handle. It was open, Jacob. You must have left it unlocked. They let themselves in before I could stop them. I-I'm so sorry.'

He thinks a moment, staring hard at her, before shoving her down and releasing her hair. His face is stony, cold, a flicker of something behind his eyes. *Did I forget to lock it?*

'Don't worry... darling,' Ella continues, feeling sick, shaking, 'you were in a hurry for work. And we were both tired from Zach crying in the night.'

Jacob makes a growling sound deep in his throat. He gets up, still holding the baby, and goes to the front door, checking he locked it on the way in just now. He had.

'You're a good dad,' Ella says when he sits down again. 'You went out and bought baby stuff early this morning as well as making bottles. Liz says new parents shouldn't be hard on themselves.' She strokes his arm, watching his face soften. 'And look, we're still here, aren't we?'

'You do know what will happen if you leave, don't you, Ella-bella?' His voice is calm, measured.

She nods, her eyes wide. 'Zach enjoyed having another baby here,' she says with a lump in her throat. 'Steph from over the road has a little… a little baby girl, and Rachel from next door has a two-year-old boy. Liz's kids have started school.'

'What did you tell them?' Jacob asks, still agitated. As expected, he goes to the kitchen for his nightly drink. He brings Ella a glass of water, keeping hold of it as he sits down.

'Nothing I shouldn't have,' she says. 'They're nice. Maybe you could get to know their husbands. We could all be friends.'

Jacob stares at her, giving the tiniest of nods.

'Liz invited us over for dinner on Saturday. Isn't that nice?' Jacob says nothing, just slowly sips on his drink. 'But of course, I said I'd check with you first. The other neighbours will be there too, and their kids. It could be fun,' Ella says. 'Couldn't it?'

'Fine,' Jacob says. 'But one wrong move and you know what happens.' Then he chucks the glass of water in Ella's face.

Later, Ella watches him nod off from the alcohol. The pain inside her cast thrums, as it does every night, getting worse from even the limited movements she's able to make during the day – going to the toilet, wheeling herself into the kitchen, shifting positions on the sofa to reach the baby's changing stuff. She's done two nappy changes since Liz left. Would be feeling quite proud of herself if she wasn't in this unthinkable mess. If it wasn't someone else's baby.

After her bottle, the baby fell asleep at the same time as Jacob. Ella fights her own drowsiness, knowing she'll be carted upstairs to bed before long anyway. If nothing else, she's formulating his patterns of behaviour, figuring out his schedule.

Work, swim, eat, drink, sleep. Repeat.

Somehow, it's familiar. Comforting.

She resolves that tomorrow she'll find her backpack, use the pad and pen inside to make notes of times, log Jacob's schedule, identify a pattern, a window of opportunity. She wonders whether to write a letter to Harry, to see if he'll forgive her, help her, though she knows it's futile. He can't help her now. Wouldn't *want* to help her now.

Then she's thinking about her old life, what they're saying about her at work, if they're missing her, if she's been sacked yet or, worse, perhaps her boss has called the police when they can't reach her, when they discover her flat is empty and she's actually missing. A tear escapes her eye. It's as if she never existed.

As her eyelids grow heavy, her mind drifts back to her desk, the solitude when she had her headphones on, immersing herself in a project. Very occasionally, she conversed with another human about something other than work – the weather, the cakes someone had brought in, or a chat about a TV show she hadn't seen. She couldn't deny a part of her enjoyed it, even though she knew how dangerous it was to engage.

Company.

Once, Liam invited her to take part in a sponsored run. *Imagine,* she thinks. *Me, running.* It was related to one of the charities they'd produced a film for, and, another time, he invited her to a summer fete. She'd declined both. Anyway, she wouldn't have known what to talk about. She could have chatted about work, she supposed, going into technical detail about colour grading and bit depth, perhaps even transcoding or the rough cut she was working on. But that would only last so long. When it came down to it, she'd be going home alone. And she was content with that. Didn't need anyone interrupting her life. Throwing her off course.

'Wake *up!*'

Ella jumps as she's shoved roughly in the shoulder. Jacob is standing over her, hands on hips. The baby stirs on her chest and, after her prolonged naps today, Ella thinks she could be in for another sleepless night.

She watches Jacob gathering up the nappy things, prising the baby away from her and carrying everything upstairs. Then he comes back down for her, hoisting her up in his arms. Ella remains silent as he goes through the process of undressing her, washing her. Her limbs go weak and heavy, like that time when she had flu. She felt so ill, she thought she might die alone in her flat. Didn't care if she did. Just like she wouldn't care now, as she watches him take off all his clothes and climb into bed beside her, naked, curling his arms around her body, pulling her close, whispering how much he loves her in her ear.

CHAPTER TWENTY-EIGHT

Liam

All the next day at work, Liam couldn't concentrate, kept making basic mistakes – losing an hour's work because he'd forgotten to save it, sending attachments to the wrong client, turning up late for a team meeting. The part of his mind he kept available for being organised and on the ball had become occupied – or rather *preoccupied* – with Ella.

'You all right, Li?' Wendy, another of the post-production team asked as she came past his workstation. 'You didn't seem quite yourself in the meeting.'

He looked up. She was pretty. Probably a lot prettier than Ella – but only because she used a ton of make-up, had her nails a different colour each week, wore clothes that showed off her figure without being too trashy (though they were a bit, he thought). Ella didn't do any of those things, yet she still seemed pretty to him. She was natural and genuine, and that counted for a lot in his book.

Wendy would have gone out for a drink with him in a heartbeat if he'd asked her. She'd given him all the signals. But he wasn't desperate for a girlfriend. Far from it. Rather he was desperate to get to know Ella, find out what makes her tick. He had an inkling it could be the same things as him.

The annoying thing was, he'd only truly realised all this in her absence. And it was now driving him mad not knowing where she was. Ella had always just, well, *been there*.

'Not feeling so great, truth be known,' Liam replied, holding his stomach.

Wendy had given him the opportunity he needed. She pulled a sympathetic face as he made up his mind. He saved his work and logged out of the system, shutting down his workstation. He grabbed his jacket from the back of his chair, gathered his wallet, phone and keys and reported to the office manager that he needed to leave because he wasn't feeling well.

As he walked down the street, the bright autumn sun making him squint, he didn't feel too bad about pulling a fast one. For a start, there was all the unpaid overtime he'd done recently and, secondly, he *was* actually heading to a hospital.

The bus stop-started through the traffic, its final destination the Queen Elizabeth. Twenty minutes later, Liam was standing in the huge modern entrance foyer, his eyes scanning down the large board signposting all the different departments. He had no idea where to go, let alone knowing if he'd even be allowed to wander into a ward on the off-chance Ella might be there. At the information desk, he saw a sign clearly stating the visiting hours. Which weren't now, he thought, glancing at his watch.

Liam stood at the counter, waiting for the volunteer to become free. He pulled at his beard – well, more stubble now since he slipped with the razor and decided a good crop was in order.

'May I help?' the woman said, sort of smiling but not quite managing it.

'If someone had had a bad accident, say,' Liam began, 'which department would they be taken to first?'

'That's hard to say,' she replied. 'A&E probably, but if you give the patient's name to reception over there, they'll be able to help.'

Liam shifted from one foot to the other. 'But which department might they be taken to after that?'

The woman sort of rolled her eyes. Everything about her was half-hearted, as though she didn't really want to be there. 'Maybe Critical Care if they were really badly hurt or had a major operation. Or another ward. Depends.'

'Critical Care?' Liam repeated, thinking it sounded serious. He remembered seeing directions on the board. Probably as good a place to start as any. 'Thanks.'

He went to queue up at the main reception desk anyway but, as he suspected, they weren't much help. No patient registered by the name of Ella Sinclair.

He headed off to the lifts, going up to the second floor, walking briskly along the network of corridors littered along the way with trolleys, stretchers being wheeled past, and nurses and doctors either walking briskly or standing chatting. At the entrance to the ward, there was an intercom next to the hand sanitiser. He used both.

'Critical Care…' came the clipped voice.

'Oh, um, hi,' Liam said, leaning forward. He hadn't really thought this through. 'I'm here about a patient.'

Silence for a moment and then, surprisingly, he heard the door click and buzz, releasing the catch. So he pulled it open and went through.

He was in another corridor, wider now with doors leading off into what looked like a couple of small offices. He walked on, expecting someone to come and meet him, but no one did. Two nurses, dressed in blue scrubs, walked briskly past, ignoring him. Ahead, he could see the ward opened out and, as he went on, he saw the large area was populated with beds, though not as many as he'd seen in other wards before. There was so much equipment surrounding each one, it was hard to determine patient from machine. A couple of the beds, he noticed, had visitors sitting beside them, one holding the hand of a young man whose head was mostly covered in bandages, and another reading quietly to an old woman who appeared to be asleep, tubes going down her throat.

There were plenty of staff buzzing around, in fact more than in any other ward when he'd visited people in hospital. Yet still no one approached him.

''Scuse me,' he said to a passing nurse. 'I'm looking for a patient.'

'Take your pick,' she said, laughing, looking around. 'Who you looking for?'

'Ella Sinclair,' Liam replied.

The nurse quickly diverted over to a workstation, laying down the files she was clutching. She went around to the other side of the desk and began looking down a list, shaking her head. 'She's not in here, sorry,' she said. 'She might have been moved. When was she in?'

'Recently, I think,' Liam went on. 'Well, within the last month or so.'

The nurse tapped at a computer, leaning on the desk with one hand as she typed. 'Ah, it was a while ago,' she said, glancing up. 'She was moved,' she said, jotting something down and handing him a note. 'Try this one.' She smiled again, held his eye for a moment longer than Liam thought was necessary. 'Fourth floor. And ask for Sue,' she said. 'She flits between here and there, gets to know the patients. She might be able to help.'

'Thanks,' Liam said, nodding, flashing her a smile before heading back to the lifts.

Ward 418 was easy to walk straight into but he got collared immediately by a male nurse. Liam sensed they were stricter about visitors here, probably because patients weren't so critical. Not so life and death.

'Have you pre-arranged an out-of-hours visit?' the nurse asked, stepping in front of Liam.

'Well, not as such,' he replied, glancing around to see if he could spot any beds, hoping that, by a slim chance, Ella might be in one of them. 'But Critical Care sent me.'

'Visiting times are from two until four, then six until eight.'

'Thing is, I'm not sure if the patient I want to visit is here. Or ever was,' Liam added.

'What's the name?' the nurse said, heading into a small office just off the corridor where a whiteboard covered the back wall, sectioned off into rectangles with a marker. Names were written inside each space. None were Ella.

'Sorry,' the nurse confirmed. 'No one by that name here.'

Liam was about to go, not knowing where to search next, when another, older nurse came into the office.

'Sue, do you know if there's an Ella Sinclair in at the moment?' the nurse asked.

Sue, Liam thought.

She glanced at Liam then back to her colleague. 'Who wants to know?'

Despite her caution, Liam thought she looked friendly enough.

'I do,' he said. 'If she's here, I can come back at the proper visiting time.'

'And you are?'

Liam took a second to think about this, concluding they might not reveal patient information to just anybody. 'I-I'm her boyfriend,' he said, quite liking the sound of it. 'Her partner,' he added to make it seem more the real deal.

'I see,' Sue said, pulling an odd expression. 'Then you'd better come with me.'

*

Once inside another small room, Sue closed the door behind them. It was not a room for good news, Liam thought to himself, noticing the small vase of fake lilies and a box of tissues on the table.

'Have a seat,' Sue said. She sat opposite on a chair with frayed blue fabric. 'I'll be frank,' she continued, 'Ella *was* a patient here for a while. I knew her quite well.' Her face was serious.

'*Knew?*' Liam said, feeling his pulse kick up. 'Is she?...' He'd not even considered that she might be dead.

'Oh no, I don't mean that.' Sue made a sympathetic face.

Liam wished she'd just spit it out.

'I looked after her in Critical Care and also when she was transferred to this ward.'

'Go on,' Liam said.

'But I can't help wondering that if... if you're Ella's boyfriend, then you'd know all this anyway?' She tried to sound pleasant but there was still an accusatory look about her.

'Oh, yes...' Liam knew he looked guilty, hadn't properly thought this through. 'Well, you're right of course. I...' He ruffled his hair anxiously. 'It's a bit sensitive,' he went on. 'We sort of split up but then we didn't and-and then the accident. It's complicated.' He'd heard a few people in the office describe their relationships as 'complicated' and it seemed to shut everyone up. Liam hoped it would have the same effect now.

'I can imagine,' Sue said, raising her eyebrows. 'Ella went home. With her husband.' She sat back in her chair, watching him.

'Oh. I see,' Liam said, clearing his throat. He'd certainly not been expecting that, nor the strange sensation he felt in his heart. 'Like I said, it's, um, complicated.'

'I'm on the last five minutes of my break if you want to explain?' Sue softened, perhaps seeing the disappointment on his face.

'Is she OK?' he asked, wanting to divert away from talk of boyfriends and husbands.

'It was a nasty accident and the consultant suspected brain trauma so induced a coma for a few days. Thankfully there was no lasting damage. Her wrist and leg were badly broken and both in casts. She'll be wheelchair-bound for a while, but should heal right as rain eventually.'

'Christ,' Liam said, hardly daring to breathe. Poor Ella. 'What happened?'

Sue folded her arms, gave him a look. 'Boyfriend?' she said. 'Really?'

Liam leaned forward on his elbows, hung his head, looking down for a moment. 'Work colleague,' he confessed. 'But I thought you might not tell me anything if you didn't think I was a partner or relative.' He waited, saw a glimmer of a smile on Sue's face. 'What kind of accident was it?'

'She was knocked off her bike. There was an appeal on the news the next morning. I'm surprised you didn't see or hear it.'

Liam shook his head. 'No, I didn't,' he said, making a mental note to ask the others at work. It seemed no one cared at all about Ella's wellbeing or whereabouts. As if she'd barely existed.

'Anyway, when she was brought in, we found her work details on her lanyard and a message was left at her office. Then, thankfully, her husband arrived the next morning. He was by her side every day. A lovely man.'

'To be honest, I didn't know she was married,' Liam confessed. There was no way he'd have been considering asking her out if he'd known she'd had a husband. But something didn't sit right. After all these years, he reckoned Ella would have mentioned she was married. That he'd have picked up on something. And besides, he'd never seen a wedding ring.

'So did she go back to her flat?' Liam asked.

'Flat?' Sue said, glancing at her watch and standing. 'Oh no, Ella didn't live in a flat. She and Jacob – that's her husband – told me they've recently bought a lovely big house. He was showing me pictures.'

'He was?' Liam had to be careful. Sue clearly wanted to wrap things up, but he needed more. 'Do you know where? I'll send flowers and a card, get the others in the office to sign it. And yes, I remember her husband's name was Jacob, now that you mention it. She talked about him fondly. Had a picture of him on her desk.'

Sue got up, pausing with her hand on the door knob. 'I probably shouldn't be telling you this, but you seem like a decent chap. He said it was south of the city. You know, the posh part in the south-east, Solihull way... some exclusive gated development, he told me.' She pulled a funny face, glancing at the ceiling, trying to remember. 'Green something, I think. Can't be sure though.' Then she opened the door and was immediately collared by a doctor to discuss a patient.

'Thanks,' Liam said as she left. 'You've been very helpful.'

But Sue didn't hear.

CHAPTER TWENTY-NINE

Ella

Ella is numb. Floating. She remembers the feeling well.

She stares up at the ceiling.

Of course, much of her life this last decade has been spent similarly – existing in a mostly anaesthetised state with occasional forays into actual feeling, keeping herself as real as she was able to tolerate on any given day. This usually took the form of talking to someone in a shop for longer than the obligatory 'pleases' and 'thank-yous', but never much more than a cordial chat about the weather. These little interactions, perhaps one or two a month, at most, satisfied a basic need for human contact, made her still feel part of society. Just.

But this numbness is different.

It's protection.

Last experienced 17th June 2008, 12.16 a.m.

The numbness got her through then, as it will get her through now. Until she can get out. Just like last time.

The baby is crying. And Ella can smell her nappy. The tang of ammonia and a soily stink thickening the air in the bedroom. Jacob left an hour ago. She turns her head to the left, reaching out from the bed to rock the pram. The screaming gets worse.

Ella sits up, noticing the numbness is different this time. Before, she could sink fully inside herself, wrapping her soul in layers and layers of defences. But now, there's someone else reliant on her, another life depending on her actions. She doesn't like it. But she can't ignore it either.

She looks down at herself – still naked from when Jacob undressed her last night. Still covered in cells from his body – his saliva, his skin, his sweat… and worse. She didn't want him to do it again. Of *course* she didn't want him to. But how could she stop him? She said no plainly enough – though she didn't yell, didn't hit or kick or punch and scream. Not like then. But he carried on anyway – the baby whimpering beside them – him telling her it was simply a continuation of what they'd had all those years ago. As if no time had passed at all.

She screws up her face as she drags her bad leg down onto the floor. The heavy cast lands with a thud, sending a shock of pain into her thigh. She leans over the pram, lifting the poor baby out. Her towelling suit is wet through, her mouth and chin red and sore as she sucks and bites on her fist. Her eyes are a deep, dark blue as she stares up at Ella, imploring her.

'I was like you once,' Ella says, whispering through the cries. She starts to quieten a little when she hears Ella's voice. 'A little baby, all innocent.' She places her on the bed, reaching down for the bag of nappy things. 'And now look at me,' she says, the baby staring up, seemingly enthralled by what Ella has to say. Her little legs thrash and pump as her suit is unpopped. Excited by the prospect of being cleaned. 'Goodness me, you smell bad,' she says, thinking her voice sounds like someone else's. Someone she doesn't recognise.

Just like ten years ago. All those screams, the panic, the terror – none of them seemed to be coming from her.

Numbness.

Ella takes off the dirty nappy, cleans the baby's bottom, smears on some cream (it's been helping with the redness, she notices) and puts on a new nappy and sleepsuit. She sits there, watching girl-Zach wriggle and writhe, never still, occasionally emitting little squawks, meaning she's hungry, Ella supposes.

Jacob didn't carry them downstairs this morning like he usually did. He left early with hardly a word.

She'd woken to him leaning over her, him dressed in a suit, his face up close to hers with a satisfied expression as he pulled back the duvet, exposing her. His breath had been warm on her skin, his tongue warmer still as he'd run it slowly up from her belly button, between her breasts and up her neck. 'Don't fucking try anything today,' he'd said, kissing her slowly on the lips. Then he'd shoved her on the shoulder and left.

She grabs her robe from the end of the bed and pulls it on before lifting the little bundle of clean baby, holding her in the crook of her left arm. She hooks the plastic bag of nappy stuff over her wrist, and, using the bed as support, she slides down the side of it, landing on her bottom with a thud.

The baby's head jolts a little and she lets out a whimper, staring up at Ella, totally trusting. 'It might take me a while,' she says, 'but we'll get down. There's something I need to do.'

*

Twenty minutes later and Ella is down the stairs but exhausted. Shuffling along the bedroom floor and across the landing was painful enough on her leg, but since she needed her good arm to hold the baby, she'd been forced to use her plaster-cast arm to push herself forward. Then, stair by painful stair, she shifted herself down one step at a time, worried she would slip and not be able to stop herself. At least Jacob had removed the protective carpet covering, but it was still sheer agony.

'Made it,' she whispers, thankful that the hall floor is wooden and easy to slide along and her wheelchair is in sight in the living room. There are things she needs to reach in the kitchen later.

'And you need a new name, baby,' Ella says, laying the little girl down on her back on the rug beside the fireplace. Calling her girl-Zach doesn't seem right. 'Don't move. I'm going to see if he left you any bottles in the fridge.'

Ella climbs up into her chair and wheels into the kitchen.

He didn't.

She slams the fridge door shut, a few wine bottles rattling. Her stomach churns and rumbles – she's not been eating well herself. Just the stuff he gives her and that's usually just a microwaved meal or soup. She wheels around the big kitchen, opening cupboards, banging doors closed, trying not to think of what he did last night.

In the larder cupboard, she finds a tub of powdered baby milk. Reads how to make it up but gets confused by all the measurements, number of feeds, age and weight of baby. In the end, she grabs a washed-up bottle from the draining board, puts in a few scoops of powder and then adds some water from the kettle that's already been boiled. She knows she has to be careful with germs. She adds the collar and teat to the bottle before giving it a good shake.

Back in the living room and she's surprised to see girl-Zach has moved about three feet and is lying on her front, playing with the corner of the rug, trying to get it in her mouth.

'No, no don't eat that,' Ella says, reaching down and scooping her up. She cradles the baby in her left arm and the bottle is almost snatched from her when she sees it, urgent whimpering noises gurgling up her throat. She wonders how her real mother is feeling right now, how she is coping with the worry, the sadness and guilt. Ella wishes there was some way she could contact her, a way to let her know she's looking after her baby, that she'll do everything she can to get her back to her.

'I should probably just alert the police and be done with it,' she whispers down at the baby. But that would mean involving

Liz or one of the other women in the street as there's no landline handset here – just her useless flat mobile. 'Oh God, but then...' she adds with a deep sigh, thinking briefly about her old life. Her job. Her flat. Her colleagues. Liam.

She shakes her head. Sentimentality is not what she needs now. Determination is.

There's only one way out. And to do it, Ella needs to be able to walk. No, she needs to be able to *run*.

She flashes a few glances at the CCTV camera in the corner of the room while the baby stares up at her, suckling. 'If it wasn't for those damned things...' she says, mulling it over, wondering how she can disable them without him noticing. But she knows he will. Knows he spot-checks throughout the day, watching everything she does. She needs to be cleverer than that.

After the baby has finished her bottle, Ella makes a nest on the floor out of cushions, placing her in the middle of them so she can't roll away. She instantly starts to cry, reaching out her arms.

'Here, have this to play with,' she says, giving her the remote control to Jacob's new TV.

While the baby is preoccupied, turning the remote over, sucking on the corner, she wheels herself out into the hallway, glancing at the camera above the door. The other night, while Jacob was in the shower, she had crawled into the spare bedroom to see if she could find her cycling pack. She'd come across some things from her flat – a few clothes plus some toiletries in a box, a bedside lamp, her smart padded coat that she used to wear to the park at the weekend, and her embroidery bag. It made her sad. Remnants of her life that wasn't a life. But there'd been no pack.

She wheels into the dining room but, apart from the ugly furniture, there's nothing of hers in here. The study has a desk and chair over by the window, where she's seen Jacob sit once or twice late at night with his laptop – the laptop he keeps with him at all times, never leaving Ella alone with it – but again, there's nothing of hers or of interest in here. There are two cupboards under the stairs – one she knows is locked, containing the Wi-Fi router and the security alarm panel, but the other one is open.

Ella pulls the door wide, wheeling her chair up close. And there, on a hook at the back, is her black and green bag – still splattered with dirt and blood.

CHAPTER THIRTY

Ella

'*Meggie*,' Ella says, reaching down to pick up the baby again. She's still gripping onto the remote control as if she's been given the best toy ever. 'That's what I'm going to call you. In secret, of course.' She thinks the baby has the same sparkly eyes, the same zest for life as her old friend from university. She's often thought about her, wondered what happened to her after that summer. She's even missed her from time to time, though she tries not to think about it, not allowing the feelings to creep in. Along with everything else, it's easier to lock it all away. She's a different person now and Meggie wouldn't like who she's become. The old Ella is long gone.

'And look at me now, Meggie,' Ella says, kissing the baby on the head.

She jumps at the sudden noise, unsure at first of where it's coming from. 'Oh!' she cries, laughing and taking back the remote control from little Meggie. 'Silly girl,' she says. 'You turned the TV on.'

She's about to flick it off again – she's in no mood for entertainment – but it's the news channel. She freezes, her mouth hanging open as she listens to the newsreader talking, a superimposed image of a familiar little face in the top right of the screen.

Meggie starts screaming, reaching up towards Ella, her face going red.

'Here, here, have it back,' she says, handing her the remote. Anything to shut her up while the story is on.

Police say there are no further leads in the Kayleigh Roberts abduction case, although they are hopeful of a resolution soon. The six-month-old baby was snatched from outside a shop on Salgate Lane around 7:30 p.m. over a week ago now. Investigations are nationwide, with European countries and borders also on alert. Potential sightings are coming in from as far away as Glasgow and Berlin, with Kayleigh's face now part of a Euro-wide online campaign begun by her single mother, Sharon Roberts, and her sister, in the hope of getting the baby returned soon. Fears that trafficking rings are involved are growing, with specialist police teams working around the clock.

'Shit,' Ella says, covering her mouth as the screen cuts to an earlier appeal made by a tearful woman with bleached hair sitting between two officers at a table. Camera bulbs flash constantly as she talks, black mascara winding down her cheeks. She looks exhausted.

I just want my little girl back, the woman says, her eyes wet and swollen. *No one can possibly know how much she means to me and my family. Her dad might not be around but, if he were, I know he'd be out there searching every corner of the country for her. Please, dear God, give me my baby back. Please…*

Ella stares down at Meggie. Girl-Zach. *Kayleigh.* Tears pool in her eyes.

If you know anything or if you've got Kayleigh, Sharon Roberts goes on, *I beg you to give her back or go to the police. She's got a little birthmark on the back of her neck and she's my absolute world, my little baby girl. Just please… please don't hurt her. Take her to a hospital or a police station and do the right thing… I beg you, bring my baby home.*

Ella can't stand to watch more as the woman breaks down completely. She swipes the remote from the baby, jabbing it at the TV, hitting the off button. She feels sick, hates herself for yelling at the baby when she begins to howl again.

'Oh God, oh *God*,' Ella says, reaching down and hauling her up onto her shoulder. 'I'm so sorry, I'm so sorry, little one.' She presses her face to her, nuzzling her neck. 'I promise I'll get you back to your mummy, if it's the last thing I do.' She holds her out at arm's length, looking her in the eye. 'Believe me?'

The baby's bottom lip quivers, twisting and making odd shapes, not knowing whether to smile or howl again.

'I will, Meg… *Kayleigh*, I will,' Ella says, cuddling her close. 'Everything will be OK. I promise, I won't let you down.'

But Ella is wondering if she already has.

*

Jacob is back later than usual. It's dark and there's no sign of him. Ella is being productive with her time, making notes on her pad – the one from inside her backpack. And it only occurs to her when she writes out the sequence of events so far, only really dawns on her when she sees it in black and white, tallying it with him being late now – he's late back from the *pool*.

'Of *course*,' she says to Meggie… to Kayleigh. She can't decide what to call her. 'He goes there almost every night. Obsessive,' Ella adds, whispering. 'But…' she says, making funny hand shapes above the baby's face to keep her amused. 'If he's in the *pool*, then he can't be checking the app on his phone to watch us, right?' She chews the end of her pen, tapping it on her teeth, realising the opportunities she's been wasting.

There's a window of time and she needs to use it. But for what?

Simply fleeing – whether it's in her wheelchair (useless) or on foot (impossible), is not going to be enough. He will find her. He will destroy her. And all with one anonymous phone call to the police and delivery of the tape.

'Oh, Kayleigh,' Ella says, almost in tears as she searches for answers. 'What *am* I going to do?'

The baby gurgles a reply, her made-up babbling sounding, to Ella, a lot like *Kill him.*

'My beautiful family…' Jacob says as Ella wakes with a start, trying to focus on him, read him, gauge his mood. But all she can see is his wet hair and his crumpled clothes, standing over her with sweat stains making darker patches in his blue shirt. Her eyes are bleary from having fallen asleep on the sofa with the baby. Swim or no swim, Jacob doesn't look fresh or on top of things either. She tries to wake up, be more alert, but her mind is sluggish and slow. Dragged down.

'Did you have a good day?' he asks, as if it's a perfectly normal way to address the woman you've kidnapped.

'Fine, thank you. And you?' Ella sits up, pushes her fingers through her hair.

He might look bad, but he doesn't seem in a bad mood, she thinks. Which is a good sign. Before he came back, she'd put the dirty nappies in the bin, plumped up the cushions. Hid her notebook and hung her backpack back in the cupboard again. Then, when she knew he'd be in the pool, she'd gone to the front door, wheeled right up close to it, reached out and held the handle, pretending to fiddle with the lock. She hadn't been able to open it, of course, but she'd waited there for five minutes or so, looked up towards the hall camera. Stared right at it.

'Are you in the pool?' she'd mouthed at it slowly with a questioning expression, shaking her head. 'Or are you watching me, rushing back right now because you think I'm going to escape?' Then she'd jabbed her middle finger up at the camera half a dozen times, made a face at it and spat on the floor.

Afterwards, lying on the sofa with Kayleigh just before she fell asleep, Ella had thought of ways she could use that hour of time each day, if indeed it was hers to have in the first place.

'I'm all the better for seeing you two,' Jacob says, sitting down beside her and giving her a kiss. 'I've been thinking,' he goes on. 'We should definitely accept Liz's invitation to dinner. I want to show off my lovely family.'

Ella's heart skips. He's in a good mood. He didn't see what she did.

'Liz will be pleased,' she says. 'And so will… so will little Zach. He couldn't take his eyes off Steph's baby when they were here. They'll be at Liz's dinner too,' Ella adds, trying to sound excited.

And she is, but for very different reasons to Jacob.

CHAPTER THIRTY-ONE

Ten Years Ago

Ella stepped out of the station building – a tiny little Victorian place on the edge of a village in Oxfordshire where a steam train wouldn't look out of place – and shielded her eyes from the early morning sun. The only one to disembark, she wheeled her small suitcase behind her, not knowing what to expect. Zach had already told her he wouldn't be there himself, that he had a late function with his parents the night before and would send the family driver instead.

Before she'd even got her bearings, a man in a black uniform wearing a peaked hat approached her. He was probably in his sixties, Ella thought, as she saw his friendly smile.

'Miss Sinclair?' he said, his gloved hands folded in front of him. He bowed his head slightly.

'Oh, yes,' Ella replied and before she knew what was happening, he'd taken her suitcase from her and relieved her of the large cloth bag she had slung over her shoulder.

The driver opened the rear door of a black Jaguar. She glanced at him, nodded and slipped inside the luxurious interior. Leather everywhere – cream and unblemished – with shiny wooden trims in which she could almost see her shocked face reflected. She smiled inwardly. She could get used to this, she thought, feeling a pang of guilt as she remembered her mother's battered old Escort that was more rust than car.

'We'll be about twenty minutes to Adlington Manor, miss,' the driver said through the glass hatch, before sliding it closed.

Ella nodded, allowing the seat to swallow her up, taking in the lush countryside as they cruised along the lanes. After a few more miles, the road narrowing to a single track, overhung by a thick canopy of trees, they turned down a long sweeping drive. Ella suddenly felt self-conscious, wished she'd not worn her torn jeans and a faded old T-shirt, worrying that she didn't look her best for meeting Zach's family.

'Bloody *hell*,' she whispered under her breath, covering her mouth as she locked eyes with the chauffeur in the rear-view mirror. She noticed his small smile and she sat forward in her seat, unclicking her belt and taking it all in. Adlington Manor was… well, it was *huge* – even more impressive than the photos suggested.

The car finally drew up to the sweeping gravel area in front of the house – a raised stone pond and fountain being the centrepiece of the drive. Water spouted twenty feet into the air from a giant stone fish's mouth.

'Thank you,' Ella said, getting out of the car as the driver opened the door for her. She stared around in awe as he went to the boot to retrieve her luggage, requesting that she follow him. They headed towards the steps that led up to an ornate portico carved, like the fountain, out of austere, grey stone. One side of the large double doors opened and a butler, also in uniform, appeared to greet them.

Stupidly, Ella found herself wanting to giggle. And then, to her horror, she found she *was* giggling, feeling as if she was some kind of prized possession being delivered. She wondered if, in Zach's mind, she actually was.

'*Ella*, my God, how fab to see you!'

Ella heard the shrill voice before she saw who it belonged to – although she knew the sound of it well enough. She just hadn't expected to hear it today. Zach had implied that she would be the first to arrive.

'Meggie?' Ella said, focussing beyond the door. The butler ushered her inside just as Meggie came bowling out wearing nothing but pink silky pyjamas – tiny lacy shorts and a camisole top.

Ella jolted as her friend flung her arms around her, almost knocking her over as she gave her a hug. She jumped up and down, the pyjamas doing little to cover her up.

'I can't believe you're finally *here*,' Meggie went on, squealing.

'And I can't believe *you're* here,' Ella replied quietly, though it made sense, she supposed. Meggie and Zach had both attended the same Oxfordshire prep school and the two families were close. But she'd hoped to have some alone time with Zach before the house party began and everyone descended, a chance to settle in and get used to the place. Anyway, on the plus side, she thought, as she reciprocated Meggie's hug, at least the frostiness between them of several weeks ago had finally gone. An intense run of final exams had focussed everyone's minds.

'Come, come, *come…*' Meggie said, taking Ella's hand, dragging her along. 'We're all here. We came down a couple of days ago. Actually, I can't even remember when it was. It's all a bit of a blur.'

She seemed so different outside of Durham, Ella thought, as though the unifying and equalising effect of being at university had worn off, that it suddenly wasn't an even playing field any more. Meggie was on familiar turf. Ella wasn't.

Meggie led her through the vast entrance hall that reminded her of a museum – grand, ornate and stuffed with antiques. She glanced at the three stags' heads above the big stone fireplace, each of them staring down at her as she walked by, their eyes tracking her just as someone would have once tracked and hunted them.

'Zach's a little worse for wear,' Meggie went on, regaling Ella with tales of what they got up to last night – dinner at so-and-so's followed by the private club in Oxford, the champagne, not even remembering the journey back there. 'Oh God, and he lost most of his coke in Alex's dad's car. He was none too impressed...' She squealed again then, skipping along.

Ella didn't know what to say. She stared at the oriental antique furniture as she passed from one room to the next, through long corridors spread with expensive-looking rugs. None of this was her world.

'We're all down here,' Meggie said, as they eventually reached the kitchen. It was only the black cooking range taking up most of one wall – an Aga, Ella thought – that gave away the room's use. At one end of a long table there was a cluster of familiar faces, plus a few others she didn't recognise.

'Thank fuck you're here,' Zach said, standing. She could see immediately he looked awful but, true to form, still beautiful. His eyes, even though they looked tired, still had their trademark quality. She went up to him to deliver the hug he was expecting, but stopped.

'*Harry?*'

'Hey, sis,' her brother said, staring into a cup of coffee, looking as deathly as the rest of them. Packets of food were spread out between them, the wrappers ripped off in what must have been a hungry frenzy.

'I can't believe you're here, too,' Ella said to him, a sick feeling sweeping through her. Why hadn't he told her he was coming, or offered to travel with her? And, more to the point, why had he been invited ahead of her? She glanced around the table – there were about nine or ten people in total, and most she recognised from Durham.

'He's come to keep you in order, obviously,' Charles said, shoving a cream cracker in his mouth with a huge lump of cheese on top. He laughed, spraying out crumbs. 'Want one?' He held out the bright orange packet but Ella shook her head.

'No, thanks.'

For a moment, Charles looked shocked, as though he'd never been refused before, even if it was just for a biscuit. A second later, he stood up and came right up to Ella, grabbing a cracker from the packet and holding it under her nose.

She backed away, unnerved, looking at Zach.

'Fuck off, Charles,' Zach said, drawing Ella closer.

Charles glared at him but then laughed, dropping the cracker on the floor, crunching it underfoot before blowing Ella a silent kiss. He sat back down.

'Just ignore him,' Zach whispered. 'He's been such a prick the last two days.' He kissed her then, full on the lips, making a couple of the others whoop. But when he pulled away, Ella's heart virtually stopped beating when she saw him, sitting slightly apart from the others, watching everything.

Nerdy Boy.

'What's *he* doing here?' Ella whispered in Zach's ear, hardly able to speak as she stared at him over his shoulder. The boy stared back. His eyes were empty, watching her. The last person she'd ever expected to see at Adlington.

'I'll explain later,' Zach said into her ear. 'But it's fine.' Then he plunged his mouth onto hers again, consuming her.

'Oh, get a room already, you two,' someone called out as Ella pulled away, gasping for breath.

'Let the party begin,' Zach said, not taking his eyes off her, lifting up her chin with his finger as she tried to compose herself.

'This. Definitely. *Now*,' Meggie said, passing over the dress. 'If you wear that old thing, I'll never speak to you again.'

Ella was still reeling from what had happened in the kitchen – not to mention being put in a room called the 'Alexandra Suite' by Zach's mother. She was a small and thin woman, who was probably younger than she actually looked and, for the short time Ella had met her, she seemed to never stop moving, as though she was fuelled entirely by nerves and worry, her eyebrows angled together in a permanent frown.

'We like to keep everything locked up, Ella dear,' she'd told her as she showed her to her room, turning the key. 'My husband is very security conscious,' she added when Ella gave her a puzzled look.

She could understand locking outside doors, but all the internal doors had locks too.

'Of course, Mrs White,' she said, watching the woman's hands shake.

'You seem a sensible girl,' she said, looking up at her. 'Make sure those boys lock up at the lake house, too. It's remote there and we've had a spate of break-ins. Alan thinks it's the kids in the village. They hang out in the woods, even though it's private property. He's at his wits' end with it and the police are no help.'

'Oh, I'm sorry to hear that,' Ella said. She'd supposed it was because Zach's family had a lot more to lose than most.

'My husband works hard,' she said, placing her hand on Ella's arm outside the bedroom door, as though she were confiding all her secrets. 'Has done all his life. He gets... well, he gets angry easily. He's a generous man, but doesn't like people helping themselves. He even threatened to flatten the place if it happened again, so no one could break in,' she'd added with a sort of resigned laugh.

'I understand, Mrs White,' Ella said, wondering if it was some kind of veiled threat. But she liked Zach's mother nonetheless, and thought she'd taken a shine to her, too, despite their very different lives. She sensed they had something in common, but still couldn't quite place what.

'You win,' Ella said to Meggie, feeling the excitement brewing now that she was settled in to her room. She looked around – four-poster bed, plush Chinese rugs on the floor, an ornate salon suite (she'd joked with Meggie about taking afternoon tea on it while doing tapestry like proper *ladies*), and her own bathroom that was virtually bigger than the entire downstairs of the house she and Harry had grown up in. 'I could get used to this,' she went on, her stomach deliciously full from the brunch she'd eaten earlier with the group, cooked for them by the family's chef. Thankfully, Charles had behaved himself after the cracker incident. She suddenly stopped, lowering the dress she was holding up in front of her, turning away from the long mirror.

'Megs…' Ella began.

'Mmm?…' Meggie was touching up her mascara.

'Why is *he* here? You know, Nerdy Boy from the library.'

'What, you mean Ethan?'

Ella stopped, not ever considering that he actually had a name. And that Meggie might know it.

'If that's his name, then yes, him.'

'I suppose because Zach invited him,' Meggie said, fluttering her lashes at her reflection.

'Does he even know him?' Ella said, perplexed. He certainly hadn't seemed to when they'd been in the café a few weeks back.

'No idea,' Meggie said, applying a slick of lip gloss and rolling her lips together. 'Does it bother you?'

'No,' Ella said quietly, staring out of the window towards the lake. 'No, of course it doesn't.'

'Good, then hurry up and get ready.'

'Sure,' Ella replied, going into the bathroom to change.

'Stunning,' Meggie said when Ella emerged, wearing the short black dress with tiny shimmery stones stuck around the neckline. 'Expect it to be muddy and torn by the morning,' Meggie went on, laughing. 'They've got shenanigans planned down by the water.

The lake house is a favourite, but it's a bit of a trek and there's no road. We have to walk through the woods.' She said the last bit in a spooky voice, making her eyes go wide.

'Well it sounds fun,' Ella said, trying to put Ethan out of her mind. Zach would look after her and, besides, any friend of his would have to be a friend of hers. Perhaps they could find some common ground. They'd clearly got off to a bad start in the library. 'Though I don't know why we don't just wear jeans and sweaters if we're tramping through the woods later.'

'But we're having dinner here first, *darling*,' Meggie replied in a silly voice. 'All the boys will be in black tie, Zach's parents and friends too. They like us to dress up. Besides, you'll see. The lake house isn't exactly a shed. We'll be fine. *You'll* be fine.'

Meggie took another sip of the drink she'd been knocking back at a pace and came up to Ella, kissing her full on the lips. Ella pulled away, shocked.

'Chill. You're so uptight.' Meggie sauntered up to the mirror, appraising herself in her heels. 'Besides, you're at Adlington now. Everything's different here.' She gave a slow smile before turning and leading the way downstairs.

'I'm so fucking jealous of you,' Meggie said, watching as Ella knelt nervously beside the low table made from giant polished planks. The lake house was a Canadian-style log cabin – numerous bedrooms, a kitchen, a large living area – and Ella could see it was a home from home. More than a home from home, and still way bigger than normal people's houses. Huge hide-covered sofas surrounded the roaring open fire – even though it was mild, Nerdy Boy had taken it upon himself to light it as soon as they arrived – with each sofa draped in real furs to sink in to. The walls were hung with hunting trophies and the floors covered in yet more fur – white sheepskins, Ella had thought, as she'd kicked off her painful and muddy shoes after they'd staggered through the woods following dinner. She'd allowed her toes to sink into the deep pile, while Zach's arm was firmly fixed around her waist. As if he was marking his territory, showing the other boys she was his. She'd never belonged to anyone before and she was growing to like it. It made her feel… *safe*. And, after the couple of glasses of wine she'd had with dinner, she thought she might even be enjoying it.

His bow tie was hanging loose around his neck as he watched her kneeling at the table, his hair falling across his face, part covering his boozy eyes.

They'd all dropped down onto the rhino-like sofas when they'd arrived, laughing, jeering, talking about everything from politics to sex as they grabbed sticky bottles from the drinks cabinet, chucking their cigarettes and dope into the centre of the table alongside Zach's camcorder. He'd been randomly filming their antics all night.

Boozy, silly, privileged fun.

'You promise me one thing?' Zach had said to Ella as they'd walked up to the lake house through the dark woods. They'd only had one torch between them. He'd held her back for a moment, his hand gripping her arm.

'What's that?' she'd giggled, staggering in the stupid shoes she was wearing, clinging on to him.

'That you'll try to be one of us.' Zach's voice was deadly serious, despite all the alcohol he'd put away.

Ella was silent for a moment, fighting back the tears. She'd had more wine than usual and was in the middle of nowhere. Her sluggish brain couldn't decide if she felt completely safe with Zach or utterly vulnerable. 'Sure,' she said quietly, grateful it was so dark and he couldn't see her glistening eyes.

And then, when they'd settled into the lodge, someone had got out the cocaine.

'Virgins first,' Stan had said, pushing her forward.

She wasn't completely certain his comment had been about the drugs. Did Zach and his mates have private jokes about her, about what she had and hadn't done?

She'd sat next to Stan at dinner and several times she'd removed his hand from her leg under the table as she was discussing poetry with Zach's mother. Even when dessert was served – a huge pile of strawberries, cream and meringue (Eton mess, she'd learnt it was called) – Stan still persisted, his hand lingering as he ate greedily.

Maybe things at Adlington *were* different.

She made a face at the camera when Charles grabbed it, hitting record and pointing it right at her. 'Give us a good show,' he said, squinting through the viewfinder.

Ella wasn't sure what he meant until Stan's hand was on her shoulder, loosening one of her straps. She saw Zach's face, how he tensed, leant forward, watching. But he didn't say anything. His words echoed through her mind: *Try to be one of us…* Ella wanted to catch Meggie's eye, but she was busy talking to Alex, the pair of them curled up together at one end of the sofa. And then she saw Ethan watching on from the fireplace, an unnerving smirk on his face.

Ella batted Stan's hand away and slid her shoulder strap back up. 'Behave,' she said in a silly voice that wavered a little, rolling her eyes at him. It seemed an inoffensive way of making her point without making a fool of him (or her) yet meaning what she said.

But Stan drew up close, his lips against her ear. 'No one fucking turns me down,' he whispered. '*Ever.*'

For a moment, Ella couldn't move and it seemed as if the rest of the room had fallen silent around her, as if she was suspended underwater, just her and Stan, his hands pulling off her clothes in slow motion.

'Which is why I fucking envy you so much, Ella,' Meggie continued loudly. 'You get to have your first time in front of us. After this, it'll never be the same again.'

'Just like sex for the first time…' Charles slurred from behind the lens, fixing it on Zach as the others chimed in with laughter. He flashed Ella a look.

'You going to cut that shit or what, Stan?' Zach said, grabbing his camera back from Charles.

'On it, boss,' Stan replied.

Ella watched as he crushed up the coke with the edge of his credit card, making the little salt-like lumps into a fine powder. Then he cut it into lines and passed her a straw. She'd seen it done in movies, of course. Read about it in books and had seen them all do it countless times before. But she'd never done drugs of any kind herself. Two or three drinks was her limit. And she'd already gone way over that tonight.

'All yours,' Stan said, giving her a look. Sophie, another girl who'd joined them just for the evening, had draped herself over his knee as he sprawled back on the fur sofa. Beautiful, blonde, elegant and well-educated.

Try to be one of us…

'OK, I'll do it,' Ella said, though by then no one apart from Zach was watching. Filming. She leaned down and pushed the straw up her nose, blocking her left nostril closed. She sniffed – gently at first but then harder as the line disappeared. Meggie was right. Everything *was* different at Adlington.

CHAPTER THIRTY-TWO

Ella

Jacob rings the doorbell. 'Best behaviour,' he says, leaning down and whispering in Ella's ear as she sits in the wheelchair holding the baby.

Zach and Jacob, Jacob and Zach, she repeats over and over in her mind. *Baby Zach, adult Jacob.* One slip and she knows it's over.

'Of course,' she says, looking up at him, forcing a smile.

'Of course, *darling*,' Jacob reminds her. He'd drummed it into her a hundred times as he helped her into the dress he'd bought for her. A nasty thing made from royal blue floral fabric. He'd positioned her in front of the mirror before they left, appraising how they looked together.

'The perfect couple,' he'd said, smoothing down his navy blazer, straightening the collar on his Oxford shirt beneath. His trousers beige, his brogues polished. His eyes shiny and bright. He'd kissed her before carrying her downstairs to the wheelchair, next to which the baby was squawking in its pram.

'Ella, Jacob – hel-*lo*!' Liz sings out as soon as she opens the front door. 'I'm so glad you came.' Her eyes dart all over the place – at the front step, Ella's wheelchair, at Jacob. 'Now, how are we going to do this?' Then she turns, calling out down the hallway. 'Mick, come and give us a hand.'

But Jacob already has Ella inside the house.

'Ooh, strong man!' Liz says, leaning down to deliver a hug to Ella and a gentle stroke on the head for the baby. 'Come on through… please.' She leads the way into the living room. 'You already know Steph and Rachel, of course, Ella. Everyone, this is the lovely Jacob, Ella's hubby. And this is Pete, Rachel's other half and Andy, Steph's husband. My two kids are buzzing around somewhere.'

Ella's head swims as she's introduced, as hands are shaken above her and all around her. She grips onto Zach, jiggling him on her lap, forcing herself not to call her a girl or Meggie or, worse, Kayleigh. As it is, she's had to apply thick smears of concealer over the birthmark on the back of the baby's neck. The whole country will be on the lookout for it since it was mentioned on the news. Ella doesn't wear make-up but thankfully always kept a concealer in her backpack for the days when a rogue spot or two would flare. She hated people staring at her, even for something so silly as a blemish.

'And who's this little chap?' Pete says, bending down to stroke the baby's cheek. He's a tall man, broad, clean-shaven. Goodlooking, Ella thinks, until she remembers what Rachel said her husband does for work.

A *police officer*.

'This is… this is Zach,' Ella says, her throat closing up. She catches Liz's eye, then Rachel's. Both women give her a little nod, as if to say: *Don't worry, we understand… we won't say anything.* She prays that's what it means, anyway. Prays that they can't possibly know the truth, haven't made the connection.

'Lucky man,' Pete says, eyeing Jacob. 'Wait till he turns into a little monster like this one, eh?' He ruffles his young son's hair as he toddles past, a toy car in his hand, pretending it's flying.

'It's a Jaguar,' Jacob says, his eyes glinting as he reaches out and catches the toddler's wrist. The boy stops suddenly, swinging around, staring up and looking frightened. 'My favourite kind,' Jacob goes on, squatting down next to him.

Little Joey's face relaxes then, not looking quite so scared as Jacob makes zooming noises while the adults continue to chat above them. Ella watches, though – sees how Jacob pushes the toddler's car around the floor. She thinks that, in reality, he's not much more than a kid himself.

Stuck.

Liz hands around drinks, Ella taking a glass of Prosecco even though she knows she shouldn't. Not while on the painkillers. But she's not sure how she'll get through the evening otherwise. The temptation to find the landline or escape while no one's paying attention is strong. Not to mention confiding in Liz or one of the other women, asking for their help. But what would she say? *My husband is not my husband. He's kidnapped me, he's kidnapped the baby, and he's got evidence showing I did something terrible.*

No. Of course she can't say that. There's a police officer in the room and Jacob could have her put away for the rest of her life. She'd rather die than let that happen.

'So, how long have you been living here?' Ella asks Liz instead, trying to stop her hand shaking as she sips her drink.

'We bought off-plan. So not long. It's just the friendliest place to live. We love it. And much of Mick's work is around here, too. So if you need anything doing, you know, an extension or conservatory, my Mickie's your man,' Liz says, excusing herself to check on the food.

'Mates rates?' Jacob says to Mick, laughing. Ella sees a part of him she's not witnessed for a long time – cordial, friendly, able to get along with anyone. And even then, it was something he turned on and off. She stifles the shudder.

'Well, if all your babies turn out as cute as this one, then I suggest you have many more and fill the place up,' Steph says, leaning down to give Zach a tickle on the tummy. 'Do you mind?' she says, reaching for the baby, not waiting for an answer.

For a second, the way she looks at her, Ella wonders if she recognises Kayleigh from the news. She hopes it's true what they say, that all babies look the same.

'Dinner's served,' Liz says, poking her head around the door.

Everyone goes through to the dining room, with Jacob wheeling Ella. She finds herself seated at the head of the table – Liz having left a space for her chair. Her worst nightmare, she thinks, looking to Jacob, studying his face, trying to remember some kind of etiquette or conversation from way back. All those summer balls, the black-tie Christmas parties at St Mary's College, the spring flings with muddy gowns and champagne, the casino nights in London, stopping over at Meggie's plush family apartment in Chelsea, the sailing trip… Jacob smiles back. It was a different world.

As Ella looks at the people seated around the table – Steph still holding baby Zach with her own baby beside her in her pram – she realises that this, in many ways, is just the same as those crazy, hedonistic days. People being people. Just doing what they know.

Yet it couldn't be *more* different. Because these are *normal* people, Ella thinks. People with regular jobs. Regular problems. Pleasant houses. They've all worked hard. Respect each other, take nothing for granted. Steph has baby sick on her shoulder, Mick's shirt stretches at the buttons from his beer belly, Pete has the flaky tell of psoriasis on his elbows, and Rachel, Ella notices, has a strange tic in her eye every few seconds.

She watches, looks around. Studies them, as she's learnt to do over the last ten years. And she tells herself that, after everything, she can handle a suburban dinner. *This is the middle*, she thinks, smiling, feeling oddly warm inside. *Not the bottom. And not the top. But slap bang in the middle.*

'And I *like* it,' Ella says, meaning to keep it to herself. She claps a hand over her mouth.

Liz laughs. 'Tell me that after you've tried it,' she says, spooning a huge portion of something brown and meaty onto a plate.

'Pass this down to Ella,' she says. 'You look as though you need feeding up.' Then a look exchanged between them. Ella smiles back. 'Help yourself to veg,' Liz goes on, pointing at the serving dishes dotted around.

A moment later, there's chaos as everyone dives in, Liz's kids squabbling over the potatoes. But good chaos, Ella thinks, as food is served, plates are passed around, more wine poured, and conversation and laughter shared. Someone knocks their cutlery onto the floor, Joey squeals that he needs a wee-wee, and Mick jeers loudly when the football result is mentioned. Everyone tucks in.

For dessert, Liz brings in a huge bowl of Eton mess. Ella stares at it, not knowing what to say when Liz serves her a huge portion. *It's just a name*, she tells herself. *A stupid name for a bowl of strawberries, meringue and cream.* She glances across at Jacob, forces a smile when he tucks into it. They both know; are both reminded.

Afterwards, Liz suggests coffee in the other room, so they all troop through. 'Aww, bless him,' she says, looking at little Joey asleep on the sofa. 'Carry him upstairs to the spare bed, if you like,' she suggests to Pete. 'And it's time for the pair of you to go up now, too,' she says to her own children, giving them each a kiss. Jacob wheels Ella right beside the living flame gas fire, as close as he can get her. She looks up at him with a frown.

'Darling,' she says, clearing her throat when it comes out as a croak. 'It's really hot sitting here. Can you move me back a bit?'

Jacob stares down at her before leaning close. 'Nonsense,' he says, stroking her cheek. 'I know how much you love fires,' he whispers, making sure his breath goes right inside her ear. Jacob moves away then, leaving her there. Ella's left side heats up quickly, burning her skin so much she feels her face and arm might blister. The warmth also magnifies the stink coming from Zach's nappy as she cradles the baby on her lap.

'Would you like me to change… to change him for you?' Liz asks, stumbling over her words.

'Oh…' Ella doesn't know what to say.

'Not a hands-on dad then, eh?' Pete says, nudging Jacob. His coffee sloshes into his saucer.

'He's brilliant,' Ella says quickly, seeing something flare in Jacob's eyes. 'He gets all the bottles ready for me before he goes to work, brings home nappies and milk.' Truth is, Ella thinks, he only did that stuff once, and thank God he's never bathed the baby. Neither has she, for that matter. The poor little thing has to make do with being cleaned with wet wipes.

'Come on,' Liz says, coming up and grabbing Ella's wheelchair handles. 'Let's go in the other room and do it together.'

Ella feels like a goldfish as she's wheeled out, her mouth flapping, silently protesting, no one noticing, but she's glad to be away from the fire.

Liz takes them through to the study – cool and quiet – and unhooks the bag of baby stuff from the back of the chair. She sits down opposite at the desk, gently lifting the baby from Ella.

'Now,' she says, 'why don't you tell me what's going on?'

Again, Ella is unable to talk. It's as if she's sinking into a hole – the huge hole that's inside her. Unfillable.

Liz lays the baby on her knee, unpopping the sleepsuit and wriggling out limbs skilfully. She undoes the nappy tapes, pulling the front flap down underneath the baby's bottom, grabbing a load of wipes with one hand while holding the baby steady with the other.

'I'm waiting,' she continues, glancing down between the baby's legs.

'I told you already,' Ella says, 'Jacob's got… well, he's got a few issues. It's hard to talk about. But please, *please* dear God don't say anything or I'll be the one to get it.'

'Ella,' Liz says, pulling a face that makes her want to cry. 'I have to ask. Does he ever… you know, hurt you? I was wondering how you got that bruise on your face.'

'Oh God, *no*,' she says quickly, adding a laugh. But inside, she feels the sting of Jacob's fist around her head. She touches her cheekbone. 'It was just me being clumsy with the kitchen cupboard door.' She sighs. 'Look, he'll accept that we have a baby girl soon enough. Maybe one day we'll even have the boy he's always dreamed of. Until then, he just needs time to adjust. To process everything.' Ella swallows down the lie. 'So please, *please* don't mention it.' Her flat is suddenly on her mind again and she wishes – *oh how she wishes* – that she was back there, all by herself. Reading, listening to the radio, doing her embroidery.

'You're crying,' Liz says, reaching out, putting a hand on hers. 'Oh, *Ella*, you've been through such a lot – a baby in the last six months. A house move. A terrible accident. And your husband not accepting that your child is a girl…' She shakes her head. 'He needs professional help with that, love. This situation is really not OK for either of you.'

'Sorry,' Ella says, wiping away the tears, sniffing. She hangs her head. 'I'm fine. He's fine. We're all fine.'

'How long have you been married?'

Christ, Ella thinks, pulling herself together. Jacob didn't tell her how to answer *that* question since they now have a baby. 'About… well, a few months now.' She supposes that still counts as being newlyweds.

Liz raises her eyebrows, squinting and tilting her head.

'It was February,' Ella says without thinking. 'I always wanted a white winter wedding.' But then she realises she would probably have been heavily pregnant then. A bad time to plan a wedding. 'Actually no, it was Christmas time,' she adds, thinking that sounds more plausible, but Liz looks confused.

Then Ella's reminded of all the Christmas carol services at Durham – as well as the final leavers' service at the end of exams. They were all in the cathedral – the chamber choir ringing out 'Lord of All Hopefulness', the stained-glass windows looming above them, the vaulted roof reverberating the sopranos, and the vibrations of the huge organ resonating through their hearts – when Zach announced they would one day get married in that very place. When they were seated again, he'd slipped his hand up Ella's skirt, his fingers almost getting to where they wanted to be. But she'd slapped him away, crossing her legs, making a silly but firm face at him. Still, she'd been thrilled by the prospect of marriage. Of finally being his.

'Ella?' she hears Liz saying. 'How about it?'

'Sorry?'

'A shopping trip. Just you, me and the baby.'

'Sure…' Ella hears herself replying, though in reality, she knows she can't, that she'll have to make excuses. Her head is pounding from the memories, everything swimming before her.

Swimming… she thinks, overwhelmed by possibilities.

'OK, that's… that's Zach changed,' Liz says, handing back the baby. 'And look, your secret is safe with me. And you can trust Steph and Rachel too. I'll help you get through this.'

Ella gives a little nod. 'Thanks. But about the shopping trip,' she says, looking up at Liz as she wheels her back through. 'Please don't mention that in front of Jacob either, OK? He worries.'

'Sure,' Liz says nodding after a pause.

When they go back into the living room, peals of laughter ring out, everyone turning to look at Ella. The baby startles in her arms, buries its face in her side as she strokes its head, cradling her close.

'We've been talking weddings,' Rachel rings out, a tipsy glow to her cheeks. 'Turns out Pete and I have been at it the longest with ten years under our belt. Ten fricking *years*,' she says, laughing loudly.

Ella smiles, accepting another drink from Liz. She's already feeling light-headed.

'Ella, you and Jacob are in second place,' Steph chips in. 'Liz and Mick are each on their second time round, positive newly-weds compared to the five years you and Jacob have racked up.'

'Oh no,' Liz says, settling herself down after topping up everyone's drinks. 'Ella's only been married a few months.'

Ella smiles, wincing inwardly as she envisages the blow she'll get when she's alone later with Jacob.

CHAPTER THIRTY-THREE

Ella

He stands above her, holding out his phone. 'You have a call to make,' he says, his face blank.

Ella lies frozen on the sofa, the baby half-sitting, half-dropping sideways in the mound of cushions beside her, playing with the crinkly wrapper from the remainder of a packet of biscuits – the only thing Jacob has given her to eat in twenty-four hours. Since they returned from Liz's house the night before last, he hasn't spoken a word to her. But he didn't hit her either. It was just nothing, blank – him acting as though she didn't exist. In a way, that was worse, not knowing how he was feeling, what he was going to do.

Now, it's Monday morning and he hasn't left the house for work yet. It's already gone 9 a.m. It's unsettling. 'A call?' She doesn't like that she sounds grateful that he's speaking to her again. But she is.

'They're going to ask questions,' he says.

'Who are?' Ella forces herself up to a sitting position. Her leg itches and throbs within its cast, though, thankfully, her broken arm has been less painful the last day or so.

'The people at your work. You're going to phone them and tell them you're not coming back. Ever.'

'But—' She stops when she sees the look on his face, her head already stinging in anticipation of the clout she'll get if she disagrees. When she pulled back her hair in front of the mirror earlier, her bruise had turned greeny-blue. Her scalp is still tight and swollen.

Ella hangs her head, takes a breath. 'You're right, of course,' she says, smiling, reaching out for the phone, but he whips it away.

'Tell me the number,' he says, dialling 141 first to conceal his phone's number. 'And don't pull any stunts. You speak to the correct person, tell them you're recovering very slowly, that you won't ever be back. And that's it.'

Ella nods, knowing the number off by heart – it's an easy one to remember. Besides, she has a knack for recalling information such as postcodes or dates or numbers. Perhaps because there's been little else to occupy her mind these last ten years.

Work, home, sleep…

She recites it, pausing after the city code and the first three digits. She knows the main reception number, and she knows the last few digits of the direct line to HR. But she also knows most of her colleagues' direct numbers, too. 'Zero four seven nine,' she adds quickly, giving Jacob an earnest look as he hands her the phone. He stands over her.

'It's ringing,' she says, smiling, stroking the baby's head – a little comfort as she braces herself.

'Oh…' she says when he answers, the sound of his voice making her stall. 'Hello…' She's transported to another place, another time – as though she was last at work a million years ago. 'This is Ella Sinclair here,' she says, trying to sound formal, praying he doesn't exclaim loudly when he hears her voice. She doesn't know why, out of everyone in the office, she called him. She imagines him sitting at his workstation, a few spaces down from hers. Sees him hunched over his screens, working his way through the day's editing projects, perhaps looking forward to lunch with the others at the deli, stopping by her desk to start up a conversation.

'This is the HR department, right?' she adds, nodding at Jacob. She doesn't know what's possessed her to do this or, indeed, how Liam can possibly help. He won't have a clue what she's talking about.

Suddenly, Liam is firing a load of questions at her, tripping over his words.

'Ella, where are you? How are you? What the hell happened? When are you coming back?'

She needs him to stop talking, so she coughs loudly, trying to cover up any chance of Jacob overhearing. He's watching her every move. But then Liam throws her, makes her heart skip.

'I've been looking for you... desperately worried... Ella...'

'I'm really sorry, but I won't be coming back to work,' she says, speaking over him, ignoring everything he's saying. Her fist is clenched so tight that her fingernails dig into her palm. 'I'm afraid my injuries after the accident were... they were life-changing and I'm in a wheelchair.' She looks up at Jacob. Blank-faced, he nods his approval. 'I'm left with no option but to resign.' Ella's heart is thumping. She just wants to get this over with. 'No, no, it's fine. I'm staying with my family. They're looking after me.' She notices the smile spreading on Jacob's face, watches as he goes to sit down in the chair opposite. '*Very* well looked after,' she adds, closing her eyes for a few seconds when she hears Liam's concern.

'I've been worried sick... something's not right here, Ella... Your flat is empty... I don't understand... You love your job...'

He cares. He really cares, she thinks, fighting back the tears.

'No, I'm absolutely fine, but as I said, I won't be coming back to work. I'm sorry.' Silence on the line. She can almost hear Liam's mind whirring, sensing something's wrong. 'Please make sure you let Diana McBride know about... about my situation. Goodbye.' Ella hits the call-end button and hands back the phone.

'All sorted,' she says. 'They were fine about it.'

Jacob stares at her. 'Who is Diana McBride?' he says, his mouth twisting into an ugly shape.

'Oh, she's the head of HR,' Ella says, smiling. 'It's important she knows for everything to be final.'

The baby is squawking and fussing, gnawing on her fist, dribbling.

'I see,' Jacob says, staring at her for a few moments before grabbing his jacket off the chair. 'I'm going to work.'

And it's only when Ella hears the front door lock behind him that she lifts the baby from her nest and drops back onto the sofa, the baby lying on top of her thumping heart.

'Diana McBride,' she whispers, putting her finger over her lips, wondering if Liam picked up on what she was trying to say.

It's later. Much later. The television is on but the volume is down – just so she can keep track of the time. Meantime, Ella has kept busy. The baby has been fed and is as clean as she can manage, plus she's eaten the food left out for her by Jacob. More cold soup, but she knows she needs the strength. Anything she can get. As ever, she fell asleep for a few hours after eating it, waking in a fuggy state, her thoughts dragging, her eyes barely able to stay open. She drinks some water, hoping it will wake her up. It's nearly 6 p.m.

'Please don't cry,' she says, peering into the pram. Ella thinks she must be sick to death of the one toy that was in there when Jacob stole her – a blue plastic ring, the top half of which is shaped like a rabbit. The baby likes to chew on it, then chuck it down again, howling when it's gone from her hand. Ella always patiently picks it up, sometimes passing her other things to gnaw on that are safe – the remote control, a wooden spoon from the kitchen. But she soon gets fractious.

'It's time,' she says. The baby stops its staccato cries, listening to Ella's voice. 'I have something important to do.' She glances at the TV again. 'And I only have an hour. Maybe only forty-five minutes to be on the safe side.'

The baby almost replies intelligently, Ella thinks, making a gurgling noise that sounds as if she's saying: *Yes, do it.*

'I'll have to work fast,' she says, getting into her wheelchair, glancing at the cameras as she does so, praying he's not watching, that she can rely on his rigid swimming schedule. He told her it's the adults-only swim at his gym between six and seven, that he can't stand screaming brats in the pool while he's doing his laps.

Ella forces the chair across the thick carpet, her arms trembling, going into the kitchen and up to the worktop, pulling herself out of her chair, standing up as best she can on her good leg. Her broken one throbs as the blood rushes into it. She stares at the knife block, wondering if it's even feasible. She knows they use electric saws in hospital, watched them when they changed her original full-leg cast to this slightly smaller one. But she needs to get mobile, needs to learn to put weight on it, be able to walk. And while Jacob is training in the pool, she will be doing her own exercises here.

She reaches over and takes out the long, serrated bread knife, running her thumb across the blade. Shuddering as she remembers. It's sharp. *Very* sharp. And while she knows what she'd like to do with the knife, she knows she has to bide her time. Get stronger, get fitter.

She sits back into her chair and unwinds the great length of gauze bandage that Sue reapplied before she left hospital, rolling it up neatly as she goes. Underneath that is another sock-like tube bandage, which she slips off. Then there's the raw plaster – crumbling around the top just above her knee.

Ella hears the baby let out a few frustrated cries from the other room as she positions the serrated blade at the top of the cast, the tip pointing down towards her foot. From what she remembers, there's thick cotton wadding underneath the plaster. If she can just saw down to that, she thinks, she can snip through the rest with the big kitchen scissors.

She sets to work, making mini-hacking movements as fast as she can. She can't waste time, but has to be careful too. White dust falls from where she's cutting, getting all over the leg rest of her chair and, worse, all over the floor. She must allow time to clean up, she thinks, moving the knife down another inch or two as she makes progress. It's easier than she imagined, but she can't help glancing down the hallway every few seconds, watching the front door.

She prays he's still in the pool.

For another twenty minutes, Ella hacks at the plaster. She has a clean line running from the top down to her ankle and toes. She does the same to the other side of the cast, but is quicker this time, knowing how deep to saw without hurting herself. When she's done, it makes a satisfying cracking sound as she eases the two halves apart, taking care not to tear the wadding inside. Instead, she reaches into the drawer and grabs the scissors, making clean snips, keeping the padding neatly inside the cast when she pulls the whole lot away.

Ella stares at her leg. It's pale, thin and toneless. A small dressing covers the wound site on her bruised and swollen knee. She wants to cry.

After a few deep breaths, she hoists herself up, standing on her good leg. She attempts a few slow twists of her ankle to see how it feels. Tingling sensations shoot up her leg, transforming into pain. But that's nothing compared to the agony she feels when she dares to lay her foot on the ground, attempting to bear weight on it.

'Owww… *nooo*…' she cries, dropping back down into her wheelchair and reaching into the cupboard where he keeps her pain medication. 'Oh… wait…' she says, rummaging through the many boxes. She's been taking the painkillers he's been dishing out, but, judging by the many empty blister packs, it seems she's been taking something else too. 'Diazepam?' she whispers, staring at the empty packets. But there's no time to wonder, no time to do anything except pop a couple of paracetamol and reach for the damp cloth sitting by the sink, wiping the floor as best she can to get rid of the plaster dust. Standing on one leg, she rinses the cloth and goes at the floor several times more, cleaning up the dust on her chair, too. Then she slides the knife back into its block and the scissors into the drawer.

Another quick try of bearing weight on her bad leg tells her she's going to need a miracle to ever walk on it. Then, conscious of the cameras, of time ticking on, Ella picks up the plaster pieces and positions them back on her leg, securing them in place with the tube bandage, sliding it on. She winds the gauze around and around again until it looks just the same as before. No one would ever know. But now it's ready for next time.

It's only as Ella is swinging her wheelchair round, ready to go back to the now screaming baby, that the lock in the front door clicks and turns. Within seconds, Jacob is in the kitchen, looking around.

'What's this?' he booms, pointing at the floor. His voice is as tight as the muscles in his jaw.

'I'm so stupid,' she says, her heart thumping. 'I was making another bottle for Zach and spilt the milk powder. I'm sorry, it was hard to clean up properly.' She watches and waits, her chest releasing just a little when, after a moment, he nods and slips off his jacket.

Smiling.

CHAPTER THIRTY-FOUR

LIAM

Liam hung up the phone and pushed back in his chair, shivering and suddenly covered in goosebumps. *Really?* he thought to himself. *Had it really been her?* It didn't even sound like the Ella he knew – her voice was different for a start; almost confident, assertive, decisive and in control. She'd even spoken over him. Not like the Ella he knew. And *life-changing injuries*, he thought, shaking his head in disbelief. Poor, *poor* woman. After what he'd discovered at the hospital, he supposed this could be the case. And family looking after her? Her husband, he supposed. He just couldn't believe she'd never mentioned him, or family, before.

'Utterly dreadful,' he said to himself, folding his arms, thinking about how her life had changed so drastically.

'What is?' came a voice from behind.

Liam swung around. Forced a pensive smile. 'Oh… just this clip. I can't seem to get it right.' He batted a hand towards his monitor. Wendy was more and more persistent these days, stopping to chat every time she passed.

'Think you need one of these,' she said, raising the large paper cup of coffee she was holding. 'I can fetch you one, if you like?'

Liam stared at her. No, actually, he was staring beyond her. She just happened to be caught in his line of sight. He shook his head slowly in reply and, eventually, Wendy took the hint and went off, leaving him with a comment about the weather.

'Diana McBride,' Liam whispered to himself, swinging back around in his chair. *What the hell had Ella meant by that?* He knew the name rang a bell but couldn't immediately place it. *And why had she told him to let her know?* In fact, why had Ella even phoned him, and so formally, about her situation in the first place? He wasn't HR or even her boss. He was her equal.

Pondering, he tapped away at his keyboard, running a search in past files for the name. It was on the tip of his tongue and he knew he recognised it from somewhere – a project, perhaps – he just couldn't remember which film. But, just as the results popped up onscreen, it dawned on him – that short piece they'd worked on not so long ago.

Both he and Ella had been involved with it from the start – with Ella, he'd thought at the time, taking far more interest in the project than anything else they'd worked on together. He'd seen the way her expression changed when she viewed the raw footage over and over. Embracing every frame, making it scream out its true meaning, making sure none of the client's vision was lost to heavy-handed editing or tight budgets. They'd sat through meetings together with the rest of the team, thrashing out ideas about how best to get the charity's message across, brainstorming long after the clients had left, injecting their creative input from all angles. It was the most passionate he'd ever seen her.

Crimes like that, he'd thought at the time, were something that happened to other people. Not normal people like them. How would they interpret their client's brief? 'Diana McBride never had a voice,' Ella had said. 'And it is our job to give her one.'

And, ultimately, it was Ella's idea to switch them. The voices.

When the client came in for yet another viewing, with a strong likelihood that the account would be lost if it wasn't right this time, someone – *Ella* – had masterfully overlaid the victim's voice with the perpetrator's on the soundtrack, giving the victim's words to her abuser.

Afterwards, everyone sat in shock, reeling from the impact.

'Genius,' the client had said, vigorously shaking hands with each of them.

Ella's hard-hitting take on their message through the telling of a true story did indeed raise the charity's profile, gaining the exposure they needed, prompting the client to sign up for three more contracts.

'Diana McBride,' he said to himself, reading the title of the file onscreen. He glanced at his watch, knowing that the colour grading work on the clip he'd been assigned needed finishing within the hour. But he clicked it open anyway, playing the film several times.

There was no doubting it, Diana McBride was in a mess.

Made even more poignant after Ella had worked her magic on the film.

But more importantly, Diana was in grave and imminent danger. And, despite her many pleas for help, not one person had taken any notice.

'There's a group of us going to the River Club tonight if you fancy coming along,' Adam said, scrunching up the wrapper from his lunchtime bagel. He drained his Coke can, peering over the top.

'Busy, mate, sorry,' Liam replied. Google Maps had already thrown up a few possibilities and he fully intended to check out as many as he could just as soon as he finished work. *Green* something; he'd been sporadically tapping into the app, making notes for later, underlining the streets that were closer to the south-east as that nurse, Sue, had thought. But more streets than he'd bargained on had 'Green' in their name.

'Anything I should know about? Or, rather, any*one*?' Adam said, adding a playful punch to Liam's shoulder.

'Yeah, she's called "Early Night",' Liam replied, deciding he wasn't good at lying or humour. But Adam didn't seem to care. He was already chatting to someone else in their group, talking about a band, a sports team, some kind of rumour about the company moving offices.

Liam gathered up his rubbish and chucked it in the bin on the way out. As far as he was concerned, 5 p.m. couldn't come quick enough.

Buses weren't going to cut it. As ever, Ken was in the Dog, chucking darts at a board that was mostly filled with holes made by him – many on the surrounding wall. The barman looked up as Liam walked in, reaching for a pint glass, his hand immediately on the Guinness tap – Liam's usual. But he flicked a shake of his head, going over to the oche where Ken stood, taking aim.

'Aye up,' Liam said, hand on Ken's shoulder, making him halt mid-throw. 'Need a favour, mate.'

Ken reached for his virtually empty pint glass, draining it, holding it out. 'See me right,' he said, winking. 'And I'm all ears.'

A new drink bought, a bit of banter, and Liam was soon holding the keys to Ken's van, with his wallet lighter by only a couple of pre-paid drinks and a cab fare home for Ken. Seemed like a fair deal to him, even if the streets of the area he'd driven to were unfamiliar and he'd had to pull over several times to check Google Maps. He squinted at the screen of his phone. Green Acres had proved useless – too far away from the area Sue had described, and Green Fields Avenue and Green Lane, while sort of in the right location, were both filled with old houses, mostly terraced and small. Sue had talked of modern, new, detached and exclusive. To keep focussed, he had to bear in mind what she'd told him. He'd be out searching all night otherwise.

Having said that, none of the things he'd learnt about Ella's home from Sue seemed, well, very *Ella* at all. The place he'd already been to, her little flat in the bland 1970s block, was far more akin to the woman he knew. It was just more *her* – neat and tidy while also, inadvertently, seeming slightly undesirable. As if it – and *she* – didn't want to be wanted.

He ran another street search, again focussing on anything that had the word 'Green' in its name. Green Ways, Lower Greenfield Avenue, Green Street, Greening Lane, Greenleigh Walk… the list was endless, even for the locality and surrounding suburbs. In the end, thirst made him pull into a parking bay and dash into a corner shop opposite. He needed water, perhaps a Mars Bar, too.

'All right,' he said to the lad at the till, handing across his items plus a £5 note. They were rung up, change given back as Liam stared at his phone, shaking his head. He glanced up. 'Any idea if there are any street names with the word "Green" in them around here?' he said, having pretty much written off the list on his phone.

The boy paused, offering up a receipt as the till spewed it out. 'Not really,' he said, glancing at the growing queue behind, scratching his cheek. 'Sorry, mate.'

Liam offered a quick nod and turned to go, stopping as the woman behind him chimed in.

'Green Leys, do you mean?' she said.

'Maybe. Is it near?' He reckoned he was close to the area Sue had hinted at, but it had so far seemed devoid of Green anything that he hadn't already checked out, according to his version of Google Maps, making him think he may not have the latest update.

'Not far,' she said, flicking her hand behind her. 'It's posh. Fairly new.'

'Can you give me directions?' Liam said, listening intently, trying not to get his hopes up.

Even as the surrounding houses gradually changed from average semis and red-brick terraced places into larger, smarter detached homes, Liam felt out of place. Mainly because of Ken's van spewing out a trail of black exhaust and making a loud knocking sound every time he changed gear. The grubby white bodywork – mostly made up of rust and filler – was a stark contrast to the plethora of shiny BMWs and four-wheel drives parked symmetrically in front of the suburban dreams.

Liam slowed and ground down through the gears to second, eventually forcing it into first before the engine cut out completely. The light wasn't good – that awkward place between dusk and darkness – making his eyes see things that weren't really there. He restarted the engine and pulled away, suddenly slowing down again.

Ella?

There was a woman walking a little dog along the street. Her height was about the same, perhaps an inch or so either way. Her hair was the same colour too – nondescript and mousey until you looked closer, saw the magic in the half-light. Liam wasn't sure if Ella had a dog, but he imagined she might. A companion. Someone to talk to, someone to love and be loved by unconditionally.

'Shit!' Liam jammed on the brakes, even though he was only crawling, but it was too late. The screech and blaring horn behind him showed how close to causing an accident he'd come, so he revved up again and continued on. 'Green Leys,' he muttered to himself. 'I *swear* that's what the sign said.' He glanced back over his shoulder but was met with the V-sign from the driver behind.

Up ahead, he found a turning point, swung the old van around and prayed he'd spot where the concealed turning had been when he cruised back. It was only chance that had made him look across to the other side of the street, because of the woman who looked like Ella.

This time when he braked, there was no one behind him and, indeed, he confirmed that the little lane – all block-paved and flanked by sweeping brick walls, large iron gates – was labelled 'Green Leys' on a carved stone plaque set into the wall. There was black iron scroll writing set into the top of the gates, too.

'Christ,' he whispered under his breath, thinking it didn't look at all like somewhere Ella would live – nor likely be on any street maps. But then people can be deceptive, he thought, thinking just how much that might be true. Though he had no idea how Ella's little flat fit into the picture he was forming of her.

He sat at the top of the gated drive, glimpsing the dozen or so properties lining the exclusive-looking street beyond as it dipped down a hill. Trees and landscaping made it look picture perfect – a place inaccessible to the likes of him. To the right, just out of reach from where he'd pulled in, was a panel with a number of brass buzzers on it. One for each property, he assumed. He had no idea which one Ella's house might be and could hardly ring them all. But, just as he was contemplating reversing back out onto the busy road, a black Mercedes came cruising up from inside the gates. They swung open as it approached, narrowly missing the front of the old van as they arced out. And, because the Mercedes pulled away before the gates were fully open, slipping quickly into the main road traffic, Liam was able, on the spur of the moment, to jam the van into first gear and get through before they closed again. Just. He heard a scraping sound down the back panel.

'Ouch, sorry, Ken,' he said, wincing, his heart thumping. He felt even more out of place now he was inside. But he reckoned he could always say he was a tradesman, lost. He was hardly committing a crime.

He slowly drove down Green Leys, peering at the houses in the failing light – each one unique in its own way, though all oddly similar. And something told him, deep inside, that he was one step closer to finding Ella.

CHAPTER THIRTY-FIVE

Ella

All day, Ella has kept the baby awake, stimulating and playing with her even when she wanted to nap, tiring her out so that when six o'clock came, she'd be ready for a long sleep. Even though she's tired herself, Ella can't risk being distracted by the baby's cries.

'There, there,' Ella croons, breaking into a lullaby she remembers from way back. The words are still etched inside her from when she was little, from when her own mother used to sing it. Though Ron soon put a stop to that. 'I love little pussy… her coat is so warm… she sits by the fi-re…'

Finally, the little girl's eyelids grow heavy, her body relaxing and moulding into Ella's shape. Tears fill Ella's eyes as she stares into the gas fire, switched on with the remote control. The flames are mesmerising, drawing her in, taking her back, filling her head with shouting and screaming, the roaring and cracking as timbers collapsed, the intense heat as she realised what she'd done. What she could never *un*do…

Ella gasps suddenly, as though she can't breathe, choking, remembering. She flicks off the flames with the control, wishing it had been that easy back then. The baby startles but soon settles again. When she's finally asleep, Ella risks moving her into the pram, cradling her head, laying her down. She breathes a sigh of relief, sliding into her chair and wheeling into the kitchen. It should buy her half an hour – all she can spare anyway, now that it's just after six, praying that Jacob is in his swimming session.

She unwinds the bandaging, taking the cast off again, placing the pieces of plaster carefully on the floor. Then she hoists herself upright, leaning on the worktop for support. She dosed herself up with pain medication an hour ago, knowing she wouldn't manage without.

'OK,' she says, bracing herself as she rests her bad foot on the floor. Little by little, she allows her weight to shift onto it, gritting her teeth through the pain as her ankle stretches out, followed by her calf muscle, her knee cracking into place – the patella sliding and grinding over the swollen tissue surrounding it – and then the agony as the leg takes her full weight. She bites her lip, scratches her nails against the worktop as she breathes through the pain.

Keep going, keep going, she tells herself, shifting to her good leg then back onto her bad one until she convinces her brain that the biting, crippling shots of torture are almost normal. Then she takes a single step sideways, gripping onto the worktop in case her leg gives way. It won't be her resolve that breaks, she thinks, knowing her body will give up long before her mind.

Slowly, Ella walks herself around the kitchen against the worktop, not daring to let go. It could be her imagination, it could be her determination, but she swears that, by the time she reaches the fridge on the other side of the room, the agony is perhaps one per cent less than when she started. Her cheeks burn scarlet from effort as she walks herself back around to where she began. For the final few steps, she manages to do it without holding on to the worktop.

Then she hears something. Not the baby. Her heart thumps. The noise was more of a bang. A clunk. A car door, perhaps, though the first she hears of Jacob coming back is usually the key in the lock. Ella lets out a whimper – she has no idea how long it's taken her to navigate the worktops but she can't risk Jacob finding her without her cast.

Shit…

She drops down into the seat again, panting, reaching for the cut halves, messily fixing them back in place with the bandages as fast as she can. Then another noise… she pauses, listening. Holding her breath.

All quiet again.

Exhausted and terrified, she wheels herself into the hallway, glancing up at the camera, trying to look unfazed. Back in the living room, she peeks into the pram, watching the baby's little chest rising and falling steadily as she sleeps soundly. But then her attention is suddenly drawn to the window – the curtains still wide open even though it's virtually dark outside now, a thin skim of drizzle winding down the panes of the bay. Two cones of light sweep through the room as a vehicle reaches the end of the cul-de-sac, swinging around outside the house.

For a few seconds, Ella is dazzled, blinded by the full-beam lights in the darkened room. Instinctively, she sinks down in her wheelchair, squinting and blinking as the room grows dim again. It's not Jacob's car, she thinks, wheeling a little closer to the window. Not many people drive this far down the street.

Ella peers out, cautiously sitting to one side of the window, catching sight of the tail end of a white van – like something a builder might use. The throaty engine noise suddenly cuts out as if it's stalled, then the red brake lights come on while the driver turns the ignition a few times. To begin with, it sounds as if it won't start but, after several loud bangs, the engine growls to life again and the van heads off. She didn't get a glimpse of the driver.

Ella lets out a sigh, remembering that Mick, Liz's husband, is a builder. It could be something to do with him, she thinks, doubting it's the police. They'd hardly be looking for a stolen baby in a rusty old van covered in dents. But to be on the safe side, she reaches up and drags the curtains closed.

Then the familiar click in the front door, making her wonder if it *was* Jacob in the van.

Her body tenses and the usual shudder sweeps through her as he comes in, standing there, his eyes flicking around the room, sizing up everything.

'Hello, darling,' he says, beaming at her, his hair still damp. 'How was your day?' He comes over and kisses the top of her head. Ella closes her eyes. 'The baby smells bad,' he says, wrinkling his nose.

'Sorry,' Ella says, leaning into the pram to lift her out. She makes several annoyed cries, curling up her knees and batting at her face. 'Come on, little Meg…' Ella freezes, cursing herself.

'What did you just say?'

'Nothing,' Ella replies, staring down.

'You said: "Come on, *Meg*". Why are you calling the baby Meg?'

'No, no, I didn't,' Ella says, her eyes wide. 'I-I said: "Come on, *mate*". You must have misheard me. Would you like me to fix you a drink?' she adds, holding her breath, desperately trying to appease him.

Just like she always did.

CHAPTER THIRTY-SIX

Ella

Gradually, Ella's routine takes shape. A form of its own. A way of life. A new reality.

Work, home, sleep…

Except now it's different.

Wake up, look after the baby, wait until 6 p.m., mobilise leg, pretend.

And while Jacob is swimming, Ella has managed her own training sessions – shuffling around the kitchen, sweating through the pain as she forces her leg to work. Perhaps, she thinks, she's noticed a little difference in the muscle tone, the lessening of bone grinding on bone. But it could just be a rise in her tolerance to the pain. Tonight, she plans to walk across the kitchen unaided, though the ten or twelve feet might as well be measured in miles.

She lets go. Puts her bad leg forward. Then she bears her weight on it, biting her teeth together, grimacing. She takes a step forward. It's painful but it holds up, so she takes another, and then another. Her heart races and her temples thrum with the pressure of her blood, her body almost catching fire from what she's putting it through.

'Oww…oww-www…' she cries, trying to contain the screams. She takes a couple more lurching steps, arms flailing, making the halfway point. She reckons she's got another fifteen minutes until she has to put the cast back on, before she's in for it.

'In for it,' she whispers through clenched teeth. It drives her on, remembering, seeing his face the very first time he threatened her, the pure bitterness in his eyes where, before, she'd seen nothing but love. It seems like eons ago now.

Ella-bella...

She remembers the first time he ever called her that, too. No one had ever given her a pet name before, not even her mum or Ron, and she'd soaked up the affection. The familiarity, the closeness. It was special. Private between the two of them.

She takes another agonising step, focussing on the fridge, only a couple of feet away now.

'I... can do... this...' she says in laboured, breathy gasps.

Another step.

Then the cry from the other room, knotting up her heart.

Suddenly, she feels dizzy... something triggered. More memories playing through her mind. She puts it down to the pain.

'Let's put things right,' he'd said, leaning on the flimsy wall to her cubicle partition. Ella had turned around at the sound of his voice – half pleased to hear it yet also annoyed that her space had been invaded. She hadn't felt like talking. 'Do you know what I mean?'

'No,' she'd replied. Her chair creaked as she'd turned back to her screen again.

'The overall look of the film... it's just too...' Liam had hesitated then. Searching for the right word. 'Just too fun. It's about bullying, for Christ's sake. The whole look is wrong. It belongs in *The Sound of Music*. Not this brief.'

He was right, Ella knew. But it wasn't her account. She was just the sidekick on this job.

'OK,' she'd said, shrugging, focussing on her work.

But when she'd watched the clip again, Ron had been on her mind. She'd always tried to block him out when the thoughts came, she really had. But all she saw onscreen, then, instead of the actor, was Harry being hauled against the wall by the scruff of his collar. And it was Harry who felt the knee shoved in his young groin, his face spat at, his cheeks filling with blood as Ron threatened him. Touched him. Made everything bad.

'Stop!' Ella had screamed the first time it happened, pushing up between her brother and stepfather. It had made no difference. Ron had swiped her aside. Their mother had been out, of course, working at the hotel, doing long hours to make ends meet. Cleaning, serving, folding.

Afterwards, Ron usually passed out from booze. That's when Ella comforted her brother, let him hug her, sob on her shoulder as she dabbed at his cuts and bruises with wet tissue. She talked to him for hours, told him it was going to be OK, that one day they'd escape, together, that things would change. Harry had sobbed silently against her, hugging her, his cries gradually turning into plans far greater than their miserable existence with Ron and a mother who'd failed them for so many years. As they plotted, they spoke of their real dad, what he would have been like, how much he would have loved them. Neither of them remembered him, only knew his name.

'Ella?' someone said. She'd jumped, turned.

'Oh, sorry.' She'd forgotten Liam was even there, waiting for an answer that wasn't really necessary. To her horror, he'd come into her workspace and sat down on the spare chair.

'You OK?' Liam went on. 'You're…'

'I'm fine,' Ella replied, but then felt the tears on her cheeks. Damn.

'I'm a good listener,' he'd said. 'And I've got a few minutes.'

Ella had laughed then. 'It would take more than that,' she'd said, wishing she hadn't. It was all the opening he'd needed.

'Then how about a drink after work, somewhere quiet. We can chat.'

Ella felt the blood pumping wildly through her heart. That had sounded too much like a date to her. And whatever else she did in her life, she had vowed there would never be any of those again.

'Busy later, sorry,' she'd managed to get out as chirpily as possible, feeling hateful when she'd seen the flicker of sadness register on his face.

But what was worse, was that he had never asked again.

CHAPTER THIRTY-SEVEN

Ten Years Ago

The water shimmered blue-green as Ella gazed beyond the bows of the boat, trying not to feel nauseous. She hadn't come prepared for sailing, had no idea the week-long house party would entail a trip to Southampton, cruising through the choppy waters of the Solent as they headed to Cowes. She sat upfront, pulling her anorak around her. The others were all kitted out in sailing gear and, even though the weather was fine, the wind just enough to fill the sails, it was still chilly and blustery out at sea.

Ella sat on the deck, looking back along the yacht's length. She'd never been on one before. It was a racer, Zach had said, one of his dad's passions, and he'd invited the group of friends along too, although with all of them on board, space was limited. The plan was for some of them to stay overnight in a B&B in Cowes when they arrived. She and Zach would remain on board with his father and a couple of his friends, who were crewing.

She startled as someone came up beside her. 'Deep thought?' Zach said, leaning down and nuzzling her neck. He grabbed onto a winch for support as a wave hit the bows, lowering himself down to sit beside her.

'Trying not to puke, more like,' Ella replied, making a face as the boat heeled even more. Several other yachts were cruising nearby, with their bright tenders bobbing behind as they followed the same tack to port.

'But you're having a good time, right?' Zach said, looking concerned.

Ella frowned. 'Well,' she began. 'It's just…'

'Go on…' Zach tensed, withdrawing his arm from around her waist.

Ella looked at him, noticing something in his eyes. Something not *right*. It reminded her of that time Ron had belted her for laughing at something on the telly. Then he'd kicked his foot through the screen before booting her and Harry off upstairs to bed. They'd held each other for comfort all night long.

'It's just I don't understand why you invited *him*,' Ella said, glancing back down the boat.

Ethan was sitting alone halfway along the port side, coiling and uncoiling a rope. Every so often he'd glance up, stare at her, not looking away until she did. It had happened about five times in the same number of minutes. She didn't want to sound confrontational or ungrateful for being here, but he was creeping her out. Zach had seen how he'd behaved towards her in the coffee shop a while back. She didn't understand.

'You mean Ethan?' Zach said, winding his arm around her waist again.

Ella swept her hair off her face, holding it in a ponytail at the nape of her neck. The wind was getting up.

'He's harmless.'

'No, he's creepy,' Ella said, staring down at her feet. She daren't look at Zach *or* Ethan now. 'He… well, he stares at me all the time. Never says anything to anyone. Why did you invite him?'

'Honestly?' Zach said, sighing. 'Because I felt sorry for him. We shared some lectures together and he seemed lonely. He never spoke to anyone and didn't seem to have any friends. A couple of weeks ago, I approached him and we got chatting. Harry was there, too. He seemed OK and didn't have plans for the summer, so I invited him. That's it really.' Zach shrugged, clearly not thinking it was a big deal. 'I dunno, maybe I felt a bit bad after what happened in the café that time.'

'I think he's got a thing for me,' Ella said. 'You know, like *that*.'

'What, Ethan?' Zach sprayed out laughter. 'I don't think he's got it in him, to be honest.'

'But he was—'

'All right, mate?' Zach suddenly said, glancing behind Ella. 'Not too green, I hope.'

Ella looked up. Ethan was right beside them, clinging onto the side railings. He shook his head. 'I like it,' he said, staring at Ella. 'Nice views,' he added. His face was expressionless, his mouth barely moving.

Ella felt herself shaking, looking to Zach for reassurance. But he gave her none – rather, he was chatting to Ethan about wind direction and nautical miles. Perhaps it was her after all, and not him. All in her mind. Perhaps she'd also imagined that Ethan had been following her, how he'd seemed to be everywhere she was, encountering him at least once a day the last few weeks of term, in places she'd never expected him to be. Probably just coincidence, she tried to convince herself, as she heard Zach's father, Alan, call out that the boat was about to tack. Ella already knew this meant the boom swinging across the deck, the sails flapping wildly until they caught the wind again as the boat lurched in the opposite direction. Now wasn't the time to cause a scene, if one was needed at all.

She took a deep breath. 'Have you sailed before?' she asked Ethan, looking up at him. It was the first thing she'd ever said to him apart from their altercation at the library.

'No,' he said, smiling, appearing grateful that she'd even spoken to him. Ella felt Zach's hand tweak her quickly around the waist before going to take over the helm from his father. Perhaps Ethan was more like her than she realised – a bit of an outsider too.

Ella was about to ask him something else, try to make amends, but he suddenly went deathly pale, his head rocking back and forth, a glazed look in his eyes. He staggered to the other side of the deck and grabbed hold of the rail, just as the sails began billowing noisily above them as the boat changed course.

'You OK?' Ella called out over the loud flapping, but he didn't seem to hear. She got up, making her way over to him. It seemed they were heeling at an even steeper angle. She grabbed hold of a winch for support as she drew up next to him, feeling helpless as he threw up over the side of the boat.

'Oh God, you poor thing,' she said, putting her hands on his back, supporting him. While he was in this state, their differences didn't matter. 'Do you want me to help you get inside?'

But suddenly, Ethan's arms were thrashing about and he stood upright again, yelling and screaming at her.

'Get off! Get *off* me! No, stop it!' His eyes were wide and his pupils huge, his lips sticky with vomit and spit.

Zach and his father quickly made their way back down the deck.

'What on earth's going on?' the older man said, looking panicked, panting, glancing up as the mainsail and jib filled with wind again. He closed up the sailing knife he'd just had to use on a caught rope, trying to get it into a pouch on his jacket, but it wouldn't go in. Stan was at the helm now, craning his neck to see what was going on.

Ethan was clutching his arms around his skinny chest, his face ghostly white, glaring at Ella. He was hyperventilating. 'She-she just went wild and tried to push me overboard,' he said, his voice on the brink of tears. 'She's crazy. I could have died.' His voice was shaking as much as his body as he stared at her, terrified.

Zach's father turned to her, hand on pocket, frowning. 'Ella?' he said, looking shocked. 'Is this true?'

'No, no of *course* it's not. He was throwing up, so I went to see if he was OK. I'd never do anything like that.'

'Oh, Ella…' Zach said, a disappointed look sweeping across his face. He reached out for her arm, but she whipped it away, scowling.

'She's lying,' Ethan said quickly. 'I'd literally just told her I couldn't swim, that I was terrified of falling in. Then she said she wanted to know if scum like me would sink or float. I swear to God that's what happened.'

'Right, enough,' Alan said firmly. 'Ethan, I'll take you down to the cabin to rest while Zach has a word with his girlfriend here. And put this bloody knife somewhere safe, will you, son?' he said, handing it to Zach. They went off towards the stern, Alan gripping on to Ethan's arm so there was no chance of him going overboard.

'What the *hell*…' Ella said, covering her face as she sat down on the deck again. She, too, was close to throwing up, and not because of the swell. 'I don't believe he just did that. And he shouldn't even be on a boat if he can't swim.'

'Ella…' Zach said again, drawing out her name as though he was eking out the truth. He stuck the knife in his own jacket pocket, zipping it up safely.

'*What?*'

Zach stared at her.

'I swear on my life I didn't touch him. You believe me, don't you?'

'When I looked around, you did have your hands on him.'

'Oh for God's sa—'

'I want you,' Zach said suddenly, giving her a look. He had that intense look in his eyes, the one she couldn't quite decipher. Didn't he even care about what Ethan had just done?

Ella stared out to sea, shaking her head, watching as Cowes harbour drew closer. Maybe it was best to let it go, follow Zach's lead. She knew the truth at least. 'I know you do, Zach…' she said. 'But…' She leaned over and kissed his cheek before staring out to sea again, not feeling in the mood.

'Do you love me?' he asked, hooking her face towards him with his fingers under her chin.

'Of course,' she said. 'You know that.'

'So this week with me isn't enough then?' Zach glanced back down the length of the ketch. Alan and his crew were now busying about with ropes, preparing for their arrival at Cowes. Dinner had been planned at a harbour restaurant.

'It's more than enough,' Ella said, the sick feeling in her belly growing. Was she supposed to feel grateful and indebted to him, give herself to him in return for a week's stay at his lavish home? The thought made her feel even more sick and she knew it wasn't just from the sea.

She silently thanked God that Harry was here, that she wasn't as alone as she felt. She caught his eye as he took a turn at the helm, Stan showing him how to navigate. She watched as he stood proud in the aft of the boat, both hands on the huge wheel. Neither of them had ever done anything like this before. He gave her a quick smile and she immediately returned it, reaffirming their connection.

'Then why won't you?…' Zach leaned in and kissed her, sending butterflies through her stomach.

As Ella had discovered many times before, all his kisses were special – each one somehow different to the last – and there had been thousands over the few months they'd been together. She never tired of them. And it seemed he never grew bored of giving them, until now. He pulled away. She knew he wanted more.

'I…' Ella looked pained, didn't know what to say. He'd mentioned sex several times before, of course, and yes, things had got heated, too. But it had only taken a semi-forceful bat of her hand to fend him off. A few giggles, an understanding look to let him know she wasn't ready, though never explaining why. She'd always

sensed his disappointment. Ella wondered if her reserve had only
served to make her more attractive to him. And that the invite to
Adlington was only for one reason.

The party of twelve was seated outside on the terrace of The Shack
– a place that couldn't have been more opposite to its name. Ella's
nauseous stomach had finally quietened. Mostly. Though she couldn't
deny she still felt a twinge of sickness, but not from the sea, or even
Ethan's ridiculous claim about her trying to push him overboard. This
time her stomach lurched when Harry decided to wedge himself in
between her and Zach as they sat at the long table under the giant
patio heaters. Ella noticed the annoyed look on Zach's face when
he pulled up a chair between them. His father was paying, after all.

'How you doing, sis?' Harry said, shifting back a bit when he
saw the warning look on Ella's face.

'I'm having a wonderful time,' she said, making sure Zach heard.

'Bring more champagne,' Zach said to the waitress, though his
stare was fixed on Harry's back.

'Shift around a bit,' Ella whispered to Harry, giving him another
look. She tried to catch Zach's eye again, wanted to give him a
smile, reassure him her brother wasn't being rude as such, but he
didn't look her way. He was chatting to the waitress about sailing.

'You really don't have any idea, do you?' Harry said under his
breath, broadening his shoulders so Zach was further excluded.

'About what?' Ella sipped her water, pretended to read the
menu, while keeping one ear on Zach and the pretty waitress.

'About those two.'

Ella looked at her brother. 'Those two who?' She was trying
to keep her voice down, but knew by Harry's tone that he was
serious. About what, she had no idea.

Harry leaned closer. 'Zach and Meggie,' he whispered, raising
his eyebrows. 'Everyone sees it except you.'

'Sees *what*?' Ella's voice wavered as she saw Zach place his hand on the waitress's arm, giving her a broad smile. She swallowed, bracing herself for what Harry would say next. But he just raised his eyebrows instead. 'For God's sake, just tell me, Harry,' she said after the girl finally went to fetch the drinks. 'You can't say something like that and leave me hanging.' She prayed Zach couldn't hear.

Harry opened his mouth to speak, had the kind of look on his face that told Ella he didn't want to have to say what he was about to but, as her brother, he felt he needed to. But he suddenly stopped. Meggie was beside them, giggling in Ella's ear.

'I'm going to the loo,' she said. 'Coming?'

Ella looked away, staring at the tail end of the sunset to the west, the orange streaks gradually diffusing into darkness below the masts. She was going to reply but stopped, shaking her head at Meggie instead, looking away quickly again.

'I don't believe you,' she whispered to Harry when she'd gone.

'Well do what you always do,' he said, raising his eyebrows. 'Deny everything, as though it's not happening. You can't go through life with your eyes shut, Ella.' He reached out to take her hand, but she pulled it away. 'Don't say I didn't warn you.'

She stared out across the water again, scanning her mind for anything that might confirm what Harry had said. She'd never found Zach alone with Meggie, or even caught him looking at her. Not in that way, anyway. They'd known each other for years, she knew that, but had only ever thought they were friends, nothing more. But then Ella was thinking about that time at Durham, when Meggie had turned moody and cold about her coming to Adlington, and how she'd arrived at the manor before her, now making her wonder if she'd been excluded on purpose or Meggie had somehow engineered it. She shook her head. She knew Zach was crazy about her. Surely Harry was wrong.

As the champagne flowed, the chatter around the table escalated with everyone in good spirits. Zach's father was sitting with his two friends and crew, Sally and Don, at the other end of the table, while the rest of the group discussed jobs and autumn plans. Ella remained silent, catching Alan's eye once or twice, knowing he didn't believe her about Ethan and the incident on board. In fact, he seemed to have taken the boy under his wing since it happened, inviting him to sit at the other end with his friends when Ethan couldn't find a seat. Perhaps, Ella thought, Alan disapproved of his only son's choice of girlfriend, imagining that a girl from a council estate in Birmingham wasn't suitable wife material. Then Meggie was on her mind again – beautiful, rich, the two families close.

She took a large sip of champagne as her eyes filled with tears, refusing to think about what Harry had said, grateful that he had finally moved his chair. And, by the time their food arrived, Ella was chatting and laughing again, making herself join in as if nothing was wrong. She didn't want to spoil the evening.

'OK, you lot,' she said to the group after they'd eaten. 'Photo time.' She reached down into her bag, feeling around for the digital camera Zach had bought for her in Durham. She'd not used it much yet and wanted to capture the moment. But then her hand felt something strange in her bag, making her pull it up onto her lap, peering inside. Her mouth dropped open. It was filled with… with *crumbs*. There was what looked like almost an entire packet of broken crackers smashed up and dropped in her bag – the wrapper too. All her stuff was covered in the mess.

Ella froze, trying not to react, feeling tears prickle her eyes again as she scanned around the table to see if anyone had noticed. The only person looking at her was Charles, sitting a few places away and eyeing her from over the rim of his champagne glass, his hand resting on the table, a cigarette burning down between his fingers. She quickly looked away again, zipping up her bag and placing it on the floor, praying the shock hadn't shown on her face. The photographs would have to wait.

CHAPTER THIRTY-EIGHT

Ella

Ella takes the bowl from the fridge just as the doorbell sounds, the loud chime making her jump. She startles at the slightest thing these days, even flinching if the baby raises her little arm, clenching her tiny fist. She's torn, doesn't know what to do as she sits in her wheelchair in front of the fridge, the door wide open, the chill from inside wafting down on her as she stares at the bowl in her hand.

'Coo-*eee*,' comes Liz's familiar voice. 'You in there, Ella?'

Of course I am, Ella thinks, staring at the congealed porridge Jacob made for her before he left. It has powder crusting around the edge, as if something hasn't been mixed in properly. It doesn't look like sugar, she thinks, dipping her finger into it. She tastes it just as the doorbell rings again, immediately screwing up her face from its bitter taste. She shoves it back in the fridge, starving, wheeling herself to the front door, eyeing the camera as she goes.

'Hi,' she says nervously when Liz's blinking eye appears the other side of the letterbox.

'I've got the keys,' Liz says cheerily. 'Can I come in?'

Ella pauses, knowing for certain now that Jacob only puts the door alarm on at night. He can't set it from outside.

'OK,' she says, just wanting Liz to go away. But she knows she won't give up, not with what she knows about the baby's sex. The more Liz gets suspicious, the more likely it'll get back to Rachel's husband, Pete. She can't risk questions being asked.

Because she has no answers.

Ella hears the lock turning and, a second later, Liz is standing there, wearing a bright-orange padded jacket, jeans and trainers. She's got a leather handbag slung over her shoulder and her face glows from the chilly morning.

'Shopping day!' she announces with a massive grin.

'What?' Ella's tongue feels dry and sticky from whatever she's just eaten. It reminds her of… of being in hospital.

'I'm taking you out shopping. It's cold but lovely out there. You get yourself ready and I'll sort little… little Zach, eh? I won't take no for an answer.'

Ella stares at her, already feeling exhausted. She can't possibly go out.

Can she?

'I don't think…' She pulls a face, glances to the living room where the baby is stirring. Heart-wrenching sounds building up to a full-blown cry.

'Well, I *do* think,' Liz says. 'And it's time you got out of here. For a start, your little one needs some toys. I know it's been tough lately, and that Jacob works long hours, but you could do with a break, right? It's like you're a prisoner in this house.'

Ella's eyes fill with tears before she can stop them. She gives a little nod. 'That's kind,' she says, her voice weak. 'But Jacob prefers it if I stay home. He-he worries about me.'

'Well he needn't worry while you're with me. Let's call him now and tell him where we're going. And you can text him while we're out to tell him you're OK.'

'It's not that simple,' Ella goes on, wheeling through to the living room. She scoops the baby from her pram, rubbing her back.

Liz follows her through, sits down on the sofa.

'Oh, I think it is,' she says, reaching out and touching Ella's arm.

*

It's been weeks, no months, *years*, even, since Ella has done any-thing like this – gone out to a big shopping centre. She can hardly breathe. Not only did leaving the house in full view of the cameras send her heart racing, but driving all this way with a stolen baby in the back of Liz's car, strapped into a car seat borrowed from Steph, has sent her into a flat spin. And Liz keeps on chatting as if nothing's wrong.

'Oh my God, I just have to get one. Don't you agree?'

Ella stares out of the windscreen. Rigid. Not listening.

'Plus I'm in dire need of new shoes. Maybe you can help me choose. Mick's a darling but he hates shopping. I totally need advice. Something comfy and good for winter yet stylish as well.' Liz glances across. 'Maybe you could treat yourself, too. Is there anything you need?'

Ella concedes a look in return, wishing Liz could read her mind.

'Not really,' she says, as they pull into the underground car park. Her stomach lurches as they go round the spiral ramp, downwards. Ever downwards.

'How about you call Jacob now, let him know where you are?'

Ella clenches her fists. 'Oh, I'm pretty sure he already knows I've left the house,' she says, biting her lip, gripping onto her cycling backpack that Liz had foisted on her as they left, assuming it was her day-to-day handbag. She'd stuffed a few nappies and provisions for the baby in there, going on and on about how they were going to the baby shop to get more stuff. Then she'd helped Ella into the car, packing up her wheelchair and the pram. There was no stopping her.

'I saw your phone in your bag,' Liz goes on. 'You could put his mind at rest. He obviously worries.'

'It's out of charge,' Ella says, grateful for the reprieve. 'In fact, I don't have a charger any more. It kind of... well, it got lost.'

'Then we shall buy you a new one,' Liz announces. 'So you can stay connected. You're cut off enough as it is,' she goes on. 'Nothing quite so isolating as having a young baby and being stuck at home. We have a Green Leys WhatsApp group you can join, and there's the local Facebook page for various goings-on. You'd be most welcome.'

Ella tries to smile but it won't come. 'I don't have Facebook or stuff like that,' she says, which is at least the truth.

Liz pulls into a space, wrenches on the handbrake and gets out of the car, busying behind it with the wheelchair, the pram, helping both her and the baby get settled. As they head for the lift and the shops, Ella wheeling herself, which is hard with her bad arm, she looks up at Liz as she pushes the pram beside her.

'Thanks,' she says, actually forcing a little smile this time. And, as they wait for the lift to arrive, Ella can't help glancing up, spotting the CCTV cameras positioned all around them.

*

'Oh. My. God,' Liz says. 'This is just so utterly adorable.' She holds up a little coat and matching knitted hat in the baby shop. 'Do you have one of these for winter? She… I mean *he's* going to need one,' she adds, blushing at her mistake. 'And it's the perfect colour, all things considered.'

Ella stares at the cream and green jacket, suitable for a boy or a girl. She forces a smile. 'We can keep looking,' she says, catching sight of the price tag. Nearly thirty pounds. Apart from a bit of loose change in her pack, she has no money and, despite looking, she couldn't find her purse anywhere at the house. Besides, she doesn't think she's even spent that much on a coat for herself. She closes her eyes for a second before wheeling away, staring at the door of the shop and the crowds beyond, wondering how she could somehow lose Liz and get away.

Half an hour later, they leave the baby shop with several carrier bags of stuff hooked over the handles of Ella's chair. Liz insisted on paying.

'I know Jacob will pay me back,' she said, winking. Half a dozen brightly coloured and noisy toys, the same number of new sleepsuits, several day outfits and the padded coat and hat are all in the bags, not to mention the extra nappies, wipes, various creams that Ella doesn't even know what to do with, and new bottles and, to Ella's horror, little jars of baby food.

'He's meant to be eating actual real food?' she asks when they stop at a coffee kiosk near the escalators in the mall.

Liz looks down at her with a kind smile. 'Yes, *she* is.'

Ella takes the coffee gratefully. 'I-I didn't know.'

Liz sits down at one of the bistro tables set around the kiosk. 'Jacob can get help, you know, for his issues. Can you talk to your health visitor about it?'

Ella looks away briefly. 'Please don't tell him I told you. He'd be so embarrassed.' So *mad*, she thinks.

Liz rolls her lips together. 'I won't. But you need to get support, Ella. This won't just go away on its own. Especially when it's time to think about nurseries or school.'

'I know,' Ella says, praying to God she'll be long gone by then. She sips her coffee, watching other shoppers. Mothers with their pre-school children in tow, some pushing prams or pushchairs too, a couple of guys in suits walking briskly past – phones pressed to their ears. A group of teenagers who look to Ella as though they're bunking off school, loitering at the top of the escalators. Lots of normal people going about their normal lives. None, that she can see, with broken bones or a stolen baby. And definitely none with a secret as huge as hers. Tears fill her eyes.

'Right,' Liz says, when they've finished their coffees, 'let's go in search of shoes.'

The baby is getting restless, so Liz grabs one of the toys from the shopping bags and tears open the packaging. 'Here you go,' she coos, shaking the bright green and yellow rattle. It's the same colour as the zigzags on the pram, or rather the colour they once were, Ella thinks, noticing the grubby marks on the luminous flashes.

'Oh! I'm *so* sorry,' Liz says, accidentally knocking into a couple of lads with the pram as they head off.

'Watch it, yeah, lady?' one yells back, rubbing at his leg, scowling.

'I really didn't mean to,' she replies, raising her hands as the boys yell out obscenities, making a scene. 'I'm out of practice,' she says to Ella, looking worried as the boys walk off, still shouting.

But Ella is more concerned by the two security officers patrolling nearby – their heads craning to see where the commotion is coming from. She's not sure if they saw what happened or if they spotted Liz, her, or, indeed, the baby. But they keep on going regardless, Ella wheeling as fast as she can until they're swallowed up by the crowds, disappearing into the lift, the doors finally closing behind them.

CHAPTER THIRTY-NINE

Liam

Liam didn't sleep. After driving down Green Leys last night and discovering nothing useful, he felt angry at himself for getting cold feet. It had been nearly dark by the time he'd found it, and he was still drawn to the place this morning, sensing he'd got so close to Ella. It had been the curtain twitching in someone's front window that had made him turn around at the end of the cul-de-sac and head off. He'd made enough of a spectacle of himself with the old van stalling, refusing to start immediately, chugging out exhaust. Green Leys was so quiet, so exclusive, that he'd reckoned someone like him would stand out like a sore thumb. He needed a different tactic, he'd thought.

And it was his mum, early this morning who, inadvertently, had come to the rescue.

When he'd taken her a cup of tea in bed, he could see she still wasn't feeling very well – she'd been bad for a few days and her cough had turned into a chest infection. She'd been prescribed antibiotics and signed off work for a week. Her face was pale and drawn, yet he could see she was fretting about all the things she had to do.

'Mum, I'm here, OK? I'll help. I just want you to rest.'

'And the car's supposed to be having it's MOT tomorrow,' she went on, half-covering her mouth. 'I'll get into loads of trouble if—'

'Mum, stop,' Liam said, plumping up her pillows. 'I'll take it to the garage for you.'

Then Liam's mind was whirring. If his mum was off work and she wanted him to run a few errands for her, it surely wouldn't be unreasonable of him to borrow the car? The cat had to go to the vet for its vaccinations, she'd promised a friend a lift to the station, a package needed picking up from the post office... these were all things he could do, if he had wheels.

'Thanks, son,' she said, coughing again. 'It's the MOT that's the most important. My insurance will be invalid if—'

'Mum, I've got it covered. But I'll need to borrow the car for a couple of days, if that's OK?'

She nodded, smiling briefly before resting her head back down on the pillow and closing her eyes. Liam felt her forehead, adjusted her bedding before he left. He loved his mum and promised to check on her later.

Liam called the office from the car, leaving a message that he was off sick, that he was going to the doctor's, adding in a few coughs for good measure. He felt guilty, of course, but would feel more guilty if he didn't head back to Green Leys to find out if Ella was there.

Three times he cruised past the entrance to the gated estate, the autumn sun angling low, dazzling him, and three times the gates were closed. He'd struck lucky last night, of course, with that other car coming out, him slipping in afterwards. But not so much luck now. He would need to wait it out. He glanced at his watch as he sat in a bus stop, seeing a double-decker approaching in the rear-view mirror.

The bus hooted, looming large behind, so Liam drove off, going up and down the same stretch of road, waiting until someone came in or out of Green Leys so he could slip in. He did yet another U-turn and, as it happened, he didn't have to wait much longer.

He'd lost count of the number of times he'd cruised by but, just as the turn was coming up on his left yet again, the car in front put its indicator on. Liam's heart kicked up as he tailgated it, watching as the gates slowly swung open, hoping the driver of the car in front didn't get suspicious as he stayed bumper-to-bumper.

As he drove through, he supposed the crunching sound wasn't *too* bad as the gates closed behind him, that he might be able to have a word with the garage when he took the car for its MOT. But for now, he was just relieved to be inside Green Leys again, in a decent-looking vehicle, and that it was daylight.

He'd come prepared this time. Briefcase, mobile phone, smart jacket and trousers. Even put on some aftershave, just in case. Midway down the cul-de-sac, he pulled over in an unobtrusive place under a couple of trees and got out of the car, looking around. There was only one way to recce the street and that was on foot. In his head, he tried to think like a door-to-door salesman, though he had no idea what he was actually selling.

'Hi,' he said cheerfully when a woman opened the door. He'd decided to pick a random house rather than starting at the top of the road. 'I'm, um, doing a local survey about streetlights,' he said, quite proud of himself for literally thinking of this as he approached. He reckoned the sales tactic would get the door slammed in his face.

'Oh, OK,' the woman said, looking bored already.

It didn't matter. It wasn't Ella.

The next house wasn't her either and, thankfully, the woman – the cleaner, he reckoned – seemed to be in a hurry to get back inside. The couple of doors he knocked on after that didn't answer, but then he spent the next ten minutes in conversation with a very nice lady, about the same age as Ella, with a baby in her arms. She clearly felt passionate about lighting in the area. Liam pretended to make notes.

'And what's it going to be like when Milly grows up and wants to go out with her friends? I can't have her walking back from the bus stop down a dark street, can I? We moved here with the knowledge that the council had plans to adopt the street and put in better lighting.'

Liam found himself switching off. All he could think was that her baby was, well, just a *baby*. It was almost a lifetime away until she'd need to be walking alone down a dark street, but he pretended to be interested anyway. He'd started it, after all.

'Thank you, you've been very helpful, Mrs?...'

'Steph,' she said. 'And you've got Liz who lives over there.' She pointed to a nearby house. 'She'll have a lot to say about this; though, she's not home at the moment. She's gone out with the girl from next door but one to her. If you come back later and knock at number 11, make sure you give her a chance to answer. She's in a wheelchair.'

Liam felt the ground move beneath him.

Bingo!

'Ok*aay*,' he said, forcing himself not to hug her. 'Number 11, you say?'

Steph nodded, suddenly looking more cautious, as though he could be some weirdo stalker. 'She doesn't always answer.'

Liam thanked her and walked off down the drive, veering to another house first, one he'd already visited that he knew was empty, just until Steph gave up watching him and closed her front door.

The number 11 plaque was hidden behind a twiggy, leafless clematis that climbed up the front of the house, but Liam could identify it well enough. It was the last house of the street, one of two down at the end of the cul-de-sac. Right where he'd turned the van around last night, making a meal of it, drawing attention to himself. He wondered if Ella had seen.

He was about to ring the bell but something stopped him. Possibly Steph's words about Ella not always answering, or maybe something else – a feeling that he wanted further confirmation it was actually her house.

Liam crept up to the front bay window. At first glance, there was no sign of anyone inside, though the sparse contents of the living room made it seem as though someone had not long moved in – which would fit with what Sue had told him. Two large sofas, a low table. A rug. Some packing boxes over in one corner. A few other bits – including a baby's half-finished feeding bottle on the table, a mug, a packet of disposable nappies on the floor, some wet wipes. Ella had never mentioned a baby.

It wasn't particularly homely, Liam thought. And then he spotted the camera up in the corner of the room, right next to the sensor for the burglar alarm.

He walked back past the front door again, noticing a tall wooden gate leading down the side of the property. He tried it, but it was locked. Locked and with very sharp spikes across the top. Someone here was certainly concerned about security. At the front door, he was about to knock, but decided to be cheeky and peer in through the letterbox. Just to see.

The first thing he spotted, when he looked up, was another camera at the other end of the hallway, aimed right at him. Likely filming him, he thought, judging by the red light on it. Then he glanced around – a pair of men's black shoes were placed neatly beside an under-stairs cupboard, a sweater draped over the bannister rail, a couple of large framed photographs on the wall – from what he could make out, they looked quite old but seemed to be taken on a sailing boat.

And then he saw the waterproof jacket on the floor at the bottom of the stairs, as though it had slipped off the bannister. It was black and orange with white visibility bands around the arm. But, more recognisable, was the wording emblazoned on the back. *Team Durham*. It was undeniably the jacket that Ella wore to cycle to work. Every single day.

Liam rang the bell. Then he rang it again and again, waiting in case Ella was struggling to get to the door. After he'd knocked a few times, rang yet again, he pulled out a notepad and pen from his pocket, scribbling down his name, phone number, followed by a quick message.

Came round to see how you are. Give me a call. L x

And then he posted it through the letterbox.

CHAPTER FORTY

Ella

'Oh fuck,' Ella says, unable to help herself as they pull up outside Liz's house. She doesn't like swearing, but seeing Jacob's car on their drive, she can't help it.

'What's wrong?' Liz says, turning off the engine. Ella knows she's turned pale, feels her entire body is shaking from its core. 'Love?'

Ella just stares at the silver BMW, noticing how it's not parked neatly as it usually is, rather, it has been left haphazardly and diagonally across the driveway, almost as though he's handbrake-turned onto the paving. And the driver's window is down. Jacob would never normally do that. She knows his habits, the precision and order by which he lives.

'Is that Jacob home already?'

Ella gives a tiny nod.

'Were you not expecting him?'

'No, no I wasn't,' she whispers, even though, deep down, she was. Of *course* she was expecting him, she thinks to herself. She went *out*. Cameras don't lie. Now she will pay the price.

'You should have called him,' Liz says, way more cheerfully than is warranted. 'He's probably worried about you.' She reaches out and strokes Ella's arm. 'Once he knows you're home, he'll be relieved. Besides, you won't ever have a flat phone battery again now, will you?' She reaches behind into the back, retrieving the bag containing the new charger. 'Here. Don't forget it. I'll fetch your wheelchair and get… and get Zach sorted.'

She's about to get out of the car but stops, letting out a little sigh. 'I'm always happy to talk, Ella. Figure out how to get you some help, if you need it,' she adds, pausing. 'My sister, she had something similar going on for years. She never said a word until… well, until things got really bad.'

Ella whips around. 'It's fine,' she says with a smile, unclicking her seatbelt, forcing her shaking hands to be steady, her racing heart to slow. She stuffs the phone charger inside her backpack.

Liz nods. 'OK,' she says finally, getting out.

When they get to the door – Ella in her wheelchair, Liz pushing the pram, the shopping inside it as she cradles the baby – Jacob is standing there, a thunderous look on his face. Though Ella doubts Liz notices. To everyone else, he will look as though he's just waiting to greet his wife. Relieved she's home.

'My fault!' Liz sings out cheerily. 'I stole her away for a few hours. But look, we got a good haul.' Liz points to the pram contents, offering up the baby to Jacob. But he just stands there, glaring down at Ella.

'Wow,' he says flatly, without looking at the bags. 'You *have* been busy.' Then, reluctantly, he manoeuvres the pram inside, and comes back for Ella – shoving her chair up the ramp. Finally, he retrieves the baby from Liz, blocking her way inside when it's clear she wants to come in.

'Bye, then,' Jacob says, closing the door and locking it.

He strides inside, the baby fretting in his grip, before he dumps it in Ella's lap. Then he lifts his leg high, kicking the pram hard, sending it onto its side, stamping on a couple of the bags. 'Fucking stupid bitch,' he spits at Ella, his face up close.

He goes to the kitchen and pours himself a large drink. It's only three thirty.

'What the *hell* do you think you're doing?' he says, following her into the living room, grabbing her wheelchair handle, shaking it so her whole body lurches.

Sobbing, she steadies the baby perched on her lap.

'Nothing. I—'

'*Nothing?* I don't call leaving this fucking house *nothing...*' Jacob paces about, going up to the window, whipping the curtains closed. 'I checked the cameras from the office. You weren't here. I came home and...' Jacob's face turns beetroot. '*Anything* could have happened,' he says, his fists balled by his side, his shoulders heaving up and down. His breaths are shallow, laboured, rasping. 'Do you *want* me to turn you in?'

'I'm back, aren't I?' Ella says quietly, instantly regretting it.

He comes up to her, looming over her wheelchair. Ella covers the baby's head. Cowers. Closes her eyes, waiting for the blow.

It doesn't come.

'You risked all this, Ella. Our life together. Everything we ever wanted.' He sweeps his hand around the room, sounding calmer, almost remorseful. 'I just couldn't stand to lose you again.' He glugs the last of his drink. 'And if all this isn't bad enough, a *friend* of yours stopped by.'

Slowly, Ella looks up, opens her eyes. The baby squirms on her lap, so she hoists her up, settles her on her shoulder, patting her back.

'Friend?' she says. 'What friend?'

She doesn't have any friends.

'He even left his number,' Jacob goes on, smirking down at her, back in control. 'But it's OK. I phoned him. Told him you were fine.'

Ella wants to speak, but can't. Her throat has closed up, useless. Filled with fear. Choked.

'And you know what else I did?'

She gives a tiny, terrified shake of her head.

'I invited him to our house-warming party.' Jacob grins, his mouth twisting into an awkward slash, igniting memories. She can hardly stand to look at him.

'Party?'

'I thought it would be nice. What a shame you weren't here when he stopped by. What a shame that you were *out*. This is not how things should be, Ella-bella.' He crouches down beside her. His breathing loud. 'No, no, *no*.'

Ella's heart pounds – just the same as it always used to when he got angry – that swollen thump in her chest, nothing like a normal beat. 'A party might be nice,' she says, behaving the only way she knows. 'We can invite the neighbours. We're settling in around here, Jacob. Becoming part of the community.' Her voice is shaking, terrified that someone's found out where she is.

'Aren't we just,' he says, striding off to the kitchen. He returns with another drink for himself and the bowl of cold porridge that Ella left. 'Eat.' He thrusts it at her, grabbing the baby away.

Immediately, he – *she* – begins to cry.

'Eat!' Jacob yells.

The baby cries louder.

Ella does as she's told, staring up at him, trying not to retch as she takes morsels of porridge off the spoon. It tastes vile – *diazepam*, she thinks, remembering the empty packets in the kitchen, silently praying that tonight, of all nights, she stays alert. The drugs don't take long to work.

'I don't want you ever, *ever* to leave this house again unless it's with me. Understand?'

Ella nods, porridge stuck around her mouth. She can't take her eyes off Jacob, holding the baby like he is, her head hanging down from the crook of his arm.

'You do know what will happen otherwise?'

She nods again, her cheeks full, her lips sticky.

'The tape has *everything* you did on it. And it's safely hidden away.' His eyes flick upwards involuntarily, suggesting to Ella it's in this house somewhere.

She screws up her eyes as thoughts of that night thunder through her mind – *the alcohol, the drugs, the blood, the flames. The camera.*

The baby screams even more – wriggling, thrashing about.

'Please, don't hurt her,' Ella pleads.

Jacob tenses, scowls. '*Her?*' He holds the baby out in front of him. 'What are you talking about?' Then he lays her down on the floor, pulling off the all-in-one suit, about to peel back the nappy.

'No, don't! Zach doesn't need changing,' she says. 'I just did it. It's time for his nap now. Give him to me.' She reaches out her arms.

But Jacob ignores her, unsticks the nappy tabs, pulling forward the front. Stares down at the baby.

Then he spits on the floor, narrowly missing Kayleigh's bare tummy, before getting up and swiping Ella around the head, almost knocking her out of her chair.

CHAPTER FORTY-ONE

Ella

Ella lay on the sofa for the entire night, drifting in and out of sleep, the baby in the pram beside her, fidgeting and whimpering for hours at a time. She tried to settle her but couldn't. Jacob got drunk, eventually staggering upstairs around midnight, leaving Ella relieved she didn't have to be pressed up in bed next to him.

Now, at dawn, she wakes – sweating, still wearing the tracksuit she had on yesterday. Early-morning light filters in through the gap in the curtains and there's a bad smell in the air. The baby's nappy. She hauls herself up, her limbs stiff and sore, her neck worse, and hobbles the couple of steps across to the wheelchair, managing to use her broken leg a little more since she's been doing the exercises. But underneath the bandages, the cast is unstable, not providing support.

Ella lifts the baby from the pram and sorts out her nappy, forcing herself to go into the kitchen, the baby on her knee as she wheels through, mixing up a feed as best she can. It looks lumpy, but she guzzles it down greedily, making contended noises, her hands pawing at the bottle.

'How are my two favourite people,' Jacob says, startling her as he comes into the kitchen. She cowers as he leans down and kisses her head, giving the baby one too. 'My little boy,' he says, stroking her cheek. 'Well?' he says, staring directly at Ella, hands on hips.

'Fine,' she says, forcing a smile, wondering how his mood can change so quickly. She watches as he busies about, making himself coffee and toast – just like any normal husband – before he grabs his jacket and work bag, heading to the door.

'See you tonight, my darling,' he calls out, blowing her a kiss.

Ella doesn't say a word, just watches him leave, hearing the key turn in the lock afterwards. It wouldn't make a difference if he left it wide open, she thinks. She can't go anywhere. Then she's reminded of the videotape again, wondering if she could somehow find it. Destroy it.

Back in the living room, Ella lays the baby down on the rug with some of her new toys. She's discovered she likes lying on her front, pushing herself along with her back feet and knees, sometimes rolling over then back again.

While the baby's preoccupied, Ella decides she will charge her phone. She daren't call anyone, of course, but wants to read back through a few work messages, reconnect with her old life. Plus, she's kept all the messages from her mum, even though she died eleven months ago, just before Christmas. Not that they were in touch very often – just the occasional text here and there. The twice-yearly duty visits. Forgiveness was hard.

She fetches her pack from the hallway and rummages through it, pulling out the new phone charger Liz bought her. Digging deep, her hand fishes around, feeling for her phone – she knows it's in there somewhere. Jacob knew it was useless without a charger. Didn't bother taking it from her. Tissues, a pen, loose change, her book… then her hand hits something cold, hard, unfamiliar. She pulls out whatever it is.

Keys.

Ella frowns, staring at them. She knows for a fact there were no keys in there before she went out yesterday – Jacob had sent her old flat keys back to her landlord. She'd been through the entire bag several times before, looking for anything useful.

Yet now she has a set in her hand. One for a Yale lock and one for a deadlock.

She glances at the front door, then at the camera above. She will bide her time until he swims. No point in trying them yet. If they fit, then there's only one place they've come from.

Liz.

*

For the next three hours, Ella sits on the floor playing tirelessly with baby Meggie. It was hard to get down there with her casts, but she's learnt to use the sofa to haul herself up again. She tickles the baby until she giggles, sings to her, tells her stories, plays with the new toys over and over and over until Meggie hurls them away.

Then it's time for her lunchtime feed. She guzzles the bottle, falling asleep while doing so, though Ella keeps waking her, makes her take all the milk. When there's no hope of rousing her, she places her in her pram and covers her up. She's never seen her so deeply asleep.

'Right,' Ella whispers, wheeling out of the room. 'The tape,' she says, knowing that finding it is a long shot. She's pretty much searched through everything kept on the ground floor since she's been here, but she gives the study a quick check again before the task of heaving herself up the stairs.

She pulls open the desk drawers, but is sure Jacob wouldn't be so careless leaving it there. It could even be at his work or stored in the bank. Every time she thinks of it, her stomach burns, her heart races. By the time she knew it was filming, it was too late. The damage had been done. Blood spilled. And then the terrible aftermath. A smoke-filled haze in her mind, not something her brain can piece together or make sense of. She's blocked it all out for the last decade, gradually believing none of it had ever happened.

Ella opens the only other cupboard in the room – hopeful for a moment when she spots a few CDs, some books. But there are no tapes. No home movies from when camcorders were popular. She gives the kitchen a quick once-over, but she's already familiar with the skeleton contents.

She wheels herself to the bottom of the stairs, listening out for Meggie. She hears the soft wheezes of her breathing, she's still soundly asleep, so Ella manoeuvres herself out of her chair and onto the bottom step ready to push herself up.

A mountain she thought she'd never have to climb.

Ella kicks back with her good leg, balancing on her unbroken arm, hoisting herself up the first step. Then she does it again and again, dragging up her semi-useless leg behind her. She thinks the bone has healed enough to support a little of her weight, but she remembers Sue saying it would be at least three months before she'd be able to walk unaided. She can't stand the thought of being trapped here that long.

Sue… the hospital… it seems so long ago now.

Her mind drifts back even further – a movie on rewind. Year after year of her life streaming by in reverse, everything she's ever said played back – her voice fast and high-pitched, her actions a speeding blur.

Work, home, sleep…

Then it slows… to that night. To when everything turned bad. Perhaps she's got it wrong, she thinks, touching her head, closing her eyes. Perhaps none of it ever happened. Or, if it did, maybe there's some way she can edit it, make it not seem so bad in her mind. Manipulate the footage in her mental post-production suite. Rewrite history. Undo everything. Make it all better.

She didn't mean it… It wasn't her fault…

And then Ron is on her mind, everything he did to her and Harry. Her mum, her job, her little flat with its lino kitchen floor and the shower that leaked so she had to mop it up with a towel after she'd used it. Her bike, wherever that is now, and the embroidery piece she was working on, her sandwiches in the fridge at work that didn't really chill anything properly, the women in HR who always gave her a cheery hello, the bald guy in the corner shop where she'd sometimes buy chocolate, Wendy, the girl in the office whose nails were always so perfectly painted, Liam – his chats, his smile, his kindness…

Something feels wet. Ella realises it's her face.

She wipes the tears. Sniffs. Keeps on climbing.

On the landing, she crawls from one room to the next, searching through the couple of boxes in the spare room, though she only finds her own pathetic belongings, shoved in by Jacob – not caring if her clothes were creased, her books damaged, a vase cracked. There are a few other things of his there, too – shoes, winter coats, yachting magazines, photography equipment, old university books. She moves into their bedroom, managing to stand up just enough to reach the cupboards above the wardrobe.

No tapes. Not even a whiff of a camcorder.

She crawls back to the landing and lies on her back on the floor, staring up. It's hopeless. It could be anywhere.

Then she sees it. The loft hatch. Slightly displaced and with grubby handprints on it, as though someone has recently opened it. Everything else in the house is freshly painted. Barely a mark. Pristine.

Except the hatch in the ceiling.

For a while, she lies there, studying it, drifting between the past and the present, not knowing what's real, what's not. There's no way she can get into the loft. Not with her leg like this. The tears come again. This time, in frustration.

Then a noise makes her jump.

Chiming.

The doorbell.

She sits up. Nothing. She listens, waits.

It rings again.

She covers her ears, not wanting to face another visit from Liz. Not after yesterday and the trouble it caused. The closer Liz gets, the more questions she'll ask.

She's knocking now, banging loudly. Then the letterbox flaps open.

'Hello?'

Ella sits bolt upright. Not Liz.

It's a man's voice.

She shuffles to the top of the stairs, edging down onto the step below. Then the next, then the next.

Halfway down she stops. Listens again, hears the letterbox open.

'Hello, anyone there?'

Ella's mouth is dry. Her heart on fire. Her limbs shake as she forces them to work, bumping herself down the last few stairs, wincing as the pain in her leg shoots up into her thigh. But she doesn't care. As she nears the bottom step, she holds back, peeking around the corner so she can spy on the door without being in full view.

'Hello?…'

There's something about the voice… something that sets her heart alight.

The doorbell again.

Then, whoever it is, tries the handle, wiggling it a few times.

Ella covers her mouth, hardly daring to breathe.

'Ella, are you in there?' the voice calls out.

When she peeks around the edge of the wall, she sees fingers poking through the letterbox, holding it open.

'I know you're home. I saw your…' he hesitates. 'I saw your baby through the front window.'

Ella hangs her head, cradling it in her hands, knowing exactly who it is.

'It's me, Ella,' he says, knocking loudly again. 'It's Liam. I'm worried about you.'

Shaking and terrified, Ella musters some courage, giving one quick glance up to the camera – praying to God he's not watching – before sliding into her wheelchair and pulling the keys from her pocket.

CHAPTER FORTY-TWO

Ten Years Ago

'I love you, Ella,' he said, looking into her eyes as they lay on his bed at Adlington. 'And I want you. I really, *really* want you.'

They'd been together a few months now, but Ella still struggled with the word 'couple'. She knew that's what they were, knew how relationships worked, of course, but being one half of a whole – the complementary piece to the puzzle of *them* – still sat awkwardly with her. She'd spent her entire life being one half of a whole with Harry. Even before they were born, she'd never been alone. So admitting to being in a relationship with Zach, giving herself to him fully, was the ultimate commitment. And she knew she wasn't ready.

That's what she told herself, anyway.

The evening had been warm and pleasant, the group of friends spending it in the village-pub garden until the night turned chilly and they'd ambled back up to the manor. They were over halfway through the week now and, since the boat trip, Ethan had been avoiding Ella, though she was still aware of him watching her.

'Does he do it to you?' she'd whispered to Meggie in the pub garden earlier as they'd shared a bag of crisps. They'd each got half a cider, their legs stretched out in the evening sun. Zach had been sitting the other side of her, his hand idly running up and down her thigh, stroking her smooth skin as he chatted to Stan and Charles. 'Ethan,' Ella added when Meggie looked puzzled.

'Can't you just let it go?' Meggie had said, glancing at him. 'Sure, he's a freak, but he's Zach's guest. Don't sweat it.' She'd tipped the remains of the crisps into her hand. 'Anyway, more to the point, have you seen how Stan's been staring at me all day?'

Ella had made a vague noise, not sure that she had noticed. 'You do know that I was trying to help Ethan on the boat, not push him overboard, don't you?'

'I *would*, you know,' Meggie had said, fluffing up her hair as she stared in Stan's direction, ignoring Ella's question. 'I so, so would.'

Ella had poked Meggie in the ribs. 'You're incorrigible,' she'd said, finishing the last of her cider. The others had been making noises to leave. 'And Ethan might be a creepy twat, but there's no way I'd ever hurt anyone, let alone try to kill them. You believe me, don't you?'

'Of course I do,' Meggie had said, stretching out her long legs as she stood; she'd gone up to Stan, asked if she could borrow his jacket, pretending to be cold.

After saying good night to the others back at the manor – everyone a little worse for wear after the last few nights' indulgences – Ella had agreed to go up to Zach's room briefly. Since arriving at Adlington, she'd only been in there once and was grateful that she'd been given her own suite – Zach's mother's propriety, she supposed, but, of course, Zach had still come knocking on her door late at night. She'd sent him away with a smile and a good night kiss in the doorway; but the night they'd stayed at the lake house, they'd actually shared a bed together, with Ella making it quite clear nothing would happen. They'd both been fast asleep when Harry had burst in drunkenly, waking them, mistaking it for his room.

'I mean it, I love you,' Zach said now, holding her closer.

Ella was mildly tipsy – just enough for her inhibitions to have melted. She allowed herself to be held, smiling up at him, her head resting on his shoulder. She smelt his scent on the bedsheets, turned to snuggle against him as she looked around the room he'd grown up in – so different to the room she and Harry had been forced to share. Compared to how things were just three years ago, she was living a dream she never believed possible.

'And I love you too,' Ella replied, staring up into his eyes.

Zach's hand trailed up her thigh, leaving it there as if he wanted her to get used to the feel of it. She giggled as they kissed, wrapping her arms around his neck.

'Crazy times, eh?' she said, with a twinge of sadness. Everyone was aware that the bubble they'd lived in these last three years was coming to an end. It was a looming, yet unspoken, reality. 'Being here with you is just amazing.'

Zach kissed her more deeply, rolled on top of her, pulling at the buttons of his shirt, exposing his chest.

'What's going to happen?' Ella said, turning her head to the side.

'Now?' Zach said, kissing down her neck. He made a deep growling sound in his throat, making Ella giggle again.

'No, silly. After this. After graduation.'

Zach ignored her, his hand slipping inside her clothes. Ella moved it away, putting it on her shoulder instead. It went straight back down.

'I'm serious, Zach. You'll walk into some hotshot banking job in London. And me? I'll probably have to…' She trailed off, hardly daring to say the words 'go home'. It was unthinkable. 'It just feels like an ending. Too much of an ending.'

But Zach wasn't listening. He was losing himself – his hands all over her body, while Ella's mood turned maudlin. She wanted things to stay like this for ever – the university and all it had given her, her course, her tutors, her friends, the weekends in London at Meggie's flat, the crazy clubs, Adlington, the lake house. Even the drugs and alcohol, while she rarely indulged, had played their part in this wild existence. She supposed, if she thought about it, she'd always known it wouldn't last. *Couldn't* last. All good things must come to an end, she remembered her mother once saying, though she couldn't recall about what. There'd not been much good in anything when she was growing up.

'Zach, *no*!' Ella said, more forcefully this time, letting out a squeal. He always stopped when she asked, eventually conceding. She knew how much he wanted her, sometimes felt bad for denying him. There was no doubt she wanted him, too. Just not like this. Not while they were still in the bubble.

Ella tried to wriggle out from underneath him, but when she put her foot on the ground, he hoisted her leg back up on the bed, forcing himself between her thighs.

'God, Ella, I want you so much… don't tease me like this…'

The weight of him bore down on her chest as he kissed her mouth, her face, her neck, her breasts – everywhere he could get to. She pushed her hands against his shoulders, levering him up as hard as she could, but she was no match for his strength.

Part of her kissed him back, yes, her hands feeling the muscles in his upper arms, gripping on to him, and her body responding by pushing against him.

But she'd said no several times now. And she needed to be heard.

'Zach, *no*!' she yelled as loud as she could.

He stopped instantly, sitting up, swinging his legs over the side of the bed, cradling his head in his hands, sweating, taking deep breaths. 'God, Ells, I'm so sorry. I got carried away.'

Ella sat up then too, pulling her top down, pushing her fingers through her hair, shaking it out. She ran her hand down the length of Zach's back. 'It's OK,' she said, kissing his shoulder. 'You know I love you,' she added, seeing the look of hurt on his face.

He glanced sideways, gave her a quick smile.

'Let that be enough. For now.'

'Yeah,' he said, patting her knee. He paused, staring at her in such a way she thought he was trying to see inside her soul.

'C'mon,' he said, standing, 'it's late. Time for bed. We've got a lot of partying to do tomorrow.'

Suddenly Ella felt like the abandoned one, the one being rejected. She was in two minds whether to pull him back down onto the bed, let him have his way. Instead, she found herself slipping on her shoes, grabbing her bag and being ushered to the door. They exchanged a quick peck on the lips before she left.

As she walked towards her room, she heard the click of Zach's lock behind her.

She wasn't sure if he was locking himself in, or her out.

CHAPTER FORTY-THREE

Ella

'*Ella*,' Liam says, his face lighting up. Then it crumples from worry when he sees her. But she isn't bothered about that, the state she's in. She's staring at the keys in her hand – marvelling that they worked. She peeks out towards Liz's house, silently thanking her. It feels as though she has a friend. *Another* friend, she thinks, as, finally, she focusses on Liam.

But the gratitude is short-lived.

'You have to go,' she says, feeling the camera burning into her back as she sits in her wheelchair by the open front door.

Liam looks hurt. 'I brought you these,' he says, holding up a bunch of chrysanthemums. The price is half picked off the cellophane.

'Thank you but I can't accept them. I'm unable to have visitors right now.' Her voice shakes, her heart thumping. It's only a matter of time before Jacob checks the cameras. If he hasn't already.

'Are you here alone?' he asks, peering beyond her.

'For now,' Ella replies, putting her hand on the door, ready to swing it closed.

'We miss you at work,' he goes on. 'I would have got everyone to sign the card but... well, I took a sick day to come here and bought it on the way.'

'I'm missed?' A strange feeling rushes through her. Something she doesn't recognise.

Liam nods. 'Ella, I'm a bit worried about you. All this...' he gestures to the house. 'It's different to what you said. And... and to be honest, you don't look well. Really pale and you've lost loads of weight. You look really tired, too, and—'

'I'm fine,' Ella says. 'Well, apart from...' She points to her leg, raises her broken arm.

Then Meggie cries – her sudden wail deafening even at the front door.

'I-I didn't know you had a baby,' he said, looking shocked. 'And I thought you said you lived in a flat.'

'I'm a private person,' Ella says. 'And the baby's adopted, before you ask,' she adds quickly, knowing he'll wonder why she was never pregnant. She just wants him to go.

Doesn't want him to go...

'Why don't you sort the baby while I put the kettle on? We can have a chat. I've got some time before I have to take my mum's car for its MOT. I'll fill you in on work and you can say as much or as little as you like. Deal?'

'Sorry,' Ella says. 'I'm busy.' She goes to shut the door but Liam puts his foot in the way.

'Ella,' he says kindly but firmly, 'you called me at work, when really, we both know you should have called HR. Do we need to talk about Diana McBride?'

She stares at him, cursing herself for having dropped in the name when Jacob forced her to make the phone call. It was foolhardy and spur-of-the-moment, but what's done is done. He knows as well as she does what it means.

'I was confused,' she says. 'It was the drugs. I really meant to say Helen or Jan in HR. Not Diana. The film must have been playing on my mind.' Ella lowers her eyes to the floor, her hand still on the door.

'Ella,' Liam says, reaching forward and lifting up her chin. When she meets his eye, he glances at the camera behind her. 'Let me in. Please.'

He makes a good cup of tea, she gives him that. His coffee at work was always up to par, too.

'I'm sorry,' Ella says.

Liam raises his eyebrows, smiling at the baby as she sits contentedly on Ella's knee.

'For?'

'For never making you a drink at work. For never even asking if you wanted one. For always being so aloof, so wrapped up in myself.'

'No rule says you have to socialise in the office,' he says, making cooing noises at the baby. She responds by gurgling, flapping her hands excitedly. 'Though to be fair, you did take isolation to a whole new level.' Liam's face creases with smile lines. 'Anyway, it looks as though you have enough going on here to keep you busy – a big house, a baby to look after. And in your condition.'

'It's not always been like this,' Ella says, wishing she could tell him everything. 'But I'm happy. We're happy.' She jiggles the baby, waves her rattle about.

'Your husband's a lucky man,' Liam says. 'And it was kind of him to invite me to your party this weekend. Anything I can bring?'

You, Ella thinks, horrified that what Jacob said was actually true.

'How did you even find me?' She's touched he did, but scared too.

Liam nods, looking awkward. 'I was worried, OK? No one seemed to know how you were or when you were coming back to work. And then that weird phone call from you. So I decided to track you down. It wasn't too hard, but you were out when I came, so I left a note.' He sips his tea. 'You certainly made an impression on Sue at the hospital. Anyway, she told me you're married.' He makes a sad face then, shrugging and winking. Adds a little laugh to hide his embarrassment.

Ella covers her mouth.

'Anyway, you made an impression on me too, over the years.' He looks away briefly. 'You might have *tried* to be invisible all this time, Ella Sinclair, but you didn't succeed. People notice someone like you. Someone... *lovely*.' He drops his head for a moment. 'Sorry, I shouldn't have—'

'It's OK,' she says quietly. 'It's nice.' She can't help the tears in her eyes, can't help it that one or two roll down her cheek. She sniffs.

'So, anyway, how long will you be like this?' Liam clears his throat, leaning over and tapping her leg cast.

'It's hard to say,' she says, knowing she's missed follow-up appointments at the hospital.

'Is there anything I can help with while I'm here?' he asks. 'Groceries? Things fetching or carrying? Any jobs in the garden? Your husband is at work, I take it?' Liam flicks his eyes to the hallway.

'He'll be back soon after seven. He swims every day. He likes to keep in shape.'

'While you're stuck here like this?'

'It's OK,' Ella says. 'I like the time alone.' She can hardly say it's the only opportunity she has to practise walking, for when she escapes, or that she wouldn't care if he never came back ever again. That she hopes he drowns. Then she has a thought. 'Actually, there is one little job you could help me with. I've been looking for something and I think it might be in the loft. I can't get up there like this.'

Liam downs the rest of his tea and is suddenly on his feet, hands on hips. 'Point me in the right direction and tell me what you need.'

*

After hauling herself up, with Liam's help, Ella sits on the top stair, watching as he balances on the bannister rail, his bare feet curling around the wood and his hand reaching out to the wall for support. 'Good job I'm tall,' he said breathlessly. 'And that I go climbing twice a week. Turns out I'm rather good at it.' He winked down then. Unfazed. 'I like a challenge.'

Ella thought about this, about him climbing, maybe with friends. She likes hearing snippets of his life that she didn't know. Adding layers, dimensions to him. If she'd gone out for lunch with the others, accepted the occasional invitation to the pub, or even bothered to respond to conversation over the years with more than a few words, then she'd probably know a lot more. But the trade-off would have been revealing things about herself.

Liam reaches up and pushes the loft hatch aside. Suddenly, his legs are dangling above her as he grabs the frame, hauling himself up. His hips and legs wiggle wildly as he pushes his feet against the wall, the muscles in his arms and shoulders standing proud as he deftly gets his upper body through the hole, his legs following soon after. Then she hears the click of a switch and suddenly the dark roof space above is lit up.

'Wow,' Liam calls down. 'No wonder your house is so tidy. There's a load of stuff up here.' His voice is muffled and distant but Ella hears him laughing. 'A lot of boxes,' he says. 'Any idea which one it's in?'

'Try looking for one with other videotapes and maybe some old photographs?' Ella pauses, not wanting to sound too urgent, even though she is. 'I… I really need to find it as I have a feeling there's some footage on it I can use for a work project. Old clips are just the best, right?' She screws up her eyes as she swallows the on-the-spot lie.

'Work project?' Liam appears at the hatch, smiling. 'So you're coming back then?'

Ella hears the hope in his voice. 'Sure,' she says, lying again. 'Which is why I really, *really* need this tape.' She glances down the stairs to the front door, digging her nails into her palms. 'It could be labelled "the Lake House", something like that. And dated June 2008,' she says, wanting to sound vague. She knows how meticulous he was about labelling his footage, keeping his pictures in albums, how ordered he kept everything in his life. And then it occurs to her that he might have taken a copy.

Ella's heart thumps while Liam rummages around up in the loft. She hears him swear when he bangs his head on a crossbeam, then sneezing as he rifles through the stuff.

'Oh, wait up,' he says, coughing. 'Might be onto something here.'

Ella holds her breath, listening to the noises above, while also keeping an ear open for a car pulling up, the door slamming, the key in the lock.

Liam appears at the hatch again, laughing, holding something out. 'Want this bringing down for the baby?' His smiling face is framed by the hatch.

Ella feels sick when she sees the teddy bear. 'No, no you can leave that up there. It's old,' she says. 'Not safe for little Zach.' She just wishes he would hurry up.

Liam pauses, staring down at her. 'Are you OK? You've gone very pale.'

'I'm in pain. Will it take much longer?' She pulls a face, hoping it will hurry him up.

Liam disappears again. She hears him muttering to himself, the clatter of things being moved about. She bites her nails, hears Meggie whimpering in her pram downstairs.

'Liam?' she says, realising it's gone quiet up there. 'Any luck?'

Nothing. Just silence.

She forces herself upright, using her good leg, supporting herself on the bannister. 'Liam?' she calls out again. 'Are you OK?'

Another few moments of silence. Just the sound of her own breathing.

'Yeah…' comes Liam's slow, thoughtful reply. 'Yeah, I'm OK.' Then another long silence before Ella hears a load of clattering, a box being moved again. Then he's at the hatch, shrugging, pulling a face. 'I'm so sorry,' he says. 'I couldn't find anything. There were just a few photograph albums and a load of old CDs.' He pauses, seeing the disappointment on Ella's face. 'And judging by the bands, you wouldn't have wanted them anyway.' He adds a laugh.

Ella sits back down onto the top stair again, watching as Liam swings down from the loft hatch, standing on the bannister rail as he pulls the cover closed again. When he jumps down, he brushes himself off, staring at Ella. Seeing her tears.

'The tape's that important?' he says, crouching down beside her, his hand on her shoulder.

'It is,' she says, sniffing, unable to help the sobs.

Liam tentatively wraps his arm around her, staring over the top of her head, rocking her gently.

'It's literally a matter of life and—'

But Ella doesn't get a chance to finish. Instead, she turns rigid, sits upright, her breathing quickening as she stifles the scream.

The front door opens and, when she looks down, Jacob is standing in the hall.

CHAPTER FORTY-FOUR

Ella

'Jacob,' Ella says, wiping her tears. 'You're-you're back early.' There's no hiding the fear.

Jacob says nothing. He slides off his jacket, discarding it on the floor with a whipping motion. Slowly, he puts his keys in his trouser pocket and takes a step towards the stairs, his eyes fixed on Liam the whole time.

'Hi there,' Liam says, flashing looks up and down the stairs between Jacob and Ella. 'Good to meet you, mate. I'm Liam, Ella's work colleague. Just called round to see how the patient was doing.' He grins. But it quickly drops away as he sees Jacob's steely expression.

Ella, sitting on the top step, shaking, is aware that Liam now has his hands under her arms, is hauling her up, helping her get further back onto the landing. Almost having to drag her as her muscles refuse to work. She feels like a dead weight. *Is* a dead weight.

Jacob, still silent, puts his foot on the first step, slowly advancing. His jaw clenches and his eyes glaze over – dark and intense, assessing the situation.

He's halfway up.

At the top, Liam extends his arm, ready to shake hands; but when Jacob draws close, he puts his hands flat on Liam's chest, shoving him hard.

'*Oi*, mate. Unnecessary,' Liam says, staggering, making a noise as he bumps the wall behind. 'I was just trying to help—'

But he doesn't get a chance to finish because Jacob takes a swing with his right fist, punching him in the face. Liam's head slams back against the wall as he cries out, clutching his jaw. Blood oozes from his split bottom lip.

Ella screams.

'What the?—' Liam yells, reaching out and grabbing Jacob's arm just as he goes for another punch. But he only manages to deflect him for a moment as Jacob's other fist hits him sharply in the guts.

'*Ooof*—' Liam doubles over, sliding down the wall just in time to receive a knee in the face from Jacob. His head slams back.

'Stop it, Jacob! Stop it *now*!' Ella cries out, hyperventilating, crawling across the landing to get to them. She grabs onto Jacob's ankle but he kicks her off. She lies on the floor at his feet, hysterical.

Jacob still hasn't said a word.

Liam manages to haul himself upright again, but only to find himself grabbed by the collar of his shirt, lifted up and slammed back against the wall again. Blood streams down his chin, onto his clothing, mixed in with Jacob's saliva now as he spits at his face.

'How fucking *dare* you come into my house,' Jacob booms up close. 'How fucking *dare* you interfere in our lives, you shit. You have no idea what you've done.' His chest heaves up and down.

'Jacob, stop it, please. Liam is my friend. And you invited him to-to our party, remember?' She claws at his legs, staring up, imploring him. The skin under Jacob's eye twitches and, for a moment, he has a faraway look, as though Ella's words have almost got through to him.

While he's distracted, Liam takes the opportunity, shoving him hard – away from both him and Ella – returning the punch to his face with a hefty swing of his arm, ramming Jacob against the bathroom door. It swings open and he falls back through it, going down, cracking his head against the edge of the vanity unit.

Ella screams again, covers her mouth as a trickle of blood dribbles from Jacob's skull onto the white bathroom floor.

'Shit,' Liam says, staggering in, standing over him, terrified of what he's done. But there's no time to react as Jacob's foot whips up, kicking Liam between the legs with full force. Immediately, he goes down, yelling out in agony, clutching himself while Jacob scrabbles to his feet, grabbing Liam's hair and ramming his face over and over against the side of the bath. Blood spatters up the tiles, on the floor – everywhere.

It's Ella who finally gets Jacob off him – dragging herself across the landing, sinking her teeth into the fleshy part of Jacob's calf as hard as she can, not letting go even though he howls out, swiping at her.

He yanks at her hair, forcing her to release and is about to throw her back but Liam is on Jacob now – punching, kicking, grappling.

Ella cowers between the sink and the toilet, watching as the men wrestle, throwing punches at every opportunity, staggering across the landing and towards the top of the stairs. Grunts and the sound of fist on bone drown out the sound of Ella's shrieks as she sits shaking, her body refusing to move.

She hears the baby screaming in her pram downstairs.

'Jacob, *stop* it, for God's sake let him go!…'

All she can do is watch as the two men lurch towards the top of the stairs, punching and shoving as they get closer and closer. It's Jacob who takes the final swing, aiming again at Liam's jaw, hitting him squarely. Stunned for a moment, teetering on the edge, Liam loses consciousness and falls backwards, tumbling over and over as he drops down the staircase. His head hits the wall at the bottom.

Ella screams, screwing up her eyes, tearing at her hair. Her lungs are on fire as she gasps for breath. Seconds later, she feels a hand on her shoulder, Jacob's breath on her cheek as he strokes her back.

'There, there,' he says. 'Everything will be OK now, Ella-bella. Just like it was before.'

She doesn't say a word. *Can't* say a word as he lifts her easily from the bathroom floor, carrying her down the stairs over his shoulder, stepping over Liam, before putting her in her wheelchair in the hallway. She's shaking, terrified, prays that she'll soon wake up from this nightmare.

Jacob kicks Liam's lifeless body.

Nothing.

'People should learn not to interfere. Isn't that right?' he says, a tight smile on his face. He looks adoringly at Ella; all she sees is pure evil.

She nods frantically, glancing down at Liam, willing him to move. He doesn't.

'You're in the way,' Jacob says, spitting on him. 'Disgusting man,' he says, reaching down and pulling his arms from under him. He grips onto his wrists, dragging him across the hallway towards the kitchen, disappearing around the corner, leaving smears of blood in his wake. Ella follows in her chair, her arms weak as she pushes the wheels.

'What-what are you doing with him?' she asks. 'Is he dead?'

Jacob says nothing; rather, he reaches on top of the high wall cupboard, feeling around for a key. He unlocks the door to the garage, dragging Liam through, bumping him down the steps.

'What are you going to *do*?' she pleads, wheeling close to the door. A waft of cool air hits her as she squints into the dark space beyond. 'You should call an ambulance. He needs help.'

Jacob stops and turns, looking back at her. 'Do you love him?' he says coldly.

'No… no, of course not, but he's hurt, he—'

'Do you love him more than me?'

'Jacob—'

He drops Liam's body onto the concrete garage floor, striding back to Ella, his face close to hers. 'Who do you love, Ella? Tell me!' he growls, his expression filled with panic. '*Who?*'

'You,' she says quietly. 'I love you. You know that. But please, just call for help. Say he had an accident and fell down the stairs or something. I'll vouch for you.'

Then the swipe around her head before he goes back into the garage, rummaging in some boxes before pulling out a length of rope. He binds Liam's wrists tightly and then his ankles, tying all four limbs together. He shifts more stuff about, swiping things off shelves, finding a roll of silver insulation tape, winding it round and round Liam's mouth. Then he kicks him again, leaving him lying on his side. He doesn't make a sound.

Jacob comes back into the kitchen and locks the door, pouring himself a large whisky. 'There,' he says calmly. 'All sorted now. But what *am* I going to do with you, Ella-bella? Your behaviour is—'

Before he can finish, the doorbell chimes, followed by Liz calling through the letterbox. 'It's only me, Ella. Are you OK in there? I was out in the front garden and heard shouting and noises.'

Ella stares at Jacob, her eyes wide. He puts his finger over his lips, silencing her, before wheeling her away from the kitchen door. He indicates for her to stay put. Ella nods, terrified, as Jacob strides out, drink in hand.

'Liz,' Ella hears him say as he unlocks the front door. 'How nice to see you.'

'Oh,' Liz says, clearly shocked by Jacob's dishevelled appearance. 'I heard…' She hesitates, no doubt silenced by the stern look Jacob will be giving her. Ella knows it well. 'Well, as long as you're here, that's the main thing. I was worried about Ella, thought she might have taken a tumble judging by the commotion.' Liz laughs then, but she's not giving up.

'Everything is fine. Ella is sleeping and I was moving furniture. A large cabinet toppled over...' He injects a laugh. 'I'm afraid I lost my temper and yelled when it fell on me.'

'Ah,' Liz says. 'Do you need any help? Ice for your head?'

'No.'

'I'll-I'll leave you in peace then,' Liz says, sounding agitated. Ella hears footsteps, but then they stop. 'It's just that there's no way for me to get in now if she needs help. Rachel gave me the house keys, you see, so in turn I gave Ella...' Liz trails off.

'You gave Ella what?' Jacobs says.

'I just thought—'

'*What?*'

'It was just a spare set.'

'I'm sure that was very thoughtful of you, Liz. But Ella will be fine. Goodbye.'

Ella drops her head down, covering her face as she hears Jacob lock the door. She's desperate to cry, but can't. She's beyond tears. When she looks up, he's in front of her, holding out his hand.

'Give them to me,' he says, quite calmly.

Ella raises her eyebrows.

'The keys, Ella-bella.' Surprisingly, he smiles. 'Now.'

Ella nods, wheeling past him to her pack lying on the hallway floor. She reaches inside and pulls out the precious keys, handing them over.

Jacob shakes his head. 'Stupid girl,' he says, before another blow comes.

Ella reels, gathering her senses as her world spins for a few seconds.

No DV tape in the loft. And now no keys. A single tear escapes her eye.

CHAPTER FORTY-FIVE

Liam

Liam doesn't know where he is. Or how long he's been here. All he knows is that it's dark and that everything hurts.

He tries to move. Impossible. He's not even sure if his eyes are open because he can't see anything. Just blackness. Then there's a sound – a muffled voice, incomprehensible words. *His* words, he soon realises, stuck inside him because his mouth is sealed shut.

He blinks furiously, spurred on by a flash of something... over there. He cranes his head upward. A chink of light. Something rough and cold presses against his cheek. The floor. He wants to cough, but can't. Instead, a choking sound rumbles down his throat.

Fuck, he says in his head. *Fuck, fuck, fuck.* Snatches of what happened begin to come back – his mum's car, driving to Ella's place, knocking on the door, going inside, a baby, the loft... searching.

And then that man. He screws up his eyes as he recalls the fight, his face hitting the side of the bath over and over. His nose feels as though it's broken and his entire body aches and cramps, not least from being stuck in this uncomfortable position. He's been tied up, thrown somewhere to die. Right now, that would be preferable to feeling like this.

And then he remembers. The tape. The DV tape Ella had sent him up to find. The urgency in her voice, even though she was trying not to show it. There's more to her story than she's letting on. Her maniac husband is proof of that. *Diana McBride…*

Liam squirms and rolls on the floor, his bomber jacket flapping open at the front. He manages to get onto his opposite side, his head bumping into something, and he can feel it in there – still feel the hard, rectangular shape in his pocket.

The tape.

Good.

Light suddenly floods around him, making him screw up his eyes. When he opens them, he sees a figure standing above him, feels the shoe thwacking into his side. He groans as the wind is kicked out of him.

He blinks, staring up as that man – Ella's husband – comes into focus.

'Well, well. You're alive. Tenacious little fucker, aren't you?'

'Jacob, *no*,' Liam hears Ella cry from beyond the door. Warmth and the smell of food floods in around him, making him feel sick. He swallows it down, can't allow himself to puke with his mouth sealed up. With the extra light, he sees he's tied up in the garage, notices the up-and-over door at the other end, various clutter and boxes stacked all about.

'Please, just let him go,' Ella pleads.

Then Liam sees her in the doorway, sitting in her chair. Her eyes are bloodshot, ringed with bruises. A far cry from the quiet woman he saw every day at work – the woman who kept her head down, intent on minding her own business, who did her job well. The woman he wanted to befriend.

'Who knows you're here?' the monster above him says.

Liam shakes his head as best he can, knowing his eyes look demented from fear. He doesn't want to die.

'Liar!' he roars, kicking him again. 'Did you call the police before you came? Did you tell anyone you were coming?'

Liam thinks of his mum – her quiet and modest life, how she keeps everything in order, even down to getting her MOT sorted while she's sick. He knows he's long since missed the MOT appointment at the garage, that they've probably phoned his mum asking if she's still bringing the car in. He imagines her anxiety when they tell her he didn't show up, her face crumpling with worry. She knows her son would never let her down on purpose, that she'll suspect something has happened to him. She'll be ringing his phone, over and over, getting more and more frantic when he doesn't answer, perhaps even calling the police when she can't get in contact. But, of course, he left his phone in the car outside, didn't expect to be at Ella's for long, let alone get into a fight. Right about now, he imagines his mum will be calling the hospitals to see if he's been in an accident, or worse.

There's a sudden searing pain across his face as the tape is ripped from his mouth. It feels as though his skin has been torn off.

'Who knows you're here, I said?'

'No one, I swear,' Liam rasps, panting, realising how thirsty he is. He has no idea how long he's been like this. 'I only popped by to—'

'Shut up!' Jacob growls, kicking him again.

'Jacob, let him go, *please*. You can trust him. He won't tell anyone. He's just a mate from work. My *old* work. We'll never see him again.' Ella's voice in the background is urgent and frightened, yet Liam still detects strength, some fight left in her. He prays she can escape but, seeing the extent of her injuries, he knows it won't be easy.

Or, perhaps, he thinks, she doesn't *want* to escape.

'No, I will not be letting him go,' Jacob says in a taunting voice. Though Liam suspects he doesn't know what to do with him either. 'This man was here all alone with my wife. He deserves punishment.'

'But, I'm *not*...' Ella trails off. 'Look, just give him this then,' he hears her say. She holds out a water bottle. 'Please... darling,' she adds.

Jacob falters for a moment, whipping the bottle from her, pulling the cap off before squirting ice-cold water in Liam's face. He screws up his eyes but his mouth gapes wide, trying to catch some of the jet. Then the bottle is dropped down on the garage floor beside him, just out of reach.

'Die for all I care,' Jacob says, bending down and re-sticking the tape across Liam's mouth.

Then the blackness again, even darker now because his eyes had just got used to the bit of light from beyond.

*

Sleep. He thinks it was sleep. Though he could have been unconscious. Either way, his thoughts are back with him, his senses semi-working. There's a pain in his head, slicing from one temple to the other as though a knitting needle has been pushed through his skull and left there. His eye sockets ache, his guts hurt, his lip smarts under the tape, and he's pretty certain he's got a broken jaw and a broken nose.

He listens. Is that a television? He holds his breath and listens again – yes, the chatter of voices, laughter, applause. A show on the TV in a room beyond the kitchen. He's trapped in here and they're watching television. Part of him even wonders if Ella is in on this. If she, too, is some kind of monster with a twisted mind who lures men in for her husband to mistreat. He can't stand to think what might come next.

But then he overlays those thoughts with what he knows about her from work and it's ridiculous. Even through his pain and thirst-fuelled fog, the two don't match up. Ella is not bad.

Diana McBride, Liam thinks, drifting in and out of his semi-conscious state. Her story affected them all at the office – a real-life drama, played out by actors to get the charity's message across, to raise awareness. Long-term domestic abuse, starting with a single incident many years before, then slowly, insidiously, escalating into a situation where Diana's husband wouldn't allow her to leave the house, have a job or any money, see friends or even a phone… Her food was restricted, she wasn't allowed to wash or see daylight – she barely had an existence. In fact, Liam thought, her freedom only came after her husband killed her and buried her body in the back garden.

'Imagine dropping a frog into a pan of boiling water,' the charity's media director had explained to the team in the boardroom at the initial brief. 'What does it do? It naturally jumps out. It's hot and painful. It doesn't want to be boiled alive.'

Everyone had nodded, exchanged glances. Seemed reasonable so far, they'd thought, though they had wondered about the relevance.

'Now, imagine that same frog placed into a pan of cold water on a slow-burn gas stove. The water gradually heats and the frog sits there, perhaps feeling a little uncomfortable, though it's not sure why. The water gradually warms, eventually boiling, but the frog still doesn't notice. Not until it's too late, that is.'

Everyone had remained silent, imagining the frog. Imagining Diana McBride.

CHAPTER FORTY-SIX

Ella

Ella takes a deep breath. She has no choice, needs to act. Can't just sit here, doing nothing, while Liam dies of thirst or his injuries on the garage floor. She sees the baby happily flapping her little arms, pumping her chubby legs as she sits on Jacob's knee while he watches the news. He's behaving as though nothing's happened, casually waving a coloured rattle about to amuse the baby.

Ella wheels back to the kitchen and returns shortly. 'Hey,' she says, touching his arm, 'I made you this. It was no mean feat carrying this through,' she says laughing, wiping the underside of the glass with her hand. 'I wanted to do something nice for my man.' She beams her best smile, knows she looks a state with her black eyes, her tear-soaked face. She hopes seeming happy will make him overlook all that.

Jacob turns, looks at her before his eyes flick to the drink. 'Ella-bella…' he says in a crooning voice more suited to the baby. 'How kind. You are a darling.' He takes the drink – a very strong gin and tonic, with a slice of lemon and a few ice cubes added.

'You're welcome,' she says. 'Oh, and I've just made a salad to go with the chicken. I figured that it's time I started doing a bit more around here. You know, being a better… a better wife.' She swallows down the word. 'You know, now that I'm feeling a bit more like myself. And I won't be in this for ever,' she says, tapping the wheelchair.

Jacob glances down at her cast, as though it's the first time he's actually considered that one day she'll be able to walk again.

'And tomorrow, I'll even tackle the washing. I can make the ironing board go down low so I can press your shirts. I don't want people in the office thinking I don't look after you.'

She leans forward, puckering up her lips, waiting for Jacob to reciprocate. She wonders if she's gone too far, if he suspects that she's being odd, too nice, but then she feels his mouth, warm and moist and tasting of gin, pressing down on hers in a deep kiss. She shudders, and not only from the bitter addition to the drink that she can taste on him – the three 10 mg diazepam tablets she crumbled and stirred in – but rather from everything he did.

'You are learning, Ella-bella,' he says, cupping her cheek in one hand. She tries not to flinch as his fingers dig into the most recent bruise. 'Learning to do things right.'

'I want to be a good wife and a good mother,' she says, giving the baby a gentle tickle on the tummy. She admits, the baby is a problem. She can't stand the thought of abandoning her, leaving her here with him, but including her in the escape is going to make it even harder. To give her strength, she focusses on the child's mother, how she must be feeling right now. Bereft and in pieces.

Then, before Jacob can reach for the remote control or press the button to change channels, the news presenter suddenly catches their attention. Ella wonders if he read her mind.

In a press conference earlier today, the senior investigating officer in the missing Kayleigh Roberts case, Detective Inspector Doug Jones, confirmed that the round-the-clock team is working on new leads, one of which includes a recent possible sighting. DI Jones revealed earlier at the short conference that a security guard at the Colonnades Shopping Centre reported seeing two women with a pram matching the description given by the baby's mother, Sharon Roberts. The sighting happened only four miles from where the infant was snatched. The short statement released by detectives confirmed that enquiries—

Jacob jabs a button on the remote, switching to a documentary about clean water supplies in Third World countries. Ella stares straight ahead, forcing her breathing to stay steady as she waits for the blow to her head. But it doesn't come.

'It's OK,' he says, turning, stroking her hair. 'We'll be OK – me, you and our baby. No one can touch us. No one can hurt us. No one will find us.'

'That's right,' Ella says, watching as he downs the last half of his drink in one go, not taking his eye off the screen. She sees the tightness of his jaw, how it unclenches and clenches – a sure sign he's twitchy, nervous. 'Shall I make you another?' she asks.

Jacob nods, holding out his empty glass.

In the kitchen, Ella makes the same drink again, standing up to do it, testing out the weight of her body on her bad leg. Agony, but doable, she thinks, wincing, thankful that she's kept up her exercising when she's had the chance. It's helped a little. Quickly, she reaches her hand to the top of the cupboard where Jacob put the garage door key. Too high. She'll need a chair, but daren't risk making a noise right now or, worse, falling off.

She crunches up another four or five diazepam tablets, grinding them into powder with the back of a teaspoon in a saucer as quickly as she can. White frothy fizz appears in the glass as she adds them to the gin and tonic, stirring them in. She daren't risk putting in too many at once in case he tastes it, so she sloshes in another slug of gin, plus a good squeeze of lemon and a slice, plus more ice too. She holds the glass up to the light to check the tablets have dissolved.

'Here you go, my darling,' she says, going back in and handing him the drink. 'Dinner won't be long. I have a surprise for you.' She smiles and kisses his cheek, turning her chair around to leave.

But he reaches out, grabbing her wrist.

'I love you, Ella-bella,' he says, the hard lines on his face softening into a relaxed expression. 'I really, really love you. This is all I ever wanted. All *we* ever wanted. Don't you remember?' He kisses the baby's head, leaving a wet mark.

'I do. And I love you, too,' she replies, smiling, swallowing down the lump in her throat. The grip on her wrist loosens then, as though his muscles are relenting, and his face looks more relaxed, his eyelids drooping.

Ella wheels back to the kitchen to throw some salad in a bowl. She doesn't care how it looks, doesn't bother washing any of the ingredients, just wants to get on with grinding up more tablets. She has no idea how many it will take, what with the codeine added in for good measure.

Then it occurs to her that she might actually kill him. Again. That he might never wake up. She doesn't want him to die, and couldn't live with herself if he did, however much she hates him. The guilt has been torment enough to live with these last ten years – work, home, sleep, repeat.

No, she just wants him to pass out for a few hours. Get Liam and the baby safe. It's her fault they're both here. And then she'll deal with the aftermath. Face her punishment. She knows the truth will have to come out.

Ella opens the oven, flinching as the roar of hot air scalds her bruised face. She takes out the pot – filled to the brim with chicken in a creamy sauce, one of those ready-made things in a jar that Jacob had in the cupboard. He put it in an hour ago, as though he was oblivious to what he'd just done to Liam. She serves a single portion onto a plate, then mixes more crushed tablets into the main pot, stirring them in well.

*

'Dinner's served, darling,' Ella says from the doorway, pointing across the hall to the dining room. 'Why don't you put Zach in his pram? He looks sleepy.'

The baby's head lolls and her eyes roll closed as Jacob lays her down, looking drowsy himself.

'Candles,' Jacob says flatly, hands on hips staring at the table. Ella has put out a cloth and lit half a dozen tea lights in little coloured jars. She's dimmed the main lights and even put on some music. 'Appropriate,' he says, bending down and kissing her on the head. He sits down.

'Oh,' Ella says, panicking. 'No... no, that's not yours. This one is,' she adds, pointing at the other plate.

Jacob stares at the table. 'But I always sit here.'

'Do you?' she replies, her voice squeaky. He nods, making no move to change places, so Ella forces herself to half-stand and lean across the table, swapping the dishes. 'I gave you more,' she says, thankful that her plate has less on it. 'I don't want my man going hungry,' she adds, grinning.

Jacob stares at her before unfolding his napkin. 'Delicious,' he says with a big yawn, tucking in.

'Bon appetit,' Ella says, taking a sip of water, watching him over the rim.

CHAPTER FORTY-SEVEN

Ten Years Ago

Ella soon decided the lake house was her favourite place in the entire world. The tranquillity, the nature, its raw surroundings reflected in the ever-still surface of the expanse of water chimed with her own inner energy, her values – honest, true, peaceful. During the week she'd been at Adlington, they'd come down here a few times and she'd never felt so happy – more so than any other time in her life.

And it was all because of Zach. She smiled at him across the huge low table sitting between the fur-strewn sofas.

They were all drunk, of course – the group of them sprawled around the living area – laughing, relaxing, having fun. It was their last night and they wanted to make the most of it. The boys were still full of tales from their fishing trip earlier that day, joking about the ones that got away as they cast lines from the opposite banks. They decided there must have been something wrong with their rods or the bait as no one, apart from Ethan, had landed anything. He'd had four fish in his haul. It seemed, Ella thought, that he was good at catching things.

Zach made a silly but fond face back at her, one of those 'love-you-hate-you' looks, ending with Ella poking out her tongue. Of course, he still had his camcorder glued to his palm, his fingers clamped through the strap. He'd been randomly shooting snippets of film all night.

'One day,' he'd said earlier at dinner, standing on his chair at the end of the table up at the manor. 'One… day…' He was slurring, wobbling from side to side.

'This will all be yours?' Charles had chipped in, sucking on a fat cigar.

Everyone roared with laughter.

'No, you twat,' Zach said from behind his camcorder, one eye closed, shaking from laughter, nearly losing his balance again. 'One day… *one* day, we'll all look back on these times with great fondness,' he said, slurring while feeling around on the table below him for his glass. The camera was still held up to the room. He raised his drink high in the air. 'I propose a toast. To all of us, in our youth, our prime, and *finally* at the end of our fucking exams…'

'To us and the rest of our lives!' came the unanimous chime from everyone as glasses were chinked. Ella looked among them fondly. Dear friends. How on earth, she wondered with a small smile and a wink to Harry, had they ended up here, a part of this? Judging by the warm look he gave her back, he felt the same.

But then she felt something stroking against her leg under the table – the third time in a few minutes. She glanced down, trying not to make a thing of it, but not liking it either. Ethan was sitting opposite, watching as she surreptitiously flashed him a look. She felt her cheeks redden as she crossed her ankles, tucking her feet under her chair so he couldn't reach. Stan, who had previous form for this, wasn't anywhere near. It could only have been Ethan touching her.

*

'Do you *have* to?' Ella said to Zach, giggling, flopping back onto the furs in the lake house after they'd all tramped down there in the dark. It was a fifteen-minute walk through the woods down a narrow path littered with tree roots and ferns. As ever, they'd only had one torch between them. Now, Zach was up close to her with the lens again, having been told to sod off by Charles while he was doing a line. He'd nearly sent Zach flying. 'I'm sleepy and I look a state,' Ella said, covering her face. But she was giggling beneath her hands, secretly liking the attention.

'I already told you,' he said, coming close, whispering into her ear, 'one day, we'll show these tapes to our kids. And then we'll look back when we're old and grey and see ourselves as the reckless and carefree youth we once were and it will make us feel young all over again. Perhaps even turn our hair back to its original colour.' Zach kissed her. 'If nothing else, my son will have a good laugh at his dad.'

Son, Ella thought warmly.

'You've got to get her into bed first, mate,' Stan said, prodding Zach in the side.

'Fuck off, Stan,' Zach said. 'Just give me some of that shit,' he said, kneeling down by the table where the coke was.

Ella was behind him on the sofa, her legs wrapped around either side of his back, her dress hitched up even shorter. She dug her fingers into his shoulders, trying not to react to Stan's comment, even though her stomach knotted from it.

'Haven't you had enough?' she whispered in Zach's ear. 'Booze and now that?'

He glared up at her with a frown. 'You should have some,' he said. 'It might help you chill out a bit.' He leant forward, sticking the straw up his nose, leaving Ella wondering if Stan's comment had got to him, too.

She sighed. She didn't like the effect that stuff had on her and, besides, Harry would be so disappointed. He'd already warned her off, worrying it was going to become a regular habit.

'Please, just watch yourself,' he'd said upstairs at the manor. They'd been on their way down to dinner but he'd cornered her.

'What are you talking about?' she'd said, shocked. 'You're not my dad,' she added, instantly regretting it when she'd seen the hurt on his face.

'No, Ella, but I'm your brother. I care about you. Just don't be pressured into doing things you don't want. Their lives are so different to ours.'

Ella'd had an urge to shove him, but gave him a little nod instead, even though, not so long ago, she'd have agreed with him entirely. Three years at university had changed her. Given her a voice. 'I'm not stupid, Harry,' she'd said, thinking she heard a nearby bedroom door open.

'And I worry about…' he said, trailing off, looking her up and down. She was wearing yet another of Meggie's many dresses – short and revealing.

'Well, you needn't—' But she'd stopped suddenly, flashing a glance over Harry's shoulder. Ethan had come out of his room, was standing there with his arms dangling by his sides, watching the pair of them.

'You OK?' he said meekly, looking at her. He'd barely said anything all week, let alone asking how she was. She couldn't help thinking that Zach had invited him along as a plaything, something to be made fun of. Sport. In a way, she'd been grateful. It was a role that could so easily have been hers.

'She's fine,' Harry said. 'What is it to you anyway?'

'Harry, don't,' Ella said, seeing the look on Ethan's face. She'd wondered if that's how things had always been for him – every time he spoke up, he got slammed down. She could relate to that.

Ethan had turned to go, also giving Ella's dress a sweeping look before he went.

After Harry had gone too, she'd rested her head back against the wall, exhaling, reminded of something Zach had said at university. *Sex with Ella Sinclair – the final frontier.* He'd laughed then, making her choke on her wine as they'd been chilling together in the student bar. Outwardly, she'd been smiling, finding it funny, but his remark cut deep. 'And that's the way it'll stay until I'm ready,' she'd replied. Though it hadn't stopped him pushing his luck more and more when he thought she might give in.

But he was always met with the same answer.

I will be ready when I'm ready.

But, she had to admit, she thought now, watching as Zach felt the effects of the drugs kick in, that she liked talking about their future – him mentioning a son, growing old together. They just hadn't decided what to do in the meantime – how to get from where they were now to that. With their final exams over and graduation only a few weeks away, plans for after the summer were on everyone's minds – especially Ella's, given she didn't have a rich family to fall back on. Fact was, she didn't have *any* family to rely on, with her mum in poor health. Neither she nor Harry had much to do with her these days, knowing their aunt took care of her needs. The guilt cut deep for Ella, but Harry told her she didn't deserve anything from them, that the tables were turned now.

'Fuck, that's sweet,' Zach said, wiping his nose as he lolled back next to Ella.

Meggie had put on some music – lazy Ibiza chill-out tunes – and Ella got up to open the big glass doors that led out onto a wide deck overlooking the lake. She could just see the remains of the sunset behind the trees as the last of the orange streaks fizzed out in the darkness above. From the wooden deck, there were steps down to a scrubby beach area – flanked either side by the thick woods. She went and stood outside, the music pulsing gently in the background, breathing in the night air.

'Almost midsummer,' Meggie said, joining her outside. 'The witching hour,' she giggled. She was high, Ella knew, but it was always a happy place for Meggie. 'Beautiful, isn't it?'

'Mmm,' was Ella's reply. She leaned on the wooden railing, her drink to hand, condensation running down the glass. Like the tears she realised were rolling down her cheeks. 'It's the end of an era, Megs,' she said, knowing that she and Harry would feel it especially hard.

But then she corrected herself. *She* would feel it especially hard. Harry had already got himself a decent job – as long as he achieved his 2:1, which he easily would because Harry was, well, Harry. A worker. Ridiculously clever with a first almost guaranteed. The internship he did last summer had paid off. Ella, however, had done no work experience at all and had little idea what she was going to do for a job or money. She couldn't face going back to Birmingham, *home*, but she supposed she might have to, even if it was to work in a bar until she got on her feet.

'But it's the start of a new one, too,' Meggie said, pulling her friend in for a hug. Ella looked at her – her pretty face, her long blonde hair, her effortless beauty. She was going to work in her dad's firm in London from September, do a Law conversion degree. She'd be OK. She'd be *fine*. Her parents would buy her a flat, take care of all her expenses.

'Yeah,' Ella said, wiping her eyes. 'You're right.' She knew Zach was London-bound, too, which made her stomach tighten, to think that he'd be close to Meggie, that they'd see each other regularly. And of course, like the others, he could afford to live there. It would only take a phone call or two from his father and he'd walk into some hotshot banking job easily enough. So far, he'd not asked her to join him. And, after the seed Harry had sown in her mind, she was beginning to realise why.

'Zach spoke to me the other night, you know, Els,' Meggie said in that voice of hers. The serious one, despite the drugs.

Ella's heart skipped a couple of beats. 'Oh…' she said, trying to sound chilled about whatever was coming.

'He really likes you, you know. *Loves* you.'

Ella raised her eyebrows, smiling. She'd not been expecting that. She glanced back inside, catching Zach's eye. He looked away.

'But he's not sure you feel the same.'

'Wait…' Ella said, shocked. '*Why?*'

Meggie pulled a face, shrugging. 'Because you won't have sex with him.'

It was a punch in the face. He'd been talking to Meggie about it? Ella glared at her, then glared harder at Zach inside, though he didn't look her way. Instead, he had his damned camcorder pointing at everyone and was making a nuisance of himself by filming Charles and that girl Zandra.

'Did you offer to fill in for me then?' Ella said, instantly regretting it. She stared out across the lake, counting the flickering reflections of stars to calm herself, to slow her seething breaths. Why couldn't Zach just accept that she did love him but being forced to prove it in *that* way wasn't how she was hardwired? Not after everything. And she couldn't talk to anyone about *that*. Not even Harry.

'I'm going for a walk,' Ella said, feeling hurt and angry. 'It's turning into a bloody orgy in there.' She glanced inside again.

'Ooh,' Meggie said, fluffing up her hair. 'Time for me to go back in then. Stan's had the hots for me all night. That Zandra's a bit full of herself though, don't you think?'

Ella shrugged. Another glance showed her that Zandra's top was half off and she was making out with Charles. 'Seems to be,' Ella said, and the last thing to catch her eye as she went down the steps was Zach sitting on his own by the fireplace, turning the camera round and round in his hands, looking up and smiling at Meggie as she went back inside.

CHAPTER FORTY-EIGHT

Ella

'Jacob?' Ella says, softly at first. 'Jacob… are you awake?' A little louder. Then she touches his arm, prods him gently. Nothing. He's lying flat on his back on the sofa, his head lolling to one side, his lips vibrating every time he breathes out. 'Jacob!' Ella says, almost shouting now. 'There's a fire!'

If anything will wake him, that surely will.

Nothing. Jacob's breathing is slow – the rise and fall of his chest barely visible – and each in-breath is shallow. She wonders if she overdid the drugs, if he will stop breathing completely.

The baby makes a sudden cry from her pram. She was restless half an hour ago, so Ella put her down to see if she'd settle after yet another bottle. While she's been waiting for Jacob to fall asleep, she's been getting as much milk into the baby as possible. Less chance of her making a sound when Ella makes her move.

Except she's making a sound now. A big sound. Ella doesn't understand. She's fed, has a clean nappy, is soon to be reunited with her real mother…

She wheels over quietly, lifting the baby from the pram. 'Sshh, little one,' she whispers. *Please don't wake up*, she prays, glancing over at Jacob. He doesn't move a muscle. Not even an eyelid flicker.

Ella sniffs at the baby's nappy. It seems clean, she thinks, holding her over her shoulder. But then, almost as if she read her mind, the baby's discontented squawks turn high-pitched and her little body tenses as she draws up her knees to her chest. Ella now knows this is a sure sign her nappy is about to be filled, that she's perhaps in discomfort. *Please no...* she thinks. *Not now...* But it happens.

Ella slowly wheels over to where she left the plastic bag of nappy-change items, hooking it up with her finger. She puts it on her knee, along with the baby, and pushes herself towards the door, wheeling into the kitchen. It's precious time wasted and it takes her a good ten minutes to clean up the wriggling baby on her knee.

A noise. She stops, listening, but the baby is fussing too much for her to hear. Or perhaps it came from the garage, she thinks. A sign that Liam is still alive. She gently cups her hand over the baby's mouth but that just sends her into more of a frenzy. All Ella can do is put the nappy on and get her dressed again as fast as possible. Her hands are shaking and the tabs of the nappy won't stick because she's got cream on them. Then she buttons up the towelling suit all wrong. She lets out a little sob – it will have to do. She doesn't have time to be perfect.

Slowly, she wheels back into the doorway of the living room. Jacob is still out cold.

Back in the kitchen, still balancing the baby on her lap, she closes the door and pulls off the sock bandage from her cast, unwinding the longer bandage that has been fixing it in place. Kayleigh grabs hold of it, shoving it straight in her mouth, chewing on the soft fabric. At least it muffles her occasional squawks, Ella thinks, prising the two cast pieces off her leg. Her leg feels stiff as she stretches it out.

'OK, Kayleigh,' she says, holding the baby up on her shoulder. She stands up out of her wheelchair, tentatively placing her weight on her bad leg as she takes a single step towards the kitchen counter. She's done this many times before, but never while holding the baby. 'Sshh-shh…' she whispers, screwing up her eyes for a second as pain shoots through her knee and up into her thigh. She nuzzles Kayleigh for comfort, takes a deep breath.

Ella grits her teeth as she slowly slides a chair over to the kitchen cupboards. Every second of weight borne on her bad leg is agony. Using her good leg first and keeping a tight hold of the baby with her left arm, she steps up onto the chair, making sure to stand in the middle so it doesn't overbalance. She fishes around on top of the high cupboards and, for a moment, she can't find the key anywhere, but then breathes out gratefully as she feels the coldness of it under her fingers. She lowers herself down off the chair, wincing, but it's worth it to have the garage-door key in her hand.

She puts it in the pocket of her tracksuit bottoms before opening one of the drawers, taking out a large pair of kitchen scissors and a large cook's knife, her eyes fixed on the door leading to the garage. Ella clenches her teeth again, bracing herself for the agony as she makes her way over. Her main priority is not hurting Kayleigh, keeping her safe. And freeing Liam, she thinks, getting closer to the door.

She stops, wondering if she heard another noise, but it's nothing but her own rasping breaths and the baby's snuffles in her ear as she sucks on the bandage, the ribbon of it trailing down behind them.

As she reaches the door, Ella holds the baby tightly on her shoulder. Her jaw clamps together, chewing away the pain, helping her forget. She fishes in her pocket for the key, tucking the scissors and kitchen knife under her arm as she fights the tears, trying to get the key into the lock, her fingers trembling. She keeps thinking she hears noises from the other room, but convinces herself she's imagining it – just as she convinced herself, as a child, that she was imagining it when her mattress dipped down as he climbed in beside her late at night. Pretending to be asleep never worked.

The lock finally turns and she opens the door, pulling it back and revealing the black space of the garage beyond.

'Hello?' she whispers into the darkness.

The baby chortles and Ella feels her drool on her neck.

'Liam, are you here? Can you hear me?'

Nothing for a few seconds. Just silence and darkness.

Mmm…gahrrr…

'Hello?' Ella says. 'Liam?'

Then another choked, muffled noise. It barely sounds human. With her free hand, she feels around the inside of the door for a light switch. Before turning it on, she waits, listening out again for Jacob. Nothing.

The garage floods with light. It takes Ella's eyes a moment to adjust, as well as Liam's. And then they're staring at each other – him foetal and on the floor, his hands and feet bound and his mouth sealed up with tape. There's a bloodstain around his head on the concrete floor.

'Oh *God…*' she says, seeing him properly for the first time since Jacob threw him in there. 'Liam…' She grabs hold of the door frame, navigating herself and the baby over the couple of steps down into the garage. She could never have done it in her wheelchair.

Liam watches on, staring up at her, his eyes revealing as much fear as she has in the pit of her stomach. She inches closer to him, the pain making her feel dizzy.

The baby lets out another annoyed cry just as Ella bends down and pulls the tape off Liam's mouth.

'Fucking hell,' he says, as soon as it's off, shaking his head and spitting. 'What the hell's going on, Ella? I mean, what the actual…' He trails off then, noticing the steely look in her eyes, the way she keeps looking back over her shoulder as she tries her best to lower herself down to the ground. Not easy with the baby. 'Your leg,' he says, seeing there's no cast.

'Shh,' she whispers. 'Keep quiet. No time to explain,' she says, slipping the knife and scissors out from beneath her arm. She tries hacking at the rope binding up Liam's wrists, knowing that if he has his hands free, that's a start. But she can't get enough grip with the fingers of her broken arm, so she swaps the baby over to the other side, but it's almost as hard doing it with her left hand. 'We-we need to get out. And soon,' she says, sawing through the fibres as fast as she can. As soon as the last nylon strand is cut, Liam pulls his hands apart, flexing his wrists, watching his blue-grey skin colour up again.

'Thank fuck for that,' he says, grabbing the knife from Ella. It's easier for him to hack away at the rope binding his ankles, which he does furiously. 'Just tell me,' he says, glancing up, panting, as he keeps cutting. 'Are you coming with me?' he asks. 'And the baby?' he adds, finally cutting through the last of the rope. Suddenly, he's up on his feet – a bit wobbly at first, but he soon gets his balance.

'Yes, of course we're coming too,' Ella whispers, bundling up the bandage for the baby to chew on. She's whimpering again. 'And-and she's not actually mine,' she says, wondering how they're going to get out of the garage. She'd not considered that part, but it seems Liam has.

He's already at the up-and-over door at the front, fiddling with the catch on the inside, frantically looking for the release.

Ella limps up to him, the baby getting heavier by the second. 'Liam,' she whispers, just as he finds it, trying to force the heavy electric door up manually. 'The baby is stol—'

But she doesn't get a chance to finish. The booming voice fills the entire garage, his rage echoing around them.

'What the *fuck* are you doing?' Jacob roars, bracing himself in the doorway, flashing a look down at the cut ropes. Then his eyes go wide, his anger building, as he spots the other things lying there.

A videotape and a set of car keys.

Ella screams when she sees him – and the things – her heart missing a few beats, catching up in a rush of palpitations as Jacob staggers closer, his fists balled in front of him.

CHAPTER FORTY-NINE

Ten Years Ago

'Hey…'

Ella looked up. She was sitting alone on an old log at the shore of the lake, the water lapping around her bare toes as she pushed them into the sandy mud. She could still hear the others inside the lake house partying, the beat of the music filtering through the night. She smiled. Zach had his camera, of course, but at least it wasn't pointing at her, recording something she'd regret saying years later. She couldn't imagine what their future children, if indeed they had any, would think if they saw footage of the wild week they'd had. But it made her happy to think that one day she might have a home and kids with him. That he was considering that far ahead.

Zach sat down on the log. 'I remember this old tree coming down years ago,' he said. 'Lightning struck it. It blazed for hours. We thought the whole wood was going to go up.'

'Did no one call the fire brigade?' Ella asked. 'The lodge could have gone up too.' She looked back at it – entirely made from wood, inside and out. A tinder box, she thought, shuddering.

'No way a fire truck would get down here,' he said. 'When it was built, the original track was only just wide enough for construction, but now it's completely overgrown with trees. Dad's paranoid about privacy and security anyway, and wanted it secluded, but there's no access for cars any more, let alone anything bigger. Anyway, thankfully the tree fire just burnt itself out. The next winter it fell down and here it still lies.' He kicked the trunk. 'It made a good climbing frame for a while, though,' Zach said, smiling fondly.

'I like hearing these stories,' Ella said. 'And you know how much I love it here.' She slipped her hand inside his as they stared across the lake. 'I've had such a wonderful week, Zach. I wish we could stay here for ever.'

'Me too,' he said, laughing, leaning across and kissing her. 'Though we'd have to get rid of that rowdy lot first.' He gestured back up towards the house. They heard the faint beat of the music, the occasional wave of laughter, could just make out the warm glow from the candles that Meggie had gone around lighting when they'd arrived. 'Can you believe, I just got told off in my own house. My *dad's* house,' he added quickly.

'That's funny,' Ella said, laughing, splashing her outstretched feet in the water. 'But I'm hardly surprised. You've been shoving that camera up everyone's nose all night, including poor Zandra's. I'm surprised Charles didn't punch you.'

'It wasn't Charles,' Zach said. 'It was Harry.' He laughed as Ella tried to conceal the frown. She didn't like the thought of him and Zach having cross words. 'I was looking for you, actually, and found him crashed out on my bed, drunk, convinced he was in the guest room where he usually sleeps. He looked very green. I left him there, telling him not to puke.' He lit up a cigarette, the glow of the match making his face look eerie. His eyes – dazzling, intense.

'He'll be right as rain in ten minutes,' Ella said, laughing again. 'You know what Harry's like.'

'Yeah,' Zach said, staring at her. 'I do.' He tilted up his head and blew out smoke, watching for a reaction. 'He cares a lot about you, you know.'

'He sometimes worries,' Ella said, feeling embarrassed. She didn't want Zach to think that she needed her brother to look out for her.

'Worries or something else?...' Zach trailed off, standing and picking up a flat stone from the shore, skimming it across the lake. The moonlight picked out the ripples on the water as it bounced four or five times off the surface.

'What do you mean?' Ella said, drawing up to his side. She'd never thought Zach the jealous type before, and certainly not when it came to Harry. He and her brother were mates.

'Nothing,' Zach replied, looking at her. 'Let's go for a walk.' He took her hand. 'Maybe we'll spot an owl in the woods.'

As they set off, they glanced back to see what the sudden noise was. The entire group had come out onto the deck and were stripping off their clothes – arms flailing, bodies staggering and hopping about as they giggled and pulled off dresses and shirts. Then, one by one, they ran down the steps and into the water.

'C'mon,' Zach said, and they disappeared into the woods that edged the shore, leading away from the lodge. For a moment, he looked at Ella – eyebrows raised – perhaps wondering if she wanted to join in with the others, but she could think of nothing she'd rather do less. She gave a quick shake of her head and Zach led her on. 'I've got a favourite spot,' he said, guiding her to a little clearing in the treed area further around the shore – a small curve of soft, grassy sand right at the water's edge. It was completely private.

'They sound like they're having fun,' Ella said, laughing at the whoops, catcalls and splashes carrying through the night.

'Sit,' Zach said, taking off his jacket and laying it on the ground for her.

But before she'd even settled down, he had his hands on her shoulders, easing her back into a lying position. He lay beside her, half on top, his mouth coming down on hers, moaning gently, his passion resonating into her mouth. 'God, Ella,' he said, his hand running all over her, as though he couldn't get enough of her. 'Tonight would be so perfect…'

Ella smiled, looking up into his eyes, the moon bright even through the trees. 'Zach…' she whispered, kissing him again. Her hands felt out the shape of his body – the thick muscles across his shoulders, the soft hair at the nape of his neck, the stubble on his jaw, and his slim hips as he hoisted himself on top of her.

'I know you want your first time to be special… and surely this is it, right here?' He unhitched his belt, pulling roughly at it, barely able to control himself as he undid his jeans. Ella felt him shudder as he pulled his T-shirt off over his head, exposing his lean, fit body.

She turned away.

'Zach, please…' They'd been through this so many times before – him pressuring her, her feeling guilty, him getting moody for a while until things went back to normal. He always understood and, in turn, she understood his frustration. 'I still want to wait,' she said, but was silenced as his mouth plunged onto hers again. This time he was rougher, more urgent, her head pressed back into the ground as his hands fumbled with her clothes.

Then she heard a ripping sound. The straps of her dress.

'Zach… *Zach*, what are you?—' She felt her heart kick up. Something was different this time. 'Zach, no *stop*, you're drunk. Let's go back to the others.'

Ella tried to sit up, but he wouldn't let her. Instead, he grabbed her hands, pinning them above her head while, with his other arm, he tore at her clothes, ripping down the top half of her dress to expose her bra. He pulled at it, kissing and biting her naked skin, a strange animal sound coming from him that Ella had never heard before. His eyes looked different, as if he wasn't inside them. As though someone else had taken him over.

'*No!* Stop, Zach!' She thrashed her legs about, writhing from side to side, but he climbed on top of her, pinning her down, his jeans around his thighs.

'Tell me you want it too,' he said urgently, panting, sweating, even his voice sounding different, not like him.

'*No*, no, not like this!' Ella cried, almost ready to give up and resign herself to what was coming. 'Please, don't…' She began to sob, beating her feet uselessly on the ground.

Then, suddenly, Zach let go of her arms, his face still seething, staring down at her, his expression somewhere between shame and anger.

He leapt to his feet, pulling up his jeans, kicking at the dirt on the ground and sending it showering over her as he threw on his T-shirt. 'Fucking hell, Ella,' he said pacing about, tearing his hands through his hair, sweat pouring from him. 'You lead me on, then you turn me down. Look what you do to me…'

He walked off into the trees, then came back again. Ella was on her feet, sobbing, trying to fix the straps of her dress. He grabbed her by the shoulders, kissing her again, growling, fighting more urges. She froze, praying for it to be over. And in a few more seconds, it was, because he swiped up his jacket and camera and strode off again.

So she thought.

Exhausted, scared and not knowing what to do, Ella dropped down onto the soft ground by the water's edge. With her knees drawn up under her chin, she buried her face, sobbing. Was she being unreasonable? Perhaps she was. But she couldn't bring herself to, not yet and not with everything from her past still hanging heavy over her. It was too soon, as though she wasn't yet back to herself. She wondered if she ever would be. Zach believed he would be her first. And, indeed, he *should* be her first. But that was a lie and she didn't know how to tell him. He would never be that.

Choked sobs bubbled out of her as she sat there, reliving the shame, her shoulders shaking as she curled herself up into a ball of self-loathing. She loved Zach dearly, and he loved her but—

'Oww…' Ella's head whipped back as his hands grabbed her hair. '*No*—'

She was flung to the ground, her torn dress ripped from her again as he undid his jeans, a look in his eyes she'd never seen the likes of before. As he forced her legs apart, as she writhed and thrashed beneath him trying her hardest to get him off, Ella gradually gave up, knowing that this time there was no use in screaming or fighting. So she fell silent. Waited for it to be over, thinking of other things, as she always had.

CHAPTER FIFTY

Ella

'Jacob...' Ella says, her eyes wide, her mouth agape. She can't feel herself – her skin, her feelings, her thoughts. She's trapped in a bubble. As though it's him and her. Just the two of them. She knows by the look on his face that there'll be no appeasing him now, no talking him round. They just need to get out.

Jacob staggers into the garage, scuffing over the cut ropes, crashing into the clutter that's stacked up in the garage – old gardening tools, boxes of stuff, things from a decade of life Ella knew nothing about.

'So this is how you repay me,' he says, glaring at her. His voice is slurred – almost sad, Ella thinks. His movements are unco-ordinated and clumsy as he comes towards them, one unsteady step at a time. But then he stops, staring down at the things on the floor again.

'*Shit*,' Liam says, seeing them at the same time as he wrenches at the electric up-and-over door. It's stuck, not operating properly without the remote control. He grabs Ella, pulling her away from Jacob; she stumbles, clutching the baby, protecting her little head. Her bad knee buckles but she saves herself. Just.

Ella has her eyes fixed on the two things as well – the DV tape, lying next to a set of keys on the floor where Liam was tied up.

It happens so quickly, she's not sure who lunges first. A flurry of fists and arms knot and thrash as Liam and Jacob fight, each of them hurling punches and kicks, yanking the other round, headbutting by Liam, a punch in the guts from Jacob. Ella screams, not knowing what to do. It's hard enough holding the baby, let alone intervening as the two men crash into everything. But as they wrestle, all she can focus on is the tape. And how she can get it – if it is indeed the one she's been looking for. She has no idea how it got there.

'You're *crazy*,' Liam yells, his face red from the twisted headlock.

Jacob brings his knee up, planting it in Liam's back, sending him to the ground. He kicks him several times in the guts as well as the face for good measure, even though he's still uncoordinated and drugged.

'Jacob, stop!' Ella cries. 'What the hell are you doing? What are you doing to our *family*? I'm your… I'm your *wife*. This is your baby. We'll make things OK again, right?' She pants, the thump of her heart pounding up her throat.

But he doesn't hear her. He's way past reason, driven by something much deeper – a hurt Ella has never witnessed before, something that's been festering inside him for years.

She cries, can't help herself. Then the baby starts up too – high, pitiful wails that fill the garage. Ella limps towards Jacob as Liam hauls himself up off the floor, his face bloody and grazed. He looks around, reaching out for the keys, but Jacob follows his line of sight, kicking them out of the way.

'You're not leaving me,' he booms at Ella. 'Ever!'

Slowly, almost imperceptibly as Jacob focusses on Liam again, Ella inches towards a stack of tools propped in the corner. A gardening rake, a fork, a broom, a spade – all leaning against a wheelbarrow from a life she never knew he had.

Liam, trailing blood, crawls after the keys, reaching out for them, but Jacob's boot is quicker as it hits him squarely in the jaw, sending him flying backwards again, crashing into a pile of flowerpots. A suitcase comes tumbling down, landing on top of him. He shoves it away and, with a second wind, launches himself to his feet, rushing at Jacob and throwing another punch. Jacob staggers backwards with a grunt, allowing Ella just enough time to lay the baby in the wheelbarrow – carefully resting her head down on the metal – before grabbing the shovel. It's shiny, looks as though it's never been used. While the men tear into each other, Ella advances slowly. One agonising step at a time.

For a few seconds, she hallucinates, perhaps induced by the pain, perhaps by fear, but she sees herself pedalling hard. It's raining, sheeting down, and all she wants is to get home. It's times like that – the *between* times, as she used to call them – when she felt most vulnerable. Not at work, where she was distracted and engaged by technical stuff, deadlines or listening to the banter in the office. And not at home – her sanctuary, even though, if she was honest, it was her prison.

Slowly, she raises the shovel, holding it firmly in both hands.

Another step. Gritting her teeth until she thinks they'll crack from the pressure. That, or her jaw will break.

She tries to focus on both men – separating them. Pulling apart their bodies, their heads, as she lifts the shovel higher, taking breath after breath, pedal after pedal, as she advances. Leans into the roundabout.

The windscreen wipers of the van, the man's face, the rain blurring her vision, skewing what's real and what's not as she focusses on Jacob's skull, taking aim. But all she sees is her own head as it hits the tarmac, the taste of grit in her mouth as the dirt gets in, the crack of bones in her leg and wrist as she goes down.

Blackness.

Then the beep, beep, beep of hospital machines.

In that one moment, as her shoulders tense ready to take a swing, she sees everything. The cobbled streets of Durham, her room at St Mary's, happy, excited freshers' faces, the lecturers, the formal dinners, the bars, the kiss, the drunken nights, the essays, the library, Meggie, fancy clothes, private limousines, exclusive restaurants, Adlington, the lake house, the trees, the friends, the water, the lightning, Ron, her mum, Harry, Zach and how much he told her he loved her, the furs, the football, the wine in the shed, crying in her room, the longing to escape, the hard work, the freedom, her job, her desk, birthday cakes, sandwiches in the fridge, her embroidery, microwave meals for one, exams, the celebrations, the water's edge, the loneliness, the despair, the hope…

Yes, most of all, the *hope*.

Jacob's eyes bulge, his face a twisted, bloody mess as he prepares to launch himself at Liam for a final attack. Ella screws up her eyes just as the baby cries – another wail that seems to come from her own heart, not that of the child.

Then she does it. With all her strength, she brings the shovel down cleanly on the side of Jacob's head, almost feeling the pain herself, as if she's been hit, not him.

For a moment, he staggers. His arm frozen mid-air, ready to punch. But he stops as his eyes roll back in his head, his tongue poking out of his mouth as he registers the blow. Ella takes another hit, harder this time as his legs give way and he goes down. His head hits the concrete.

Then, unable to stop herself, she hammers him with the shovel again and again, grunting with each blow as she lays into him with full force. She doesn't care about the pain in her leg, doesn't care about the consequences, the blood spattering everywhere. She only cares about what's gone before, about everything she suffered. About getting out.

'Ella, stop!' Liam yells, dragging himself up and grabbing her arms. 'Enough!'

She freezes, looking down at what she's done. He lies there, blood flowing from his nose, mouth, ears. His eyes are flickering, staring up at her, as he fights to keep consciousness.

'Let's get out of here,' Liam says, pulling her away and grabbing his keys and the cracked video box as they go, shoving them in his jacket pocket before wrenching at the up-and-over door. He glances up at the mechanics of it, jiggling it frantically, knowing there must be an internal override button inside somewhere.

Ella limps back to the wheelbarrow and scoops up the howling baby, cradling her head, nuzzling her, whispering to her. For a blissful second, her sweet baby scent is all she can register.

Then the garage door raises and a cool rush of evening air floods in.

'Quick,' Liam calls. 'Let's go.'

But Ella is frozen. Staring at Jacob, writhing on the garage floor.

She can't move.

'Ella! Hurry, *now*!'

She feels the pull of Liam's hand on her arm, thrown off balance by his urgency. She wobbles on her bad leg, grimacing from pain.

Jacob twitches, dragging himself up onto all fours.

He won't give up. She knows this.

This was the fight they should have had long ago, but never did.

'Ella! *Now!*' Liam yells, snapping her back to reality.

She turns, hobbling on her bad leg towards the exit of the garage as fast as she can. She sees the driveway and Liam's small blue car parked under the streetlights beyond. He's already bleeped it unlocked, opened the passenger door for her.

Ella gets in with the baby, not even caring about the pain any more, watching in horror as Jacob staggers out of the garage towards the car. She hugs the baby close as Liam leaps into the driver's side, shoving the key in the ignition. He starts the engine, flicking the central locking just as Jacob hurls himself at the side of the car, yanking at Ella's door handle. She screams, his face leering at her through the glass, smearing it with blood. When it doesn't open, he thumps the window, kicking the car, yelling and spitting at her.

Liam rams the car into gear and speeds off, just as Jacob launches himself at the bonnet, flying off it as they pull away.

Ella daren't look back. She focusses on the street ahead, the electric gates at the top as Liam shifts through the gears, hammering the engine up the hill, halting only for the gates to swing open.

'Hurry up, hurry *up*...' Ella whispers, expecting Jacob to appear at her window any moment. Finally, the gap is wide enough to get the car through but, just as they're about to pull away, a police car with its blue light flashing speeds towards them, screaming through the open gates and down the hill.

'Oh God, *no*,' Ella cries, glancing back as they head out onto the main road. She knows it'll all be over soon – that Jacob will tell them everything, not to mention that she's run off with a stolen baby. She can't help the tears, hot and fat, as they dribble down her cheeks and onto the baby's head. Her shoulders bounce up and down in time with her sobs as Liam pulls out onto the main road, driving more steadily now. It's all over for her – the only comfort that Liam and the baby are safe.

'Oh, *Ella*,' he says, sighing out a huge breath. He reaches across and takes hold of her hand, squeezing it. 'Everything's going to be OK.' He glances in the rear-view mirror, wincing when he sees the mess of his face.

Ella rests her head back against the seat, closing her eyes for a moment, not thinking everything's OK at all. She's free but not free. Probably the most trapped she's ever been.

'Liam,' she says, sniffing, looking across at him as they merge in with the traffic. 'The videotape that was on the garage floor... was that the one I was looking for? How did you?—'

He glances across at her. 'I was going to tell you, but I didn't want to get your hopes up either. You seemed so-so *panicked* about it. As if it was a matter of life and death.' He grips the wheel, his knuckles white.

Ella covers her face.

'It was wrong of me, I know. And I'm truly sorry.' Liam slows up at the traffic lights, drumming his fingers. 'Truth is, I was going to watch it on the kit at work then let you know what was on it. I didn't want to raise your hopes.'

'Jesus Christ, Liam. That's *not* OK.' Ella stares over at him. 'That tape is private and nothing to do with—'

'Fine. You really want to know why I took it?' he says, flashing her a look again, colour flooding his cheeks.

Ella checks herself, letting him speak even though she just wants to thump him. 'Why?'

They sit, motionless, at the traffic lights, waiting for the signal to change. Kayleigh lets out an indignant squawk, not enjoying being pinned to Ella as she grips her tightly – useless in an accident, but for now she has no choice.

'Because I wanted to know just *one* fucking thing about you, Ella Sinclair.'

She can't help the gasp. 'But—'

'We've been working together for what now, five, maybe six years? And I still have no idea about you – what you do in your spare time, what your hobbies are, if you have any siblings or even what you have in those bloody sandwiches you bring to work every day. Do you know how long I've been waiting for you to forget your lunch box so there was a chance you'd come to the café? Years. Fucking *years*, Ella.' He raises his hands off the wheel before shoving the car into gear. 'So I'm sorry. Taking that tape was wrong, I know, but I figured something in your life was wrong, too… I just sensed you weren't telling me everything and that, somehow, the tape was to do with it and that I might find out something about you. Be able to *help* you.'

As they slowly pull away, he glances in the rear-view mirror again, touching his split lip and cheek, rubbing at the dried blood.

'You're right,' Ella says quietly, staring out of the side window. 'I haven't told you everything and-and I can't.'

Liam nods.

Ella sighs, wanting nothing more than to confide before the police catch up with her. Then at least one person in the world would know the truth. She'd quite like it to be Liam. But how can she? She imagines Jacob now – the police helping him, calling for medical backup, him describing how she went crazy, attacked him with a shovel and fled with a stolen baby and a violent intruder. And then he'll tell them all the rest. What she did.

'I understand,' he says, pausing. 'So, where are we going? I'm just following the road here. Do you want me to take you to hospital? We should both get checked—'

'No, definitely not,' Ella says. She wants to enjoy her last moments of freedom, not be prodded by doctors.

'Then where?'

Ella thinks, staring across at Liam. Then she slips her hand into his jacket pocket, pulling out the DV tape. 'Turn left up here,' she says flatly. 'Take me to work. There's something I need to do.'

CHAPTER FIFTY-ONE

Ella

Liam pulls his pass from his wallet and swipes it at the door. Ella stares around the deserted office as she hobbles inside, not even sure how many weeks have passed since she was last here – that fateful day when she walked out of work, unlocked her bicycle from the rack and headed off home.

'Ella, you're really struggling. Let me carry the baby.' Liam holds out his arms to take Kayleigh, who smiles up at him as she's passed across. 'And look, lean on this. It might help.' He pulls out a large umbrella that someone's left in the stand. Ella glances back outside through the glass doors, checking.

'It's OK. He was in a bad way. He won't have followed us.'

'It's not him I'm worried about,' she says, knowing that Jacob will have likely remembered Liam's car's number plate, or part of it, and told the police. Their investigations, prompted by the shopping centre sighting of the pram, and no doubt CCTV of Liz's car, must have led them to Green Leys. They're hardly going to ignore a blood-covered man lying on the ground a couple of driveways down. There's probably an alert out on them right now. She lets out a little sob.

'Let's go up,' Liam says, pressing the lift button. While the pain in Ella's leg makes her want to throw up, it's incomparable to the pain in her heart. It seems she's never going to be allowed a go at life. Even if she gets away with kidnapping Kayleigh, she's still an accessory. And anyway, there's no escaping murder. She can never undo what she did – even if she destroys the tape, even if he didn't take a copy, she and Jacob still know what happened.

'Here,' Liam says when they reach the editing floor, 'put your arm around my waist, let me support you.'

Ella looks at him. She's not spoken to him this much in all the years they've worked together, and now he wants them to wrap their arms around each other.

'Thanks,' she says, allowing him to tuck his arm under hers, while she does the same to him, holding her up as they step out of the lift. Liam swipes his pass to the editing suites, holding the door wide open.

Ella stops, looking around, her eyes coming to rest on her workstation halfway down the office. Her eyes fill with tears as she sees the place she sat for just under a decade, day in, day out.

'You want to go over?' he asks.

She shakes her head. 'No, I need to play this,' she says, holding up the tape and pointing down to the edit suite. She has no desire to see what's on her desk, what she left behind.

Liam nods, helping her along, holding Kayleigh in the crook of his other arm. As they approach the small room, racked up with equipment, sound decks and monitors, Ella can't help wondering what people would think if they saw the three of them. A family – an injured wife, a loving husband helping her, and their much-loved little girl. Perfect.

In reality, she and Kayleigh are none of these things. But she can't help thinking that Liam would make someone a good husband, with his kind eyes and caring nature. Or, she wonders, perhaps he already has a wife or girlfriend. She hopes if he does, that his wife is as lovely as him.

He opens the heavy soundproof door, allowing Ella in to the small room first. She stops and turns, halting him gently with her hand, staring up at him. 'I need to do this alone,' she says, holding up the tape. 'It's kind of... well, it's personal,' she adds, thinking that's at least the truth. Murder is indeed a deeply personal experience, woven into every strand of DNA, each cell of her body living with the consequences ever after.

'Sure,' Liam says, giving her a small smile. 'I'll show the baby the office.' He touches her arm, so lightly Ella's not sure if he even did. She shuts the door, wondering how long she's got before the police track them down. Liam's car is parked right outside the office.

She flicks a few switches, thankful they have the right equipment even though most of their work is digital, and inserts the tape into the DV player, powering up a monitor too. She twists the blinds closed on the glass partition to the main office. If it's the right tape, the contents are for her eyes only.

She sits down, feeling faint, her heart pounding, as she presses play. She watches as the monitor flickers and jumps to life, the ten-year-old footage immediately showing old technology, poor quality.

'It might not even be the right one,' she tells herself over and over, biting on her lip as the leader runs. She studies the cassette box, spotting the faded pencil scrawl on the paper insert – *his* writing.

Lake House 08.

Then she sees familiar faces onscreen, making her startle, cover her mouth as she's hurled back in time. She feels twenty-one again. Or, rather, not quite twenty-one. That birthday was spent alone, holed up, hiding, avoiding, waiting for the inevitable knock at the door. But it never came. She only ever allowed herself to read one newspaper report – *Two Die in Student Inferno* – and refused to look after that, isolating herself more and more.

She can't help the tears, her vision blurred as she sees Meggie's sweet face onscreen, pulling crazy expressions as Zach films her from all kinds of angles, turning the camera on its side, upside-down. That's what he was like – wild, happy, carefree. He's not like that any more, she thinks, swallowing.

Ella dares to tweak the volume up and the sounds of Adlington fill the small editing suite. She's plunged back there.

'We had dinner first,' she says, nodding, remembering, her hand still covering her mouth, unable to take her eyes off the screen. She recalls Zach's mother, how she insisted they were all fed properly, sitting around the large, formal dining table. She'd seemed to have had a soft spot for Ella. It was after dinner that they'd gone down to the lake house for their last night. Where everything turned bad.

Suddenly the camera wobbles and tilts on its side, as though it's been put on a table and left there, filming by mistake. She hears chatter and laughter, sees people walking past, only their middles showing. Then, a few minutes later, expletives as Zach realises he's left the camera on, moaning about the switch not working properly. Then he's up on his chair, pointing the lens down the table as he makes a drunken toast to them all.

She remembers it as though it were yesterday. Goosebumps cover her body.

Then she sees herself sitting at the table and wants to throw up. It's like seeing a different person entirely, even though she knows it's her. She remembers the dress she was wearing, how she'd done her hair, her make-up, and worn the perfume Zach had given her. Meggie is sitting to one side of her with Charles the other side, next to that girl he'd brought along just for the weekend – Sandra or Zandra or something. And then there's Ethan, looking disinterested and aloof, and Harry, Stan and Alex mucking about.

She stares at herself – her beaming smile, the light in her eyes, the shine on her hair. Only ten years ago but it may as well be a hundred. 'I look *happy*,' she whispers. Little did she know that she only had about three hours of happiness left. After that, everything changed.

To the lake! she hears Zach calling out from behind the camera, filming as everyone gets up from the table, staggering, merry, in good spirits. Then the camera is switched off, and Ella holds her breath as she sees a few seconds of blackness before it switches to the next scene.

CHAPTER FIFTY-TWO

Ella

Ella hardly breathes, can't take her eyes off the screen as she watches everyone chilling out in the lake house, the alcohol flowing, the air hazy from the joints being smoked. Charles is on his knees at the table, doing his beloved lines before pushing himself on Zandra who, judging by her expression, doesn't seem to mind. In fact, she's encouraging him. The film is erratic, jumping all over the place as Zach zooms in and out, the focus blurring then sharpening as the old camera struggles to keep up in the candlelight. She sees herself, sitting comfortably on the sofa, but also looking out of place, as though she's feeling awkward, on edge. It was the thought of everything coming to an end, she remembers – and not just the blissful week she'd spent at Adlington. She was worried what would happen to her and Zach when he went off to London, Meggie too, as well as the uncertainty of her future. The others, even Harry, had everything mapped out.

She sees herself get up from the sofa, walking past Zach as he points the camera right at her face. She pokes out her tongue playfully, notices how much healthier she looked then – flesh on her bones, a sparkle in her eye – rather than the grey, skinny creature she's become now, surviving on microwave meals for one and little sunlight.

'I went outside next,' she says to herself, biting her nail, remembering how she stood and stared at the lake, thinking, counting the stars. She adored that place, wished she and Zach could have spent time alone there.

Don't film me when I'm shitfaced, Harry says, looming large at the lens, joking, laughing, although Ella sees something sad in his eyes. The image shakes then as Zach laughs, panning around, then it goes black and crackly for a few more seconds when he switches it off.

Ella pushes back in her chair, gently rubbing her throbbing knee, tears rolling down her face. She's sweating – fever or fear, she's not sure – and the light-headed feeling is getting worse as the tape goes on. She knows it's the right one – the evening it happened. She's just not sure she can stand to watch. The ultimate self-punishment.

Seconds later, the tape starts up again, but this time the footage is much darker and grainier, almost as if it's in black-and-white, the lighting dim. Ella thinks she hears someone mumbling in the background, swearing as they crash about, but the sound quality is poor so she can't make out words. Wherever the camera is filming, it's not the living room any more, and whoever's holding it obviously doesn't know it's recording. She hears breathing, footsteps, sees a window with the moonlight glowing behind the glass, but then the camera gets puts down on its side, the footage at ninety degrees. It's one of the bedrooms at the lake house.

Ella tilts her head, hearing more footsteps before a light comes on nearby – perhaps in the adjoining bathroom. She knew he'd already got into bed before she went in. A few moments later, a figure comes past the lens, too out of focus to see clearly – although Ella already knows who it is. Then he falls onto the bed, lying semi-naked on top.

That's when she sees his face. Covers her own as she watches, peeking between her fingers. His last moments alive. She sits there for a good ten minutes, watching his chest rise and fall as he quickly drops into an alcohol-fuelled sleep, his foot twitching, his head occasionally turning from one side to the other. She can't take her eyes off him – the goodbye she never had. She sits there staring, entranced, sad beyond belief.

'Wait, *what?…*' Ella says, leaning forward for a closer look. She didn't expect someone else to walk past the camera lens just moments later – again, too close for it to focus properly. She sees the grainy shadow of the second person pacing back and forth, hears them as they curse and yell, making a din. It's clear they're drunk – staggering, slurring, not in control. Then there's a crash, making Ella jump in her chair. She squeals as objects fly onto the floor, stuff being swept off surfaces as he lashes out. The camera jogs as it's knocked but the bed still stays in view.

She hangs her head for a second, remembering tripping over those same things when she came in, possibly only minutes later. Ella can hardly breathe as she watches.

You're in my fucking room, you stupid bastard, he says, slurring, staggering over to the bed. He kicks it but misses, wobbling, trying to regain his balance. He kicks again, the film resolving into focus as he comes into full view from behind. She recognises him instantly, of course – his shape, the aggression piled up in his tense shoulders, his fists clenched by his sides. *I fucking hate you, you know that? All this time, I've loathed you. I'm only nice to you for her sake.*

The figure on the bed doesn't move. Just a small twitch. Out cold to drugs and alcohol.

Ella watches, hardly daring to breathe. She had no idea he came into the room *before* her. Her heart thumps harder as she sees how pent-up he is, despite what he'd just done to her down by the lake while the others were swimming. The time flashes in the corner of the screen – 1:03 a.m. – less than an hour after he'd raped her. His shirt is still untucked, dirty on the back from where she put up a fight, tried to get him off. And she nearly did at one point – kicking, scratching, biting as she'd writhed on the rough ground with him tearing at her clothes, forcing himself into her. She'd screamed out, of course, but he clamped his hand over her mouth and, besides, the others were too far away and making too much noise in the water themselves to hear her cries for help. In the end, she'd fallen silent.

Ella watches intently, thinking, frowning, trying to work it out. Was she still down by the lake at this point – lying on her back, shaking, terrified, broken? She remembers the water lapping nearby, her body aching and destroyed after he'd torn her soul to shreds.

Ella cries. Full-blown sobbing, her chest heaving and her heart breaking as she watches the monitor, confused. She's certain that, in a few moments, she'll see herself bursting into the room, a girl tormented, a girl destroyed – filled with rage and shame.

Afterwards, he'd left her lying there, and she'd stayed, perfectly still, frozen, for what seemed like an age. Then, gradually, she'd forced herself to move, to stand up, before stumbling back up the slope, shaking as she climbed the steps to the house with a sore body, a broken heart, unable to comprehend what had just happened. She hadn't felt real, as though her soul had left her, was looking down from above, disowning her because she was dirty.

Again.

She remembers it was quiet inside the house, with the others having swum out to the little island that lay off the shore. She had just wanted to hide away before they all came back. There was no way she could face anyone, let alone *him*. Yet she'd known she was stuck there until morning, would never be able to find her way back through the woods in the dark. She flicked on the light in the kitchen. She'd wanted water, perhaps find some antiseptic for her cuts, some painkillers. But, as she stood at the kitchen counter, leaning on it, head down, trying to stop the tears and pain, she'd seen the knife. Lying there on the chopping board, left out by someone earlier. It had spoken to her, whispered to her, told her everything would be OK, that her pain could be taken away once and for all. That she never need suffer again. It was then she'd known she wanted him dead. That she couldn't carry on living if he was still alive. She'd imagined the knife sliding into his body over and over and over, like he'd just done to her so violently down by the water. Because that's what it was – a knife going into her. Killing her. She'd dragged her hand across her face, sniffing, sobbing, wiping her nose on her arm. Pure anger.

And then she'd heard a noise.

'Hello?' she remembers calling out. But there'd been no reply.

She listened, straining her ears, but all she could hear were the faraway catcalls of the others as their splashes and squeals echoed through the night. Then she'd heard the relaxed notes of the chill-out songs still playing in the other room, which had somehow calmed her, helped her believe she was doing the right thing by wrapping her fingers around the knife, picking it up. It was protection, that's all. Then a noise again, as if someone was walking about. Ella had known which of the many bedrooms was his. She'd seen him in there earlier, lying on the bed, arms up behind his head, looking like a lord, king of the castle. She'd crept from the kitchen, the knife raised in front of her, her bare feet making no sound on the wooden floor as she went down the corridor towards the back of the lodge.

On the way past, she'd glanced in the living room – empty, as she'd thought. Just the remains of their drinking, their smoking, the drugs, a dozen candles flickering on the low table. She'd carried on walking.

Ella cowers at the workstation, quickly checking through the blind behind her to see where Liam is. She doesn't want him bursting in, doesn't want him to see what happens next. She spots him standing at the other end of the office, jiggling the baby on his hip while waving a little stuffed toy about, plucked from someone's desk. She's reminded of the Valentine's teddy left on hers. More tears as she turns back to the monitor.

Any moment now, she knows she will see herself appear onscreen, coming into the bedroom with the knife. She glances at the timestamp – 1:08 a.m. Five minutes of nothing – just a grainy image, the occasional moth or fly flicking past, upsetting the focus.

Still no sign of her coming in.

Suddenly, Ella cries out in shock, thankful the edit suite is soundproofed. 'Oh my *God*,' she says, cupping her hands over her mouth. 'What the *hell?*…'

The other figure is back – launching himself at the bed, unable to help the rage. It was just the same when he raped her, his muscles tight as steel, no chance of her getting away. He slings his fist at the bed – a wild punch – and despite the grainy film and poor light, Ella sees there's a struggle. Grunting and swearing. But it's useless. He's pinned down and, like her, he didn't stand a chance of getting free.

And then she sees the glint.

'*No*…' Ella whispers, her heart thumping as she covers her mouth again.

The sailing clasp knife opens easily – she recognises it from their trip to Cowes earlier in the week. It sinks into his belly so swiftly, so easily, there's barely a sound. Just a pool of dark blood spilling out as Harry stabs Zach with one deep thrust. The drugs, the alcohol… he doesn't even put up a fight. *Can't* put up a fight as her brother climbs off him, standing, staring down at his work, wiping the knife down the sheets before flicking it closed, putting it in his pocket.

Ella can't move as she watches him throw the duvet over Zach, covering his lifeless body. And then he leaves, unaware that everything has just been filmed. As her eyes fill with tears, she tries to work out what this means, tries to understand as she watches the now motionless screen, stares incredulously at the shrouded figure in bed, no indication of the carnage beneath. It just looks like someone's asleep. But she can't think clearly as she sits in the booth, shaking, shivering, waiting.

And there she is. Bursting into Harry's room in a rage – the room she saw him lying in earlier. But, of course, she now knows it *wasn't* his room – that there was a mix-up, Harry getting confused again, them swapping. He'd done it before. Ella watches herself on the monitor as she goes up to the bed – a girl broken, a girl intent on revenge. It's not self-defence any more, it's cold-blooded murder as she thrusts the knife through the duvet, plunging the blade into her brother – the person who she *thought* was her brother – stabbing wildly, wanting nothing more than for him to die as she screams out *I hate you, I hate you, I hate you*, over and over.

She couldn't live with what he did to her down by the lake.

Couldn't live with what he did to her when they were children, coming into her room night after night, climbing into bed, his needs changing from solace and comfort to far worse as they became teenagers. Ella had no choice as he pinned her down, covered her mouth. If she ever told anyone what he did to her, he said, she'd be dead.

Ella hears the sobs bursting out of her as she watches herself, her hair flying everywhere, the tears streaming down her face. She remembers thinking she hadn't even hit him with the blade, that it didn't even feel as though he was under there. That she'd missed him completely.

Though, when the voice had come from behind, when the hands had pinned her arms to her side and the slap across her face had come, she'd known it hadn't been her brother under the covers. Couldn't have been. He was standing right beside her.

Harry?... she screams on the film, looking up at him, terrified.

That one word changing everything. Changing the next ten years of her life. In the dim light, she sees herself almost passing out, sees Harry catching her as her legs buckle, allowing her to drop onto the bed. Then he whips back the covers. The sea of blood from the carnage beneath still spreading out, soaking the bedding.

See what you've done, Ella-bella? he yells, hitting her around the head again. *You've killed him.*

She remembers it as though it was yesterday, can still smell it in her nostrils – the metallic tang of Zach's blood, the empty look in his eyes, his skin pale and lifeless.

She watches herself crumple from shock when she realises what she's done. *Zach!* she screams, lunging forward, shaking him, trying to wake him up, covering herself in his blood. *Please, don't be dead, oh my God, Zach, wake up!* Her tears come thick and fast then as Harry watches on. *Harry, help me. I didn't mean to. What shall I do? What shall we do?* She's hysterical.

Ella sits watching, aghast, wanting to pull her twenty-year-old self into her arms, tell her that she didn't do it – she didn't kill Zach – that he was already dead. That Harry had killed him first.

She didn't do it.

And what she'd *intended* to do, she thinks, sobbing, was because of what Harry had done to her. She couldn't take any more. It wasn't Zach who'd come back to her when she was by the lake – as ever, he'd taken control of himself and gone off to cool down – rather, it was Harry who'd found her down there; it was *him* who did what he'd spent their teenage years inflicting on her. All she'd ever wanted when they were growing up was to protect him from Ron. It was a twisted triangle of abuse. Him creeping into her room at night as a little boy, disturbed, frightened, Ella protecting him, comforting him, while he told her that everything would be OK once they were older and could get away. Together, they'd planned their escape, with Harry promising that they'd one day have the perfect family they'd always wanted. The family they'd never had, just the two of them. They were meant to be together, he'd said. *For ever.* And now she knows he meant it.

We do nothing, Harry says on the screen, laughing, turning so Ella can see the depth of his smug smile. But then he stops, notices the camera, sees the red light glowing on the front. He comes up, snatching at it, swearing loudly as the footage goes all over the place – the floor, the ceiling, his face close-up. And, finally, with one last shot of Ella sobbing hysterically over Zach's body, the film cuts.

Ella stops the DV player. Sits staring at the blank monitor, silent tears streaming down her face, allowing what she's seen to sink in, letting her mind process that she's lived the last ten years believing she'd killed Zach by mistake. Not only that, but he'd filmed his own murder. Ella had no idea Harry was already on the footage, what he'd done before she'd gone in to the room.

She rests her head down on the editing desk, remembering how Harry had pulled the tape from the camera then, his hands shaking as he shoved it into its box, his anger visible, as she'd lunged for it. The evidence. He'd told her he was going to destroy it but obviously he never had.

'You're crazy,' she'd said. 'And I *hate* you!' she'd yelled, staring at him through swollen eyes, finally seeing him for who he really was, despising that they were twins. Whenever she looked at him, she saw herself superimposed – him and her, one and the same.

Something had flicked inside her as she stood in Zach's bedroom, her entire body shaking as Harry came closer, the tape tucked inside his pocket, coming for her. It was her only chance.

Quick as a flash, before he could grab her, she was out of the bedroom, pulling the key from the inside with trembling hands and locking the door behind her. She just needed to get away. One of the others would eventually hear him banging on the door and unlock it. By then, she'd be long gone.

Panicking, terrified and not thinking straight, Ella had run back to the living room to grab her stuff – her bag, her phone, her shawl. She hadn't known where she was going to go or what she would do, but she'd known she needed to get out, get away from Harry. Everything had been strewn everywhere and she couldn't see properly for the tears streaming down her face. She'd spotted her bag on the sofa and had whipped it up, not immediately realising she'd toppled a couple of the candles until it was too late, that they'd fallen on to one of the old furs.

By the time she had realised, had stood up from searching for her phone on the floor, feeling around under the sofa, the flames had already caught some newspapers, were smouldering the old furnishings. The room had quickly filled with black smoke. She'd tried to put out the fire, she really had – beating at the flames with a cushion – but had had to give up when she couldn't breathe any longer, coughing and choking, her eyes smarting.

She'd run to the big glass doors leading to the deck but someone had locked them from the outside. Stumbling, she fled to the main hall, pausing briefly when she heard banging and yelling from down the corridor. She had imagined Harry trying to get out of the bedroom. She'd glanced back to the living room where, by then, a fierce fire was blazing, smoke billowing out, flames licking at the doorway.

She'd screwed up her eyes for a second, making her decision. Then she'd fled, locking the front door behind her before charging back down to the lake. The others had been out in the water. Oblivious.

By then, they'd all swum over to the little island some distance away, were sitting on the other side of it with the lodge well out of view. Ella remembers the freezing water biting into her body as she swam, fully clothed, washing the blood off herself on the way, dragging herself up onto land when she got there, joining in with the others as if she'd been there all along. They'd been so drunk, they hadn't even noticed she'd not been with them. And by the time anyone had spotted the flames leaping out of the roof of the lake house, lighting up the surrounding woods, and stumbled back to the manor in the dark to call for help because their phones were inside the lodge, the inferno had destroyed the timber building and everything inside it.

The fire service had come, of course, but the trucks couldn't get access. It was the plastic jerry cans of gasoline for the backup generator, the thick, dry timbers of the lodge that had, the investigators said, effectively turned the building into a kiln. Traces of bone were later found, analysed, but with two boys missing, both were, eventually, presumed dead.

For the next ten years, Ella had believed that she'd murdered Zach, and that she'd allowed her brother to be burnt alive. And, of course, she believed the camcorder tape had been destroyed with him, too.

'You think I'd leave *that* behind?' Harry had told her one evening at Green Leys, bouncing Kayleigh on his knee, a drink in hand. 'You underestimated me, Ella-bella.'

She'd listened, hand over mouth, imagining what it would have been like for him, smoke quickly seeping in under the bedroom door as he tried to kick it down. 'Even I wasn't strong enough for that, not in the short time I knew I had. Of course, if it wasn't for Zach's father's obsession with security, the window would have been an easy escape. But the bars prevented that.'

Ella remained silent as he'd told her, detaching herself from the horror as he recounted that night. She hated him with all her soul, yes, but he was still her flesh and blood, still her twin. Still a part of her.

'If I hadn't shoved his body off the bed and hauled the mattress to the door to help block out the smoke, I'd never have seen it.'

'Seen what?' Ella had whispered nervously, her face buried in her hands.

'The trap door in the wooden floor, of course,' he said with a smug smile. 'Turns out it led down to the storage area under the house, where they kept the dinghies. I knew there was another way out. Imagine, Ella, me crawling on my belly, the roaring fire above me, the heat so intense I couldn't breathe, feeling my way through the blackness.'

Ella had let out a whimper, rocking back and forth in her wheelchair. Harry had pulled open his shirt then, forcing her to look at the burn scars across his chest and shoulder. 'I thought it was all over when the floor above caved in, when burning wood fell on top of me. But I kept going, dragging myself to the exit hatch under the deck at the front. Someone had left it unlocked.'

Ella said nothing then, just sat there listening as he told her that he'd intended to call the emergency services. 'I've never failed before, Ella, but that night I did.'

She listened as he told her how he'd finally fallen down some-where in the woods, lost and exhausted as his body had given up. He'd been heading back to the manor to get help, his lungs burning with every breath, his skin bubbling with blisters.

'It was already light when I came round. Thick black smoke was still billowing into the sky and the place was swarming with police, the fire service. Even though I had the tape, I didn't know what they'd find in there, Ella-bella.' He'd stroked her cheek; she hadn't fully understood, then, what he'd meant. But now she realised – he'd been terrified they'd find out he'd killed Zach. As it turned out, there'd been nothing left to prove how he'd died. 'So I let them believe I was in there too. Cremated. Turns out, disappearing was easier than I imagined. Which is when Jacob was born. Or should I say, resurrected.'

Their father's name, Ella thinks, wondering what the man they'd never known would have had to say. Afterwards, Harry – Jacob – had got on with his life, while she dragged around the guilt of what she'd done. What she *believed* she'd done.

There's a knock at the door. It opens. 'Ella?' Liam says.

She jumps.

'Sorry, I'm done,' she says, wiping her face, trying to stop herself shaking.

She takes the tape from the machine, staring at it before slipping it back in its case. She shuts down the equipment, turns off the light. 'We should go,' she adds, wondering where to.

CHAPTER FIFTY-THREE

Ella

'Mum, hi,' Liam says, answering his phone as they head out of the office towards the lifts. 'Don't worry, don't worry… I'm so sorry I didn't call. I just had… well, I had a few things come up. I can't explain now.'

Ella hears a woman's urgent voice down the line as she hobbles towards the exit.

'Mum, the signal's getting bad, OK? I'm in a lift. Yes, I know, and I'm really sorry about your car. I'll make it up to you. Yes, I know it's illegal without an MOT. And yes, it *was* important. I had to help out a mate.' Liam falls silent. 'Yeah, I'm fine. Love you, too,' he adds, hanging up.

Fine-*ish*, Ella thinks, as they both spot the police officers swarming around the little blue vehicle outside on the street.

'Shit,' Liam says. 'Get back from the doors.'

'But—' Ella says. 'We haven't done anything wrong. It's not even on double yellow lines.' And for the first time in ten years, she really means it. She *hasn't* done anything wrong.

'You mightn't have, but my mum's bloody MOT has expired. I was meant to take it to the garage.'

Liam guides Ella back, lurking in the shadows behind the reception desk, watching as the police try the car door handles, wearing gloves, peering inside. Then they start taking photos of it, one of them talking into his radio.

'Christ, they *are* taking it rather seriously though,' Liam says, frowning. 'I don't want Mum to get in trouble.' He thinks for a moment. 'Wait, I've got an idea.' Ella sits down at the reception desk, taking the weight off her leg, sliding the chair further back as Liam makes a call.

'Y'all right, Ken,' he says. 'I've had better days, mate. Look, I was wondering if there's any chance of a lift? I know it's a bit late, but I'm with a young lady and she's got a bad leg. And a baby.' A pause. 'Yeah, I'll let you win at darts next time.' Liam listens again. 'Cheers, mate. I owe you a pint or three.' And then he gives out the address, telling him to come to the rear of the building, not the front.

'We'll wait out the back,' he says to Ella, glancing out of the windows, pulling a worried face. There are even more police surrounding the car now. Blue flashing lights too. 'She'll have to report it stolen or something. I dunno.' He shrinks back into the shadows, shaking his head. 'Or I'll just have to take the rap for it. I honestly was going to take it to the garage.'

Ella looks up at him, watching him worry about the car, about his mum. 'I'm not sure it's the MOT they're concerned about.'

Liam looks at her a moment, not understanding. 'C'mon, let's get outside and wait. Ken won't be long,' he says, taking the baby again.

Ella stands, grabbing his arm for support.

At the rear of the building, Liam swipes his card to let them out. A fine drizzle has started up, making Ella shudder as it hits her face. It's dark and there's an autumn chill in the air as they stand waiting in the narrow lane. Ella stares at him, clutching the tape in her hand. Liam notices her shivering and wraps his arm around her shoulder.

'Don't mind, do you?' he says, looking down at her with a small smile.

Ella shakes her head, manages a small smile back as she pulls the tape from its box, dropping it on the ground. 'Not at all. As long as you stamp on this as hard as you can,' she says, nestling against him. Liam looks at her for a moment before shrugging and doing as he's asked, the plastic case shattering beneath his foot as he pounds it over and over with his boot. Ella reaches down and grabs the broken plastic, ripping long ribbons of tape from inside, tearing it out as fast as she can before dropping it on the wet ground and getting Liam to scuff it again to make sure.

'What are you?—'

'I don't need it,' she says quickly. Liam doesn't understand yet senses her urgency, her need to do it. Then, moments later, just as the rain starts to get heavier, they hear the engine noise of a vehicle approaching from around the corner at the end of the narrow lane. Ella bundles up the remains of the tape and drops it into the dustbin, burying it under the other rubbish.

'That sounds like Ken's old van to me,' Liam laughs. 'Puffing out blue smoke, no doubt.' He rubs his hand up and down Ella's shoulder, trying to keep her warm. Pulling her close.

She's shivering more than she should be, especially when the van comes into sight, almost taking up the entire width of the alley as it approaches. Liam puts up his hand in a halt sign, then sticks out his thumb as if he's hitching, giving the driver a quick wave. A cloud of smoke belches out of the van's exhaust, filling the enclosed lane with a noxious smell.

'Oh…' Ella says, touching her forehead. 'I…'

'You OK?' Liam asks, holding the baby close.

'I-I just feel a bit dizzy,' she says, not taking her eyes off the van. 'It's probably my leg. I've been on it too long. She wobbles then, clinging on to Liam, feeling unsteady. The van gets closer, looming down on them as it approaches, the wiper blades flashing back and forth, back and forth across the windscreen.

Ella can't help that her eyes go wide, that her breathing quickens and her heart thumps. She has an overwhelming urge to get away, to flee, but she's trapped. *The van coming at her as she pedals, the exhaust fumes, the rain pelting her face, the man's face in the window, oblivious…*

She hears herself screaming – a piercing, agonising cry as she goes down, as the van smashes into the side of her, knocking her off, trapping her leg under the bike as it crunches over the rear wheel. But the sound is only in her head.

Ella can't move. She's frozen, staring at the deep dent on the front of the van. A flash of blue paint embedded in its bumper. She blinks hard against the rain, her mouth hanging open.

'Hey up, Ken,' Liam calls as he stops right in front of them, window down.

Ella stares at the face in the cabin – his stubbly grey beard, his thick glasses, his weathered skin. Then he gets out, comes up to Liam with a beaming grin for them both. He flashes a glance at Ella. A double take.

'Blimey, you're in a state,' he says, looking at Liam's battered face. 'And you've been busy, lad,' he adds, making silly noises at the baby.

Kayleigh grows restless in Liam's arms, making whimpering noises against his shoulder.

'Got time for a quick pint down the Dog? Looks like you need it. You too, love,' he says, glancing at Ella again. 'Babies are welcome in there.'

'That's kind of you, Ken,' Liam says. 'But it's been a long day. I need to get Ella…' He trails off. 'Where am I taking you?' he asks, turning to her.

'I don't know,' Ella says quietly, shrugging, flashing a look at the van again. 'Perhaps you could just drop me and the baby at the nearest police station,' she says. 'That'll do for now.'

'No problem,' Ken says, making a puzzled, yet concerned face. 'And no questions asked.' He turns and opens the door, Liam and Ella sliding onto the front bench seat, all three of them in a row.

'I'll come with you,' Liam whispers, helping Ella do up her seatbelt, while she rubs her sore knee. He clings onto the baby as tight as he can. 'I'll need to give a statement.'

'I'll probably be in there a while,' she replies. Though not as long as she'd once believed, she thinks, grateful she can tell the truth. That she and Kayleigh were both kidnapped. It'll take a bit of explaining, but if the past comes up, there's nothing to lie about. She didn't kill anyone.

'After we're done,' Liam says quietly to Ella as Ken chugs on down the alley, turning out onto another side street before joining the main road, 'you can come back to my mum's place, if you like. She's got a spare room and won't mind if it's late.'

'Thanks,' Ella says, noticing the warm feeling inside. 'That's kind.'

And then comes another smile as Liam reaches across and takes her hand in his. He leans over, whispering in her ear. 'Maybe you'll come to the Dog with me another time, if you fancy it. But not with Ken.' He laughs then, sending goosebumps down Ella's spine as she feels his breath in her ear.

Ella looks up, smiling. 'I'd like that, thanks,' she says, squeezing his hand.

'We could—'

'Oh my God, *stop!*' Ella screams, banging her fist on the dusty dashboard.

Ken jams on the brakes just as he's about to pull away from the roundabout. 'What, what is it, love?' he says, as the car behind blares its horn.

'The *bike*,' Ella says, peering out of the windscreen, trying to focus through the sheeting rain as the wipers flap and squeak. 'Didn't you see it?'

Ken looks all around, puzzled. 'There was no bike, love,' he says, crunching the van into gear again. 'Just relax. I'm a good driver. I've not killed anyone yet.'

Ella sits back in her seat, her heart gradually slowing again. She holds Kayleigh's fingers as the baby reaches out, thinking she must have imagined it. That all she really saw was the ghost of herself, a fragment of memory seeping out. She leans down and kisses the baby's head.

'Not long now, Kayleigh,' she whispers in her ear.

CHAPTER FIFTY-FOUR

Six Months Later

Ella gets off her bike, leaning it up against the stand outside the office building. She slips off her backpack and takes out the lock, stopping before she clamps the wheels. She looks around – up at the glass-fronted building above her, across the street to the café as they set up for the day, putting out the chalkboard, arranging the street tables, turning the sign to 'open'. There's a definite feel of spring in the air – the chill of recent weeks gradually growing milder. Bulbs, sunshine, showers and buds. It won't be long, Ella thinks, before she doesn't need her padded jacket at all on her trip to work. She's been back at Ghost Media three months now. Three months since she returned to her workstation, expecting to see everything exactly as she'd left it.

But no. That first day back, there'd been at least a dozen cards on her desk – some from the bosses, people in other departments, clients she'd worked with, one from Jan and Helen in HR and another massive one signed by everyone in editing. Her eyes had filled with tears as she'd read all the messages – *Welcome back, Ella!… We missed you… Hope you're feeling better now…* But the one from Liam had made her cry and smile in equal measure.

Lunch? L x

There'd been chocolates, flowers, a stationery set with her name on it, and a pretty gift box of herbal teas. All for her. Left for her to find when she returned. It's almost as if, she'd thought, that they *wanted* me back.

Out of habit, she'd been going to email Liam her reply about lunch, even though he was only a couple of desks away. But, instead, she'd got up and gone to his cubicle, tapping her fingers on the partition.

'Knock-knock,' she'd said.

He'd looked up. 'Hi.' His smile had been broad. 'I hope you got the bus to work,' he said with a wink, standing, going over and giving her a hug.

'No chance,' she'd replied. 'I love cycling. Anyway, I take a different route now.'

'Well, now I've got a car, my offer of a lift always stands if it's raining. Or if your leg hurts.' He'd looked at her, appraising her as if he hadn't been able to believe she was really there, even though they'd been seeing each other a couple of times a week since she'd been recuperating.

Liam's face was fully healed by then, just the tiniest of scars left on his bottom lip.

'Thanks. But the physio says that keeping it mobile is good. It seizes up if I don't use it. Amazing what an extra bit of metal in a knee can do, eh?' Ella flashed a familiar smile at him – the smile she'd been using daily for weeks.

And Liam was quite used to seeing it, too.

He visited her every day for the four days she was in hospital following the second operation, and regularly after that.

Now, as she stands outside her office building, she locks up her bike and takes off her helmet, shaking out her hair, feeling content, somehow warm and settled inside. Then, on a whim, she nips across the road to the café. 'Two soy lattes, please,' she says. 'With an extra shot in each.'

She thinks back to when she was in hospital and the many conversations she'd had with Liam, how he'd told her about not getting on with dairy, that he was going on a health kick and thinking about taking up running again, and that he probably shouldn't have so many meals after work down the Dog. They'd discussed everything those few days after her operation, laughing and sharing stories in a way Ella never thought possible with another human.

Though, of course, Zach had come to mind, especially when Liam questioned her about her university days, tentatively asking if she'd had a boyfriend. She'd said that she hadn't, not really, closing her eyes briefly. That could come later.

'I got you this,' Ella says, going up to Liam's desk, coffees in hand. He has his headphones on, doesn't realise she's there until she taps him on the shoulder.

'Hey…' He pulls the headphones off, hooking them around his neck. He looks up, taking the coffee. 'Thank you. That's kind.'

'It's soy,' she says with a wink, patting her tummy. 'Thought it might suit you better.'

'Cheers,' he says, raising the paper cup at her, before showing her the project he's been working on. 'Wouldn't mind your opinion on something,' he says, pulling up a chair.

Ella sits down, a warm feeling growing inside as she takes off her sweatshirt, revealing a colourful T-shirt. No more boring uniform for her now, Ella thinks, with an inner smile. She treated herself to a few things that… well, a few things that Meggie would have likely scowled at, but that the old Ella would have once worn without a second thought. And now, she doesn't care what anyone thinks. Doesn't even care that Liam helped her sign up for a Facebook account a week or two ago, that she's actually found a few of her old university friends on there, Meggie included. To Ella's surprise, she was in touch right away after they connected, saying how she was missed at their graduation, but that they all understood. She was grieving a double loss, after all. She even suggested they should get together soon.

And of course, adding Liz as a contact was a priority. Ella sent her a message, too – asking if they could meet up soon, maybe even go shopping again. Besides, she wanted to explain. To thank her.

'They've all done so *much* with their lives,' Ella had said, wide-eyed, as she scrolled through the timelines, checking out her old friends' photographs. Weddings, babies, careers, moving countries. She lost count of how many times she'd clicked 'Add Friend' that night.

Liam showed her how to put a profile photo on her account – with Ella insisting on using a silly selfie shot of the pair of them playing pool at the Dog. To her surprise, a few people even 'liked' it. Initially, she only had one post on her timeline. A link to a national news story that had warmed the hearts of the nation:

Mum and Baby Kayleigh Reunited

Now, sitting at Liam's desk, watching the piece on bullying that Liam's working on – which starts with the face of an innocent baby transitioning through childhood and into adulthood and the effects bullying will have on her life – Ella can't help thinking about the night Ken dropped them at the police station, the rain sheeting down, wondering what the rest of Kayleigh's life would entail.

In the end, she decided not to mention anything about Ken to the police – his van, the dent in the front and the blue paint marks. Besides, the officers were far more interested in the baby she was holding as well as the state of Liam's bloody face. What was done was done. And, in a painful, terrifying, roundabout way, Ken's careless driving had given her back her freedom. If it wasn't for him, she'd still be holed up, alone in her little flat eating microwave meals for one. Living in fear.

The night at the police station had been gruelling. Walking in with a kidnapped baby that'd been all over the news for several weeks was always going to cause a stir. She'd given statement after statement, had been interviewed rigorously by different teams of detectives, transferred to the main station in the morning, where she'd had to go through the whole process again. And Liam had gone through similar, though they'd never been together. Their stories matched perfectly, of course, and they'd been believed, while the house at Green Leys had been picked apart and forensically examined for days after.

It was just before Ella was transferred to hospital that a detective broke the news of Jacob's – *Harry's* – death. The combination of alcohol, massive amounts of benzodiazepines plus the blow to his head had eventually caused coma and, finally, death.

After hospital, Ella stayed with Liam and his mum for a couple of weeks while she regained her strength, started looking for a new flat. The old one had already been let out again and, besides, she didn't want to go back there. It would have felt too… *lonely*, she'd told Liam. Too isolated. Too much like the old days.

Liam had come with her to the viewings, with the fourth place being perfect. Ella took it on the spot, particularly loving the little balcony overlooking the park and the tennis courts. Liam challenged her to a game when she was better.

'Health kick starts tomorrow,' Liam says, laughing as the barmaid in the Dog brings over a huge pie and chips. He squirts on a load of ketchup before shaking on some salt.

'Oh my God, I'll never eat all this,' Ella says when her pie arrives. She laughs, picking up a chip with her fingers.

'Can't go wrong with that in here, lass,' Ken says walking past, taking his darts from his top pocket.

Ella's come to love the place with its beery smell, slightly sticky red patterned carpet, the old varnished tables where there's never quite enough room for plates, drinks and condiments.

'Sauce?' Liam asks, holding up the tomato-shaped squeezy bottle.

'Thanks,' Ella says, smiling. She hopes her lipstick hasn't smudged. She bought a new one earlier. A pretty peach shade that reminded her of one she used to have way back.

'All over?'

'Please,' she says, trying not to laugh. She knows Liam takes his sauce seriously. She sips her drink while he douses her food.

The pub's getting busy – the usual crowd of locals, young and old, chatting, sharing tales of their days, laughing, watching the football on the screen in the corner.

Liam pushes her plate back to her, turning it round.

Ella unfolds her napkin but stops, staring at her plate. She can't help the smile. 'Oh, Liam…' she says, glancing up at him, tucking her hair behind her ear. Then she drops her head, laughing – laughing until she can't stop as she stares at the huge red heart he's drawn on the golden crust of her pie. 'That's *so* nice. Thank you,' she adds, the look shared between them lasting longer than it ever has before.

His hand slides across the table, holding hers for a moment, giving it a squeeze.

As she tucks in, somewhere deep inside her mind she hears, *Work, home, sleep…* She gives her head a little shake, getting rid of the thought. There's more to life than that, she thinks, grinning at Liam, her mouth full, her heart even fuller.

A LETTER FROM SAMANTHA

Thank you so much for choosing *The Liar's Wife*. I really hope you enjoyed it and it kept you turning the pages right to the end! I'm busy working away on my next novel, so if you'd like to keep up to date about all my books and forthcoming releases, then do please take a moment to sign up here to get all the latest news:

www.bookouture.com/samantha-hayes

As an author, I'm always on the lookout for inspiration and, while it may sound a little clichéd, the idea for *The Liar's Wife* actually came to me in the middle of the night. I'd had a bad dream and woken up terrified and unable to move. I was literally paralysed from fear.

To begin with, I didn't know where I was and, as I lay there, trying to figure everything out, I heard a 'beeping' sound coming from somewhere. It turned out it was just an appliance (!) but for a moment, I wondered if I was in hospital, that I'd perhaps had an accident and the noise was a medical monitor. It took me a while to remember who I was or even open my eyes and recognise my surroundings, but gradually details began to filter back.

I felt rattled for the rest of the day so, like a typical author, I began to ask some 'What if' questions. What if I *had* woken up in hospital? How had I got there? What if I gradually remembered things about my life – my name, where I worked and lived – but someone else was telling me differently? What if they said I was married, when I knew that I wasn't? What if, to my horror, I was wearing a wedding ring? What if my 'husband' came to visit?

And so *The Liar's Wife* began to take shape. I usually begin with planning the story itself, rather than developing the characters, making sure everything is plotted out in detail. But even as I was doing that, Ella sprang to life in my mind. I wanted her to feel the same fear I'd felt when I'd woken from the nightmare, and knew she had to be damaged and vulnerable in some way, but a fighter too. And while she was literally living through her nightmare (thankfully, I couldn't remember mine!), I knew I wanted her to have a happy ending – which is where Liam came in.

I actually chose the Rudyard Kipling quote at the start of the book after I'd typed 'The End'. For me, it sums up the entire message in my story perfectly – that the worst liars are often our own fears. Once we realise this, we can take back control, just like Ella did.

So that's a little insight into how *The Lair's Wife* came about. If you enjoyed reading Ella's story, I would be so grateful if you wrote a quick online review. I read all of them and really value my readers' thoughts – plus it's a great way to let others know about a book you've enjoyed.

Also, if you want to join me on Facebook, Twitter or Instagram, it would be great to 'meet' you and chat, or perhaps take a look at my website for details of all my other books.

Meantime, happy reading and I'm looking forward to sharing my next story with you too.

Sam x

samanthahayesauthor

 @samhayes

 @samanthahayes.author

 www.samanthahayes.co.uk

ACKNOWLEDGEMENTS

As ever, I want to give my heartfelt thanks to the brilliant team behind my books. Firstly, Jessie Botterill, my fantastic editor – working with you is an absolute pleasure and all your hard work on this book is so very much appreciated. You never fail to add the perfect 'magic'! My sincere thanks and gratitude to all the fantastic team at Bookouture – I feel very honoured to be one of your authors. And huge thanks to Kim Nash and Noelle Holten – what can I say, apart from do you ever sleep?! Your boundless energy and passion for all the books you put 'out there' is incredible. So, thank you.

Big thanks, too, to Oli Munson – I honestly couldn't wish for a better agent! And of course, everyone at AM Heath. Cheers for everything you do!

Tracy Fenton's passion for books is just amazing and, as ever, I want to say how grateful I am to you and your fab admin team at THE Book Club (TBC) on Facebook for all your support. You realise that every time I brainstorm new book titles, they have to fit the 'In My Pants' game!

Huge thanks to you, my readers, for investing your time in my book and spending a few hours with my characters. I hope you'll come back for more! Plus, my sincere gratitude to all the lovely book bloggers who read and review my books, helping to spread the word. And finally, much love to my dear family, Ben, Polly and Lucy, Avril and Paul, Graham and Marina, and (last but not least!) Joe xxx

9 781786 816696